PRAISE FOR CHRISTINE NOLFI

The Season of Silver Linings

"An enchanting, impossible-to-put-dow e truth of family. This heartwarming story r reminds us that love is what keeps hope alive."

— Bette Lee Crosby, bestselling author

"Charming and sincere, Jada's journey to reconcile the past left me with a smile on my face and hope in my heart. The idyllic setting only adds to the joy of reading this heartwarming tale of past mistakes and glorious futures."

— Heather Burch, bestselling author of *In the Light of the Garden*

"In *The Season of Silver Linings* we see love on every page. Each novel in the Sweet Lake series offers a special experience for the reader, and the third book may be your favorite yet."

— Grace Greene, *USA Today* bestselling author

Sweet Lake

"[This book] has such a charming small-town vibe and endearing characters that readers will find themselves falling in love with quirky Sweet Lake and hoping for a series."

— *Booklist*

"In this uplifting and charming story, each room of the inn is filled with friendship, forgiveness, and love."

— *Kirkus Reviews*

"Craving a literary trifecta of romance, small-town drama, and soul searching? That's exactly what you'll find in Linnie Wayfair's life as she tries to restore an inn in Sweet Lake, Ohio, to glory—all while navigating the affairs of the heart. This is the literary answer to *Gilmore Girls* withdrawals, and we don't give that compliment lightly."

—Marina Kendrick, YourTango.com

The Comfort of Secrets

"Welcome back to the Wayfair Inn, where discovering secrets and overcoming human frailty are the ingredients for finding love and happiness. Reading Nolfi's *The Comfort of Secrets* feels like coming home."

—Kay Bratt, bestselling author of *Wish Me Home*

"Poignant, honest, and filled with heart, *The Comfort of Secrets* has it all. With a natural talent for lyrical prose, Christine Nolfi sweeps you away."

—Heather Burch, bestselling author of *In the Light of the Garden*

"This is a surprise-filled page turner, right to the end. Brilliant!"

—Patricia Sands, author of the Love in Provence series

Second Chance Grill

"Nolfi writes with a richness of heart that is incredibly endearing."

—Renee Fountain, *Book Fetish*

"An emotionally moving contemporary novel about the power that relationships have to transform lives."

—Susan Bethany, *Midwest Book Review*

The Tree of Everlasting Knowledge

"Poignant and powerful, *The Tree of Everlasting Knowledge* is as much a saga of learning how to survive, heal, and forgive as it is a chilling crime story, unforgettable to the very end."

—Margaret Lane, *Midwest Book Review*

The
Season of
Silver
Linings

ALSO BY CHRISTINE NOLFI

The Sweet Lake Series

Sweet Lake (Book 1)

The Comfort of Secrets (Book 2)

The Liberty Series

Second Chance Grill (Book 1)

Treasure Me (Book 2)

The Impossible Wish (Book 3)

Four Wishes (Book 4)

The Tree of Everlasting Knowledge (Book 5)

The Dream You Make

Heavenscribe: Part One

Heavenscribe: Part Two

Heavenscribe: Part Three

The Shell Keeper (Kindle Worlds Novella)

The Shell Seeker (Kindle Worlds Novella)

The Season of Silver Linings

A Sweet Lake Novel

CHRISTINE NOLFI

LAKE UNION
PUBLISHING

Text copyright © 2018 by Christine Nolfi
All rights reserved.

Published by Lake Union, Seattle

www.apub.com

Amazon, the Amazon logo, and Lake Union are trademarks of Amazon.com, Inc., or its affiliates.

ISBN-13: 9781503903395
ISBN-10: 1503903397

Cover design by Rachel Adam Rogers

Printed in the United States of America

To my children and stepchildren,
Brian, Christian, Jameson,
Julie, Marlie, and Marguerite,
with all my love

Chapter 1

Tilda Lyons rushed into the Wayfair's kitchen. "I have wonderful news!"

An unlikely prospect. Jada Brooks muffled a groan. This morning there wasn't time for interruptions by the Sweet Lake Sirens. The members of the eccentric women's group were needed upstairs. All manner of chaos had seized a corner suite of the historic Wayfair Inn.

Jada placed a swirl of icing on the chocolate cake she'd baked for the dinner menu. "Tell me Linnie has made a decision on her wedding gown. It's the only kind of 'wonderful' I'm looking for this morning."

"Not yet," Tilda said.

"Is she close?"

The pint-size Realtor put her excitement in lockdown. "Do you want the truth?"

"No, Tilda. Lie to me."

"She told the Sirens that only a woman with a deathly allergy to carbs and aerobics could enjoy an experience this hellish."

"No decision then." Jada rolled her aching neck. The gesture did nothing to alleviate the tension brewing in her muscles. "Do me a favor, Tilda. Save your news for a happier day."

"Don't be such a party pooper. This can't wait." Recovering her excitement, Tilda shimmied her shoulders with the energy of an overly caffeinated elf. Her cinnamon-colored locks were still swinging as she added, "You'll love this. We began comparing notes while we were upstairs helping with the gowns and—bingo!—we deciphered the meaning, at long last."

"Is this about another dream?" Jada asked, thinking, *Go away, please.*

The Sweet Lake Sirens believed their dreams were prophetic. Jada didn't know why they insisted on adding her into their REM sleep. Why didn't they pick on Linnie Wayfair instead? Given her upcoming wedding, she'd become the craziest white girl in three counties.

An opinion not worth sharing as Tilda said, "Last night, four of the Sirens had nearly identical dreams about you."

"Copycat dreams? That's hard to believe."

"Well, they did. We made a comparison and stumbled upon the meaning. I can't believe it's taken us this long to work it out." Tilda paused a dramatic beat. "Are you ready?"

"No."

"Don't be frightened. We're here to help you."

"That's what scares me." Jada wasn't sure why the Sirens were dreaming about her lately. Chances were, they'd now arrived at a silly solution for a problem she didn't have.

Not that Jada didn't have problems aplenty.

For nearly a decade, the historic Wayfair Inn had been on the edge of bankruptcy with little hope for survival. Those dark years were now a memory. The three women in charge—Jada included—were breathing life back into the golden sandstone mansion that stood on the highest hill in the area, with the town of Sweet Lake nestling at its feet. Once again, tourists from across the Midwest were arriving at the retreat in southern Ohio to enjoy the mineral-fed lake and the lush forest.

With the Wayfair's newfound success, problems bred like alley cats in heat. Each day brought a whole litter of headaches. Usually they began raining down on Jada the moment she entered the lobby. Deliveries arrived late, or new waitstaff left entrées growing cold in the kitchen. New employees in Housekeeping forgot to replace bath towels in the guest suites, and the expanding kitchen staff was still learning the ropes. Most days, Jada felt like a drill sergeant whipping a group of dizzy recruits into shape.

"Why don't we discuss this later?" she asked Tilda. "Thanks to the mayhem upstairs, I'm way behind schedule. Half of the desserts for the dinner menu aren't finished, and I haven't stepped foot in my office. I'll need a snow shovel to dig through the paperwork on my desk."

Penelope Riddle came into the kitchen. "Jada, hold on." Behind thick eyeglasses, her watery eyes registered worry. "You need to hear us out."

The gentle request pinged guilt through Jada. It was one thing to nix a conversation with a caffeinated elf. Penelope, however, possessed a chewy nougat center.

"Fine, Penelope," she said, relenting. "Fire away."

Permission had been granted, yet the elderly Siren went silent like the moon at midnight. Her attention flitted across the counter and the kitchen staff before dancing to the tall windows above the sink. The trees outside fluttered with spring's first leaves.

The picturesque scene was lost on Penelope as she drew a tremulous breath.

Goose bumps sprouted on Jada's arms. Whatever the Siren believed the dreams foretold, the prediction wasn't good.

On her exhale, Penelope said, "You're suffering beneath a psychic burden."

"A psychic burden?"

That was the big reveal?

"One not of your making."

"If I didn't make the burden, who did?"

"Someone no longer in your life."

Jada swiped at the curls escaping from beneath the bandanna on her head. This morning, there hadn't been time to coil her curls or steam away the tension in her body with a long, leisurely hot shower. A short, utilitarian one was all she could manage. She was burdened, all right—from lack of sleep and the deprivation of anything resembling a social life. She was a black woman's version of Atlas, carrying the world with flour-dusted cheeks—and seriously needing a visit to the salon.

"That's your great insight?" she asked Penelope. "I am burdened, but mostly by the people *in* my life. Tell me something I don't know."

The kindhearted Siren missed the sarcasm. "All right," she agreed, clasping her hands at her generous waist. "You won't escape the burden until a stranger brings news from the past."

"Why should I care about the past? Because, you know, it's passed."

"An event in the past created the burden," Penelope said. "It has brought you regret."

Jada sighed with exasperation. She didn't need pointers on dealing with regret. A woman didn't make it into her thirties without suffering the sting of missed opportunities or foolish choices. Live long enough and you discover that no one has a flawless track record. Assuming she bought into the dream interpretation—a proposition still up for grabs—Penelope wasn't offering enough specifics to solve the mystery.

Jada zeroed in on the second part of the prediction. "The stranger who'll bring news from the past . . . this isn't a tall, dark, and handsome stranger, is it?" Along with their quirky ideas about spirituality, the Sirens liked to play matchmakers with the town's unsuspecting residents. Usually this worked out. But, at times, they created romantic mayhem in Sweet Lake, Ohio. "Because if it is, cast your spell on someone else. I don't have time to date. If I ever hang out my shingle, you'll be the first to know."

"Sending out good vibrations isn't the same as casting a spell. Sirens aren't witches, you know. We're wise women. Our combined wisdom can help you."

"Are we done here?" Jada pointed toward the confections lined up on the counter. "I'm nowhere near finishing the desserts."

"Wait." Penelope dug around in her purse. "Keep this with you. It will help resolve the burden."

She withdrew a homemade sachet. The string knotted around the small bag boasted the familiar feathers and stones used to decorate Siren tokens. From beneath the colorful fabric, a sharp green scent perfumed the air.

Jada took another sniff, relishing the aroma. If accepting the gift would get Penelope and Tilda out of the kitchen, there was no harm in playing along. "Mind telling me why I should wear a sachet with rosemary inside?"

Tilda put in, "We do mind." Beside her, Penelope nodded in solemn agreement. "Mostly because we don't have the answer yet."

"You don't know *why* I should wear rosemary?"

"We know the herb is important," Tilda said. "Every time we dream about you, we also dream about rosemary."

"I'm a pastry chef. Why not put me in dreams with chocolate sprinkles or crème fraîche?"

"Would it matter if we did?"

"Probably not."

From the corridor, a commingling of voices filtered in. The sixtyish Norah Webb swept into the room. Her graceful carriage was a remnant of the years of runway modeling during her youth. The much shorter Ruth Kenefsky marched in behind her.

The look on their faces sent Jada's mood spiraling downward. *Another disaster with Linnie upstairs?*

Whatever the setback, she didn't relish hearing the play-by-play.

A center island dominated the Wayfair's kitchen. On the opposite side, three members of the morning staff inched toward the sink. A wise move. Norah gave them an imperious glance before setting her sights on Jada.

"You're needed upstairs immediately, if not sooner." Norah peered down her hawkish nose. "We have another problem."

"I've already gone up twice." Jada reached for the rolling pin. On the marble pastry board she'd chilled prior to her last sprint upstairs, the pie dough wept silently. Leave it much longer, and it would become soggy mush. "Can't the rest of you deal with this? Narrow Linnie's choices down to three wedding gowns. Once you do, I'll go back upstairs."

"She insists on hearing your opinion."

"Norah, I can't race upstairs every ten minutes to lend an opinion. Who made me an expert? I've never been married."

"As if your sad excuse of a private life matters. She's demanding you go up, *ASAP*."

The remark about her private life was a low blow, but Jada let it slide. Summoning the last of her patience, she said, "Tell her to wait. I'm working with butter, which *will* melt. I'm not throwing away half a pound of the stuff because I'm forced to watch the fashion show." She got in Norah's face. "Am I making myself clear?"

"Like crystal." Norah leaned into the stare-down. Then she invaded private space to tap impatient fingers on Jada's head. "What's with the bandanna? Don't you own a silk scarf for bad hair days?"

The attractive Siren had no patience for *any* breach in the fashion code, but Jada didn't care. "Who has time to dig around for a silk scarf on a workday?" she countered.

Cutting in, Ruth Kenefsky unleashed her gravelly voice. "Norah, back off. Jada isn't the problem. Who cares how she looks when she's roosting in the kitchen with her pastries? Besides, her BFF doesn't need help picking out what to wear when she gets hitched in April."

"I'm sure I'll regret asking." Norah compressed her lips with impatience. Then she gave Ruth her full attention. "What do you think Linnie needs?"

"The girl needs a tranquilizer. Something that'll take her down fast, like the sedatives used to tag big game." Oddly girlish braids of stark white framed Ruth's face. She flicked them off her shoulders as she drove the point home. "I say we keep Linnie on high doses. If she's this nutso already, what guarantee do we have she'll make it down the aisle?"

"You're suggesting we drug the bride-to-be?" Norah sputtered.

"We need an insurance policy, or she'll hightail it when the band strikes up 'Here Comes the Bride.' Why are you convinced she'll carry through with the nuptials?"

"Because she's in love. Why else?"

Ruth snorted. "As if a healthy sex drive is any guarantee of common sense. When doesn't Linnie second-guess every decision? Why, she never makes up her mind until Jada does her King Solomon routine and walks her through the options."

"Oh, please," Jada put in, her patience fleeing for the exits. "I don't do a wise man routine with Linnie . . . not all the time."

"You do, and you're needed upstairs," Norah said, motioning toward the door. "Are you coming?"

Ruth stomped her foot. "Norah, why don't you stick to fashion advice? You don't know the first thing about human nature. Can't you see we're past the easy fixes? Let's drug the bride."

The women continued arguing, and Jada leaned heavily against the counter. There was no disputing Ruth's dour opinion. Only a miracle would carry Linnie Wayfair through the prewedding jitters and deposit her safely on her wedding day, at the end of April. Her fear of making the wrong decision would never abate until Jada soothed her with commonsense solutions. The responsibility weighed heavily on Jada.

She pitched the pie dough into the garbage.

Coming to a decision, she said, "Lead the way, ladies. We're going upstairs."

∽

Each gown is a disaster.

Jada vanquished the pessimistic thought. She'd already shooed the Sirens from the suite. Too many opinions had become counterproductive. She was having trouble hearing herself think.

7

Searching for optimism, she steered the zipper up the back of the latest selection. Her weary fingers caught on the zipper's teeth, and an equally weary sigh drifted from her lips. With care, she readjusted the veil's gauzy folds. Jada wondered if the outfit was another no-go, and if they'd find something among the remaining options. The untried gowns pressed together on the rack reminded her of virgin maidens, pure and unscathed. They were nothing like the molested frocks heaped on the bed in the reject pile.

If the perfect gown lay hidden on the rack, she'd find it.

Linnie deserved gorgeous attire, something with foamy yards of tulle and lace or reams of creamy satin that would glimmer in the sunlight when she waltzed down the aisle. It was just a matter of unearthing the perfect choice to complement Linnie's God-given beauty. Tawny hair fell in abundant waves around her shoulders. Her hazel eyes were bright and thickly lashed, her skin creamier than the pecan praline cookies Jada had added to the spring menu.

Yet, after helping Linnie step in and out of gowns, it seemed they'd never find a selection she liked.

The reasons were obvious. The majority owner of the Wayfair Inn lacked the statuesque height Jada took for granted. No one in Sweet Lake would describe Linnie as athletic, or trim, or very tall, for that matter. Nor did Linnie glide in the slow, sultry way many women perfected, drawing male attention by simply crossing a room. Linnie chugged along at an uneven gait like a clunky locomotive clacking down the tracks. She swerved or changed speed without notice. If the great changes that had come to the inn preoccupied her thoughts—or her penchant for sweets kept her focused on whatever baked good she'd snatched from the kitchen—she could walk three full turns through the lobby before remembering where her feet meant to carry her.

Worse still, she wasn't on friendly terms with gravity.

A fact on full display as she started toward the full-length mirror in the corner of the suite. She'd barely taken a step when the heel of her satin pump grabbed maliciously at the gown's frothy hem. The heel spiked the hem to the floor, halting her forward movement.

Shock lifted her brows. Fighting for balance, she flung her arms out. She resembled a scarecrow overdressed for a day of warding off crows.

Her tether to gravity snapped, and she pitched forward.

Jada leapt into the fray of shuddering fabric. She caught Linnie before her nose hit the floor.

Cat Mendoza, lounging against the wall, rushed in to help. Together, they righted the fear-frozen plank of Linnie's body.

With a growl, Linnie pulled out of their grasp. A wisp of the lacy veil caught on her lips.

Spitting the fabric out, she glared at Jada. "This gown should come with a hazard sign. Look at the length. Are you trying to kill me?"

"A seamstress can take up the hem. Don't you like it at all?"

"This is the worst pick so far. Why did you insist I try it on?"

"Jada insisted because she's getting desperate," Cat said, trudging back to her post by the wall. "You've done nothing but veto every option. Plus, we've run out of coffee. I'd go down and get a refill, but I'd never make it back without the Sirens barging in. They're all eager to see what you choose."

"No more Sirens." Linnie untangled her pump from the hem. "This is hard enough without a bunch of women leering from the sidelines. I can't deal with a million opinions on what looks good and what doesn't."

"Lately, you can't deal with anything. You've become a Grade A chickenshit." Cat picked up her coffee, glared at the dregs at the bottom of the cup. "Ask Jada. Since you decided to marry, she's been hand-holding you on a daily basis."

Insult spread a pink tinge across Linnie's face. "I've been preoccupied for all the obvious reasons. Jada isn't managing me." Her eyes searched out Jada's with a gentle plea. "Are you?"

The rosemary sachet was still tucked in Jada's pocket.

You're suffering from a psychic burden.

Was the Sirens' pronouncement valid, if slightly off base? Was the burden *still* in her life? Was the burden . . . *Linnie?* Guilt took a swipe at Jada. She adored Linnie. But lately, her oldest bestie was exhausting.

"C'mon, Linnie. Chill. You've been more nervous than usual. Not a big deal."

The half-truth bothered Jada, and she nervously plucked at the jeweled strip encasing her friend's waist. An ivory bead, apparently dismayed by the manhandling, popped loose. It sprang across the suite and fled into the walk-in closet.

Unzipping the dress with care, she added, "Can we please stay focused on the task at hand? Frances went to a lot of trouble bringing in all these gowns. She drove to Cincinnati personally and convinced Ballantine's Department Store to send over the entire lot. We only have twenty-four hours before the gowns must be returned to the store. You've only tried on a handful."

"What's the use? Nothing looks right."

"The mermaid gown was okay." The dress needed major alterations, but the sleek cut worked better than the beaded mess Linnie was currently extracting herself from.

"You like the mermaid dress? If the best I can do is look like a fish on my wedding day, I'm screwed." Linnie waved impatiently at Cat, who was examining her fingernails with a look of intense boredom. "Cat threw together a Christmas wedding without trouble."

Jada sighed. "That was different."

"No, it wasn't. She found a dress requiring minimal alterations. And she looked divine. Why does everything make me look frumpy?"

The complaint appeared to strike Cat as a challenge, and she angled her hip. "You're not frumpy—you're short. There's a difference."

Playing the honesty card with a woman frantic to unearth the perfect wedding gown wasn't a great move. Jada shot a warning look, but not in time to stop the sassy Latina from adding, "I'm a size six. I walk right into clothes. You're shorter, Linnie. And, well, stockier. You just have to try harder."

"*Stockier?*" Linnie yanked the gown to her ankles. "Don't hold back, Cat. Why not call me a lumberjack? A short, *stocky* lumberjack." She scooped the dress up and dumped it on the four-poster bed. "Here's an idea. I'll find something plaid for my wedding. In lieu of flowers, I'll carry an axe."

"I didn't call you a lumberjack."

"You did mention you're a size six. Talk about cruel."

"Hey! I'm only telling it like it is."

"Thanks for the news roundup. Next, you'll announce you're a perfect 36C. Or that you wear thongs because they're comfortable. Like there's a woman alive who enjoys wearing slingshot material across her butt."

"I *am* a 36C."

Jada stepped into the fractious air brewing between them. "Both of you, stop—"

Stepping around her, Cat gave her opponent a thunderous look. "What's wrong with thongs? They're nice." The honeyed skin of her nose scrunching, Cat rolled her eyes before appraising the yellowed slip that had been part of Linnie's neglected wardrobe for just about forever. "Geez, Linnie. What do have you on under there? Big-girl panties? The kind that go all the way to your waist?"

"Cat, leave her alone. Linnie's choice in undies is none of your business."

"It is now." Cat wasn't usually this blunt, but her frustration was palpable. "If she's still dressing like a Girl Scout, we need to perform an intervention."

Linnie glared at her. "Zip it, Cat."

Curiosity, a treacherous companion, got the better of Jada. She eyed Linnie ruefully. "You're not wearing big-girl panties—are you? Like the day-of-the-week undies we wore when we were kids?"

Anger shuddered down Linnie's back. Clearly the wrong question, and Jada searched for an escape route from the conversation. She couldn't stand there all morning while her two closest friends bickered like moody adolescents. For months now, neither one had been behaving normally.

It occurred to Jada that *she* should be the one foisting complaints into the suite's chilly atmosphere. Once, the three women had eagerly shared management duties at the Wayfair Inn. No longer. Lately, Jada handled the majority of the work.

Linnie wasn't the only guilty party. Since Cat's marriage to Ryan D'Angelo on Christmas Eve, she'd been suffering from newlywed fever. At inconvenient times, she disappeared from the inn, sneaking home to make whoopee whenever Ryan wasn't on the commute for the advertising accounts he managed.

Getting her groove on was one thing. But she left the bulk of her workload in limbo, or forgotten altogether.

Linnie was no better. She'd left Jada with the unhappy duty of juggling the day-to-day operations—while baking all the confections required for the menu—and while the staff, quickly expanding, looked to Jada for leadership. Since agreeing to set the date with attorney Daniel Kettering, Linnie's management skills had gone AWOL.

In her pocket, Jada's smartphone vibrated. She'd already taken a call from the staff in Housekeeping, and another from an employee manning the front desk. Absently, she rubbed her temples. That morning, she had awoken with a headache that still hadn't abated. A bad hair day *and* a four-alarm headache: it was just her luck.

"In case you've both forgotten, we're running out of time," Jada said. "Linnie still has to mail out invitations, settle on the menu for the reception, pick a band, write her wedding vows, select flowers—if we don't get past this task, the Sirens will make all the decisions." Although Linnie hadn't requested their assistance, she'd surrendered weeks ago beneath the group's determination to help plan the wedding. "Let's stop arguing, all right?"

Jada was rewarded with silent nods of consent. Relieved, she returned to the rack. Sifting through the gowns, she selected a frock with glass beads spiraling down the sleeves. They'd just finished zipping the back when Jada's smartphone vibrated again. She thumbed through the texts, an entire list of SOS messages from the staff.

Torn between loyalty to Linnie and to the inn that bore her name, Jada returned the phone to her pocket. The problems would have to wait.

Chapter 2

"You're getting an early start." In the doorway to Jada's office, Linnie offered a tentative smile.

Looking up from the paperwork, Jada felt relief. Linnie appeared calmer this morning, well rested. In the corridor where their offices stood side by side, waitresses drifted past. They were on their way to the Sunshine Room, to set up the restaurant's tables for breakfast service.

Jada motioned her inside. "I meant to get to this yesterday," she confided, nodding at the paperwork. "Employee applications. We're still short two bussers for dinner service, and we need more help in Housekeeping. We could also use another employee at the front desk. I'd like to get the positions filled before we're any further into spring."

"Should I plow through the apps?"

The offer was unexpected. "I'll let you know when I've narrowed down the field," Jada said, glad to see Linnie getting back into the swing of things. Any effort she made would be better than the previous weeks of no effort at all. "If you want to take something off my plate, make a decision on the menu for the wedding reception. I gave you a list of suggestions last week."

"I'll get to it today."

Linnie shifted from foot to foot, her attention drawn to the corridor. Nervous fingers traced the one-carat engagement ring her fiancé,

Daniel Kettering, had presented to her in January. The pear-shaped diamond scattered light across the office as she rubbed her lips together.

The pose—Linnie wavering in mild distress, hunting for the right apology—sent warmth through Jada. A flurry of memories followed. How they sealed their friendship in fourth grade with a bag of sweetheart candies on Valentine's Day. How Linnie borrowed Jada's Ford Taurus in eleventh grade and promptly drove it into a ditch. How they both learned the basics of proper makeup application thanks to Cat, who was younger but always more sophisticated.

Jada got to her feet. "The talented men from Unity Design won't arrive for another half hour. Why don't we go out back and check on Philip's progress?"

During his youth, Daniel's younger brother, Philip, had broken the hearts of many of the girls he'd dated in Sweet Lake. Back then, Jada viewed the tall, dark-haired Casanova as shallow. Ancient history. Philip Kettering now owned the landscape firm installing a new patio behind the ballroom, where Linnie and Daniel planned to hold their nuptials.

Linnie was saying, "The stone for the patio was delivered."

"Last night?"

"About ten minutes after you left. Philip's crew worked until nightfall, ferrying the pallets to the back of the inn. There was a problem with the skid loader. Philip was covered in engine grease by the time he got the contraption up and running."

"What about the azaleas?" Philip had selected a variety sure to bloom in late April.

"They came in too, along with a bunch of boxwood plants." Linnie's expression brightened. "You're sure you can spare a minute? I'd love to show you everything."

Yesterday, Jada had finished work with a full-on headache. She didn't feel much better this morning, but she managed a cheery expression. "I can't wait."

As they walked through the lobby, an older couple shuffled toward the cozy seating area that looked out at the rolling hills surrounding the inn. Outside, the rocking chairs on the veranda stood empty. Sunlight glinted off the building's golden sandstone exterior. Linnie led the way across the grass, toward the area behind the ballroom.

The crisp morning air seemed to lend the confidence she needed. "Jada, I'm sorry—for everything. I have no idea how you've put up with me." From over her shoulder, she darted a glance. "I've been temperamental and just plain snotty. Especially yesterday, when you and Cat were only trying to help. I swear I'll do better."

The apology came as a relief, and Jada smiled. "Stop viewing every decision like a chore," she suggested. She was eager to help Linnie subdue her worrywart tendencies. "Planning your wedding is supposed to be fun."

"For most women, I'm sure it is. I don't like being center stage."

Stepping into the limelight never bothered Jada, but Linnie had arrived in the world with a more reticent nature. She was more comfortable behind the scenes.

"You're an introvert," Jada said.

"Yeah, and getting glammed up isn't my thing. Why aren't yoga pants and comfy T-shirts all the rage for a wedding day?"

"Perhaps you and your handsome groom should've skipped the frills and eloped."

Linnie puffed up her cheeks, then blew out a stream of air. "Daniel wants a traditional wedding. And don't forget about the Sirens. They're determined to pitch in. I'm sure they'll come up with the cutest wedding favors and flower arrangements for the ballroom. I'd gladly skip the hoopla, but they're having a blast with the preparations."

"Then enjoy the hoopla."

"I feel like I'm drowning in details. The Sirens gave me some meditation tapes, but they don't really help." A smile crept across Linnie's mouth as she slowed her gait. "I hear they gave you a sack of herbs. Something to do with the dreams they've been having about you."

"They didn't haul a sack of herbs into the Wayfair's kitchen. Penelope made a sachet with dried rosemary."

"Why rosemary?"

"The Sirens haven't figured out the significance." Presumably they'd unlock the mystery once Tilda abandoned late-night viewings of *The Wizard of Oz* for movies featuring world-class sleuths. "I'm supposed to keep the sachet with me at all times. Don't tell Penelope I stuck it in a drawer in my office. I can't carry it everywhere. People will wonder why I smell like a dinner entrée."

"Penelope will forgive you. Tilda and Norah? Probably not. They've been the most spooked by the dreams. Better keep the sachet on you when they're at the inn."

"Will do." Changing tack, Jada said, "Listen, if you get overwhelmed, I'll make some of the wedding decisions." Given all her responsibilities, taking on more work didn't appeal. Yet she'd rather increase her workload than watch her oldest friend backslide into constant worry. "We'll split up the tasks to reduce your stress level. Easy peasy. Call it an early gift from the maid of honor."

"I've dumped too much on you already. The best man isn't stuck weighing in on Daniel's every decision."

Jada nodded in silent agreement. Between managing Unity Design and single parenting, Philip Kettering's days were hectic. More difficult too, since last summer. Once Linnie and Daniel began living together, Philip lost the homemade meals and babysitting help he'd relied on from his older brother. The change was also difficult for his six-year-old daughter. Fancy missed her uncle Daniel's attentions and eating dinner at his house on a regular basis.

Thanks to Linnie's urging, Jada had begun picking up the slack last winter when Linnie and Daniel got engaged. Now the trips to Philip's house were a normal part of Jada's weekly routine. The frequent visits to drop off meals or spend an hour playing with Philip's ultrafeminine daughter left Jada battling complicated emotions. No doubt Philip shared her discomfort; the constant interaction dredged up memories they both wanted to forget.

Linnie was saying, "Ballantine's sent a van to pick up the bridal gowns, but not before I picked out Fancy's dress from the flower girl options." She'd asked Philip's daughter to join the wedding party. "Last night, after the men finished moving the pallets to the new patio area, I dropped by Philip's house to show Fancy the outfit."

The six-year-old owned a closet jammed with dress-up clothes. She put together a different princess outfit for each Halloween, complete with a crown, faux-jewel scepter, and assorted jewelry culled from Cat's glitzy collection. When she wasn't in a Disney sort of mood, she regaled her doting father with ballerina tutus and feather boas.

"Did Fancy like the dress?" Jada asked.

"She wouldn't try it on. The dress is covered with ribbons and bows, exactly the sort of fluff she adores." A hint of injury sent Linnie's attention roaming across the grass. "You would've thought I was the evil stepmother, offering her a poison apple."

"That's a little extreme, isn't it?"

"I get the impression Fancy isn't my number-one fan," Linnie said. "Which makes sense. She loves her uncle Daniel, and I've horned in on her playtime. They used to spend lots of time together."

"They will again. You and Daniel have only been a 'thing' since last summer. Once you settle into your new life, you'll find time for his niece."

It seemed best not to address the bigger issue: Fancy's wariness around Linnie. Unlike Jada, or Cat for that matter, Linnie seemed clueless about how to interact with children. Often she behaved too formally around Fancy, making it hard for the child to relate to her.

Jada was happy to offer a few pointers. "Linnie, stop acting like you're walking on eggshells when you're with Fancy. I know you want her to like you, but sometimes you're too formal." She caught the note of impatience bleeding into her voice and sweetened her tone. "A small child doesn't know how to relate to that."

"Easy for you to say. My cooking skills are on par with Philip's, meaning they're nonexistent. And I can't bake to save my life. You've won Fancy's affections through years of luring her with killer brownies and other treats."

"I also talk to her on her level. You should too."

They'd reached the back of the inn. A large section of the lawn was carved away, revealing the dark clumps of earth beneath. Tall pallets of sandstone surrounded the perimeter like sentries. The unreliable skid loader, an expensive piece of equipment Jada knew Philip couldn't afford to replace, stood behind a cluster of plant stock.

Approaching the nearest pallet, Jada ran her fingers across a slab of cool stone. "Did Fancy explain why she wouldn't try on the dress?" There seemed more to the story, something Linnie had missed.

"She was probably tired." A reasonable explanation, yet doubt inked Linnie's voice. "I stopped by close to her bedtime."

"Not the best timing."

"I left the gown with Philip. He said he'll call if it needs alterations." Linnie circled the pallet of golden stone. She looked up suddenly. "Do you think he'll forget to have Fancy try on the dress? He's forgetful sometimes."

A small seed of concern lodged in Jada's stomach. "Should I ask if he wants me to come over?" she asked. "Men are rarely experts on little girl outfits."

"Like you need me hoisting more on your shoulders."

Head bowed, Jada absently toed the grass. No, she didn't need more on her shoulders, but what choice was there? Her bestie was getting married, and she'd never let Linnie down. Relief over Linnie's apology threatened to morph into anxiety as Jada quietly went over her expanding to-do list.

"I'm going with Daniel to hear another wedding band," Linnie reminded her. "You promised to deal with the furniture delivery. Are you sure you have time to handle Fancy too?"

"The furniture for the south wing should arrive by noon." Fending off the anxiety, Jada resolved to call Philip after the movers finished outfitting every suite. "Assuming we get everything in place by late afternoon, I'll have time to help Fancy."

"You're sure?"

"It's fine—honest." Not even close, but Jada drummed up a cheerful expression.

Linnie nodded with satisfaction. Then she spread her arms, to indicate the long rectangle of dirt Philip and his men would soon transform for her wedding ceremony. "So, what do you think?"

By late morning, Jada had narrowed down the employee applications. After placing phone calls to set up interviews for later in the week, she returned to the Wayfair's kitchen. With the lunch rush over, the sous-chef was setting out vegetables on the long center island to begin prep work for the dinner menu. At the far end of the room, the windows were flung open to let in the fragrant spring air. Birdsong supplied pleasant background music as Jada prepared a marble cheesecake.

The warm weather should've lifted her spirits. Since meeting with Linnie, she couldn't set aside her concerns regarding Fancy. Children behaved unpredictably, especially around adults they didn't know well. Although it was doubtful Fancy disliked Linnie, their interactions weren't frequent enough to forge a solid relationship. Pouring the cheesecake into a pan, Jada wondered if it had been wise to add Fancy to the wedding party. Linnie and Daniel had struck upon the idea soon after announcing their engagement. They'd done so without the child's consent but with Philip's approval.

Along with her worry about Fancy, Jada suffered the uneasy feeling that today marked a date when she must undertake an important task, something critical.

What am I forgetting?

None of the Wayfair's bills were due. She'd paid most of the invoices at the beginning of the month, a task she'd assumed in February, when Linnie's wedding jitters became too obvious to ignore. Striding through the lobby, she wondered if the forgotten item was personal in nature—a family birthday, an anniversary? Nothing came to mind.

The sense of unease followed her through a hectic afternoon.

After Jada went over the dinner menu with the night chef, she spent grueling hours darting up and down the stairwell, directing the movers on where to place beds, dressers, and chaise lounges in the newly renovated south wing. After the furniture was in place, she helped the Housekeeping staff ferry linens to the new suites. The work was a refreshing change of pace after the wedding gown fiasco of the day before.

Late in the afternoon, Cat found her inside the largest suite, sprawled across a chaise lounge. Minutes earlier, the last men from Riggin Movers had thumped down the stairwell. Down the corridor, two maids were making up beds in the suites Jada, Linnie, and Cat had occupied during the dark years before the inn became profitable.

"All finished?" Cat asked.

"Finally." The muscles in Jada's shoulders burned from hours bending, reaching, and repositioning furniture closer to windows or farther away.

Cat offered a sheepish grin. "I meant to pitch in. I was . . . delayed."

A telltale patch of red bloomed on Cat's neck. More newlywed fever, with the love bite an indication that her husband was working from home today.

"You're just now getting in?" Jada asked. She made no attempt to hide her disapproval.

"Stop looking at me like I'm a truant." Cat huffed out a breath. "I came in this morning. You were in the kitchen. I went home at lunchtime to see Ryan."

Tamping down her irritation, Jada nodded at the evidence. "Is there concealer in your purse? You need some."

"Oh. Right."

Cat dug into the purse swinging beside one slender hip. She produced a mirror from the bag, and padded her fingers across the plunging neckline of her silk dress. Unlike Jada, who preferred jeans and casual tops, Cat always appeared at work in high fashion—with all the right accessories.

Peering into the mirror, Cat dabbed concealer on the blemish. "It feels strange up here, doesn't it?" she said.

"Like we've erased the past," Jada agreed.

"I'm afraid to step into my old suite and check out all the changes." Snapping the concealer shut, Cat glanced toward the corridor with misgiving. "What if seeing the changes alters my memories? We had some great times when the three of us lived up here together. I don't want to lose those memories."

"Then don't look. I hardly recognized my old suite. It was hard being inside the room." An emotion like homesickness throbbed in Jada's chest. With a rueful laugh, she added, "I didn't offer to help the girls in Housekeeping make up the bed in my old suite. Everything looks so pretty and bright, ready for the first guests. I wanted to cry."

The three women had spent the better part of their twenties rooming together in the south wing, struggling to drag the Wayfair out of the red, sharing the best years of their youth in drafty suites laid out side by side. A sense of loss still lingered in Jada for all those times they chatted long into the night, sharing their deepest thoughts and secrets. Back then, the wing's heating barely worked, and they never knew if the Wayfair would soon be shuttered, sending them and the depleted staff into the unemployment lines. But Jada cherished every trial they had overcome, how the sense of working for the higher good of the town deepened their friendship. Cat and Linnie were more than besties now. They were her sisters, forged to her heart forever.

Settling deeper in the cushiony fabric of the chaise lounge, Jada said, "All the time we spent living here—we were lucky. We were given a chance to make a difference in the town, and we did." Her heart shifted as she added, "Remember when Treat Wayfair's stroke forced him into an early retirement? Few people believed his daughter could bring the inn back from the brink, especially with only the help of her two besties and a skeleton crew. Saving the Wayfair from ruin seemed impossible, but we stuck it out. I'm proud of us."

"We grew up here, became women. Shared dreams, and made them come true."

"Look how many new employees we've hired in just the last quarter. We're having a real impact on Sweet Lake."

"I'm glad." Cat hesitated, her eyes darkening with concern. "Jada, do you think Linnie will follow her dreams?"

"With Daniel? I hope so."

"I'm afraid she'll ditch at the last moment. Break his heart—break the hearts of every Siren. They're working overtime on the wedding arrangements."

"If she calls off the wedding, the Sirens will survive. Daniel is another matter. He's incredibly patient, but even he has limits."

"We should've suggested they elope. It would've been easier on Linnie."

Jada recalled making a similar comment when Linnie had shown her the progress on the new patio. "She never would've agreed to elope. Daniel wants a big wedding with most of the town in attendance." His parents would fly in from their retirement home in Texas; Linnie's parents, now living in Florida, would do the same.

Jada swung her feet to the floor. Cat was more emotional than her by yards, and a light sheen of tears was collecting in her eyes. If Linnie nixed the wedding, it would upset Cat too. Now that she'd found the love of her life, she wanted Linnie—and one day Jada—to join her in marital bliss.

Steering the conversation to lighter topics, Jada said, "Memories aside, guests will like the south wing's new look. We spent more money than reasonable, but I can't fault the end result. This place now reeks of elegance."

Over the winter months, an elevator had been installed behind the lobby to accommodate guests. It was a minor undertaking compared to the other upgrades. The south wing was now completely renovated, the roof repaired, and a portion of the interior gutted. The fine carpentry had been finished in February, and new paint gleamed on every wall.

Cat turned in a slow circle. "Everything looks great, and without a moment to spare."

"We have a reservation?"

"For this room, in fact. The front desk got the call this afternoon. The guest asked for the largest suite on the grounds."

This early in the season, half of the rooms in the main inn were empty.

"What's the duration of the reservation?" Jada asked. She'd assumed they wouldn't have bookings for the south wing until May at the earliest.

"Two weeks, confirmed. She might stay longer."

"Who is she?"

"A retired college professor from Chicago."

"A *wealthy* professor, if she might keep the room into April."

"There is one catch." A curious light settled in Cat's brown eyes. "She asked to speak with you. She was rather insistent."

For reasons beyond logic, the comment brought back the sense of unease that had dogged Jada all day. Something she'd forgotten, a neglected task she'd rue forgetting once she extracted it from her over-taxed brain.

Why would a retired college prof wish to speak with me personally?

The request made no sense.

Cat was saying, "Before you ask, she didn't explain why she wanted to talk to you. She just began rattling off questions. I got the impression she's used to getting her way."

"A demanding guest. How delightful." With so many new employees on the Wayfair's staff, Jada wasn't looking forward to an overly demanding guest intimidating them.

"Will you call her tonight?" Cat handed over a slip of paper. Her distinctive handwriting raced across the page. "She's strong-willed, but totally legit. I googled her. Millicent Earhardt, PhD. She taught American history before her retirement. She's written a few books."

"Which might explain her extended stay with us." The Wayfair Inn was a landmark with a rich Ohio heritage. Linnie's ambitious forebears had opened the first trading post in the area back in 1822. They had owned the first lumber mill, and carved the town of Sweet Lake from the dense forest surrounding the lake that shared its name. "Are you sure our curious historian doesn't prefer to speak with Linnie? She's the one with famous ancestors. Why would the guest ask to chat with me? I'm only the co-manager."

"And our superb resident baker." Cat shrugged. "Maybe she's writing a book on minority women in business."

"Then why wasn't she content to speak with you?"

Cat chewed this around for a moment. "What if she's finished her research on Latina women in business? Geez, I hope not. I'd love to give an interview. I mean, why should you get all the glory?" Once Cat latched onto a theory, she was capable of spinning it to ridiculous proportions. "How cool if we both end up in a history book!"

"Don't head for the footlights just yet. The woman is a historian, not a sociologist. If she wants to speak with the Wayfair's superb baker, I'm guessing she's a foodie." Jada decided she'd whip up any confection the historian craved if doing so would secure a long booking for the inn. "I'll call her tomorrow. I can't tonight. There's a good chance I'm heading over to Philip's house to help Fancy with her dress for the wedding. I need to give him a call after work."

Jada rose with her emotions in flux.

A vague sliver of a memory flirted with the surface of her mind, then sank back into the muddy depths. It dawned on her that the name *Millicent Earhardt* seemed familiar. She wasn't sure why. Jada's reading preference ran toward fiction, not history, and she'd attended college in Ohio, not Illinois.

In the doorway, Cat paused. "What's the matter?"

"I wish I knew." There wasn't an easy way to explain about the familiarity of Millicent's name, or why the upcoming call made her anxious. Instead, Jada said, "There was something I was supposed to do today. I can't recall what."

"Check Linnie's calendar. Heck, you should take the calendar and keep it in your office. You've been handling most of the management tasks for weeks."

"The missing task isn't on the calendar. I've already checked."

Cat lifted her shoulders in a careless shrug. "Then whatever it is, it'll wait. You never forget the important stuff." She patted Jada's cheek. "You're too responsible."

The scent of fresh linens wafted through the corridor. A singsong of conversation followed. Jada glimpsed two of the maids inside the suite she'd once called her own.

The walls, no longer a dull grey, sported spring-green paint. New draperies in pale yellow festooned the bay window. The maids hurried to either side of the bed, still immersed in conversation. The taller girl snapped out the sheet, a fluttering sail that rippled in the air, and Jada recalled the countless times Cat or Linnie helped her put clean linens on the bed, the sheets old and threadbare. They'd never permitted themselves the luxury of using the better linens reserved for the inn's guests.

The maids unfolded the new comforter, green like the walls. The fabric was decorated in a swirling pattern meant to give the room a modern feel. From a distance, the pattern reminded Jada of snowflakes.

Gooseflesh sprouted on her arms.

"Cat . . . ," she said slowly. "What is today's date?"

"I'm not sure. Is it important?"

Queasy, Jada retrieved her smartphone from her pocket. Of all the days—how could she have forgotten this one?

The memories rushed over her. They were a chilling onslaught, like the snowstorm that struck Sweet Lake six years ago, crusting the streets with ice and drowning the houses in layers of white. She recalled the panic that had gripped her on that fateful day. She'd raced out of the inn and down the hill, blinded by the pelting snow, guided only by a premonition of disaster.

With effort, Jada pushed the memory away. She stared blankly at her smartphone.

At last, her brain processed the date on the glowing panel. *March thirteenth—unlucky thirteen.*

The day tragedy befell Sweet Lake.

Chapter 3

Of all the Sweet Lake Sirens, Penelope Riddle was his favorite.

On a day he dreaded each year—and Philip certainly hadn't expected to receive a call from his daughter's elementary school—the owlish and sensitive Penelope supplied a patch of sunshine.

The sixtyish Siren wore her heart on her double chins, which shuddered violently if she caught one of the boys at Sweet Lake Elementary threatening to drop an earthworm down the back of a girl's blouse. Her chins danced with doughy goodness when she helped the children make bells out of Styrofoam cups recycled from the retirement home outside of town. Penelope spent hours washing out the used cups in the kitchen of her odd and charming house before repurposing them with the help of the first graders in Miss Wilson's class.

Penelope believed a benevolent force underpinned the natural world. During Philip's long-ago childhood, he'd marveled at her stories of fairies living in the forest near the blue waters of Sweet Lake. He clung to her animated voice whenever she described how the earth would sing to you if you pressed your ear to mossy ground and listened hard enough.

Long before tragedy cut a groove in his life, she convinced him that any wish—no matter how outrageous or impossible—was sure to grace his life if he ventured outside on a night when shooting stars streaked the skies, and he prayed with all his might. He'd believed the canard all the way to tenth grade, when a meteor shower burst over the town in racing pinstripes of silver. The following morning, a red Corvette did not appear in his parents' driveway.

Philip had suffered actual remorse.

He shifted his large body in the chair where he was imprisoned before the principal's desk. The skinny and high-strung Geneva Sauls hadn't arrived, and he welcomed the chance to compose himself. Seated next to him, Penelope continued to dab at her head with paper towels. On a normal day, the streaks of white sprouting from her auburn hair gave her the look of a mad scientist. Today, orange finger paint dripped from the wispy strands.

How *any* of this had happened was beyond his grasp. Principal Sauls had called while he was up to his knees in dirt, helping his men position the first sandstone pavers for the Wayfair's patio installation. Compounding his embarrassment over his daughter's infraction at school, he'd trailed clumps of dirt all the way from the lobby to Sauls's office.

A roll of paper towels leaned against Penelope's calves. Tearing off a sheet, he said, "Penelope, I am sorry. I don't know what got into her." He took a hasty swipe at the paint dripping from her chin.

"Oh, stop. You've apologized repeatedly."

"Not nearly enough."

Blots of orange speckled her eyeglasses. Tearing off another sheet, he dabbed the mess away. Behind the thick glass, her rheumy eyes sparkled with affection. She leaned closer.

"Fancy was fine when we started the project," Penelope confided. "The teachers always let me devise my own projects when I volunteer, and all the children were working with the finger paints like busy little bees. We're making a panorama—it's nearly fifteen feet long. We had to push desks out of the way to make room on the floor."

There seemed no limits to the Siren's imagination. Landscapes crafted from papier-mâché, under-the-sea dioramas built from discarded boxes—recently, the children had begun collecting plastic bottles around town for a project she was planning for later in the spring. It didn't escape the notice of Philip and the other parents that Penelope was teaching the children how to recycle items usually tossed into the garbage.

"The panorama you were doing with the kids . . . ," he said. "What was the subject of the painting?"

"Linnie and your brother's wedding."

Philip arched a brow. "Not a topic I'd expect a bunch of first graders to choose." Usually the girls went for fairy-tale themes. The boys preferred superheroes or anything related to sports.

"The children couldn't agree on what to paint. I made the suggestion. Talk about a heated debate! The boys put up a fuss, booing down the idea as too lovey-dovey. They relented once I explained they could paint the scenery, including the Wayfair and the new patio you're installing."

"And the girls?"

"They cheered when I assigned them the task of painting the wedding party. At least they all *seemed* pleased," Penelope explained. Distress whispered across her features. It disappeared beneath the excitement brightening her gaze as she added, "Several of Fancy's girlfriends asked to paint her leading the wedding party. They were very enthusiastic."

"What did you assign my daughter?"

Penelope gave him a meaningful look. "She volunteered to paint Jada. I knew she would."

The remark made him feel foolish. Of course his daughter would elect to paint Jada—she'd become a daily fixture in their lives. Initially the situation had been awkward, because Philip knew Jada had only started coming around at Linnie's behest. He was put off by the thinly veiled intervention, as if he couldn't manage without his brother Daniel's help and home-cooked meals. But he'd quickly revised his opinion—Fancy welcomed the feminine attention. Much as he'd worked to give his daughter a normal childhood, she'd missed out on motherly love.

Philip lowered his gaze to his work boots, shedding dirt on the floor.

Last night, Fancy had turned her nose up at the dress Linnie wanted her to wear for the wedding. Why, he wasn't sure. She'd stomped off to her bedroom in little-girl fury. After Linnie departed, he tried to enter his daughter's bedroom to get a fix on the problem. Fancy's stuffed animals were barricading the door.

The situation should've been funny, but he hated the idea of disappointing Linnie and Daniel if his kid put a kink in their wedding plans.

"You're sure Fancy liked the idea of painting the wedding scene?" he asked doubtfully.

"She seemed eager," Penelope said. "I hope I didn't misread her. All the girls in her class are so excited about Fancy being the flower girl. Isn't she excited?"

"I thought so. Now I'm not sure." Philip realized his feet were tapping a nervous rhythm, showering more dirt on the floor. He stilled them. "I should've run the idea by her before telling Linnie and Daniel she'd participate. All things considered, I'm wondering why I didn't. Fancy is in a big-girl phase. She insists on making her own decisions."

The door to the principal's office squeaked open, then shut with a bang. Startled by the noise she'd created, Geneva Sauls flinched. Muttering apologies, she trotted to her desk.

"Philip, hello." The principal landed her skinny arms on the desk. Her elbow nicked a mason jar brimming with pens. The jar rolled toward Philip, then toppled to the floor.

Pens skittered in all directions. Retrieving all within reach, Philip skipped the pleasantries. "Where's Fancy? I thought I was taking her home."

The principal smiled too brightly. "Let's talk alone first."

Straining nearly out of his chair, he caught the mason jar before it rolled into the dots of paint by Penelope's loafers. "She's still in her classroom?" A chunk of the jar's rim had broken off; he found it beneath his chair.

"I asked the school nurse to take her to the infirmary to calm down," Geneva said. "She refused to go back to class."

The concern shading the principal's words slowed his movements. Carefully, Philip returned the jar to the desk. "Fancy refused to go back to her classroom?" Usually she was obedient, especially at school. Always at school.

Or so he'd assumed.

Principal Sauls seemed incapable of meeting his eyes. "Frankly, she's been . . . unruly," she elaborated. "Quite a bit lately. I'm concerned."

"I wouldn't describe Fancy as unruly," he said.

"She wasn't, earlier in the academic year."

"Are you implying my kid has become a troublemaker?"

A challenge, and Sauls appeared ready to leap from her chair. "She has seemed troubled. Lashing out may be her means of expressing emotions she can't process well."

"Fancy processes her emotions just fine," Philip shot back, and the fierce, protective love he reserved for his daughter put him on the defensive. "Listen, I can't explain why she dumped paint on Penelope in the middle of an art project. The behavior is totally out of character, especially when you take into account how much she loves Penelope. All I'm asking is for you to go easy on my daughter. I promise I'll get to the bottom of this."

Penelope rested her hand on his wrist. The touch of her fingers made him aware of the erratic beat of his pulse. He felt off-balance, a reaction he usually suffered on the thirteenth of March. The problems with his daughter managed to amplify his unsettled emotions.

"Philip," Penelope murmured, and the pressure of her hand increased until he lifted his eyes to hers. "Geneva has no intention of punishing Fancy. Your daughter is a joy in every class, one of the best students."

"Then what is the problem?" he asked.

"She's wondering—we're both wondering—if Fancy chose to act out this afternoon. This *is* an upsetting day. You and Jada are very stoic, grieving in your own ways. Both of you carry your sorrow admirably, as you've done every year. However, Fancy is older now. Children *are* like sponges."

The comment knotted the muscles in Philip's back. "I'm not following." Nor did he wish to follow the conversation's dangerous turn. "Why don't you spell out what you're trying to tell me?"

"Children absorb the emotional climate of the adults around them. They sense grief, sorrow, even anger."

"Penelope, be realistic. Fancy isn't picking up bad vibes. Jada would never discuss the anniversary with her. I wouldn't either. We both know she's too young."

She patted his hand. "Calm down," she murmured, with a quick glance at the principal. Sauls was sitting stock-still on the other side of the desk, apparently glad to let them hash this out without her intervention. "Philip, I'm not implying you or Jada would discuss today's significance with Fancy. You're both responsible adults. Jada loves your daughter as much as you do. There's another issue to consider."

"Which is?"

"Every year, the anniversary brings heartache. For you, and Jada too. Which is a problem because Fancy is old enough now to sense something amiss."

"No, she's not," he said, mortified when his voice nearly broke. Fancy didn't have the slightest inkling of the day's significance. The possibility was ludicrous. He had every intention of steering her through the precious years of childhood—and all the way through the dangerous teenage years—before being forced to explain the loss marked by March 13. He refused to share the excruciating details before Fancy was mature enough to hear them.

At six, she understood nothing of the world's ugliness. She didn't understand the sorrow that drove an unbalanced soul to the edge of an emotional precipice, as if self-inflicted suffering were an irresistible lure. Nor did Philip grasp the motivation—and he'd spent years rehashing the memories of his short marriage with grim precision.

Stiffly, Philip rose. "Are we done here?" He searched for a pleasant tone sure to mask his unease. "I appreciate your concern. I'll talk to Fancy, spell out my expectations for her behavior at school. Now, if you don't mind, I'd like to take her home."

When the school nurse materialized with Fancy, he was pacing in the reception area with ill-suppressed frustration. Smudges of paint covered the bodice of the green-and-pink plaid dress his daughter had chosen that morning for school. Wisps of lemon-colored hair fell around her face. At the sound of his approaching footsteps, she hung her head.

Sadness washed through him. Whatever impulse had driven Fancy to act out, she regretted it now.

Taking her by the hand, he led her past the office staff.

In the parking lot, he lifted her into the passenger side of his pickup and latched the seat belt. Warily, her cornflower-blue eyes followed him around the hood of the truck. She looked small and defenseless on the passenger seat, a delicate wisp of a girl awaiting her daddy's reaction to her bad behavior. Philip slid in behind the wheel and brought the engine to life.

"Daddy?"

He drove out of the lot, turned right on Orchard Lane. "What, sugarplum?"

"Are you mad?"

Houses streamed past. Stopping at the light in Sweet Lake Circle, Philip regarded her. She twirled a lock of her long hair around her fingertips.

His heart lurched as she stopped twirling and began sucking on the strands. "I'm not mad," he assured her. Removing the strands from her mouth, he rested his fingers against her cheek. "Worried is more like it. Why did you dump paint on Penelope?"

The light changed. Fancy scooted out of reach. She looked out the window.

She began swinging her legs up and down. "Penelope showed my class," she muttered.

"Showed them what?"

"A picture of the dress."

"Your dress for the wedding?" He couldn't imagine why it mattered.

"She showed *everyone*. She even showed Andy McFee."

The boldly freckled Andy McFee had a crush on Fancy of major proportions. With typical male finesse, he expressed his devotion by growling like an ape when he chased her across the playground. In the lunchroom, Andy threatened to put worms in Fancy's PB&J. Last September, the lovesick boy stuck a marble in his nose for the shock value of hearing Fancy scream. The stunt didn't amuse his parents; it took a visit to the pediatrician to extract the marble.

Fancy despised him.

Philip pitied the kid. He hadn't been much older than Andy when his first stealthy stirrings of love for Jada caught him in a stranglehold. He recalled the twigs he'd buried in Jada's corona of dark curls during his shrimp years. Gum wrappers followed, and then a paper airplane he constructed in sixth grade study hall and aimed perfectly at her head. A sensation like triumph swam through his veins every time her chestnut-colored eyes locked onto him in a death-stare. Jada never put up with his shit. It didn't matter if they were on the playground or, later, stuck inside a classroom going cross-eyed over algebra—he'd always possessed a special talent for drilling through her composure.

Later still, in high school, he lived for the days when she forgot to subdue her undisciplined curls. If he made the bull's-eye, she'd launch after him in furious pursuit.

Thank God, he'd always been faster.

Dismissing the reverie, he told his daughter, "I don't care if Penelope showed Andy a photo of all your baby dolls *and* your stuffed animals. You're a big girl now. Big girls restrain their anger."

"What's *restrain?*"

He steered the pickup into the driveway of their compact brick house. "It means you can't dump paint on a grown-up. Not even if you're angry."

"I didn't mean to get mad."

He helped her climb down. "Tomorrow, we're stopping by Gift of Garb. You'll march into Penelope's store and apologize to her."

"Okay."

"Why don't you draw a picture for Penelope to show you're really sorry? She loves your drawings." A clutter of Fancy's artwork hung behind the cash register of Penelope's consignment shop. "You'll tell her you'll never be mean again."

"Okay!" Slipping from his grasp, Fancy trudged up the drive. "My tummy is rumbly. Can we go to Uncle Daniel's house?"

Dinner. That afternoon, he'd meant to break from work at the inn for a trip to the grocery store. The call from the school derailed the plan.

Philip scraped the hair from his brow. "No can do, sugarplum. Uncle Daniel went out with Linnie to hear bands play. They have to pick a band for the wedding. He isn't cooking tonight."

His daughter stared at him accusingly. "We don't have food in the house," Fancy informed him, as if he needed the reminder. "We *never* have food around."

"Let me grab a quick shower. I'll root through the freezer and scare up some good eats."

Disbelief scuttled across his daughter's face. "*You'll* make good eats? Daddy, you don't know how."

In her office, Jada dialed Philip's number again.

It was past six o'clock. Why wasn't he picking up? She'd already walked outside to check with the landscape crew on his whereabouts. The men were finishing up a section of the patio, setting in the heavy sandstone with sweat-streaked faces before knocking off for the night. According to the foreman, Philip had left the site during the afternoon without explanation.

The phone continued to ring. Impatient for Philip to answer, Jada gazed absently at the paperwork on her desk. The note with Cat's distinctive handwriting lay beneath the desk lamp. With reservation, she picked it up. She'd promised to call the historian from Chicago tomorrow, although she still had no idea why the task was necessary. The woman's suite was already booked. She was scheduled to arrive later in the week.

More pressing concerns occupied Jada's thoughts. Philip wasn't in the habit of disappearing without notice, not with a daughter who required dinner at a normal hour and a bath afterward.

Worried now, Jada considered driving over.

The idea held no appeal. Too often lately, she found herself coming to Philip's rescue, spending pleasant hours ensconced in his home playing with Fancy or whipping up dinner. So much time together only increased the uncomfortable mix of emotion brewing between her and Philip. She wasn't sure how to cool things down.

The obvious solution? Stop visiting so often. Jada would've already followed the plan if she hadn't grown close to his daughter. When she'd first begun dropping by last winter after Linnie and Daniel got engaged, she hadn't bargained on how quickly her relationship with Fancy would grow. The first grader still missed the constant interaction with her beloved Uncle Daniel, but she'd taken quickly to Jada.

Fancy came on the line. "Hello?"

"Fancy, it's Jada. I've been trying to reach your daddy. Is everything okay?"

A breathy silence, then, "No."

"What's going on?"

"The smoke is making my nose itchy."

Smoke?

Apprehension pulled Jada to her feet. "Sweetie, where are you? Is your daddy with you?"

"He's in the kitchen, burning dinner." Fancy's voice dropped to a whisper. "Come save me. He's making smelly food."

"I'm on my way." Jada tossed the note back onto her desk. "Tell your daddy I'm bringing dinner."

Waitstaff streamed in and out of the kitchen, placing orders and ferrying meals to the guests in the Sunshine Room. The evening's special of chicken with rosemary scented the air with a savory aroma. Jada filled three carryout boxes with generous portions, adding mashed potatoes and green beans on the side. She was placing the boxes in a bag when the connection struck her.

Rosemary.

According to the Sirens, the pungent herb factored into their dreams about Jada. They believed the handmade sachet they'd given her would resolve a burden from the past. The odd gift was still tucked away in her office. Jingling the keys from her purse, she released a nervous laugh.

A dish featuring rosemary included on tonight's menu—wasn't that just a coincidence? Did it matter if she was bringing the rosemary-infused dish over to Philip's house on March 13, the unluckiest day of the year? Jada didn't need Siren tokens or their mysterious pronouncements to point out the obvious.

If she carried a psychic burden, it belonged to Philip too.

Driving down the hill leading into town, she dismissed the strange coincidence. A fluke, really—while she liked the distinctive flavor of rosemary on poultry and Italian breads, she remained unconvinced the herb held any importance on a personal level. As for the burdens in her life, she handled them well enough.

On the patch of lawn before Philip's house, Fancy stood cradling a baby doll. Waiting for rescue, presumably.

Coming across the grass, Jada buried her gloomy thoughts. Seven o'clock was past Fancy's dinnertime. No doubt she was famished.

The child trotted up and leapt into her arms. She clung tight.

Jada balanced the carryout and one anguished first grader. "What's the matter, girlfriend?" she asked. She rubbed her nose across Fancy's cheek, which smelled faintly of peanut butter and tears. "Tough day at school?"

"I was bad." Nuzzling close, Fancy hid her face. "In art class."

"You got in trouble?"

"I hurt Penelope."

Jada angled her neck. "You hit her?" The notion was foreign. Fancy never displayed aggression.

"I painted her."

The explanation came as a relief. "Why did Penelope care if you painted a picture of her? She loves your pictures." Fancy owned more art supplies than Picasso.

Fancy gave a heavy sigh. "I threw paint *on* her."

"You did?" A bizarre summation, but Jada let it go. She carried the remorseful child into the house. Whatever the details, Philip would supply them.

In the cubbyhole foyer, she gasped. Grey threads of smoke drifted through the living room like ambling snakes. They trailed an acrid scent across the secondhand couch and the milk crates that stood in for side tables. In the kitchen, black smoke belched thick plumes around the stove.

Philip was swatting the air wildly.

"What's for dinner?" she asked dryly. She lowered Fancy into a chair and placed the cartons of rosemary chicken on the table. Snatching the towel from his grasp, she nudged him aside to retrieve the pot from the oven. A terrible stench came from beneath the lid.

She placed the pot on the stove. "What's inside? I'm afraid to look."

"Pot roast," Philip told her. He darted an embarrassed glance at the fridge. "I found it in the freezer."

She lifted the lid, studied the charred remains. "Did you defrost?"

"Was I supposed to?"

At the table, Fancy rustled through the bag and flipped open a carton. "Chicken!"

Philip watched his daughter place the cartons on the table before returning his attention to Jada. "You brought dinner . . . again?" he asked.

"Tonight's special at the inn. Rosemary chicken."

"I love rosemary chicken."

Appreciation made his voice husky and low, sending pleasure through Jada. "I know you do," she murmured, dredging up a casual tone. To Fancy, she said, "Grab some mashed potatoes while the getting's good. Don't wait. Your father will plow through them."

Aside from his lust for barbecue, there wasn't much Philip enjoyed more than mashed potatoes.

The advice put Fancy in motion. Tossing her doll aside, she scrambled to the silverware drawer.

Gratitude washed through Philip's strong features. "You're a lifesaver, Jada. Thanks."

"Thank your daughter. She requested the rescue operation."

"She did?" He looked briefly at Fancy, rooting through the silverware. "When?"

"She picked up when I called."

"Right." He rocked back on his heels. "May I pay you this time? Actually, I insist."

A typical response whenever she brought dinner over. "Stop offering, all right?" she remarked, smiling. "I'm not taking your money."

Cash was always tight in Philip's household. The equipment he cobbled together for his landscaping company was bought on the cheap at auctions. Rarely did his income allow for the extras, like new clothes for his threadbare wardrobe. His daughter fared better. Philip often took Fancy into Penelope's consignment shop, allowing her to choose from the new batches of dresses as they appeared on the racks. Fancy's outfits were secondhand, but usually looked brand-new.

Or the dresses *weren't* secondhand: Jada suspected the Sirens were hoodwinking their favorite single dad. It was a safe bet they were purchasing the stylish little-girl dresses on shopping sprees to Cincinnati or Columbus, then slipping the outfits onto Gift of Garb's racks whenever Philip strolled by with his daughter. Although he despised charity, he loved treating his daughter like a princess.

Jada retrieved the milk from the fridge and poured three glasses. "When I buy my first house, plan on helping with landscaping, big-time," she told him. Pride creased the lines around his mouth, hastening her to add, "Philip, I don't want your money. I'm happy to help."

"Lately, you've been helping a lot."

"My pleasure, totally."

"Well, thanks. I'm not sure what I'd do without you."

The kitchen wasn't much larger than a shoebox, and he was standing too close. Philip's dark-brown hair was damp, presumably from a quick shower. He smelled deliciously minty from the soap he purchased because Fancy loved the fragrance. In tandem, they reached for the glasses. Her shoulder brushed against the sturdy wall of his chest. The contact thumped unwanted delight through her veins.

The disconcerting emotion urged her to move back a safe distance. "What's going on with Fancy and Penelope?" she asked, searching for neutral ground.

"I'll tell you when little ears aren't present." He nodded at his daughter, plopping a scoop of mashed potatoes onto her plate. "We're having another big-girl issue."

"Worse than the skirmish over TV?" Fancy had won that battle. They now split weekend viewing between Disney movies and sports channels.

"This debate is a whole lot more interesting," Philip said.

Jada started for the table. "I'm not sure if that's good or bad."

"Me either," he said, chuckling.

They ate in companionable silence. Fancy plowed through her meal, battling with her father over the last of the potatoes. When she hopped down from her chair to plunk her silverware into the sink, she made a wide berth around him.

Sensing discord between father and child, Jada pushed away her unfinished meal. "Fancy, may I help with your bath—if your father doesn't mind?" She recalled the conversation with Linnie about the flower girl dress. Bath time would allow an opportunity for a girl chat.

The offer seemed a reprieve, and Fancy eagerly took her hand. "Daddy won't care." She tugged Jada away from the table.

Philip held his palms up. "Go for it." He eyed Jada's half-finished meal. "Do you mind?"

He was wolfing down the remains as Fancy steered her into the bathroom. Condensation glazed the mirror. Philip's jeans, boxers, and work shirt were heaped on the floor. No one working in the landscaping trade came home looking neat and tidy, but the amount of grunge on his clothes was impressive. If Jada didn't have a bead on his chosen occupation, she might have assumed he spent his days rolling in mud like Porky Pig.

The clothes were a harbinger of worse to come. Summoning the courage, she yanked back the shower curtain.

"Fancy—"

The duet they performed was long perfected. The six-year-old opened the cabinet beneath the sink, then slapped a bottle of bathroom cleaner into Jada's hand. Next came the sponge. Bending close, Jada began scrubbing the scum left behind by a hardworking man.

Backing away from the tub, Fancy wrinkled her nose. "Icky." She untied her pink tennis shoes.

"You said it."

"Why do boys like dirt? Dirt is scummy."

Jada finished scrubbing, leaned back on her haunches. "Scummy. Nice word choice. Where did you pick it up?"

"The third graders. At recess, one of the girls told a boy he was scummy for picking his nose."

"Yuck." The mock shudder she gave made Fancy giggle. "You're smart to listen in, and pick up new words."

The compliment brightened the child's impossibly translucent cheeks. "Do you like dirt? My daddy loves it."

"Actually, I do. I like the scent of the earth after a rain, and the end result when your father and his crews finish a job. Plants need dirt to bring them food. We'd never have flowers if they didn't have good soil to grow in."

"I like flowers." Daintily, Fancy tucked her shoes against the wall. "I help Daddy plant them in our garden."

"You're a good helper." The eager child had been trotting behind Philip with plastic gardening tools since she took her first baby steps. For such an outwardly rugged man, Philip displayed remarkable gentleness with his child. "I don't know what your father would do without you," she added, aping the sweet comment Philip had made to her before dinner.

"He'd be sad without me."

"He would."

A fan of lashes hid Fancy's eyes as she removed her socks. "Jada, will you tell me something?"

"Sure."

"Why is March the weepy month?"

The question lingered between them. Checking her expression, Jada turned on the tap. Thrown by the query, her mind went blank.

"Daddy hates March," Fancy offered. She stuffed her socks in her shoes, then approached. "He told Uncle Daniel. He said March makes him sad."

Jada reached for the bubble bath.

What else had Fancy overheard?

The flowing water rushed and churned, building a mountain of bubbles. This was shaky ground, with no clear path in sight.

While she searched for a proper response, Fancy wiggled the dress over her head. She folded the garment and placed it on the counter. "Uncle Daniel doesn't like March either. I could tell. He looked weepy too."

"I'm sorry," Jada murmured.

"Me too," Fancy said. The animal instinct small children possessed sent her gaze slowly across Jada's face, weighing her reaction. Fancy resembled a fawn poised at the forest's edge, fearful of the danger in open ground. "Do you hate March, Jada? Like Daddy and Uncle Daniel?"

"I don't hate March." Her heart throbbing, she helped Fancy into the tub.

"Then why do you look sad?"

"I'm not sad." Jada stirred the bubbles, glad for a way to dispel her emotions. "You might have misunderstood what your father said to Uncle Daniel."

"What's misunderstood?"

"It means you didn't hear right. Sometimes grown-ups talk about stuff kids don't get."

"They shouldn't do that."

"Not everything grown-ups talk about is meant for you to hear. Don't worry about it. Your father and Uncle Daniel don't have anything against March. Spring begins this month. Who wouldn't love that?"

"*I* love spring."

"Your daddy does too." Dropping the subject, Jada decided to tackle the issue of the dress for the wedding and Linnie's fear that she wasn't in like aces with her fiancé's niece. "Here's a question: Is there anything *you* don't like?"

Considering, Fancy scooped bubbles over her knees. "I don't like Andy McFee." She trailed water across the caramel-colored skin of Jada's forearm. "He's bad. He squishes worms for fun."

"The monster."

"Boys are stupid." Fancy picked up the mermaid Barbie wedged against the bath tile. One of Jada's more recent gifts, a favorite bath time toy. "Not Daddy. He's only stupid when he tries to make food."

"Linnie isn't a very good cook either, but she's not stupid," Jada offered, taking a more direct approach. She picked up the washcloth. Gently, she cleaned the delicate oval of the child's face. "What do you think of Linnie? Do you like her?" She set the washcloth aside.

"Are brides supposed to be scary?"

"Linnie isn't scary."

In silent dissent, Fancy lifted her shoulders. Lowering them, she dunked the doll beneath the bubbles. "Sometimes Linnie whines like a donkey."

"She does not!"

The child demonstrated her version of a donkey's whine. The high-pitched squeal echoed off the tiles. When Jada stopped laughing, Fancy said, "Linnie whines when Uncle Daniel talks about the wedding. She doesn't like being a bride."

"She doesn't like crowds or making big decisions. But she likes *you* very much. Don't you like her too?"

The wrong question, apparently. Fancy crossed her arms, a naked slip of a girl brewing in her bath. "Isn't a wedding like a big party?" she asked pointedly.

"Sure."

"Big girls pick their own party clothes, don't they?"

"Usually," Jada agreed.

"*I'm* a big girl."

"Totally. You're the biggest little girl I know." A smile threatened Jada's lips. She fought it down. A child's rank on the mysterious steps to maturity was a serious matter. Making light of an imagined slight wouldn't keep *her* in aces with the child. "You're practically a grown-up."

"Then *why* did Penelope show my class a photo of the dress I didn't pick, and *why* does Linnie get to choose? I always pick my party clothes. Does Linnie get to pick *everything* for her scary wedding?"

No answer came to mind, and Jada allowed pleasure to crease her face. The benefits of big-girl status were a weighty matter, especially for the uber-feminine Fancy. She'd been selecting her own party clothes from age four onward—long before first grade, when she achieved the designation of "big girl."

The discussion was still ongoing when Philip joined them in Fancy's bedroom. Jada had just finished helping his daughter fill her play crib with dolls and seat most of her stuffed animals around the small table that occupied a corner of the room.

"All set?" He drew back the covers and helped Fancy into bed. He sent Jada a curious glance. "What were you talking about in the bathroom? The discussion sounded pretty animated."

Jada handed Fancy the doll she'd decided to sleep with tonight. "Offer me a glass of wine, and I'll dish," she murmured.

"Deal."

She kissed Fancy on the forehead. "Sweet dreams."

"I love you, Jada."

The endearment pulled Philip's attention off his daughter and over to her. His gaze roamed across her face with the intensity of a lover's caress. The desire to meet his eyes rose unexpectedly in Jada. Heat tickled her neck. Her movements felt awkward, clumsy, as she bent toward the bed.

"I love you too," she replied, giving Fancy a loud, smacking kiss on the forehead. Laughter rang out, cooling the supercharged air surrounding Philip.

She went out, to give him a moment alone to say goodnight.

Two glasses of Chablis were waiting when he sauntered into the kitchen. They went out back, to the deck he'd added to the house last summer. Mismatched outdoor furniture from the local Goodwill provided an inviting seating area.

Politely, Philip waited for her to seat herself. "What's the deal?" He lowered his wine to the small table between them. "Between water splashing and what sounded like my kid's donkey imitation, the conversation seemed interesting. What were you discussing?"

"Party-girl clothes," Jada supplied. "In particular, what a big girl should wear to the wedding."

Alarm flitted through Philip's greenish-gold eyes. "Damn. I promised Linnie—"

"Forget about the flower girl dress," she said, cutting him off. "Your daughter wants to pick her outfit for the big occasion."

"I'm taking her shopping for a dress? By 'shopping' I mean a quick tour through Gift of Garb? Penelope will scare up something presentable for a wedding."

"You're not that lucky," Jada said. A nervous grin tickled the corners of her mouth. Her amusement fizzled as Philip's eyes lingered on her, his expression betraying confusion and something deeper, something Jada preferred not to identify. She took a hasty sip of wine. "Here's some advice. Don't attempt to talk Fancy out of her decision. She's dug her heels in."

"On what to wear to the wedding? I'm not sure I'm ready to hear this."

Chapter 4

Night crept across the yard. Savoring the privacy, Philip listened to her explanation.

He'd always loved Jada's voice, the honeyed cadence of her words, her full, throaty tone. She'd acquired a sultry voice clear back in junior high, when most of the girls sounded like screeching hens as they complained of acne or engaged in petty fights. Jada always stood above the fray, a natural leader in any group, with her maturity and dark beauty.

He took care not to stare as she revealed why his kid dumped paint on Penelope today at school. He hid the emotions flaring inside him as she described Fancy's request for what she'd like to wear to the wedding. If he fixed his hungry eyes on Jada for too long, she'd shut tight, like a clam.

Sorrow nicked Philip. When they were young, Jada hadn't thought much of him, if she'd thought of him at all. She'd thought even less of him once Bodi Wagner crashed into his life.

An unsettling thought he dismissed.

After Jada wrapped up, he said, "Fancy was angry at school because Linnie picked out the flower girl dress without her input?"

Jada chuckled. "She's your daughter," she reminded him. "You know the rule. Big girls choose their own party clothes."

"What if the party is a formal occasion costing twenty thou?"

Linnie didn't have money to spare, not with the Wayfair only recently in the green. But Daniel? He'd gladly raided his nest egg. Philip was still amazed at how his older brother had leapt into the feminine world of wedding planning with gusto.

Life is full of weird turns.

Jada smiled. "Fancy doesn't understand the expense going into the wedding. From her perspective, this is a party like any other."

"What does she want to wear?"

"Have you fastened your seat belt?" she teased, no doubt relishing his quandary.

"No," he tossed back, grinning.

Drawing out the suspense, Jada took a sip of her wine. Darkness spread across the grass in inky pools. Slipping off her loafers, she wiggled her toes while inhaling the night air. From the corner of his eye, Philip checked out the nail polish she'd chosen for this week's pedicure. The metallic bronze shade looked fantastic against her dusky skin. She pointed her feet and the movement—lazy, languid—drew his attention like hounds to the chase.

With effort, he looked away. Having a thing for a woman's beautifully shaped feet was certifiable. He couldn't help himself.

She said, "Remember the dress-up clothes I gave Fancy for Christmas?"

"The stuff you found on Amazon?"

Jada had gone overboard, buying a large box of costumes for his kid. Princess gowns and assorted headgear—she'd even purchased a cool magician's costume with a magic set, in case Fancy was ready to expand her imaginative play.

Finally, he caught her drift. "Hold on. Fancy wants to wear dress-up clothes to the wedding? Please tell me this is a joke."

"No can do. Your kid has tons of ideas. She's mulling over the yellow gown and the magician's cape. She might add a feather boa, or the top hat. If she decides on the top hat, she wants to add flowers to the band. The jury's still out."

"Take me out behind the barn and shoot me."

"You don't have a barn." Merriment sparked in Jada's eyes, but she managed to douse it. "Should I tell Linnie and Daniel?"

"No way am I forcing you to make them cry," he joked. "Talk about an ugly scene. They're going for wedding glamour, and my daughter isn't playing along. All their plans brought crashing down by a six-year-old."

"They have been going all out with the arrangements, Daniel especially."

"Like a worker bee intent on building the hive single-handedly. Good thing he's got a soft spot for the munchkin. She'll turn the affair into Halloween." Philip picked up his wine, took a swig. "I'll assume the noxious duty of telling them."

"You're sure?" The merriment returned to her eyes. She looked warm and inviting, and he didn't want the moment to end.

Elation tripped through him. "My brother, my problem," he replied, fighting it down. "The flower girl dress didn't come cheap. I was hoping Fancy wouldn't grow too much, and we'd retool the dress for her first high school prom."

A silly visual, and he felt triumph when a chortle popped from Jada's lips. "As if she'd let you. Keep her away from Cat's fashion mags, or she'll want French couture for her first prom."

"I'd better start saving my nickels. What's the going rate for French fashion?"

"Got me."

Their gazes caught, and held. The moment drew out with silvery promise. Rarely did Philip have the opportunity to regard Jada full on, without fear of appearing impolite or caveman rude. A heady experience.

Too quickly, Jada snuffed the connection. The air between them cooled. Something about the way she searched the shadows pooling across the backyard gave him the impression she wanted to broach another subject. She seemed unsure where to begin.

In her lap, she wove her hands together. Her fingers clenched tightly.

A jumpy sensation invaded him.

"Philip, while I was helping Fancy with her bath . . . she mentioned something else. A conversation she overheard between you and Daniel."

If Jada was Linnie's rock, Daniel was his. There was little he didn't share with his older brother. Much of what they discussed was out-of-bounds for his daughter, conversations about Philip's ill-fated marriage and the events he'd never fully processed. Since the days when Fancy was a fat-cheeked toddler, he'd taken care never to excavate those memories if she was nearby.

At length, he found his voice. "What did she overhear?"

"You told Daniel you hate the month of March."

"I did," he agreed slowly. "Last weekend." They were sharing beers in the living room when the conversation wheeled to the anniversary of Bodi's death.

What if he'd been discussing his late wife in more direct terms? Altering his daughter's quixotic opinion of the mother she'd never known would've been an unforgivable breach.

Torn between relief and self-chastisement, he elaborated. "Daniel stopped by to set up a date for our tux fitting. The conversation went from the wedding to the anniversary of Bodi's death. I was feeling pretty low, but I thought Fancy couldn't hear what we were talking about. She was playing in her bedroom."

"She heard enough to wonder why March is the weepy month. She's aware we're all sad this time of year. You, me, and Daniel."

"We're not the only ones who are low this time of year. Penelope is too."

Seven years ago, Penelope had gone to Columbus to visit relatives. The big-hearted Siren was crossing a Columbus street when a sullen eighteen-year-old bumped into her. Bodi Wagner's attempt at purse snatching failed.

Most women would've shouted with outrage at the assault. Penelope, as perceptive as she was kind, barely noticed the contents of her purse tumbling across the pavement. She *did* notice the trembling thief: Bodi was paper thin, but arrestingly beautiful despite the too-tight clothes and heavy makeup.

Over donuts in a nearby coffee shop, the girl shared small pieces of her story. A nonexistent home life and parents who were uncaring, or worse. Bodi striking out on her own soon after graduating from high school, with nothing but her wits to survive on the street. After listening to the story, Penelope encouraged her to come to Sweet Lake and take a job in the consignment shop. How she put up with the daily pillaging of her cash register was anyone's guess. A less-charitable soul would've thrown Bodi Wagner back onto the street.

"Penelope does a better job hiding her grief than the rest of us," Jada said. "She's older, more experienced with loss."

"When Fancy asked why I hate March, what did you tell her?"

"That you don't hate any month of the year. I didn't go into why we're all blue in the springtime. She's too young to understand, and I'd never want to change her opinion of her late mother. Fancy views Bodi as a fairy godmother or an angel, depending on the day. It seemed wiser to change the subject." Jada unclenched her hands. Rubbing her palms together, she glanced at him briefly. "Does she ask why her mother died?"

The question surprised him. They'd never discussed Bodi. Which made sense—Jada's memories of his late wife differed starkly from his own.

"Rarely," he said. "Fancy hasn't mentioned Bodi since the start of kindergarten last year. Penelope was helping us clean out closets. We came across old photos of Bodi right after she came to town."

"The ones taken in the consignment shop?" Jada guessed.

Philip nodded. "Penelope threw together a story about how some mothers are called back to heaven for special duties, even if it means they must leave a baby behind. The story seemed to work. Fancy never asks for details about her mother's death." Sickness washed through him. And anger, for all the pain left in Bodi's wake. "I guess she'd ask more questions if she did have memories."

"I'm glad she doesn't remember. She was just a few months old when Bodi . . ." Jada's voice trailed into a hard silence. Emotion crossed her face. "Doesn't matter. Fancy now understands we're grieving. The more she senses that something is up, the higher the chances she'll ask the difficult questions."

The possibility frightened him. "We have to do better, hide our grief. She's too young to deal with the facts."

"*I'm* still lost on the facts. How did we miss all the warning signs?"

"We didn't miss them. We were burned out from the theatrics. You, me, Penelope—we gave Bodi the sense of belonging we thought she craved. How did she repay us? She took all the caring we offered, and twisted it into something ugly."

"Philip, you're being awfully harsh."

The judgment in Jada's eyes felt like a punishment. He'd tried to do the right thing. He'd married Bodi with the conviction they didn't need love to build a decent life. With a baby on the way, they needed to assume their responsibilities and act like adults. He'd tried, but during those first months of marriage, Bodi found viciously creative ways to destroy his trust.

Jada only knew part of the truth. He damn well never intended to give her the full picture. Sharing the rest would scar his manhood in ways he couldn't abide.

Overhead, the dome of stars twinkled. The flecks of brilliant light beckoned Jada's sorrowful gaze.

"We should've tried harder," she whispered. "I've always wondered if we'll ever forgive ourselves. If we *should* forgive ourselves. Aren't we put on this earth to help each other? There's so much we could've done."

53

We? The admission nearly gutted Philip.

Guilt followed.

"Jada, you did nothing wrong," he said softly.

She kept her attention fixed on the starry dome, as if the deep silence of the black universe held the secret of how to forgive herself—and him.

A responsibility he quickly assumed, adding, "It was all me."

"It wasn't."

"Yeah, it was. That first night, when Bodi came by my apartment, I should've sent her home. You're not responsible for what happened. I doubt Bodi was capable of trusting anyone, but she came the closest with you. She looked up to you like a big sister."

"For all the good it did. She needed professional counseling, not encouragement to stay in Sweet Lake. Those first weeks after Penelope gave her a place to stay, she talked about leaving a dozen times. Every time, I talked her into staying here."

"You were only trying to help."

"Changing geography doesn't change a person. All I did was keep her troubles in Sweet Lake."

The inference wasn't lost on him. Jada meant her friendship kept Bodi in Sweet Lake. It kept her in town long enough for her to land on his doorstep that fateful night. Now he wondered if Jada also blamed herself for the hellish months of his marriage. She'd always been too honorable. He couldn't recall a time when she wasn't capable of carrying the heaviest loads.

Self-loathing surged through him. The millstone of his reckless choices was his to carry.

The soft hum of Jada's smartphone pulled him from the reverie. Picking up, she walked across the porch to the railing.

"Ms. Earhardt, hello. No, I'm not busy. The girl at the front desk gave you my number?"

Jada cast him a sideways glance as if to say, *I don't believe this.* To the caller, she said, "Will you give me ten minutes? I'm at a friend's house. I'll get back to you the moment I'm home."

Philip collected the wineglasses. "Problem at the inn?"

"I hope not. Too early to tell." Irritation glazed the statement. "Why would the front desk give out my private number? I mean, seriously. What would make them think it's okay?"

"That's the point. They weren't thinking." He followed her inside.

Jada scanned the kitchen table, retrieved her purse from a chair. "Sorry about cutting our night short. I have to go."

Clutching the purse, she appeared ready to move in to kiss him on the cheek. Since she'd begun coming around more often, assuming Daniel's role of filling in with ready meals and good company, the casual affection was MIA.

Sparing her the decision, he started toward the living room.

In the foyer, she hesitated. "Will you be okay tonight? I hate to leave you alone on the anniversary." She began to add something else, then sighed instead.

"I'm good," he lied.

"You're sure?"

Her concern bruised his ego. "Don't worry about me," he assured her. "I'm used to flying solo. Been doing it for years." Not exactly what he'd meant to say, but he didn't want her to view him as weak. Shrugging it off, he asked, "Since when does the front desk give out your private number?"

"Never, but the woman booking a suite in the south wing is persistent. This morning, she told Cat to have me call her. I assumed I could put off the call until tomorrow. Obviously not."

"Why does an incoming guest want to talk to you?"

The glance Jada cast was rife with frustration. "I can't even begin to guess."

Chapter 5

Millicent Earhardt was a historian with a regrettably truncated history.

The irony wasn't lost on her. A fortune spent on private investigators, a thatching of grey invading her dirty-blonde hair, and she wasn't any closer to the truth than she'd been years ago.

On the mantelpiece, the mahogany clock chimed the hour. The sound quickened her strides past the leather couch. She trod in an impatient circle before the fireplace. Fourteen minutes had passed, and Millicent's blood pressure responded by thumping painfully in her ears. What was taking the pastry chef so long?

In the fireplace, the flames leapt and snapped. The warmth barely reached her calves. With fitful movements, she tugged at her cashmere sweater. Impatience stole the agility from her fingers as she worked the buttons, growling and muttering at her arthritis and Jada's delay in returning the call.

Unimpressed by her bad temper, Vasily strode past.

Despite Chicago's wickedly cold winter, the doctoral student did his best to keep the mansion's cavernous rooms from growing icicles. In return for cooking meals, helping with the physical therapy sessions her spouse required, and running the errands Millicent inevitably forgot each time a clue turned up, she paid the absurdly handsome Vasily Pruszynski well. He put up with her foul moods as she read through reports from private detectives scouring the United States for the smallest leads. Her moods grew fouler at each critical juncture, when closure seemed tantalizingly within reach.

Vasily sauntered to the wet bar. "Brandy?" he asked. "You need one."

"Not now."

"Something stronger, perhaps? A sedative? Keep marching in circles and you'll wear through the rug."

"It's my rug. I'll do what I please."

"Have a drink. A quick shot to ensure you aren't peevish when she calls back." He held the Waterford decanter aloft like a model in a men's magazine. "You'll scare her off in the first act, and I'll never learn how the play ends." The pose made her wonder why the doctoral student planned a life in dusty classrooms teaching American history. Six-foot-two, with defined pecs and gleaming brown hair, Vasily could earn bundles modeling for romance novels.

"Stop coddling me. You know how much I despise it." Millicent tapped her smartphone, as if demanding it awaken. "Why hasn't she called back?"

"Give her a chance to drive to her parents' house."

"She doesn't live with her parents. She has an apartment."

"Millicent, you're mixing up the Sweet Lake file with the dead end from Indiana. The woman whose name turned out to be Janelle, not Jada?" Vasily studied the decanter as if needing a brandy himself. The uncertainty was never easy on him either.

"I'm not mixing up the files," she snapped.

"According to your diligent PI, the stunning Jada Brooks of Ohio lives with her parents."

"Not now, she doesn't. She moved into her own apartment last month." On his second trip to Sweet Lake, the private investigator chanced upon Jada ferrying boxes into the apartment. The photographs he'd sent were Millicent's current obsession, but she'd forgotten to share them with Vasily. "Jada doesn't spend much time at her place. Either she works late, stops by to check on her parents, or visits at the Kettering household."

"Philip Kettering, previous loser, now the proprietor of a budding landscape firm." Vasily ticked off the basics with ease. A devilish glint entered his gaze. "Are they dating?"

"Who cares if they are? They've known each other since childhood. Friendship may characterize the extent of their relationship."

"I wish there was more personal information on the inn's website," Vasily mused. "She is about the right age for the profile you drew up."

"Early thirties, which does fit." They'd both gleaned every page of the Wayfair Inn website, searching for clues. There weren't many, and Millicent was eager to reach Sweet Lake to learn the truth. "A small town in the Midwest, an African American baker named Jada working at an inn—thank goodness we haven't been searching for a woman with a more common name, like Mary or Sarah. We never would've narrowed down the field."

"Don't get your hopes too high."

"I'm aware this may be another dead end. A reminder isn't necessary." She threw her thunderous gaze on the phone in her fist. "How long does it take a perfectly healthy woman to drive three blocks to her apartment?"

"Have patience. She'll call."

"Please. When have I ever had patience?"

"You're not too old to learn. Are you?"

Mockery tinged the comment. It was standard operating procedure for the chummy doctoral student, whose respect for his elders rarely extended past dead white men with the distinction of having signed the Declaration of Independence. Millicent wasn't sure how to react to his intimate tone, or the friendship he was determined to extend.

Confide in the young, and they assume you are BFFs for life.

Rounding the couch, Millicent laid down new tracks of frustration. "Don't you have a book on Monticello to read? Something about a dissertation you're nowhere near completing?"

"Jefferson can wait. I'm curious to hear your latest script. Have you improved the lines?"

"Doubtful. I'll ad-lib."

It was a simple enough solution. She'd acted this script a depressing number of times. This was nothing but the latest rendition with another baker, in another economically challenged town. As for how to expand the role once she arrived in Ohio, Millicent intended to concoct new lines on the fly.

Vasily opened the refrigerator beneath the wet bar, rooted around. "So, you *are* still planning the reconnaissance." He came back up with a soda. Ice clinked in a glass, and he feigned disinterest as he poured.

He was interested, all right. After she left for Ohio, he'd grow numb listening to complaints. The poor treatment on the horizon would undoubtedly give the handsome youth his first etching of crow's feet.

She nearly pitied him.

Perhaps it would be wise to give him another raise before I leave for O'Hare.

Mulling over the amount of the raise, she said, "You can't talk me out of the trip. The flight is booked. I finished packing this morning."

"When do I ever attempt to talk you out of these mad forays? You're wasting the most intellectually productive years of your retirement. Entirely your prerogative." He lifted his soda in mock salute. "Someone else, however, will have a fit. I'm not looking forward to the fireworks."

"You'll survive. If Jada Brooks is the right woman, we'll finally close the book on this." The odds of turning up real information was negligible. Too many years had passed; the trail was cold. Bad odds, but Millicent was too stubborn to vanquish all hope. Which compelled her to add, "If our pastry chef *is* the Jada we've been seeking, I'll know in a week or two. If we finally strike gold, plan on booking flights to Ohio. I'll give you the dates and times later."

"Flights, as in plural?"

"You'll also have to come to Ohio. No one wheelchair bound likes to negotiate airports without assistance."

With a frown, Vasily set down his glass. "Your better half will refuse to accompany me to Sweet Lake," he said. "Or do you suggest I search online for a straightjacket?"

"You won't need one." At least she hoped he wouldn't.

Her smartphone trilled. The sound nearly catapulted her heart from her chest. Behind the bar, Vasily lifted his brows in anticipation.

"Hello?" she managed.

"Ms. Earhardt? This is Jada, returning your call. I'm sorry to have kept you waiting. I was with a friend when you called."

Moving directly to informality was a nice touch. "Thank you for calling back. And please, call me Millicent."

"Thank you."

Vasily made a jabbing motion at the phone. *Turn on the speaker so I can hear.*

The urge to flip him the bird nearly caught Millicent unawares. An odd impulse: the last time she'd used vulgar hand signals was at a protest march in the 1970s.

She strode into the foyer, her footsteps echoing on the marble. "Jada, I'm sure you're aware I've booked a suite at your establishment. Two weeks, confirmed." A hasty glance up the stairwell sent relief spilling through her. The corridor above was empty. "If the trip proves enjoyable, I'll extend my stay. None of which is why I'm reaching out to you tonight."

"This isn't about your reservation?"

Seeking privacy, she darted into the library. "I wanted to discuss another matter with you." Through the windows, ribbons of snow whirled across the grounds.

"What *is* the reason for your call?"

"You, actually." A dreadful opener, and the statement met with a stony silence. Rushing over the gaffe, she added, "I've always been fascinated by the culinary arts—by pastry chefs in particular. Such artistry goes into the work, and the results! When I spoke with your associate, she mentioned you've worked at the Wayfair for a long time." Through the haze of nervous tension, Millicent searched for the name. "I believe her name is Cat Menendez."

"Cat Mendoza." A pause, then, "I've been with the Wayfair for close to a decade."

Ten years.

Hope shimmered in Millicent's heart.

Tamping it down, she cleared her throat. "Cat mentioned you're a remarkable pastry chef."

Appealing laughter carried across the line. "I'm not sure I'd describe my talents as remarkable," Jada said.

"Ah, you're also modest. A fine trait. But unnecessary—Cat raved about your abilities."

"Cat handles our marketing. If she went overboard on the sales pitch, my apologies."

"I'm sure she didn't."

"Are there desserts you'd like added to the menu during your stay?" Jada asked. "I'll do my best to provide them."

"I'll enjoy whatever you prepare. You're also on the management team, correct? I read the nice bio on the inn's website. And you're close with the owner of the Wayfair?" The clumsy fishing expedition trailed into an embarrassed silence.

"Her name is Linnie Wayfair, and we are close." Jada's tone became frosty. "Is it important?"

It was—exceedingly so. The scant profile Millicent had compiled indicated a close friendship between the mysterious pastry chef named Jada and the owner of the establishment where she worked.

Millicent searched her scattering thoughts, desperate to salvage the conversation. "I suppose not." With horror, she heard herself say, "Have you and Linnie always been close? Say, since childhood?"

"Millicent, I don't mean to be rude," Jada replied as her voice turned to ice. "It's late, and I need to get some rest. I'm not sure why you're curious about my background, or friendships. If you have requests for dessert selections when you arrive, I'll do my best to provide them."

"How kind," she croaked.

"Is there anything else?"

Millicent gave herself a mental kick in the keister. This was her worst performance ever.

Keep it up, and I'll never wiggle my way back into the woman's good graces.

Rallying, she got down to business. "There is one more item. A simple request. I hope you won't view it as a major inconvenience."

The remark was greeted with a thick silence. A request from an incoming guest—a guest the reluctant Jada Brooks had presumably concluded was unforgivably nosey.

Wary, she asked, "And what is the request?"

With the enthusiasm of a condemned felon, Cat tiptoed into the office.

Jada rocked faster in her chair. Anger rarely infected her even temperament, and the emotion whipping through her was dismaying. That morning, she'd already burned a cherry pie. Fifteen minutes later, she scorched a berry soufflé. She'd left the ruined desserts steaming on a counter. Let the kitchen staff discard them—she'd start over after she read Cat the riot act.

"I got your text," Cat said. Gingerly, she took a seat. "First time you've sent a message in all caps. It sure felt like you were yelling at me."

"Would you like me to start?" To punctuate her angst, Jada brought the chair to a stop. Then she resumed the furious rocking. "I'm happy to comply."

"What did I do?"

"I have to spell it out?"

"I'm not sure." Evidently Cat was the lucky recipient of morning nookie, because she padded her fingertips across her neck. The skin was refreshingly free of love bites. "It's nine o'clock. I'm on time. I swear, I won't go home at lunchtime to see Ryan. That's why you're upset, right?"

"Guess again."

In the corridor, Linnie strode past. Something in the air came across as toxic. Like a train reversing on the track, she sidled backward toward the door. Curiosity rolled her forward on her tennis shoes.

"What's going on?" Shutting the door, she took a long, hard look at Jada. "Wow. Your eyes are about to pop out of your skull. Definitely not your best look."

"Carry on, Linnie. This doesn't concern you."

"Wait. Let me guess. You're angry?"

"I passed through 'angry' ten states ago. I'm driving coast-to-coast, all the way to livid."

"You are? I'm shocked. Mostly because nothing gets past your Zen."

"Cat did," Jada supplied. "Our brainless marketing director gave out personal details of my life. A retired historian probably isn't a stalker, but I don't approve of Chatty Cathy's methods."

"Cat dished with the woman coming in from Chicago? You were on the menu?"

"They enjoyed a nice long chat."

"We only talked for a few minutes," Cat protested. Embarrassment wove her arms across the clingy dress she'd worn today. Cupping her shoulders in the silly pose, she looked exactly like her fourth-grade self on the day the teachers caught her trading kisses with a boy at recess.

"I already told you—I'll bet Millicent is doing research on minority women in business. It didn't seem like a big deal to give her background info on you."

"Cat, did she come out and *say* she's working on research? Or is this your imagination talking?"

"Well, no. But I thought . . ."

Linnie sank into the other chair before the desk. "Someone bring me up to speed. Why does an incoming guest care about Jada?"

Absently, Jada flicked at the tight curls tickling her cheek. For once, she'd risen early enough to give her hair the full-on treatment. There wasn't a strand of frizz on her head. The dark curls gleamed from the Moroccan argan oil she'd applied. She'd also put on mascara and a swipe of lipstick. Irritation at Cat, along with anxiety regarding the historian's visit, had made sleep difficult.

At least she'd arrived at work well groomed.

She told Linnie, "Contrary to what Cat will have you believe, Millicent Earhardt doesn't have an interest in me because of research for a book. When we spoke last night, it was like she was rattling off items on a list. How long I've worked at the Wayfair. How long I've been friends with you. She was hunting for something, but I have no idea what."

"That's weird," Linnie said.

Jada halted her frenetic rocking. "Here's something weirder. Her name is familiar. I'm sure I've heard it before."

"Like, where?"

"I don't know," Jada admitted. Her inability to recall seemed critical. "I've spent a sleepless night trying to remember. I almost have the feeling . . ."

Linnie scooted to the edge of her chair *"What?"* Cat did the same, leaning toward the desk with rapt attention.

Worried, Jada licked her parched lips. In the last days, too many unusual events had occurred to mark it all down to coincidence. The gift of the sachet from the Sirens. The anniversary of Bodi's death. Fancy acting out at school, and beginning to sense the grief ushered in each year with the month of March. At what point did a logical person detect signs and symbols beneath life's normal currents? Usually Jada wasn't superstitious. Now, too many seemingly connected events left her rattled.

Did an underlying thread connect the events? The notion made no sense. Yet she couldn't dispel it.

From her desk, she withdrew the rosemary sachet. It was foolish to believe a gift from the Sirens lent protection, or a means to make peace with the past—perhaps even to make peace with her guilt over the mistakes she'd made with Philip's late wife. *You won't escape the burden until a stranger brings news from the past.* Is this what Penelope meant? Was Millicent the stranger destined to bring news?

Adrift on the unanswerable questions, Jada fingered the sachet's soft cloth.

At length, she told Linnie and Cat, "I have a hunch Bodi knew the historian coming in from Chicago." She paused, and they waited with breathless anticipation. Collecting her thoughts, she added, "I think I recall Bodi mentioning the name."

Cat's jaw loosened. "Hold on. You're saying Philip's late wife is connected to the retired historian? You remember Bodi talking about her?"

"Millicent Earhardt isn't a common name. It's the sort of name *anyone* would remember. I can't recall exactly when Bodi mentioned her."

Slowly, Cat unwound her arms. "This is spooky." She flopped her hands into her lap.

"Unnerving is more like it," Jada decided. Apprehension fluttered through her as she added, "A guest is flying in from Chicago, and I'm convinced she's coming to see me."

Linnie scooted her chair close to the desk. She looked ready to do battle. "I don't like this," she muttered. For a woman incapable of making decisions without assistance, she wasn't indecisive about protecting her friends. "Jada, if you believe there's a connection between Millicent and Bodi, that isn't good news. Bodi didn't have family, at least not one that cared about her. We all caught the inferences she made—her parents were abusive. Which sure explains why Bodi didn't have much in the way of ethics."

"A lousy childhood would give anyone bad instincts," Jada said, rising to an automatic defense. "If Bodi hurt people, it was only because she'd known so much cruelty."

"I'll wager she hurt a lot of people," Linnie said. "For all we know, she bilked Millicent out of cash."

Cat rubbed her arms, as if banishing a chill. "Let's not forget how Penelope first met her in Columbus." Discussing Bodi's life and unfortunate death was never easy for her. "She tried to snatch Penelope's purse. I'll wager Bodi scammed lots of people during her short life of crime."

"Which doesn't explain why the nasty historian is bothering Jada."

"Millicent isn't nasty." Jada set the sachet beneath her desk lamp. "She's pushy, sure. When she put me through twenty questions on the phone, she seemed hopeful. Like I was giving the right answers, and she had trouble containing her excitement."

Linnie said, "I hope Bodi rests with the angels, I really do. Now I'm wondering if we should hold everything she told us as suspect, though."

"How so?"

"We may be looking at this the wrong way. Jada, you were close to her—as close as anyone got, including Philip. She looked up to you, even when she lifted cash from your wallet and burned through your trust."

"What's your point?"

"You remember hearing Millicent's name. What if Bodi mentioned *you* to Millicent? Might explain the woman's curiosity about you."

Cat, trying to keep up, leaned closer. "Why would Bodi mention Jada to someone else she scammed?"

"Cat, *think*. Even if no one in Bodi's immediate family cared about her, who's to say Millicent isn't a long-lost aunt? Or her grandmother? If I had a grandchild who deserved coal in her stocking every Christmas, I'd still want to know she's okay."

Jada weighed the theory with misgiving. "You're suggesting she's looking for Bodi after all these years?" she asked Linnie.

"Wouldn't you?"

The answer came immediately. If someone in her family went missing, Jada knew she'd never stop looking. She'd continue to search in hopes of reuniting with a loved one. No one dedicated to their family would do less.

"Say you're right. What am I supposed to do? If Millicent is Bodi's grandmother, I can only give her devastating news. Bodi isn't okay. She's gone."

Given the way she'd treated people in Sweet Lake, Bodi's grave at Walnut Grove Memorial Gardens seldom received visitors. Only Jada went out, to bring a simple bouquet of daisies, or brush the leaves off the headstone before bowing her head in prayer. Twice, she'd brought Fancy. Not recently—the child's interest in the mother she'd never known was almost nonexistent.

They hadn't stayed long at Walnut Grove either time. Jada capped off each visit by taking Fancy out for a banana split afterward.

Linnie gave her a look rife with sympathy. "I don't have good advice. We're dealing with a lot of conjecture. If Millicent is related to Bodi, you'll have to lay out the facts."

The suggestion put bile in Jada's throat. Her emotions regarding Bodi were still complicated. She'd been the only one in town to see the teen's better angels. Explaining about the girl's death to one of her relatives would prove an awful task.

"Linnie, what are you proposing?" she demanded. "Should I describe how Bodi died? Mention she was threatening suicide for months?"

"Skip the bad stuff. Just fill in the missing bits. You aren't obligated to go into enough detail to break the woman's heart."

"What about Philip? If we're right about this, he won't welcome news that Fancy has relatives on what he considers the wrong side of the family. He never met Bodi's family when she was alive—he won't want to start now. He'll assume Millicent is bad news, and steer clear."

"Philip doesn't need this," Cat said. "Bodi took a wrecking ball to his life. He's finally coming out of his shell. Anything having to do with her will set him back."

"Let's keep this between the three of us," Jada decided.

Cat nodded. Linnie said, "We'll handle this however you want."

"Good. We're keeping our mouths shut." Jada didn't relish sharing the rest of her news. The way it corroborated their theories made her apprehensive. "On a related note, Millicent asked for a favor during our chat. She wants private baking lessons during her stay."

Air *whooshed* from Linnie's mouth. "She does want to get to know you better."

"I intended to turn her down. All things considered, taking her up on the offer makes sense. The faster we become acquainted, the quicker I'll understand her motives."

"She's paying you for baking lessons?"

"Oh yeah."

"What did she offer?"

"Too much."

Cat, sold on the grandmother theory, said, "Use the money on Fancy. Look at this as an indirect way for Grandma to buy new dresses for her pipsqueak shopaholic."

"Get your facts straight. We don't know how Millicent is connected to Bodi, and *you* are the shopaholic." Jada chuckled. Cat's suggestion lent an amusing note to an otherwise somber discussion. "Good thing you married well. Or do you hide the Mastercard receipts from Ryan?"

"Only sometimes." Cat shrugged defensively. Then she switched tracks. "Speaking of marriage, what's the story with the flower girl dress? I heard a nasty rumor. Did Fancy turn her nose up at the dress Linnie picked out?"

"Jada, did you get her to try on the dress?" Linnie asked. "It's such a sweet outfit. I'll have the cutest flower girl this side of the Mississippi. Please tell me I can focus on finding my own gown and stop worrying about Fancy's."

Setting her chair back in motion, Jada rocked a nervous rhythm. Philip planned to break the news about his daughter's big-girl decision. He'd promised to drop the bomb about how Fancy planned to select her own outfit from the wild and garish dress-up clothes in her closet.

Preferably, he'd deliver the news to his older brother—not to Linnie, whose expression had become unbearably fragile.

There was no easy way to let her down.

"About your wedding," Jada said, "there's a small glitch."

Chapter 6

Within days, the problem became obvious. Contrary to her reservations about the reason for Millicent's visit, Jada *liked* the historian from Chicago.

In her sixties, with a shock of blonde hair peppered with grey, Millicent possessed the build of a linebacker and the deep, gusty laugh of a woman comfortable in her own skin.

Each morning, she hummed with a child's enthusiasm when she strolled out of the south wing. She left behind crisp bills and a handwritten thank-you note for the maids in Housekeeping. She ate solitary meals in the Sunshine Room with the *Wall Street Journal* or the *Cincinnati Enquirer* tucked beneath her elbow. On the veranda, she riffled through the newspapers; her quick, assessing regard fell upon anyone who entered or exited the Wayfair as if searching for a face she never found.

Millicent's pale, sun-deprived skin wore a bluish cast. In the afternoons, lured outside by the sunlight, she strolled the beach rimming the lake's sparkling waters. She traversed the ribbon of grass unfurling from the inn with the studious attention of a scholar who'd spent too much time indoors. If a cardinal flew past, or the rustling trees sang out, her green eyes crinkled at the corners. She plucked blades of grass and held them to her nose, marveling at the green scent of nature.

On Tuesday morning, she requested a lesson on homemade pudding. Saturday's lesson on sheet cakes hadn't gone well, nor the Monday session on the basics of quick breads. The slight palsy in Millicent's hands sabotaged her efforts to measure ingredients accurately. The clatter of dishes returning from the Sunshine Room broke her concentration. Too often, she forgot to set the timer for the treats going into the oven as she attempted in none-too-subtle ways to dig deeper into Jada's life.

"Millicent, you're doing great. Keep stirring." Stepping away, Jada returned to the oven. The brownies weren't quite done. She decided to give them another five minutes. The breakfast rush in the Sunshine Room was winding down, allowing her to extend this morning's lesson.

Millicent bent over the double boiler. "This smells delicious."

"Wait until we add the vanilla and butter. They'll go in after you finish thickening the base."

A busboy trudged in with a tray of dishes. He veered past the day cook and the sous-chef working at the center island, joining a second youth at the sink. Together they began loading the commercial-grade dishwasher Jada had lobbied for last winter. On the day the appliance was installed, she'd celebrated by preparing extra sweets for the entire staff.

Millicent asked, "Why aren't they in school?" Still stirring, she lifted her chin toward the busboys.

"They graduated from high school last year. Tony is saving for trade school. Gavin is considering a career in Hospitality Management. He hasn't made up his mind."

"Times have changed. When I became a professor, college was affordable. Back then, four years of college cost less than what kids now pay for one semester."

"Today they wonder how they'll ever get out of debt." The timer dinged, and Jada removed the brownies from the oven. "Do you miss your career?"

"Academia? Too many big egos and palace intrigue. I never learned the knack of smiling politely while stabbing a colleague in the back. It was time to leave."

"Do you miss teaching?"

"Young lady, I shall *never* stop teaching." To punctuate the statement, Millicent swirled the spoon through the thickening pudding with growing enthusiasm. "I'm no longer in the classroom, but I do make time for doctoral students. Not in a formal capacity, but they know I'm available."

"How do they find you?"

"Through the few professors I didn't alienate during my career."

"I have trouble believing you alienated *all* your colleagues." Millicent had a strong personality, but she was also charming. And generous—the Housekeeping staff now battled over who would freshen up her suite.

The compliment pleased the historian. "I don't suffer fools, and I'm too blunt," she confided. She seemed eager to share more. "The grad students learn to adapt. I don't coddle them, because I want them to work hard. In fact, one of those students lives at my estate. Vasily Pruszynski. He's brilliant, if too chummy for my tastes."

"You don't like chummy grad students?" A lie, surely. Affection laced Millicent's voice.

"There's no plausible reason why a young man four decades my junior aspires to becoming my BFF. I'm sure he can do better. Anyway, Vasily gets free room and board. Well, not free. When he's not working on his dissertation, he helps my spouse with physical therapy, runs errands—I like to joke that Vasily is an underpaid houseboy. I *do* keep him on the straight and narrow with his dissertation."

A live-in grad student, and an estate. Was Millicent wealthy? Her sensible shoes were scruffy. Her blazer looked well made, if dated. It could easily sit among the consignment offerings in Penelope's shop. And she was married. Jada had assumed she was single. It took no effort to visualize the historian tucked away in a library, happily wedded to books.

"Physical therapy . . . is your husband ill?"

Around the edges of the pot, the wooden spoon slowed its journey. Millicent lifted her head. Her long, steady appraisal made Jada worry she'd overstepped. They were treading on hallowed ground.

"We were in an accident. Not recently—the accident was nearly ten years ago." Millicent returned her attention to the pot. "The car swerved into a tree and flipped over. The ambulance took forty-three minutes to reach us. Godforsaken country roads. Snow piling up by the bucketful, and the street signs covered over. There was black ice on I-94, and lots of calls going in to 911 about fender benders. We had to wait our turn. I walked away with nothing more than a gash on my forehead."

The accident crippled her husband? Jada's heart overturned. "I'm sorry," she murmured.

"Whatever for? Good heavens, you weren't behind the wheel. Besides, we're both alive. Nothing else matters."

"You're an optimist."

"Send me straight to hell for my sins. My optimism gets me into all sorts of trouble. It always has."

"I believe you."

"You should." The grin she offered nearly took Jada hostage. Then her expression became watchful. "About college. Did you wait to go, save up to avoid running into debt? You don't seem the type to rush into anything without careful thought."

"I was lucky," Jada said, uncomfortably aware that the query represented Millicent's latest attempt to extract information. They'd been at this for days, the thrust and parry of delving questions and evasive replies. But the story about the historian's spouse was tragic, and Jada found herself adding, "I'm an only child. I'm close with my parents— they live in town. They didn't have me until their early forties. They'd saved more than enough for my education."

"Why did they wait so long to start a family?"

"They were nearing middle age when they met. Mom was born in Sweet Lake. Dad moved here to work for a building company. He was a carpenter. He retired when the company closed."

"The building company owned by Frances Dufour's late husband?" When Jada's brows lifted, Millicent elaborated. "Frances and several of her comrades stopped by my suite Sunday morning. They are an early bunch, aren't they? I was still in my robe when they rapped on the door." The pudding was adequately thickened, and Jada instructed her to remove it from the stove. "We had tea on the veranda. I particularly liked Penelope Riddle."

"Everyone does."

"Few people are molded entirely by kindness."

"Penelope is unique," Jada agreed. "She's governed by her charitable instincts."

"She complimented my necklace. In fact, she was quite taken with it."

Jada transferred the pudding to a bowl. Reaching for a measuring spoon, she explained how much vanilla and butter to add. She made a quick survey of the tweed blazer and tan blouse encasing the historian's broad frame. No earrings dangled from beneath her bluntly cut hair. If she wore a necklace, the jewelry hid beneath the collar of her blouse.

"Jada, this smells divine. We'd better hurry, or I'll start dipping in. Why are nursery foods so enticing? Smelling this takes me right back to childhood." Millicent looked up expectantly. "What now?"

"We slice bananas, toss them gently with lemon juice, and whip the egg whites. After we assemble, the pudding bakes for thirty-eight minutes. Any longer, and the meringue goes from golden to an ugly brown."

"You're very precise."

"Comes with the territory. Some recipes don't require exact timing, but others do. You learn the difference."

"It's a pity you lost your bakery on Sweet Lake Circle. Was it seven years ago? Although I'm sure Linnie is thrilled you agreed to work here. In better economic times, I'm sure you would've made a go of your enterprise. That must've been a difficult time in your life."

"It was," Jada agreed.

Fetching the cream of tartar, she demonstrated how to add several pinches to stabilize the egg whites as they whipped. Apprehension shadowed her as Millicent positioned the bowl on the mixer. This wasn't the first time the historian had steered the conversation back to seven years ago—the year Bodi Wagner came to Sweet Lake.

Was this unequivocal proof of a relationship between Millicent and Bodi? Proof Millicent was a grandmother intent on locating her missing grandchild? Jada dreaded the answer.

Her smartphone rang. She read the screen with interest.

"Hey, Penelope," she said, picking up. "We were just talking about you. What's up?"

"Good morning, Jada. I'm at the bus stop with Fancy. She wants to talk to you."

"Sure. Put her on."

At the mixer, Millicent flipped the switch to high. The steel whisk clanged around the bowl, and she flinched. Jada put her hand up like a traffic cop. Millicent lunged toward the switch. The mixer went silent.

Fancy came on. "Jada, I'm ready."

Jada knew this meant Fancy had decided which of her dress-up clothes to wear to the wedding. There was an outside chance she'd trot down the aisle dressed like a drag queen—a calamity Jada hoped to avoid.

"Do you remember the rule?" she gently asked. "Don't pick too many colors, or lots of accessories. Like, if you want the feather boa, forget about the magician's cape."

Fancy made a small sound of objection. "What if I want them both?"

"You'll have to choose. Even beauty has its limits."

"What about the fairy crown? It's sparkly. Can I wear it, and the feather boa?"

"The fairy crown we made in January?" Jada had brought over a bouquet of gently fading roses after replacing the arrangement on the lobby's front desk. Fancy had been delighted when she'd demonstrated how to dip the flowers in glitter. Then they'd glued the roses to a ring of cardboard. "I don't know, girlfriend. The fairy crown has seen better days."

They debated the merits of moldy crowns until the school bus roared up. Before finishing the call, Jada promised to stop over in the evening.

When she hung up, Millicent regarded her with amusement. "Who was that?"

"Just a friend."

"A friend who wears fairy crowns? Don't keep me in suspense."

Jada reached for the bananas. Then she slid a cutting board beneath Millicent's hands. Sharing details with Bodi's potential grandmother—and Fancy's possible great-grandmother—was a tricky proposition. Philip knew nothing about her suppositions. There was no reason to upset him until she uncovered Millicent's connection to Bodi, if any. What was the ethical course of action?

Indecision swamped her.

With unnerving perception, Millicent read her expression. "I'm prying," she announced. Grabbing up the first banana, she began chopping with gusto. It took her all of three seconds to reduce the fruit to mush. "You're not sure you can trust me. Why should you? I'm a nosey old woman from Chicago with enough curiosity for ten cats. Keep your secrets regarding fairy crowns and magician's capes. Shall we move on?"

Jada stilled her wrist. "Let's start over." She scooped up the mess and pitched it into the trash. "This isn't a coconut. You don't have to beat soft fruits into submission. They'll comply readily."

"I'm unfamiliar with the delicate approach. With bananas, and in other arenas."

"I've noticed."

"I like you, Jada. You're a quality individual. I have no right to forge ahead with the 'Do Not Trespass' sign in plain sight." Millicent rolled her meaty shoulders, clearly unable to dispel her agitation. "Forgive me."

"There's nothing to forgive."

The contrite historian peered down the counter. "Do you have abundant produce? In case I need more practice? Never flunk the student if she doesn't have time to prepare."

"This isn't a test." Demonstrating, Jada arced the knife across the second banana, producing a perfect oval. "You see?"

"What if the slices aren't uniform? There's a limit to my patience."

"Doesn't matter. They go in the bottom of the dish, beneath the pudding."

"What a relief."

Jada watched as she set to work. The palsy that invaded Millicent's hands at unpredictable moments made the knife unsteady. Gripping the handle tighter, she muttered beneath her breath. She failed to keep her movements in check, and yellow disks of uneven size fell from the blade. She seemed older then, vulnerable in ways Jada hadn't noticed. A fiercely intelligent woman, she was adept at hiding her weaknesses.

An odd calm blanketed Jada. Whatever her true motives, the historian wasn't the enemy. She was a colorful personality, a woman endowed with high intelligence and absolutely no talent for mastering the art of baking. Jada wondered if she was overreacting by refusing to explain the call. The decision continued to weigh on her as a tiny growl popped from Millicent's lips.

Her palsy increasing, Millicent brought the knife down at a bad angle, and a disk of banana leapt from the cutting board. "Blast it all," she muttered as the banana flew past her shoulder to the wall—and stuck.

Which decided the matter for Jada.

"The call was from Fancy Kettering," she said, peeling the banana from the wall. "She's a first grader at Sweet Lake Elementary. She's the daughter of the man putting in the new patio behind the ballroom."

"Philip Kettering. We met during my stroll yesterday. Nice young man."

"Fancy is into make-believe in a big way. Linnie wants her to be the flower girl in her wedding."

"The Sirens mentioned the wedding when we had tea on Sunday." Millicent took the next banana, did a better job slicing. "They're concerned about Linnie finding the right gown."

"So am I." Jada began scooping up the sliced fruit and scattering it across the bottom of a baking dish. "Linnie still hasn't made a decision, and the wedding is next month. There's still lots to do, lots to decide."

"How does a fairy crown fit into the picture?"

"Fancy got it into her head to pick her own dress for the wedding. She's determined to follow her imagination wherever it leads. I'm going over tonight to see what she's picked out from her dress-up clothes. I'm sure Philip has already hidden the crazier outfits, like the dress with multicolored spangles and the clown pants. They'd jingle when Fancy walks down the aisle, and drown out the harpist. If he didn't do a good enough job, I'll hide the worst costumes tonight when Fancy isn't looking." Jada's shoulders sagged. "I don't know what's worse. Disappointing a six-year-old who'll dress like a drag queen for the big day, or ruining Linnie's wedding. She's striving for a formal look, not a carnival sensation."

Enthralled by the telling, Millicent set down the knife. "One question," she said, and her eyes danced. "Why is this your problem?"

Jada shrugged. "I'm Linnie's best friend."

"You misunderstand. I'm curious why a child with delightfully flamboyant tastes is entrusting her decision to you."

The moisture in Jada's mouth evaporated. Until she unearthed Millicent's connection to Philip's late wife, discussing Fancy in too much detail was out-of-bounds.

At length, she said, "Philip is a single dad."

"Divorce is such a nasty business, especially for children," Millicent said, thankfully coming to the wrong conclusion. The merriment in her face increasing, she seemed oblivious to Jada's unease. Her eyes crinkled as she lowered her voice. "Are you and the dashing landscaper a 'thing'? Remind me to tell you about the girl Vasily is dating. He sneaks her into the mansion when he thinks I've doused my brain with Lunesta. She's a drama major, third year. Covered with more tattoos than Angelina Jolie."

"She sounds nice," Jada quipped. She saw no harm in adding, "I'm not dating Philip. I've known him since we were Fancy's age."

"You're old friends?"

"Not really," she admitted. "Linnie and Cat were friends with Philip when we were all growing up, but I thought he was irritating. Always teasing me in school and, later, dating more girls than I could count. Mr. Hot Body with the shallow personality." She shrugged. "That's all in the past. I suppose we're becoming good friends now."

"What changed?" The hesitancy in her voice merely increased the interest in Millicent's eyes.

She gave a short explanation of how Linnie had asked her to fill in for Daniel as they prepared for their wedding. Wrapping up, she added, "Now I help Philip out whenever possible. A good thing, because Fancy's getting to the age when she needs more girl time. It's not exactly his area of expertise."

"You're mothering his daughter."

"This is a close-knit town. Philip gets help from many quarters."

"And yet his daughter calls *you* for advice."

"It's not a big deal. I'm Linnie's maid of honor. Why wouldn't Fancy ask for my help? She knows I'm happy to stop over and see what she's picked out."

"If the whole town pitches in, why didn't she call another Good Samaritan? Why bother you?" Millicent seemed every bit the patient tutor, waiting for her student to catch up. When Jada set the baking dish aside and gave her full attention, the historian added, "You do see the problem. A little girl, a single father. A helpful young woman of marrying age. By the way, a child with a lust for fairy crowns and magicians' capes is romantic by nature. She'll have no trouble imagining the noble king and queen escorting her princess self into a bright future. Do you catch my drift?"

Jada searched the remark for veracity. Was she assuming the role of stand-in mother? A sweet emotion spun through her. She loved Fancy. Their relationship had evolved naturally. She'd never stopped to analyze it.

Then her stomach did a backflip.

Does Fancy harbor dreams of me wedding Philip?

The idea was outlandish. Until recently, Jada's relationship with Philip was best described as distant.

Would his whimsical daughter make a leap so bold?

At the bewilderment on her face, Millicent sighed. "Take care," she said. "Once a child embroiders you onto her heart, she'll have expectations."

Fancy scampered from the closet.

On the bedroom floor, dress-up clothes, headgear, and assorted jewelry sat in tangled heaps. The yellow princess gown, the original choice for the flower girl outfit, was also on the floor. The discovery of chocolate stains on the sleeves made the frock unsuitable for the wedding.

Racing to the bed, Fancy held up her latest selections.

Jada considered the two dresses wagging before her nose. "This one first." She pointed at the sapphire-blue dress with the dim hope the child would finally make a decision.

"My favorite!"

"Stop teasing me. You've picked eight favorites so far."

Placing the garment in a neat circle on the floor, Fancy stepped in. "I was pretending."

In big-girl fashion, she refused assistance, grunting and shimmying as she threaded her arms through the sleeves, even managing to close the eyelet button at the back of her neck. When she finished, she slipped her feet into purple sandals of cheap plastic that Jada decided were *not* entering the fashion semifinals.

Fancy said, "Now close your eyes. I'll get the other parts."

"Okay. My eyes are closed."

Picking an outfit had become more a game than a serious pursuit. Philip had gladly left them to it, volunteering to chill out in front of the TV while Jada worked her magic. His words, not hers. She was certain she'd misplaced her wand, along with her powers of persuasion over a determined little girl. Helping Fancy make a decision required more charms and pixie dust than presently available.

From the living room, the roaring cheers of the Cleveland Cavaliers game drifted in. Jada considered peeking to see what was taking Fancy so long. The slap of sandals approached.

"You can look now!"

Jada opened her eyes.

To the blue dress, Fancy had added a top hat, three feather boas, a pink plastic purse—and sunglasses. The sunglasses were Philip's, from his hot-bodied youth.

Amusement tickled Jada's rib cage. She rose from the bed.

Lightly, she rapped the child on the head. "Hello? Anyone in there?"

A new game, and Fancy chortled. "I don't think so!"

"No one puts on Wayfarers for a wedding. Well, unless they're getting married in Hollywood."

"What are Wayfarers?"

"Your daddy's sunglasses."

The sunglasses slid down Fancy's nose. "I like Daddy's Wayfarers." She pushed them back up.

"They're old," Jada pointed out, hoping to appeal to her sense of style. "They were cool when he was in high school, but they look kind of silly on you."

"Did you think Daddy was cool in high school?"

"Mostly I thought he was flaky." Mentioning the string of girlfriends from his teen years wasn't appropriate. Instead, she added, "He was sort of like a bunny rabbit, hopping from one thing to the next."

"Were you friends with Daddy?"

A more difficult question. Jada winced as she went with the little white lie. "Sure. We were friends." The lie was preferable to disappointing Philip's daughter.

Fancy slid the sunglasses off. "You're best friends with me now." She put them on the teddy bear seated before her dresser. All four of the pint-size chairs were lined up, filled with stuffed animals watching the fashion show.

She trotted back, giddy from the extended playtime. Her cheeks were flushed; perspiration glistened on her brow. Jada palmed away the moisture, her hand lingering against the child's impossibly soft skin. Fancy leaned into the gentle affection like a plant straining toward the sun.

The warning from Millicent tripped through Jada. Was it imprudent to display affection this readily? She wasn't a permanent fixture in Fancy's life.

Drawing away, she regarded the feather boas. "Not fair. We've already been over this. Choose one, and only one."

"Why can't I have three? They're pretty."

"They'll bounce around when you walk down the aisle."

"What aisle? Linnie and Uncle Daniel are getting married outside."

"On the patio that your father is building at the inn," Jada agreed. The installation was taking longer than expected. Philip was sending one of the pallets back due to cracks in the sandstone. The supplier hadn't yet confirmed when the replacement stone would ship. A concern for another day, and she returned to the issue at hand. "If you're going with a feather boa, you can't have more than one. There *will* be an aisle in the middle of the new patio. What if you can't see where you're going, and fall down?"

"Okay, okay." Giving in, Fancy unwound the boas from her neck. She watched them drift to the floor to join the other castoffs. Then her fickle attention landed on the bodice of her dress. She patted the narrow plane of her chest. "Jada, when will I get boobies?"

"Gosh, Fancy. Not soon."

"When did *you* get them?"

She flicked Fancy's nose, eliciting a giggle. "Why do you care about this nonsense?"

"The girls were talking about boobies at recess."

Jada frowned with consternation. "The girls in your class?" Fancy's playmates loved Disney and crafts. Sophisticated topics were beyond them.

"No, the fifth graders. They said you aren't *really* a big girl until your boobies come in. You're just a shrimp cake until then."

"What a ridiculous thing to say."

"Is it true?"

The hurt rippling through the query took Jada aback. "Fancy, did the older girls call you a shrimp cake?"

Her face fell.

Anger flared inside Jada. Didn't the older girls know that a kid Fancy's age was obsessed with big-girl status? Growing up was hard enough. She didn't need extra hoops to jump through.

Crouching down, Jada rested her hands on the child's dainty shoulders. "Sweetie, listen to me." She waited until Fancy's eyes lifted, felt relief when they did. "Who you are on the inside matters, not what you're like on the outside. If you're friendly or nice, *that* matters."

"What if you're mean?"

"It also matters, but for different reasons. Mostly people are mean because they're scared—of not fitting in, or not making enough friends. Sometimes older girls worry about dumb stuff, like getting boobies. If their friends start looking like women before they do, they're scared of not fitting in."

"They'll feel better if they look like their friends?" Clearly a bizarre concept for the six-year-old: her lemon-colored hair was a standout at Sweet Lake Elementary. The compliments that the rare blonde color elicited were a source of pride for the child.

"For some people, looking alike is a big deal," Jada explained. "It's silly, because people are all the same on the inside. We all love, and get scared. We all want to be happy, and make friends."

Fancy cocked her head like a bird. "Why are people different colors?" she asked.

The question surprised Jada. Never before had the subject of race come up. Given the widening circle of children Fancy now interacted with at school, the topic seemed long overdue. One of her new besties was Vietnamese; the other girls were white. Three of the boys in the first-grade class were black; two were Latino. As she did all the boys, Fancy avoided them because they were rowdy. Trinity Chambers was black and lived for soccer. Never would she trade in her uniform for girly playtime.

She lifted her arm, placed Fancy's pale hand on top. "People are different colors because our skin is a map," Jada said.

"Like a treasure map?"

"Even better. It tells you where your relatives came from. People with dark skin like mine? We came from places where the sun was really bright. God made our skin dark to protect us. People with lighter skin came from places where the sun wasn't too hot."

"I come from a place where the sun hides?"

"Not all the time—but sometimes. Your family came from Europe."

"Where is yours from?"

"Africa."

"The sun likes Africa more than Europe?" Fancy was very feminine, but she also possessed a competitive streak.

"No, but Africa sits closer to the sun."

"That isn't fair. Why does Africa get to sit in the front of the class?"

Wryly, Jada grinned. She needed a refresher course on how to boil down complicated subjects for a child to digest.

"The next time I stop over, I'll draw you a picture." She stifled a yawn. A quick glance at the clock confirmed it was past eight o'clock. "Can we take this up then? You still haven't picked out a dress for Linnie's wedding."

The suggestion went unheeded. "In summer, it's *really* hot," Fancy informed her. "Why doesn't the sun make me brown? I get red, like a tomato. It hurts."

"You forget to use sunscreen." She despised the stuff. "Your daddy asks you to put it on, but you say it feels slimy. You make him chase you around the yard just to get sunscreen on you."

"I want to be brown, like you." Leaning forward on her toes, she pressed her forehead to Jada's. "Then we'd be twins. I don't look like Daddy, or Uncle Daniel. Plus, you're really pretty. Did I ever tell you that?"

The unsolicited compliment was sweet and unexpected. "No, you haven't," Jada murmured, and the press of Fancy's skin against hers sent warmth cascading through her. When they drew apart, she added, "I think you're pretty too."

"Do you love me?"

"I do."

"I love you too."

"I'm glad."

"I probably won't understand why the sun picks favorites until I get boobies." She startled Jada by pointing at her breasts. "Yours are nice. Daddy thinks so too. He likes to look at them."

The disclosure threatened to knock Jada over. Since she was crouching before the alarmingly blunt child, she dropped her bottom on the floor.

Philip ogles my breasts? No. Just no.

If frequent visits to his home made for a cozy arrangement, that didn't imply Philip would allow a pesky attraction to get out-of-bounds. They were no more compatible than fire and ice. Even the casual friendship they'd embarked upon never would've come to pass if not for Jada playing stand-in for his daughter's missing Uncle Daniel.

Scrambling for composure, she said, "Sweetie, I'm friends with your father. That's all. He doesn't look at me that way."

"Yes, he does. He doesn't want you to see when he's looking. He does this." To demonstrate, Fancy widened her eyes and ogled Jada's breasts. Then she shot her attention to the wall. When she looked back, her chin lifted with satisfaction. "He's sneaky."

Jada opened her mouth, then closed it again. This had nothing to do with Philip—blame the fifth-grade girls for bringing up topics beyond Fancy's comprehension. If they'd morphed into sophisticates, the teachers needed to place them under house arrest. Bar them from recess, banish them to study hall.

What other ideas have they put in Fancy's head?

The door creaked open. "How are we doing, ladies?" Philip surveyed the bedroom. "Wow. A tornado came through. Any injuries to report?"

Fancy leapt into his arms. "We're okay!"

"Great, since I don't have a Band-Aid handy." Setting her down, he sent a jaundiced glance at the costumes heaped on the floor. "Geez, Fancy. All this crap is in the 'No' pile? How long does it take to pick out a dress?"

"I'm still deciding. There's more stuff in the closet. I'll show you."

She raced off. He regarded Jada, making a slow ascent to her feet. She felt woozy, like she'd pulled an all-nighter and then run a 5K. Philip wore a look of expectancy as he waited for her to say something—anything. Her neurons refused to fire.

When they began snapping to life, they brought a troublesome question: *Why did I stop by in a skin-hugging sweater?*

The knit clung to every curve.

If Philip *was* in the habit of staring at her breasts, sackcloth and baggy shirts were on the agenda from here on out. At the thought, humiliation rose off her like steam.

The scent of her dismay rocked him back on his heels. "What's wrong with you?" he demanded.

In a well-ingrained habit, Jada endeavored to ignore the beauty of Philip's eyes. They were nothing like the cornflower-blue wonders Fancy had inherited from her late mother, but who cared? Thickly lashed for a man, deep green with flecks of gold spinning through—his gaze transmitted emotion like a beacon. Which wasn't necessarily a good thing at the moment. He appeared bewildered.

Inside the closet, shuffling noises erupted. Fancy sang out, "Hold on. I have a surprise!"

He gave the closet a cursory glance. "Take your time." Then he surveyed Jada with concern. "Seriously. What's wrong? The mute treatment is giving me flashbacks. Eleventh grade, the day you and Linnie took your new wheels on a joyride outside town. When Bambi dashed across the road? You were upset for a week."

"For good reason—I nearly killed Bambi," Jada protested. She wasn't sure why she felt defensive. "The experience would upset most girls. I was only seventeen."

"Yeah, well, you look worse now. You look beat."

"Thanks," she snapped. "I needed a compliment right about now."

"It's no compliment," he said, misreading her, "but I totally understand. Keeping up with Fancy is a marathon. There's no shame in admitting she bested you. You're down for the count, right?"

The embarrassment scorching her neck climbed all the way to her brow. "Not down for the count," she muttered. "More like flabbergasted." The urge to hide her breasts from view was silly.

If she'd thought the remark about Philip's viewing habits was the low point of the evening, she was sadly mistaken. She gasped as Fancy sashayed from the closet. Over the sapphire-blue dress, the first grader had wound a stretchy length of fire-engine-red material.

A bra.

Philip did a double take. "Whoa, cowboy." He stumbled back, as if the fiery color posed a danger. "What are you doing with lingerie?"

"Do you like it, Daddy?" The lacy cups slid beneath Fancy's armpits. She didn't notice as she gave a wide smile. "Now I have boobies."

Silence descended on the bedroom. Dragging a palm up his forehead, Philip gripped his skull.

Then he nailed Jada with an accusatory look. "What's with the Victoria's Secret? She's too young. Like ten centuries too young. Are you crazy?"

Appalled, Jada blinked. "You think *I* gave her lingerie?"

"Aside from Penelope, you're the only woman she lets into her bedroom. She trusts you."

A backhanded compliment, but it stung nonetheless. "You're unbelievable," Jada sputtered. "Since when do I hand out bras to six-year-olds?"

"Beats me. Is this a new habit? Break it. Like, pronto."

They were perilously close to arguing. Darting between them, Fancy pulled on her father's sleeve. She looked confused, not frightened, by the debate.

"Jada didn't give me the bra," she told him. "I took it from Cat's house."

Philip's brows lowered with disapproval. "You *stole* a bra from Cat? Geez, Fancy. Why did you do something like that?"

"No, Daddy! I didn't steal. Cat was going through her closet, making bags for Goodwill."

"Fancy, you can't take stuff, even if it's meant for Goodwill."

"I didn't know."

After he unwound the offensive garment from her torso, he stuffed it in his pocket. She went to her dresser and pulled out a nightgown. "I already brushed my teeth." She tugged the garment over her head.

He gave Jada a sheepish look. "Truce?"

She knit her brows.

He winced. "Jumping to conclusions—never a good idea. Thanks for the advice. I've got it." When she continued stewing in a fine broth of outrage, he splayed his palms in apology. "Forgive me? A free pass, and I'll never ask for another?"

She was mulling over the option as Fancy, leaping into bed, sabotaged her.

"Daddy?"

"What, sugarplum?"

"Jada said you were flaky in high school. Why did you act like a bunny rabbit?"

Chapter 7

Philip left the bedroom with an air of confidence that required no inter-pretation. Thanks to Jada's faux pas, he'd wrested back the upper hand.

"You were chatting about me with my kid? Is this something you do often?" Shutting the door, he blocked her from escaping down the hallway. "Fancy is the president of my fan club, you know. If you're joining, I'll send you a special gift."

Embarrassment flamed across her face, but Jada managed to nail him with a sassy look. "Wait. Your fan club is still up and running?" she asked tartly. "I thought it disbanded after you broke too many hearts."

"Fair enough. Maybe it did."

"*Maybe?* Philip, your days as the Sun King ended around the time I bought my first iPhone."

"Is that why my kid thinks I acted like a bunny rabbit in high school? Because I had fun dating?" he teased her. "Got any other goofy opinions you'd like to share?"

"Forget it." Jada darted past him. She entered the living room with her dignity in shreds. Obviously, Fancy needed a primer on how to keep a secret.

"Stop stonewalling. You thought I was flaky in high school?"

"Please. You dated half of the girls in our class, mostly to get out of doing your own homework. Or did you fall in love on a weekly basis? Plus, you never remembered to study for tests."

"All of which falls under the purview of 'dreamy.' As in, 'the kid with his head in the clouds.'"

"Flaky," she corrected. "Whitewash the past any way you'd like, but I know what I know."

"And I was a flake?"

"You were."

He gripped his chest in mock pain. "Talk about a blow to my ego. And here I thought you looked up to me during my forgotten youth."

Arrogance wasn't a card Philip usually played. At least not with her. He did so now with a winning smile that darted pleasure to Jada's belly. The pleasure mixed nicely with her irritation.

"Dream on," she said, fending off his charisma. They were playing a new game, one she doubted she'd win. "The flakiness wasn't the worst of it. You were also obnoxious. Hard core, insufferably obnoxious."

"Is that why we were never friends?"

"In high school? Philip, I would've shaved my head and pierced my nose before I would've been friends with you."

"Keep rubbing in the salt, buddy." Philip hooked his thumbs in the pockets of his jeans. He appeared one degree shy of laughing out loud. "You're doing real damage to the memory of my suave younger self. I'll give you the bit about being a flake, but I was never obnoxious."

He really was unbelievable. "Are you kidding?" A smile tickled the corners of her mouth. "You had a special talent for obnoxious behavior. What about all the paper airplanes you shot into my hair? The paper-clips, the rubber bands—there was a day in our senior year when you went into a wind-up with a wad of bubble gum."

"Yeah, but I nixed the idea when you channeled the death-stare."

"What death-stare?"

"That thing you do with your eyes when you're really peeved. And your lips," Philip added. His attention lingered on her mouth like a caress, smooth and slow, and undeniably delicious. When he captured her gaze, her heart jumped. "You're doing it now."

If they were running a race, he was gaining on her. "If you had pitched that wad of gum, I would've beaten you to a pulp," she said, astonished by her bravado.

The remark kicked up the lights gleaming in his eyes. "I would've deserved the thrashing," he agreed, taking a step closer.

"You would've deserved more than a thrashing." Warning lights flashed in her brain. She was challenging him, and the competitive lights glinting in his eyes only made Philip more attractive.

"Yeah?" he murmured, his voice husky. "What sort of punishment would you have devised?"

The air between them sparked and snapped.

Why am I flirting with him?

The atmosphere was too inviting, too much like the interplay between a man and a woman reveling in a common attraction. Everything about Philip was comfortably familiar, yet she couldn't shake the impression she was seeing him for the first time. As if a lifetime of disliking him, which had only recently evolved into a late-blooming and sometimes awkward friendship, was nothing more than a mirage. As if she'd never before glimpsed the man standing before her now.

Common sense warned her to break off the exchange. Take this too far, and she wasn't sure where it would lead.

She couldn't manage to follow through.

"When we were young, why *did* you throw stuff at me?" she said, unable to quash her curiosity. "The antics started way back in grade school. I never got why you liked making me angry."

"Hmm. Let's see." Philip crossed his arms, clearly enjoying her interest. "Getting you riled up was a secondary consideration."

"What was the primary consideration?"

"Your crazy curls. Even as a kid you were careful and precise, never making the wrong move. Never jumping into anything until you'd calculated the odds of success. Jada Brooks, the girl in control."

He'd summed her up perfectly. "What's your point?"

"Everything about you is tidy except your wild curls. Doesn't matter what you do, you can't control them. Man, I love that. They're the one part of you that can't be tamed."

"Wait. You threw crap at me because you liked my hair?"

"The move got your attention, right?"

Was Philip admitting he'd had a crush on her? An infatuation kept on the down low all the way through high school? She couldn't bring herself to believe the cocky, love-'em-and-leave-'em youth she'd known had viewed her as anything but the most responsible teen at Sweet Lake High. Especially since she'd had absolutely no interest in viewing Sweet Lake's charming and shallow Hot Body as boyfriend material.

For all the obvious reasons.

A dazed silence followed her outside. The night breeze whispered in greeting, funneling across the daffodils bobbing in the flower bed. A car drove past as she started across the grass. She watched the taillights receding into the darkness with her thoughts colliding into one another. There were moments in your life capable of altering the most strongly held assumptions, shuffling the known facts into a new arrangement that revealed a larger truth. Was this one of those moments?

Of one thing she was certain. In the contest of bizarre evenings, tonight deserved the grand prize.

From behind, the front door clicked shut. Philip said, "What would you have done? In high school, I mean."

"About what?" Her keys jangled as she withdrew them from her purse.

"How would you have reacted if the flaky guy had asked you out?"

A sweet, nearly seductive note carried through the question. She didn't dare turn around and look at him.

"If you'd asked me out in high school? You weren't my type."

"You weren't my type either. The boring chick with the books."

The taunt lured her flashing eyes back to him for a fleeting moment. "I was serious about my studies," she countered, turning away.

"You missed out on all the fun."

"No, I decided to do the work and play later."

"How much longer are you planning to wait?" he asked, and the edgy quality in his voice coaxed her into facing him. He looked nearly smug as he appraised her. "By my count, you've dated exactly two guys in the last five years. Both dull in the extreme, and totally not your type. Keep playing it safe, and you'll never find what you need."

"Give me a break." Circling away from the car, she swatted him playfully. "Since when do you know what I need?"

Touching Philip was a mistake. She saw the error on his features, registering first her incredibly childish response of swatting him. Then his expression narrowed in an undeniably masculine way. The distance between a playful response and a sexual challenge was no greater than the space between heartbeats.

A distance he crossed as he strode to her swiftly. "You first," he murmured, crowding her, erasing the space between them by backing her into the car. Dizzy spots of color leapt before her eyes. "Repeat after me: Philip was not a flake. In high school, or at any other time in his natural-born life."

"Pass," she said, caught by the devilish gleam in his eyes.

"Last chance, Jada. Take it back."

Nervous laughter bubbled in her throat. "No!" She fought it down.

"Fine. Have it your way."

He stepped away. But only long enough for the suppressed laughter to shake her ribcage with fizzy indulgence. When he turned back to her, the revelry fled his features like sunlight before a storm. Yearning darkened his eyes.

The startling change extinguished the giddy sensation in her belly, doused it with the strength of the message he conveyed. The light attraction she'd sensed growing inside the safe confines of their friendship didn't match the fever making his cheeks ruddy with color, or the accompanying response of her heart, cartwheeling now in her chest, responding without her conscious approval. Heat built between them. With it came an unexpected hunger so fierce she froze stock-still.

With satisfaction, Philip read her face. He moved back in.

With strong hands, he cupped her face. His touch was gentle as he thumbed the sensitive skin beneath her ear. A hungry shudder rippled up her spine, and she moaned. The sound lit his eyes with desire as his gaze roamed at will, taking in every inch of her face, taking her in with a leisure she knew he'd never before dared.

The moment hung suspended out of time. Breathless, she looked up at him.

If Philip meant to deliver a tentative kiss, the decision went astray. The moment he bent his head to press his mouth to hers, his body came too. With a shudder, he sealed himself against her in a reaction that seemed equally wrought from pleasure and pain. His fingers dove into her hair, twining through the curls, a groan slipping from his throat as he angled her face up to better allow him to explore her lips. The desire carried in his kiss sent fire all the way to her toes. Beneath the onslaught of pleasurable sensation, her knees threatened to dissolve.

When he finished kissing her from earth and halfway to heaven, he clasped her around the waist. A nice move, Jada thought in a bliss-induced stupor. She'd melted against the car in a perfectly acceptable swoon.

"That," he said, "I don't take back."

Chapter 8

Philip strode past the three women and crouched before the low garden wall. "Frances, *this* is the emergency that couldn't wait? There's a shipment of azaleas coming in for the Wayfair's new patio. My crew is already on-site."

The seventyish co-leader of the Sirens had called him at daybreak. She owned a beaut of a house on Highland Avenue, and Unity Design handled all her landscaping.

"Stop whining like a mule. It's not attractive." Frances extracted herself from where she stood between Ruth and Penelope. "Surely you have mortar and the necessary tools in your truck. How long will it take you to fix?"

"I don't have mortar in the truck."

"What sort of handyman shows up for the job without proper supplies?" Feigning distress, she motioned to the three wrought-iron chairs lined up on the grass. "We were planning a nice visit while you worked."

"Frances, I'm a landscaper, not a handyman. Or a mason, come to think of it. I will help out with the wall, just not today."

Philip picked up one of the broken chunks of brick scattered across the grass. If he didn't know better, he'd conclude the morning SOS was a ruse. It sure looked like one of the Sirens had whacked the garden wall with a sledgehammer, taking care not to wreak too much damage.

He threw an assessing glance at the most ill-tempered Siren. The knees of Ruth Kenefsky's denim overalls were dirty, and she *did* look winded.

Tossing the chunk of brick from hand to hand, he got to his feet. "Mind explaining how this happened?" All three of the women looked guilty.

Frances tilted her chin. "I assume a deer gamboled into my yard."

"And rammed a two-foot high wall? Try again."

"Plant roots pushed the wall out," Penelope offered.

"We're talking about perennials, not tree roots. They didn't cleave a hole in the wall ten inches wide."

"Might have been kids," Ruth growled. Her white braids whipped in the breeze as she gestured for emphasis. "There are hooligans in these parts." When he gave her a jaundiced look, she added, "Sweet Lake's not immune to vandalism, Mr. Smarty Pants."

"Kids don't haul around sledgehammers. Mostly because they're hard to lug." Philip scraped the hair from his brow. "Ladies, keep your dirty little secrets. I'm not really interested. Frances, I'll let you know when I have time to repair the wall."

Penelope, clearly aware he was onto them, came forward. "Philip, wait." Fiddling with her glasses, she added, "We have a question."

One important enough to bring him before the tribunal of three curious Sirens? This, he decided, was not good.

"What is it?"

Her myopic gaze lowered to the grass. "Well . . . it's about Tilda."

"What about her?"

When the bashful Siren continued staring at the grass, Ruth nudged her aside. "Tilda sent a group text to all the Sirens," Ruth informed him. Her wrinkles merged into an expression of intense scrutiny. "She drove by your house last night. She swears you were putting the moves on Jada in your driveway. Is it true?"

Philip muffled a groan. He didn't need Tilda and her twitchy texting finger advertising his novice attempt at romance around town. Twelve hours later, he still wasn't sure if Jada was on board with the idea. He'd tested the waters at daybreak by sending a good morning text. In a real dipshit move, he'd added a row of purple heart emoticons. Then he'd stared at his phone with heat scalding his scalp as he wished for a "Delete" button.

Jada didn't reply.

Twenty minutes later, desperation compelled him to send a less adolescent text—minus emoticons—stating he hoped to see her again soon. As Fancy trailed cereal across the kitchen and they debated the merits of wearing a pink tutu and ballerina slippers to school, he invented a dozen reasons why Jada, who always replied promptly, was taking so long.

He never received a response to the second text either.

Snapping out of the reverie, he regarded the women. "Let me get this straight. You dragged me over here this morning to pick through my private life?"

"As if there's much to pick through," Ruth grumbled. When he began to object, she waved him into silence. "Get real, son. You're no more adventurous than a turtle hiding in its shell. Roosting alone in your house, burying yourself in work. If you laid the moves on Jada, well, I say 'Go get her, tiger.' You both need some excitement."

"And you need advice," Frances said. The comment sent horror marching across his features, and she smiled like a benevolent queen. "Don't waste this opportunity, Philip. Spare ten minutes from your schedule to have coffee with me and Penelope. We only want to help."

Ruth kicked a broken wedge of brick, pinging it against the wall. "What about me? Aren't I coming inside for coffee?"

"Would you mind if you didn't?" Frances asked sweetly. "I'm sure you understand. This conversation appears more difficult for Philip than I'd anticipated. It's best if you leave."

"Yeah, Ruth," Philip put in. "You won't be missing much. I'm having a quick cup of coffee and skipping the heart-to-heart with your comrades." He bobbed a thumb at the wall. "Besides, your work here is done."

"Fine. I'm leaving." Ruth stomped across the grass.

After she'd gone, Frances led him inside. Crafty woman that she was, she'd already brewed a pot of coffee and set out a crystal tray of cherry Danish. He had no intention of answering questions, but he wasn't stupid enough to forgo the good eats.

Grabbing a Danish, he set the ground rules. "I know you both mean well, but I'm not letting you take a magnifying glass to my private life." He took a bite, chewed thoughtfully. "And let Tilda know if she adds me to the gossip chain, I'm done mowing her lawn. She can tackle the chore on her own."

"Back to whining?" Frances poured coffee into a china cup, handed it off to him. "It's not like you to spurn our advice."

"Sure, when it comes to my daughter." The Sirens had been helping him navigate parenting since Fancy was a newborn. Their intervention was a godsend. "Lend all the advice you want about Fancy. No offense—I don't want your input on my own life."

Penelope, quivering by the Danish, lifted her head. "There was another time when you ignored the Sirens' advice—about Bodi. Do you remember?"

He flinched, stricken by the reminder.

At his reaction, she hurried forward. "I don't mean to upset you," she said, her rheumy eyes watering. "Philip, I hope you *are* planning to woo Jada. Nothing would make me happier. I've always thought you were a match made in heaven, even if the celestial lines got crossed along the way and you two lovebirds never discovered you were meant for each other."

Frances sighed. "Penelope, dear. You're jumbling your metaphors and confusing him." She patted his arm. "She's trying to give you advice once again. You'd be wise to listen."

Frances's intervention seemed to give Penelope the courage to continue. In a stronger voice, she said, "Philip, I have an awful suspicion Jada blames you both for Bodi's death. Give her a better understanding of the troubled girl she befriended and you hastily married. Do that, and your relationship has every chance to blossom."

Carefully, he set down his coffee. "Anything else?" he asked, his irritation sifting away. It was impossible to feel anger toward Penelope—she always meant well.

"Will you please do the same?" she asked.

"Do the same . . . ?"

"Forgive yourself, and let the past go."

The advice tightened his throat. With a nod, he strode out.

He pulled out of the driveway and drove all the way to the stop sign before bringing the truck to a grinding halt.

Shafts of sunlight cut across the street. Squinting through the glare, he failed to get his bearings. Penelope's well-meaning advice scraped against the guilt he'd carried for seven long years.

Forgive himself?

He didn't know how.

The following week rushed by. With the end of March nearing, Jada was thrilled to see bookings at the inn begin to rise. The lake was still too cold for swimming, but the Wayfair's increasing fortunes had sparked new businesses in town. Several of Sweet Lake's more industrious sportsmen began taking the inn's guests out on leisurely boat rides, or to fish the blue waters for walleye and largemouth bass. The baking lessons with Millicent continued and, twice a week, the Sirens hosted free yoga classes on the beach. Frances Dufour and Silvia Mendoza, when their schedules permitted, took vacationers on nature walks through the forest.

Jada welcomed the rush of the upcoming season. With more tasks occupying her days, she managed to avoid spending too much time analyzing the kiss she'd shared with Philip. They'd only spoken on the phone twice since then. Each time, she'd politely declined his invitation to stop by the house. Feeling unmoored by the change in their relationship, she needed time to sort herself out.

Mr. Uchida came into the kitchen muttering incomprehensible Japanese. One of the inn's oldest employees, he oversaw the staff manning the front desk.

"What's wrong?" she asked, wiping her hands on a dish towel. She'd just finished preparing the last dessert for the day's menu, a chocolate cream pie with fluffy peaks of whipped cream.

"I need to speak with Linnie. She's not in her office."

"She went down to the beach." They were looking into purchasing cabanas for the summer season, and she was meeting with the rep. Jada loved the idea of adding the elegant cobalt-blue-and-white cabanas for guests to enjoy during the hottest months. "She'll return soon. What do you need? I'll take care of it."

"Will you talk to the Sirens?" Mr. Uchida asked. "They're in the ballroom."

"I wasn't aware they'd stopped by." With Linnie's upcoming wedding, the Sirens were at the inn more often than usual to discuss the preparations. "Is it a problem?"

Mr. Uchida held up a note. "I have another call about renting out the ballroom. A women's club in Dayton. They're looking for a venue to host a summer retreat, and a dinner on the last night. They want to see the ballroom. I'm afraid to set up a time for the viewing."

"They're driving down this week?"

"Only if I can give them a firm time for a tour. Jada, I can't set up appointments with the Sirens dropping by whenever the whim strikes."

"They promised to give us advance notice. Linnie's reception is important, but we *will* have other events scheduled this season." Jada followed him into the lobby. "Go back to work. I'll talk to them."

Last summer, the Wayfair had ended its long decline. As guests began returning to the historic inn, Linnie made an investment to freshen up the ballroom. The dull grey walls were painted a stylish ivory color with a hint of pink at the base. With Jada's help, they'd polished every crystal droplet of the chandelier, which hadn't thrown sparkling light on partygoers for nearly a decade. A cleaning service came in to polish the long expanse of parquet flooring. Today the ballroom, where earlier generations of Linnie's family once oversaw formal dinners and lavish events, was again the prettiest jewel in the Wayfair's crown.

Twenty-five round tables formed a necklace around the dancing area and the dais beyond. Frances, Tilda, and Ruth huddled around a table near the front. Cat's mother, Silvia, who usually preferred flamboyant clothing, paced between tables in an uncharacteristically subdued beige suit. Evidently the meeting was important enough to make the accountant late for work.

Tilda was the first to notice the intrusion. "Jada, I was hoping you'd pop in. There's something I've been dying to ask you," she said, the remark earning her black looks from Silvia and Frances. "Or not," she added quickly, and they nodded with approval.

"Good," Jada said, frowning at the puzzling exchange between the women. "I don't have a lot of time."

"By the way, I've had another dream about you. Really fascinating."

"Tilda . . ."

"Oh. All right. Private chitchat. Should I find you after we're finished here?"

"Only if you give me fair warning first. You know, to give me time to hide."

The perky Realtor shimmied her shoulders, unsure if she should laugh. "You're kidding, right?"

"To be perfectly honest . . . I'm not." The Siren meant well, and Jada shifted nervously from foot to foot. She searched for a diplomatic way to let Tilda down. "Would you please do me a favor? Dream about someone else."

"You're not interested?" The prospect deflated the petite Siren like a punctured balloon.

"I'm not. I'm sorry."

The apology missed the mark. "You don't seem the least bit grateful," Tilda pouted. "Not everyone gets to benefit from Siren dreams. I can't believe you're willing to pass up the opportunity to understand the future."

"Let the future come as it will. I'll figure it out as I go along." She recalled the blistering kiss Philip had laid on her, and his six-year-old's fascination with boobies. "My life is getting weird enough on its own. I don't need your nocturnal ramblings added to the mix."

"Fine. I get it." Insulted, Tilda swished her cinnamon-colored hair. "You don't have to get snippy. I'm only trying to help."

Frances shuffled through the index cards before her. "Tilda, please. She's given you an answer. There's no need to belabor the point." The elderly Siren regarded Jada. "It's nice of you to join us. Your opinion will add zest to the debate."

"I'm not here to lend a hand."

She reminded the Sirens about the promise they'd made to call ahead whenever they planned to work in the ballroom. After the women promised to do so, she turned to leave.

Index cards were fanned out across the table. Wedding guests were listed on the heavy card stock, eight names per card. But not by family— the names appeared randomly set down on each card.

Curious, Jada picked one up. "What are you doing?" she asked Frances.

"Other than tearing my hair out? We're debating the seating for the reception. There's been some disagreement."

Ruth snorted. "Don't sugarcoat the facts. We're on the brink of outright war."

"Oh, hush."

It was unlikely Linnie would sanction a seating plan that wasn't by family. "Does Linnie know you're working on this?" Jada asked.

"She gave us permission to get started," Frances explained. "We'll show her the end result when we're finished. There's no sense dragging her into the middle of the debate."

Silvia regarded her with disbelief. "We're not debating. I'm doing my level best to avert disaster." Shorter and more robust than Frances, the co-leader of the Sirens was also more prone to anger. "Frances, you and Tilda can't alter tradition at will. How do you expect Linnie to react once she sees the seating plan? And Ruth, I can't believe they reeled you into this madness."

Ruth flicked a blank card in Silvia's direction. "I'm considering the big picture," she snapped. "Why aren't you? The wedding will give us a chance to grow the town's population. You want Sweet Lake to stay rinky-dink forever?"

Jada looked from one woman to another. "Hold on. What does Linnie's reception have to do with the town's population?" There wasn't an obvious connection, which meant the Sirens were up to something.

If the past was any guide, they were up to something crazy.

The question disappeared beneath the tension blooming between the women. War looming on the horizon, with no one willing to back down.

Tilda broke the silence. "You're wrong, Silvia. Ruth does have a point. How often do we have a party with more than half the town in attendance? None of the Sirens are getting any younger."

Silvia grunted. "Speak for yourself. I'm holding pat in my sixties, and going no further."

"Easy for you to say. Most of the Sirens have seen men come and go, or have buried husbands—or they're fortunate like you, and still *have* a husband. What about me? I'm only forty-six. I deserve to find a man who'll stick like glue. So do the other Sirens who are looking for love." Tilda skimmed a polished finger down a typewritten sheet positioned between the stacks of index cards. "Frances, I've made up my mind. Seat me by the new dog groomer."

The decision lifted Frances's silvery brows. "The stud opening up the place on Maple Street? Good heavens, Tilda. You *are* ambitious. He's not much older than Jada. Late thirties, I'd guess. Are you sure?"

"I'll take my chances."

Frances made a note. "Surprising he's invited."

"I put the idea in Daniel's head." Tilda beamed. "He's drawing up the articles of incorporation for Pampered Pets."

In lowered voices, they began discussing the dog groomer and the other eligible bachelors invited to the reception. Unsure how to stop them, Jada searched her frazzled brain for a quick fix. Like she needed one more problem on her plate.

She was still hunting for a solution when Silvia regarded her impatiently. "Why aren't you backing me up?" she demanded. "Or don't you care if the mad plotters turn your best friend's wedding into a dating service?"

"I *do* care. Perhaps I should handle the table assignments myself."

"You don't have time."

"I'll make time, Silvia. Okay?" Absently, Jada brushed at her temples and the faint pounding of a headache coming on.

"Between baking lessons with Millicent and helping Fancy settle on a dress for the wedding, you don't have spare time. Even if you did, you'd never talk the Sirens out of this. They'll only listen to me."

An accurate assessment. Jada was about to toss the problem back into Silvia's lap when Philip's name lifted from the hushed conversation at the table.

"What about Philip?" she asked Tilda.

"We're deciding if we should seat him by Daisy."

"Daisy, in Housekeeping?" The strawberry blonde was barely in her twenties, with the excitable nature of a terrier. "You can't. He's sitting at the head table with the wedding party."

With me, she nearly added.

"For dinner only. We'll have Philip move to Daisy's table before Linnie and Daniel cut the wedding cake. We've already run the idea by Daisy. She's thrilled. Wouldn't they make a darling couple?"

Jada recoiled. "In what universe?"

At her reaction, Silvia and Frances shared a meaningful glance. There wasn't time to analyze it as Tilda spoke again.

"This one," she said, laughing. "The wedding is the perfect opportunity for Mr. Lonely Heart to find love again. Since we're putting Daisy right in his path, he doesn't have to look too far."

"She's too young for him!"

The outburst made Ruth harrumph with disbelief. Or she feigned disbelief—Jada got a funny feeling she *was* missing something.

"Jada, who gave you stupid pills?" Ruth said. "Young is exactly what Philip needs."

"How can you possibly know what he needs?" she demanded.

The question deepened the wrinkles crisscrossing Ruth's brow. "Just because I never got hitched doesn't mean I haven't enjoyed intimacy now and again." She cocked her head, then stuck out her tongue with uncontained petulance. "I've had plenty of men in my time."

"Thanks for sharing. Not that I have *any* idea what your sex life, real or imagined, has to do with Philip."

"Don't get sassy. I know men, and I can tell you this—Philip is as red-blooded as they come. The man is in his prime. He hasn't been on a date in years. There's nothing more pitiful than a stud with the means to give good lovin' and no prospects in sight."

"Ruth, you're no expert on his prospects."

With a huff, the feisty Siren flipped her white braids over her shoulders. "Good grief, Jada. You're his friend. Don't you want him to find happiness? Imagine all the lust he's been saving up."

Tilda cradled her chin on her hand. "Imagining Philip's lust makes my heart jumpy. If I were anywhere near Daisy's age . . ."

Jealousy, neon green and unbecoming, gripped Jada by the throat. "Philip's lust is none of your business," she informed Tilda. "Of all the—Daisy, seriously? Her last boyfriend had peach fuzz on his cheeks and an addiction to Super Mario games. Granted, she's a sweet kid. But she's light-years too young for a mature, responsible man like Philip."

Someone tapped her on the shoulder. She spun around.

Linnie eyed her with interest. "Calm down. It's okay," she whispered. A disorienting turn of events since Jada was usually the one doling out soothing words. Linnie bounced a thumb toward the double doors that led out to the lobby. "Got a minute? There's something I need to go over with you."

"The cabanas. Right." She discovered that rage had glued her feet to the floor.

Linnie arched a brow. "Are you coming?"

Dismay ate through the rage, and Jada sucked in a breath. What was wrong with her? She was having a public hissy fit, her first ever, and the Sirens were studying her closely. Like vultures homing in for the kill.

She gave a stiff nod. "If you'll excuse us," she mumbled, turning on her heel.

Chapter 9

Jada sailed out of the ballroom with the troubling awareness that she couldn't feel her toes. The buzzing in her ears didn't help, nor did the headache ringing through her skull.

In the lobby, Mr. Uchida was helping a fortyish couple bring their luggage to the front desk. Jada veered toward the corridor that led to her office.

Linnie grabbed hold of her arm. "Let's get some air," she suggested.

"I can't breathe." Jada allowed Linnie to steer her outside.

"Yes, you can," Linnie assured her. "You just don't have much experience with anger. If I didn't know better, I'd suspect the Sirens were lighting your wick on purpose. Guess they didn't know they were lighting dynamite."

Jada trotted down the steps and onto the wide span of lawn. "I'm not angry."

A half-truth, because the jealousy simmering inside her carried a nice undernote of fury. What right did the Sirens have to meddle in other people's affairs? As if fixing Daisy up with Philip made any sense. Jada fended off the desire to march back into the ballroom and give the Sirens an even bigger piece of her mind.

Linnie came to a standstill, presumably to talk. Unable to control the emotion simmering inside her, Jada kept moving.

"We're taking a walk? Oh, okay." Puffing out breaths, Linnie jogged to catch up. She tugged her smartphone from her jeans. In a teasing voice, she talked into the device. "Code red. Meet us at the beach. Jada is having a meltdown."

Jada darted a look of annoyance. "Don't give me your comedy routine, all right? It's not making me feel better."

"Hey, let me enjoy this."

"I'd rather you didn't."

"How often do I see you at full froth? If you're curious, I knew the Sirens were doing the matchmaking thing for my reception. No harm, no foul. Why did their devious plan make you ballistic? Lots of people hook up at weddings."

Providing an explanation proved impossible. Or too humiliating. Jada couldn't decide which.

On the beach, a couple with twin boys sat near the water building sandcastles. Gulls swooped overhead.

Jada stalked past. When she'd reached a suitable distance, she kicked off her shoes. She walked into the surf with embarrassment prickling her skin. Had she actually shouted at the Sirens? She wasn't sure. Nor was she willing to imagine the conclusion they'd drawn from her behavior.

Cat approached with her shoes dangling from her fingers. "Why is Jada having a meltdown?" she asked Linnie.

"Got me. I'm waiting for her to calm down and explain."

"She's really mad?"

Linnie nodded. "Big time."

Jada gave them a thunderous glance. "Stop talking about me like I'm not here. It's really irritating. And stop joking around. Both of you."

Linnie pulled off her heels and joined her in the surf. She'd dressed up today, in a nice sweater and a hip-hugging skirt.

"No more jokes," she promised. She rubbed Jada's arm, a comforting gesture sorely needed at the moment. "Ready to talk? Or do you need more time to calm down?"

"I'm all right, Linnie." Far from it, but she was making an effort.

From the shore, Cat said, "You don't look all right."

Linnie nodded in agreement. Then she said, "Correct me if I'm wrong. I had the impression you weren't mad about the Sirens playing matchmaker with the seating chart for my wedding. You were upset about them fixing Daisy up with Philip. Mind explaining why? I mean, let's face it. Philip won't get back into the game without a push. He's been flying solo for so long, he's forgotten how to find a copilot."

"Oh yeah? The Sirens are giving him the wrong flight plan."

Linnie's eyes lit with interest. "There's someone else he'd like to date? He shared his deepest, darkest secrets with you? That's great!" Her attention bounded across the lake. Apparently the new game thrilled her. "Let me guess."

Inwardly, Jada cringed. "Oh, I really wish you wouldn't." There was no easy way to explain about the kiss she'd shared with Philip.

The objection didn't blot out Linnie's enthusiasm. "Charlene Frieze?" she guessed, caught up in the game. "They dated in high school for at least ten minutes. You remember the phase when Philip went after most of the girls on the debate team? Mr. Hot Body sure knew how to get around. I heard Charlene's divorce has finalized. Her boys are mud monsters, but Fancy can learn to bend."

Cat joined them in the surf. "You're way off base, Linnie. He's not interested in Charlene."

"Who, then?"

Heat crept up Jada's neck. "There's a strong possibility Philip is interested in me."

Silence fell between them as Linnie studied her with incomprehension. A fair enough reaction. Jada had veered from silent dislike of

Philip in the way-back-when to the recent induction as Johnny-on-the-spot with babysitting help and food delivery. As if Jada had become a helpful relative. Imagining them together undoubtedly struck Linnie as one degree short of incest.

Cat, more attuned to matters of the heart, planted her sympathetic gaze on Jada. She seemed capable of reading the flurry of emotion tumbling through Jada—excitement and fear, uncertainty and regret. And happiness at the memory of Philip throwing caution to the wind and taking her into his arms. None of her more rational objections were capable of dispelling the feather-light emotion.

Cat said, "Did something happen between you and Philip?"

"Last week," Jada supplied. "I went over to help Fancy choose her outfit for the wedding. Or at least I tried to help her—the munchkin never did make a decision. After we put her to bed, we went outside." The memory of the longing in Philip's eyes spread heat across her skin. "We were joking around. Then everything became serious—I'm not sure how it happened—and he kissed me."

The news puffed up Linnie's cheeks and made her look like a blowfish. "Wow. You and Philip. I didn't see that coming."

Cat snorted. "Linnie, you've been obsessed with your wedding. You wouldn't see a train coming if you were on the tracks."

"Hey! I wasn't prepared for this."

"You're not the only one who isn't prepared—look at Jada. She can't decide if she's happy or worried about this new development."

The observation sent Linnie's careful regard to Jada. "What's the verdict? Give us a hint."

"I'm not sure. It happened so fast. I mean, there *has* been something going on for months, an undercurrent to our conversations, and the way we've been acting around each other—too many long glances. Too many evenings spent watching TV or sharing a bottle of wine after we've put Fancy to bed."

"Like an old married couple." Linnie smiled, clearly pleased. "You even get the sweet tot without having to endure labor."

"Back to joking? Don't make me hit you."

"Well, it sounds promising."

Promising and confusing. She'd been his late wife's only real friend in Sweet Lake. Embarking on a romance with Bodi's husband seemed a breach on an unspoken pact between women. There was also Fancy to consider.

Now Philip had taken her completely off guard. He'd erased all her assumptions about their relationship with one bold act and the heat of his lips.

"I didn't give much thought to just how much time we've been spending together," she said. "Like we've accidently thrown together a makeshift family because the wedding is coming up, and we're both helping out. I assumed everything would go back to normal after the wedding. We wouldn't be hanging around together as much."

Gently, Cat asked, "How did you react when Philip kissed you?"

"I was totally into it," Jada admitted, sprinting past humiliation to give a full accounting. The scales of her relationship with Cat and Linnie had always tipped in her direction. If they got into a fix, she weighed the problem carefully and proposed a way out. Now she needed them both as a sounding board. "I almost felt like I'd been waiting my whole life for Philip to take our relationship and turn it on its head. Which is nuts. For most of our lives, I thought he was a hot mess. He thought I was too uptight."

"Your opinion, not his," Cat said confidently. "Philip had a thing for you way back in high school."

Linnie tilted her head back and gave Cat an odd look. "Philip liked Jada back then?" Linnie asked. "No way. He dated more girls than I can count. If he'd been into Jada, I would've caught on. Cat, is this your imagination talking?"

"Not even close. Philip went on the prowl because Jada *didn't* notice him. At least not in the way he wanted. He never would've chased all those girls if he could've had the one he wanted."

Skepticism drummed through Linnie's voice. "Give me a break. If Philip loved anyone in high school, it was the stud staring back at him in the mirror."

"You're wrong. Opposites attract. He would've tried harder to win Jada if he'd thought there was a chance. He knew the score. She never would've viewed him as boyfriend material."

"Because he was flaky," Jada murmured. Exactly what she'd told Fancy, right before the precocious six-year-old clued her in on Philip's viewing habits.

"My point exactly," Linnie said. "You're only attracted to serious guys. Sadly enough, all the heartbreak Philip went through with Bodi has turned him into one of those guys. Some people get hurt by a bad marriage and become bitter. Not Philip. The bad times brought out the best in him. They turned him into a great dad and a hardworking man."

Considering, Jada sank her toes into the wet sand. Linnie was correct—the trials Philip had overcome had burnished his character. He became stable and caring when Bodi went off the rails, leaving him the sole parent of his sweet daughter. And Cat's observations dovetailed with Philip's admission last week on why he'd aimed a hundred paper airplanes at Jada's wild curls—an immature ploy she now viewed in an entirely different light.

He'd been aiming at her heart.

The confusion rippling across her features prodded Linnie to say, "I can't tell if you're happy or scared about the change in your relationship. From where I'm standing, having my maid of honor fall for my brother-in-law is fantastic. Both of you have been stuck in the monastery long enough. Who knows? Maybe last week's hot kiss will lead to something better."

"I'm not sure dating Philip is a great idea," Jada said.

"Has he asked you out?"

Guilt pulled Jada's attention to her feet, sinking into the sand beneath the rippling surf. "I've been dodging him," she admitted. "Pretending I'm too busy to talk on the phone, too buried at work to stop over. Bad excuses, but he's playing along."

She lifted her shoulders to her ears, the same way Linnie did when confronted with difficult choices. The gesture used to amuse Jada, how it indicated Linnie's inability to face a challenge. No longer.

"When Philip kissed me, he uncorked this passion between us. Red hot, and totally out of control. I can't see him until I'm sure how I feel."

Cat smirked. "I'm guessing you're feeling hot and bothered."

"This isn't funny, Cat. I'm not like you. I don't leap before I think."

"I'm intrepid. You should try it."

Great advice—for someone unconcerned with the consequences.

"Hey, I'm no prude," Jada insisted. "I've felt passionately about several of the men I've dated, but nothing like this. Nothing like this need stalking me whenever I make the mistake of allowing Philip into my thoughts. When you begin dating someone you've known forever—even someone you thought you disliked—all that familiarity is dangerous. It's easy to skip past the getting-to-know-you stage and dive in too deep. I'm afraid if Philip takes me in his arms again, we'll go straight from heavy necking to intimacy. I'm worried we'll make the leap without stopping to consider if we should."

A dreamy sigh coasted from Linnie's mouth. "Kettering men," she murmured, hugging herself. "They know the moves. The first time I kissed Daniel? He literally swept me off my feet. He backed me up against his kitchen counter and kissed me senseless. Then he ordered me to go home. If he hadn't, we would've made love on his kitchen floor."

A visual of uncontrolled passion wasn't a great antidote for what ailed Jada. Not when simply thinking about Philip made her feverish.

"Thanks for sharing," she grumbled. "What if I can't trust myself around Philip? I don't want our relationship to change."

"Why not?"

"Gosh, let's see. What if we date for a few months, and everything fizzles? It's not like we can go back to the way things were."

"Don't ignore the better option. What if everything works out?"

"I'm not a gambler. I value the friendship I've struck up with Philip. I don't want to lose it. And what about Fancy? I adore her. We've become awfully close. If I start seeing her father and it doesn't work out, how will she feel?"

"Bad," Linnie supplied. With a frown, she added, "You do have a point."

"Millicent, what's going on? You're wheezing."

The call was poorly timed, but not unexpected. Millicent was accustomed to Vasily calling on a daily basis for updates. The doctoral student she'd left holding down the fort in Chicago treated her excursion to Ohio like his favorite episodes of reality TV.

"I don't wheeze, and I don't have asthma," she barked into her cell phone. The arches of her feet hurt like the dickens, a fact she chose not to share. She really was out of shape. "I'm winded."

"What are you doing?"

Millicent spotted a car ascending the road toward the inn. She trotted into the tall grass at the berm. The car whizzed past.

"Vasily, when I hired you, where in the job description did you misinterpret houseboy duties to involve hounding me to death?" A bee lifted out of the grass, and she waved it away. "You're my servant, not my son. How can a man with your level of education be so obtuse?"

"Don't go medieval on me. You're breathing hard. I doubt you're having sex, which leaves the unhappy prospect you may be having a heart attack. What *are* you doing?"

"Oh, for Pete's sake. There's nothing wrong with my ticker." She resumed her trek down the steep incline. "I'm walking into town, if you must know. I've been cooped up at the inn for a week."

"How far of a walk?"

She peered back at the Wayfair, perched high upon the road. "Too far," she grumbled. "Half a mile? Or more." Thankfully, the edge of town was in sight.

"You've left the inn to . . . look around?"

"Why do you have an emotional investment in the day-to-day operations? If there's anything worth reporting, I will let you know. Although I'm not sure why I should. But, yes, I'm taking a stroll through town. I'm here. I might as well look around."

"There's a chance you'll find something?"

"Doubtful. It *has* been a long time." Millicent walked on, despising the small threads of hope spinning through her. Even the dismal odds weren't enough to dull her natural optimism. Which hastened her to add, "I am convinced I'm on the right trail. All of the pieces fit."

"I knew it! You've found another clue? What is it? Something Jada mentioned during a baking lesson?"

The barrage of questions pinged against her eardrum as she took stock of her surroundings. The quaint nexus of the town brimmed with flowerpots set out before small shops. Further off, trees unfurling spring leaves sheltered the center green. Picnic tables were scattered across the grass. On the opposite side of the circle, the brick buildings were shuttered. Closer to where Millicent stood, she noted a drugstore, a beauty salon, and the two businesses owned by the Kettering brothers—Unity Design Landscaping and the law firm owned by Linnie Wayfair's fiancé.

"Millicent? Are you there?"

She ducked into the alleyway before the Kettering building. "There's nothing to report," she insisted.

"Nothing at all?"

"The town certainly fits the description. Same with the Wayfair. I'm sure it's the right inn." Steeling herself, she asked, "How is everything at home?"

The query seemed to dampen Vasily's mood. "Not good," he said, lowering his voice. "If you're still thinking about flying us to Ohio, reconsider. You'll need to fly home first. Do some big-time lobbying."

The prospect of returning to Illinois after making progress was discouraging. "Vasily, you have three college degrees and the eloquence of the original serpent. Can't *you* do the lobbying? Make it clear I've found good leads, the best I've ever stumbled across?"

"I've tried—repeatedly."

"Try harder!"

The command brought a discouraged sigh across the line. "It's no use. I'm getting nowhere. Your marriage, your problem. Come home and state the case personally."

"Fine," she agreed. Unexpected guilt jolted her. Debating with her spouse had never been Vasily's responsibility. It was unfair to presume he'd succeed. "I'll fly back to Chicago once I'm fully convinced. In a few days. Or a bit longer."

"What's the holdup?"

"I haven't confronted Jada yet."

"Millicent, you aren't preparing to do battle. You're merely asking for information. She may welcome the chance to tell you everything. Why wait?"

Leaning against the building's cool brick, she closed her eyes. The question had dogged her all week. During each morning's baking lesson, she sensed Jada's trust in her growing. Their conversations, once stilted and wary, now flowed easily. Tender the most important question now, and there was every likelihood she'd gain the information she craved.

Why not ask?

Sharing the truth made her feel weak, and Millicent hated acknowledging her failings. "I haven't found the courage to ask," she admitted, stepping out from her hiding place in the alley. She marched past the Kettering building. "This isn't like the other times. From the moment I met Jada Brooks, it seemed obvious she was the woman I'd been seeking. Now I'm afraid of what she'll tell me."

"Ignore the second thoughts. Follow through. Jada will help you bring this sorry chapter in your life to a close."

"I believe she will."

"Don't you want this to end?"

"What an absurd question. Who likes shelling out money for private detectives, and jumping on planes to follow clues? Vasily, I want to stop waking up at night and worrying myself sick. I want to heal the wounds in my marriage. I want this to end—happily. With tears of joy."

"It might."

Pausing at the intersection, she stared blankly at the curb. "What if my plans go awry?"

"Stay focused on the facts, difficult though they are. There's no telling how this will play out. Your efforts may not bear fruit."

"Exactly my fear. What if all I bring back to Chicago is news that won't heal my family? News that will only bring more sorrow and disappointment?"

The words came out needy and soft, like the bitter confession of an old woman incapable of erasing the mistakes of the past. Or the utterance of a child desperate for reassurance the world wasn't brutal and harsh, and that everything works out in the end. Yet another sign of weakness, and Vasily took his time responding.

When he did, his tone sheltered her with compassion. "You're under no obligation to carry on with this," he said, and Millicent wondered at his empathy, how easily he donned the best qualities of manhood despite his youth. "No one will think less of you for letting this go. You've invested years in the search. Your perseverance is admirable, regardless of the outcome. In fact, if you drop this, I won't be the only one to feel a measure of relief."

Tears of frustration burned at her lashes. "I can't let this go."

"Then you have your answer. Find the courage to speak with Jada."

From the center green of Sweet Lake Circle, someone called out to her. Finishing the call, she tucked the phone in her purse.

Four of the Sweet Lake Sirens were clustered around a picnic table. Silvia Mendoza sat behind a laptop with Frances Dufour at her elbow. A catalog lay between the blunt Ruth Kenefsky and her much sleeker counterpart, Norah Webb. They were leafing through the catalog's pages while bickering.

Frances shushed them. "Millicent, how nice to see you." She patted the picnic bench. "Won't you join us?"

"Thank you, but I can't stay long. It's a beautiful day for a walk." Ridiculously, she harbored the absurd notion that another clue awaited if only she looked hard enough. She glanced from the laptop to the catalog. "What are you doing?"

"Discussing the wedding favors for Linnie's wedding," Frances told her.

During the baking lessons, Jada frequently mentioned the upcoming nuptials. "I understand Linnie will marry next month?"

"The last Saturday in April."

Ruth looked up from the catalog. "She's getting hitched, but not without fussing over every detail. The girl has enough nervous energy to see a woman through ten catastrophes. She can't do anything without fretting half to death."

"Is there any doubt she'll follow through?" Millicent's interactions with the owner of the Wayfair were infrequent.

Frances reached for her purse. "Oh, she'll marry. She's madly in love with Daniel."

Producing a handkerchief, the elderly Siren patted her brow. Evidently Linnie's ability to stay the course was a cause of some concern.

"I've met the groom's brother," Millicent offered. "He's doing fine work on the patio installation for the inn." From what Millicent had seen on her strolls around the Wayfair's grounds, work on the patio was progressing apace.

"Not today he isn't," Frances said.

"There's a problem?"

"With the sandstone Philip ordered. Most of the stone in one of the pallets is cracked. His supplier isn't sure when the new shipment will arrive. Work on the patio may not resume until the first week of April."

"If the work isn't completed in time, do the bride and groom have an alternate plan for the ceremony?"

"They don't. Both of the churches in town are booked, and the invitations have gone out. They can't change the date."

Ruth grunted. "Philip will get the patio finished in time. He's not about to disappoint the happy couple." She stabbed a finger at the catalog. "Can we get back to deciding on wedding favors? I like the Hangover Kit. It comes with a bottle of Gatorade, pain pills for nasty headaches, and a cute eye mask."

From behind the laptop, Silvia glared. "Forget it, Ruth. We're going for elegant, not tacky."

"What's your big plan, Silvia? Making candles in teacups? I like arts and crafts as much as the next woman, but I'm not dealing with hot wax unless I'm removing the fur on my legs."

Norah Webb stared them both down with heavy-lidded eyes. "We're not resorting to crafts, or remedies for partygoers who can't hold their liquor. Leave the drunks to their just deserts. This is a formal affair. We won't stop looking until we find a wedding favor both stylish and unique."

Ruth pushed the catalog toward her. "Take it away, Norah. You've been married a grand total of four times. You're the expert."

The remark put thunder in Norah's eyes. "Ruth, I've had all of your company I can tolerate in one afternoon," she said from between clenched teeth. "Put a lid on it."

"Make me."

"Keep pushing, and I will."

"I'm scared, Norah. Shivering in my boots." To Millicent, the feisty Siren added, "Norah isn't really a marriage expert. None of her men last long. Living with her kills them of one ailment or another."

The insult brought a growl from Norah's throat. Without warning, she yanked on one of Ruth's long, white braids. As they tussled, she managed to shape the braid into a noose. Shock and a hearty dose of good sense urged Millicent to stumble back from the table.

Penelope came across the grass. "Sorry I'm late." Her greeting evaporated beneath the shrieking.

Millicent considered herself well versed in the vagaries of human behavior. Even so, she'd never seen two women go at it like demons from hell. Moving to safety behind Penelope's back, she asked, "They won't draw blood, will they?"

"Don't be frightened. They like to carry on. Frances will stop them."

"Stop them?" Frances Dufour weighed less than Millicent's thighs. There was the outside chance the elderly Siren carried mace in her purse, but it seemed unlikely. "*How* will she stop them?"

Serenely, Penelope gestured at the picnic table. "Just watch," she advised.

The words were barely out when Frances tapped Silvia on the shoulder. Silvia leaned back slightly, allowing Frances to reach past her. A silk parasol lay on the bench.

Millicent's hand flew to her mouth as Frances took up the parasol like a sword. Leaning across the picnic table, Frances popped Ruth on the top of her scalp. The dazed Siren shook her head like a wet collie. Then *pop!* Frances got Norah too.

The battling Sirens pulled apart.

"They'll mope now," Penelope confided.

Shock and dismay rounded Millicent's eyes. "Do they usually settle their differences with a catfight?" It seemed best not to inquire if Frances normally restored order through physical assault.

"Not too often, but it's never pretty when they do." Behind the thick lenses of her glasses, Penelope's eyes twinkled. "We should go. They'll get moody, and make the vibrations all wrong. I hate dreary vibes, don't you?"

She made no sense. "Of course," Millicent said.

"Are you ready?"

For what, Millicent refused to hazard a guess. A discussion on ancient healing practices?

"To visit my shop," Penelope clarified. "You walked into town this afternoon to visit Gift of Garb."

She followed up the extraordinary remark by taking Millicent's fingers in a gentle grasp. Under normal circumstances, hand-holding by two mature women fell into the category of behavior best reserved for the onset of senility. Even so, the affection seemed a happy accident, nearly a rescue. After the conversation with Vasily about her worries and fears, Millicent was feeling lost.

The Siren tugged her across the grass like a toy train.

The consignment shop occupied a skinny building tucked into a shady alcove of Sweet Lake Circle. A hint of sandalwood perfumed the store's musty air. The checkered linoleum floor was dated; long rows packed with clothing ran toward the cash register at the far end. For a secondhand shop, the place was busy. Millicent counted eleven shoppers, all women of varying ages.

"You're operating a healthy business," she said, impressed.

Penelope laughed. "You're surprised. Don't be. Most people around here can't afford to shop in Neiman Marcus or Bloomingdale's."

A chill darted down Millicent's spine. Of all the department stores to bring up, how did Penelope stumble upon her two favorite places to shop? Her interest in high fashion was nonexistent. But she insisted on quality, which explained why her conservative wardrobe came from Neiman Marcus and Bloomie's.

Brushing off the coincidence, she started down the center aisle. Penelope wasn't psychic. People didn't have special faculties, or a sixth sense. Utter nonsense.

She asked, "How do you acquire your stock?"

"People bring in their gently used outfits. There are a lot of towns in the area, and word gets around. If an item sells, I split the profit with the seller. Keeping the books straight is the biggest chore."

"You manage all this by yourself?"

Penelope noticed a blouse on the floor and hung it back on the nearest rack. "I hire kids from the high school, a few teens in foster care—once in a while, I'll get a call from social services to help a kid discharged from juvie," she said, straightening several other garments on the rack. "I like hiring kids prone to getting in trouble."

As far as business plans went, this wasn't a winning strategy. "Why not hire well-behaved teenagers? I'd imagine they'd cause less problems."

Penelope nodded enthusiastically, as if she understood Millicent's objections but found them misguided. "They would, but the kids with behavioral issues need structure," she pointed out. "A job where they must show up on time, rules to follow if they want a paycheck—a job gives them a sense of self-worth. Some don't last long—about half of the teens quit in the first month. When they do stick it out, the vibrations they create are marvelous. Turning around a young person's life is the best kind of magic."

Understanding dawned—Penelope wasn't concerned with profits. This was a noble quest. Her small enterprise gave troubled kids the chance to believe in themselves. Millicent's admiration for her grew.

"I wish I had your patience," she heard herself say, and the remark stirred the fragments of memories she'd worked hard to forget. "I can summon the patience of Job when helping college students with their academics. I never learned how to translate the virtue to my personal life."

"You mean with teenagers?"

"They operate more on emotion than intellect. They're unpredictable. I'm more attuned to the intellectual, I'm afraid."

Once again Penelope nodded, this time with compassion entering her gaze. "Did you raise children?" she asked.

An uncomfortable question, and Millicent struggled for a response. No, she'd never rocked a baby at her breast or helped a young child learn to read. But she'd navigated the difficult world of parenting once she met her soul mate.

"I didn't marry until my fifties," she said. "My stepdaughter was in high school when I entered her life."

A peculiar notion caught Millicent off guard. She sensed she wasn't telling Penelope anything she didn't already know. As if the Siren had gleaned the most painful excerpts from the book of Millicent's life. As if such a trick were possible.

"Your stepdaughter—did you get along?" Penelope asked, as if testing how much Millicent would reveal.

"It depended on the day. There were periods when she confided in me. Nearly trusted me. She had a mercurial personality."

"Lots of highs and lows?"

Millicent nodded. "There were days when she was bright like sunshine and equipped with superhuman energy. Then she'd go through periods of sleeping until noon, only to wake up in a combative mood. Overall, we didn't get along as well as I'd hoped."

Much as she enjoyed Penelope's company, lending a more thorough explanation didn't appeal. The details were too difficult for a public airing.

Which Millicent refused to offer. The retelling would over-whelm her.

Behind the cash register, a flurry of children's art covered the wall. Glad for the diversion, she let her attention drift from one drawing to the next. With an eager nod from her host, she walked behind the checkout counter. Many of the clumsy drawings featured princesses and fairy godmothers.

"You have a granddaughter?" she guessed.

Penelope smiled. "Not yet. My son, Ozzie, is single. He's a mail carrier in town. Philip's daughter is the artist."

"The little girl with the magician's cape and fairy crown?"

The Siren's rheumy gaze became attentive. "You know about her fascination with make-believe? Why, you haven't met Fancy yet."

Oddly, she didn't wait for Millicent's reply. Penelope turned away to fiddle with her glasses. Finally, she plucked them off her nose to polish them with a cloth she produced from her pocket. Sliding them back on, she brushed past Millicent and removed the tacks from one of the drawings. With trembling fingers, she straightened the artwork and then tacked it back to the wall. Millicent watched the performance with no idea what had upset the gentle Siren.

When Penelope located her voice, she said, "I'm being silly. You haven't met Fancy because the time isn't right. When you do meet her . . . Well, good things come to those who wait."

An English proverb on patience. The relevancy was lost on Millicent.

"Fancy sounds delightful," she offered. She couldn't get a fix on what was wrong. Hoping to smooth over the impasse, she added, "There's a simple explanation as to why I know about Fancy's interest in make-believe. She called Jada during one of our baking lessons. They had the funniest conversation. Quite a debate, really, over what Fancy will wear to Linnie's wedding."

"Yes, they spoke when I was with Fancy at the bus stop," Penelope said. "She adores Jada."

"I can see why. Jada is a nice young woman."

"It's remarkable, when you think about it."

"What is?" Millicent asked.

"How Jada remains steady in the fiercest wind. I've never seen her lose her temper with any of the employees. Lately, she's been dealing single-handedly with the staff. Hiring, training, work schedules—she doesn't miss a beat. Cat's newly married, and Linnie will be soon. Jada has assumed most of the day-to-day operations without complaint."

"Yet she finds time in her schedule to befriend a six-year-old."

"She finds time for Philip too." Penelope sighed. "He's crazy about her, but she's very practical. He's afraid she doesn't view him as the man he's become."

A detour into Jada's romantic entanglements wasn't appropriate. Millicent had befriended the pastry chef under false pretenses. Increasingly, the situation brought a flurry of second thoughts. Millicent loathed dishonesty, even though she'd assured herself that in this particular instance the end justified the means. Jada was the key to unlocking the secrets sure to repair her shattered family.

"There's no hope Jada will view Philip romantically?" Millicent heard herself say. Why she felt invested in the outcome, she wasn't sure.

"In most of her relationships, Jada plays the role of competent advisor. I doubt she views Philip as her equal." Penelope shook her head with resignation. "He was quite reckless when he was younger. I believe she's unaware of how much he's changed. Philip didn't truly grow up until Fancy came along. Becoming a father made him into a man. The trials of his marriage did too."

"Divorce is never easy," Millicent said. "Especially when there's a small child involved."

"Not divorced. Philip lost his wife soon after Fancy's birth."

Pity darkened Penelope's eyes. With a start, Millicent wondered if the pity was meant for her. Certainly not. There was no plausible reason for Penelope to view *her* with pity.

"His wife was in an accident?" she asked, brushing off the strange observation.

"Oh, it was no accident. A horrible situation for all of us. She had such a flair for drama and a brittle personality. How do you guide a lost soul when she refuses your help? Actually, she was making the threats about harming herself even before Philip got caught up with her."

"She followed through on the threats?"

"She did." The color drained from the Siren's face. "She took her own life."

For a perilous moment, the words refused to penetrate Millicent's uncomprehending brain. When they finally sank in, the revelation shook her to her bones. In the heavy silence that followed, she inhaled shallow breaths.

A brunette approached the counter. The woman placed a green dress before the cash register.

The interruption put Penelope in motion, her dimpled hands working quickly to fold the garment, her voice brimming with false cheer.

While she finished the sale, Millicent surveyed Fancy's artwork with a heavy heart. She liked Philip. He was good-natured and polite. As much as Jada had revealed, she hadn't mentioned that Philip wasn't divorced—he'd lost his wife. And he'd raised his daughter alone, right from the start. With dreary precision, Millicent did the math in her head. Philip must have been around Vasily's age when a birth and a death swept into his life. He'd been a young man in his twenties, in the middle of the decade of one's life when adulthood arrived with all the abundant pleasures, and few of the responsibilities to come. Yet Philip had known the sort of heartache sure to break most youths.

Millicent brushed absently at her nose. The story bothered her more than was sensible.

Loose change clanged in the register. The brunette strode down the aisle with a wave.

Penelope sifted through the paperwork nestled beside the cash register. "I nearly forgot. Ah, here it is." She produced an index card. Neat cursive, laid down with purple ink, covered the card stock. Offering a watery smile, she added, "I've been meaning to give this to you."

A recipe.

Taking it, Millicent read quickly. "This sounds interesting. Are they good?"

"They're divine," Penelope assured her. "Ask Jada to make a batch with you."

Chapter 10

April arrived like a prankster.

At eight in the morning, the new elevator installed during the winter renovations went on the blink. The carriage froze between the lobby and second floor, trapping a newlywed couple and a girl from Housekeeping. The newlyweds managed well enough, but Sally Anne Peterson was claustrophobic. Her whimpering carried through the walls until the serviceman got the lift running.

At eight thirty, the harried cook spilled pancake batter on the kitchen floor. Two members of the waitstaff slid through it. The man caught his balance in time. The woman, hired only the previous week, rammed into the industrial-size refrigerator. Jada sent her home with full pay and a goose egg on her brow.

By nine o'clock, three employees had called in sick. Cat called in late—she'd overslept. And a new employee in the laundry dumped bleach in a pastel load. Three sets of sheets were ruined.

Jada foisted the sheets back into the arms of the crestfallen girl. "We'll give them to Goodwill," she decided. They were standing in the corridor between the kitchen and Jada's office. "Take them back to the laundry. Then go upstairs and help make up rooms."

"Shouldn't I finish in the basement?"

"I'll have someone else do the laundry."

After the girl hurried off, Jada glanced at her watch. She was scheduled to meet with Linnie and Cat in less than an hour to discuss the ad buys in regional magazines Cat wanted to place for the summer months. With Cat still a no-show this morning, she wondered if she ought to send Linnie a text and reschedule.

Jada was still deciding when she strode into her office. She came to an abrupt halt.

Philip was leaning against the desk.

Despite her misgivings about the kiss they'd shared, she'd missed him. With the completion of the patio in limbo, Philip no longer appeared at the Wayfair each day. His crews were split up across town, working smaller residential jobs.

He looked good. His dark-brown hair needed a trim, but she liked how the glossy locks fell haphazardly across his brow. The sleeves of his chambray shirt were rolled up, showing off well-defined muscles beneath skin deepening to bronze from all the hours he spent outdoors. His arms and his ankles were crossed; an air of impatience surrounded him.

Stalling for time, she closed the door. "Philip." Her thoughts scattered like leaves on the wind.

When she came no closer, his mouth curved with disappointment. He pulled himself off the desk. With ill-concealed frustration, he rubbed his hands down his thighs.

"Can we push the reset button?" he asked. "Last week, when you came over to help Fancy, I was way out of line."

Jada wasn't sure what she'd expected would happen when they finally came face-to-face. Not the remorse curving his shoulders, or the hurt in his eyes. The last thing she wanted to do was hurt him.

"You don't owe me an apology," she said, upset that he thought he did. "Nothing has changed."

"Everything has changed, but I get it." A note of injury colored his words as he added, "You're not ready."

He meant she wasn't ready for a relationship beyond the easy camaraderie of the past months.

"I don't like making rash decisions," she said, as if he didn't understand the core motivations of her personality. He did, of course. Their long acquaintance guaranteed his understanding. Which didn't stop her from adding, "Philip, did we make a mistake last week? Maybe we pushed our relationship toward the wrong path. We were joking around, and it got out of hand."

"You think what happened was an accident? Some kind of error?"

"We jumped in without considering our actions." She swallowed. "Both of us."

"We weren't being rash," he countered. "We were finally being honest."

The confidence rimming his words put a bee's nest of anxiety in her belly. True, they shared a natural chemistry. It was more volatile than she'd imagined.

Philip studied her with hooded eyes. "I should've made sure I had the go-ahead before I kissed you," he offered, clearly aware of her misgivings. "We were having a good time, and you seemed open to the idea. So I went for it. I should've asked first. Or waited for you to make the first move. You would've—eventually."

She wondered if he was right. "You're awfully confident," she sputtered.

"Just honest." He lifted his shoulders in a shrug that belied the serious look on his face.

"Philip, I never would've approached you." Not quite true. The possibility that he knew her better than she knew herself was upsetting. "Not in the way you're implying."

"You're scared," he murmured, and the slow, steady way he kept his eyes locked on her made her breathless.

The statement's accuracy put a lump in her throat. As did the air growing charged between them. It seemed the unseen atoms colliding in the room carried a special chemistry, one capable of shrinking the physical space between them. Most of all, she was scared of the desire urging her to throw caution aside and let Philip take her into his arms.

All of which seemed transparent when he said, "Jada, some things can't be contained. You can only ignore them for so long. One way or another, we were going to end up at this point. It doesn't matter if you're ready. We're here now. We have to decide what to do."

"I don't want to start something I can't control," she admitted. "What we've stirred up . . . it's intense."

Her honesty eased the tension glossing his features. "Yeah, I've noticed." A sweet agony crossed his face. "I've been taking cold showers for days."

"Me too."

"Yeah? Good to hear I'm not the only one."

"Please. You know you're not the only one."

"Still, it's nice to know I'm getting under your skin." He dragged his attention from her, took a deep breath. When he'd regained his composure, he brought his darkening eyes back to hers, adding, "No one is in the driver's seat in a relationship like ours. We're leaving the starting gate with lots of emotion built in. All the feelings we've suppressed, the attraction we pretended we didn't feel. There's nothing casual about what we feel for each other. That doesn't mean we shouldn't press forward and see where this leads."

Needing to be clear, she rephrased the statement. "I don't want to start something I won't have the ability to stop."

The shadow of a grin toyed with the corners of his mouth. "Who says we'll have to stop?"

She couldn't decide if he was being difficult or didn't understand. "Most relationships don't go the distance. Two people date for a while, and it doesn't work out. They discover they aren't a good fit. Which is fine, as far as it goes."

Her defeatist take on romance furrowed his brows. "We aren't most people," he said gruffly. To underline the point, he let his gaze slowly journey across her face and down her quivering body with the intensity of physical touch, his smoldering regard sparking fire across her skin. When he again caught her gaze, the yearning in his eyes carried straight to her heart. "Jada, I've wanted you for longer than I care to admit. I should've made my intentions clear somewhere along the line—a lot faster than I did. And you want me too," he added, his lips quirking into a grin, "if what happened last week is any indication."

Balancing on the tightrope of his honesty, Jada feared plummeting—into self-recrimination if she followed his lead, into regret if she didn't. The quiet between them grew potent, and Philip waited for her decision with a trace of doubt skimming his features. She banished it when she decided to leap.

"I do want you." Voicing the truth was easier than she'd anticipated. The fear wasn't gone, but she felt lighter.

"Well, then. I know what I'm getting into. You do too."

"Yes, we're adults. We're able to choose. But this isn't just about us." Needing to make him understand, she found the courage to step closer. The movement washed ruddy color through his strong features, but Philip stayed rooted by the desk. He seemed determined to give her all the space she required. "What we choose won't affect only us. What about Fancy?" She nearly added the second reason for her hesitation— her friendship with his late wife—but her courage fled.

"Fancy will love the idea we're together."

"No, Philip. What if we change our minds in a few months? Decide this isn't working out?"

"We aren't telling her immediately."

"She won't know we're dating?"

"Not until we both agree it's time to tell her."

"If this doesn't work out, then what? I don't want to lose my friendship with you."

"You won't—ever."

He was making this too easy. "And Fancy?" she asked doubtfully. "I don't want anything to alter the bond I've built with her. She's important to me, Philip. Too often, kids get the shaft when adults screw up. It's not fair."

"Your confidence in our ability to make choices that *won't* hurt my kid is inspiring," he said dryly. Chuckling, he shook his head. "I figured there wasn't much I didn't know about you. I never would've guessed you're short on faith in yourself—and me."

"Give me a break," she tossed back. "This is new terrain. I'm not sure of my footing."

"You will be. In time."

Jada released the breath she hadn't realized strained in her lungs. The accompanying relief quelled a portion of her anxiety. A firm assurance—he'd given the matter thought. He'd taken into account how their actions might affect his impressionable daughter, and the future of their friendship.

Relenting, she asked, "What do you propose?"

"I'll make dinner for you tonight. I'd wow you with my culinary gifts, but my repertoire is limited. Lucky for me, I already know you like spaghetti."

"What about Fancy?"

"Linnie and Daniel are taking her out for pizza. We'll have the house to ourselves until nine o'clock." He approached, took her fingers loosely in his. The contact danced pleasure through her. "Are you in?"

She smiled. "Sure."

His palm glided up her forearm. "I'm going to kiss you now," he murmured, "unless you'd rather I didn't."

He didn't wait for permission.

The moment her lips parted, Philip gathered her into his arms. Tipping her chin up, he steered her lips to his. The movement was slow, languid as he brushed his mouth across hers, testing the softness of her flesh, reveling in the sigh that rose from deep inside her. She let her eyes drift shut as he deepened the kiss, but not before she glimpsed the triumph registering on his features. He'd made a very male decision to shape events to his will. Her muscles felt loose beneath the power of his gentle lovemaking, and the exquisite care he took deepening the kiss, urging her to follow his movements, to respond in kind.

When he lifted his head, he brushed his nose across hers. "I'll see you at seven," he said.

A fluttery anticipation followed Jada as she parked in Philip's driveway and started across the grass.

On the front stoop, she left her hand poised above the doorbell for a good three seconds. Ringing seemed too formal. Simply go inside? A first date presented a new quandary, one she'd never before encountered. On a normal visit, Fancy did the surveillance thing, stationing herself at the living room window to await the arrival of feminine company and good eats with her cherub's face pressed to the glass.

Soft rock drifted from the living room. A jarring clatter broke through the soothing melody, and Jada nearly jumped out of her strappy heels. It seemed a fair guess the sound came from the kitchen. On the drowsy street, a boy bicycled past and disappeared into the approaching night.

Her cell phone rang.

Retreating down the steps, she tiptoed to the curb to take Linnie's call. "What's up?" she asked.

"Jada!" Exuberance laced her bestie's voice. "Are you getting ready for your hot date?"

"Linnie, your sense of timing is more compromised than your hold on gravity. I'm *at* my date. Well, almost. I'm standing by the street, deciding if I should ring the doorbell or walk right in." She cast a furtive glance at the house. Then she frowned. "And don't call the date 'hot.' We're testing the waters. That's all."

"Yeah, sure. You're testing, Philip's throwing the life jackets overboard and planning to push you into deep waters and dive in after . . . never mind. I guess everything Daniel told me won't make you less nervous." Linnie exhaled a blustery stream of air that made her sound asthmatic, only her lungs were in tip-top shape. "Send Philip a text, say you'll be there in ten. Come over, okay?"

"No!" Jada tottered on her heels, thanks to either the life jacket remark or the woozy sensation that had been nesting in her belly since she'd agreed to the date. She decided not to analyze the cause of her dismay.

"Oh, c'mon. Daniel's place is right around the corner. Three-minute drive, tops."

"I'm not showing up late. Whatever you need to discuss, wait until tomorrow."

"This is important. Like, best friend important. The kind of news you first share with your maid of honor."

"I don't care."

"Hold on." A series of scratchy noises accosted her ear, then Linnie came back on. "Want Daniel to send the text? He'll tell Philip you're running late. Doesn't matter, by the way—your boy wonder pitched the first batch of sauce because he burned the meat. I suppose he's nervous too. He didn't get the steps right until Daniel FaceTimed him through the procedure. Guess we're eating duplicate meals tonight."

"I thought you and Daniel were taking Fancy out for pizza." That was the plan.

"Nope, we're eating in. Don't worry about us. Just get over here ASAP."

"Have I mentioned lately that you're a lunatic?" Jada checked her bra straps, felt relief to discover they weren't showing. "Do not have your fiancé text my date. Enjoy the girl time with Fancy, and try to talk to the munchkin on her level. I'll see you in the morning, okay?"

"I love you even when you get snippy," Linnie said, dragging out the conversation with irritating zeal. "Relax, okay? You aren't heading into one of those creepy coffee dates. You know, like if you connect online and aren't sure if the guy is nice or weird? There's really only so much you can tell about a potential lover if you've only shared a few e-mails or quickie phone calls."

"Linnie, have you been drinking? I'm hanging up now."

"Wait!"

Jada dunked her fingers into her bountiful curls, yanked out her hand before she caused damage. *WHAT?*

At the rumble of a car engine, she whirled around. Linnie hopped out of her Honda Accord.

"Don't be mad." Her jaw loosened. "Wow. You should clean up more often."

Tapping her foot, Jada folded her arms.

"Okay, okay—no compliments. You're too peeved to accept them. Your prerogative, totally. But you do look fantastic." Feigning stealth as she tiptoed onto the curb, Linnie took a quick peek at the house. She looked ridiculous in Daniel's extra-large sweatshirt and a pair of tights with a pattern of orange poppies woven into the fabric. In her haste to stop by, she'd forgotten to put on shoes. "Philip will stay in the kitchen, I swear. Daniel's back on FaceTime, checking the results of baby brother's menu."

Jada wasn't sure if she should laugh or cry. "You *are* a lunatic." She poked her finger into Linnie's ear, twirled. A punishment reserved for her bestie's wackiest behavior in grade school, but old tricks were the best.

Giggling, Linnie stepped out of reach. "This will only take a sec." She wagged her phone through the air like Eden's first apple. "You won't believe what I've found."

Dinner was simple, but delicious.

In a bid to provide a romantic atmosphere, Philip served the spaghetti and a tossed salad on the deck, allowing them to enjoy the spring evening while they ate. In the center of the table, a candle flickered inside a balloon lamp. Votive candles were scattered on the railing and in the deck's corners.

Jada twirled noodles around her fork, sighed as she took another bite. "This is wonderful."

"Not too spicy? It's Daniel's recipe."

"It's perfect," she murmured, secretly amused as she recalled Linnie's disclosure about FaceTime, and Daniel's intervention.

Philip's wardrobe was limited, but there was no mistaking he'd wanted to look his best. The blue oxford shirt was ironed, his cologne deliciously spicy. He'd also managed a visit to the barber sometime that afternoon—the tousled locks that usually brushed his thick brows were neatly trimmed.

Making a good impression was mandatory for a first date, and Jada caught herself smiling. She'd also gone the distance, leaving work early to return home to shower, coil her curls, and select a gold A-line dress that was attractive, but not too sexy.

Philip reached for his wineglass, caught her amusement. "What is it?" he asked.

"Look at us. Both out of blue jeans, and smelling great."

"You always smell great."

"Hardly." She lifted her fingers, sniffed. "I get tired of the scent of vanilla. Occupational hazard for a baker."

"There are worse fates. Want to switch careers? You don't spend all day working outdoors and come home smelling fresh as a daisy."

"I know, Philip. I've seen the evidence," she teased. "I can't count how many times I've scrubbed out your bathtub before helping Fancy climb in."

He raised his glass, as if for a toast. "The next time, let my kid do the honors. She gets free room and board. Nothing wrong with her pitching in."

"Here's a better idea: give the tub a quick scrub when you finish."

"I will," he promised.

He refilled her glass, and she murmured her thanks. The merlot was another surprise—rich and full-bodied, it glided down her throat. She loved a good merlot, and suspected he'd made a special trip to pick up a bottle.

Changing tack, she said, "Want some great news?"

Philip nodded. "Sure."

"Linnie found the right dress." She smiled as she recalled why Linnie had been so adamant about talking to her in front of Philip's house. With the wedding only three weeks off, Jada had begun to fear they'd resort to repurposing one of the old frocks in Linnie's closet. "Daniel took care of it. Or, more precisely, Carol Stillwell rode in to the rescue—with the help of her oldest daughter."

Last summer, Carol Stillwell had contacted Daniel after she decided to divorce her husband, Duke. Always one to take the higher ground, Daniel had refused to handle the proceedings unless the couple came to an amicable agreement. Jada wasn't sure how he'd managed it, but while directing the Stillwells to hash out their differences privately, Daniel convinced them to meet with a marriage counselor. In September, the couple reconciled.

The Stillwells' oldest daughter was enrolled in Kent State's School of Fashion.

"LuAnne helped Linnie find the right gown?" Philip asked.

"Daniel sent her Linnie's measurements, and a bunch of photos from the historical record. I had no idea he kept all those memories tucked away in his closet."

"The historical record?"

"From the Wayfair's heyday, when Linnie was a teenager. Remember the galas her parents used to host when they were in charge of the inn? Daniel must have a hundred photos of Linnie in all sorts of gowns. He sent a packet of them to LuAnne." The details Linnie had shared were incredibly romantic, and Jada was suddenly aware that she couldn't stop smiling. "It gets better."

Relishing her excitement, Philip picked up her glass and held it toward her. "Drink."

"Why, so you can change the subject? Philip, aren't you curious how a fashion student got Linnie to pick a wedding gown?"

"I am interested, mostly because you've been worrying about her making a decision. Maybe I'm also hoping you'll get a little tipsy." The expression he wore went from playful to seductive with breathtaking speed. "As good a way as any to get past your practical nature."

"Is that your best line?" If the responding jump in her pulse was any indication, the line was good enough.

"Does it need work? I'm out of practice."

She took the glass, sipped daintily. "Absolutely." She resumed her story. "Our dedicated fashion student showed the photos to one of her professors. Turns out, the man brought his wife to the Wayfair years ago, right after they married. One of the photos of Linnie dressed up that LuAnne showed him? He was standing in the background with his wife."

Caught up now, Philip pushed his plate away. "You're kidding." He appeared genuinely surprised.

"The professor contacted the VP at Dillard's in Cleveland. Together, they came up with ten wedding gowns suitable for Linnie's stature and general build. The gowns were delivered to Daniel's office this morning. When Linnie got home after work, she fell in love with the first dress she tried on."

The story was the icing on a perfectly confected day. April first had begun as a prankster. Now the month seemed full of promise. With a wedding soon—and a changed relationship Jada hadn't expected.

Contentment filled her as Philip asked, "Are you finished?" He frowned at her plate. "You didn't eat much."

"It was delicious."

Rising, Philip stretched. His attention flowed across the backyard before returning to her. "How about a walk? I'll clean up when we get back."

The suggestion was a good one. They were following the rules of a typical first date, which she suspected Philip also needed. He'd skipped the usual route to adulthood, becoming a parent at an age when Jada was dating a variety of men, and building her confidence in her abilities as a businesswoman while she and Cat helped Linnie keep the Wayfair from bankruptcy. Many of those years came with too much loneliness, and big doses of frustration—the men she dated were disappointments, and the worst years of the inn's decline brought hours of backbreaking work with little reward. Despite the challenges, she'd traveled an easier road to adulthood than Philip.

Wending around the side of the house, they strolled toward Sweet Lake Circle. The scent of lilacs perfumed the night air. Porch lights threw golden light across front lawns. The sidewalk was empty, lending the illusion they had the town to themselves.

Jada matched his strides. "Any news yet on the patio?" She considered taking his hand—a classic first-date move. She dismissed the idea as too forward.

"I'm fed up," Philip admitted. "I never did get a straight answer from my supplier. I found another company able to deliver on short notice."

Frustration rimmed the explanation. "There's a problem?" she asked.

"Not a problem exactly. The price they quoted is ridiculous. Brings my profit close to zero."

"You can't negotiate the supplier down?"

"Been there, done that. He won't budge."

Slowing her pace, Jada tried not to imagine the consequences. "What about another supplier, someone out of state?" Linnie's hopes were pinned on getting married at the inn. The excitement Jada felt over the wedding dress vanished as she imagined her best friend's disappointment.

"There's no one else, Jada. Not this close to the wedding."

She stopped, stared forlornly at the street they'd just passed. "Should I go over now, tell her? I suppose we can pull something together in the ballroom. Wedding and reception both? She's going to take this hard."

Philip looked at her like she'd grown a tail. "Hey, I'm not crazy enough to disappoint the blushing bride, *or* my brother. Jada, I accepted the bid."

"You did?" She stared at him.

"The sandstone comes in tomorrow. I've pulled my men off the jobs they were working in town. Most of my clients understand, but the decision didn't go down well with Jen Petralia over on Gardiners Avenue. Her backyard will look like a moonscape for the foreseeable future."

"Why a moonscape?" Jen and Leo Petralia owned the convenience store in town, and a beautiful Victorian house.

"We've taken out all the plant stock in their yard, and the lawn. Total redesign, but everything is on hold until Linnie's job is done." He looked pained, but he chuckled. "How well do you know Jen? I need someone to talk her out of posting a hostile review online."

"Not well enough." The trees rustled in greeting as they entered Sweet Lake Circle. Jada reached for his hand, drew him to a stop. Linnie hadn't mentioned any budget change. And they'd talked about *every* aspect of the wedding. "Wait a second. You're finishing the job without asking Linnie to pay the increase for the sandstone?"

Automatically, his fingers tightened around hers. With his free hand, Philip reached for her waist and steered her close. Evidently his first-date jitters weren't as insistent as she'd presumed.

"Yes, Jada," he said, his voice oddly calm despite the heat in his expression. "I'm allowing the highwayman to rob me blind to get the supplies on time. I'm finishing the patio. I'll take a beating on the job. It's the honorable thing to do."

"That isn't fair," she protested, doing her best to ignore the slow, delicious caresses he spread across her hip. "You've worked hard to give Linnie exactly what she wants. Tell her about the increase in price."

"I'm not telling her, or Daniel."

She stared at him in disbelief. "Linnie won't let you work for free. In fact, she'll be furious you even considered it."

He weighed her outrage with one part sincerity and two parts mirth. "Have I ever mentioned you're beautiful?" he murmured. His fingers halted their sensual journey across her waist.

Not the response she'd expected. Warmth fanned out across her cheeks. "I'm not beautiful. I'm attractive in a tall, sporty kind of way," she said reasonably. "Cat's beautiful. Linnie too, when she ditches the worrywart facade and cuts loose."

"For someone with a decent head on her shoulders, you sure are dumb."

She assumed she'd misheard. "Did you call me dumb?"

"Dumb as a doorpost. That's what my grandmother used to say. How can a woman with your brains have no awareness of her beauty?"

When she blinked, speechless, mischief sparked in his eyes. "Need another insult for a convincer?" he asked, leaning in to go nose-to-nose. "Here's one: you're dumber than mud."

"Thanks, Philip." She struggled to get free of his embrace.

He wrestled her still. "Kiss me."

Incredulous, she angled her neck. "Why should I?"

"Because I always make the first move. You're beautiful, you're in my arms, and I want you to show me how much you like it."

"Now there's a winning strategy. Insult the woman, then ask her to kiss you." But she wanted to comply—desperately. He'd gone boyish and playful so quickly, he'd thrown her off balance. The way he'd done a million times in the past, goading her on, urging her to strip off her sense of propriety, and chase after him.

Damn, he was good.

Rising to the challenge, she went up on tiptoes and kissed him hard on the mouth. Lusty, and full, and without reservation. She kissed him with her heart in her throat, draping her arms across his shoulders with a boldness she'd never before dared with a man. She leaned into his chest and he groaned, a deep, husky voicing of desire.

Hungry for the feel of his skin, she dipped her hands beneath the collar of his shirt. Muscles bunched in response to her touch, complying, willing. At the back of his neck, her fingers met with a jagged groove of flesh.

The discovery jolted her. Drawing her mouth from his, she rubbed the site.

"What is this?" The marred flesh felt about an inch long.

"Nothing." He caught the concern in her gaze and added, "Old war wound." He nipped the skin beneath her ear, and she shivered with delight. "Can we get back to what we were doing?"

"No." She rubbed the spot, and he flinched. "Is this a scar? I've never noticed it before."

"Compliments of Bodi." Mention of his late wife doused the passion they'd stoked. He released her. Rocking back on his heels, he rubbed his forehead as if banishing a memory. "Do we have to go into this now?"

The regret in his voice seemed a warning—of heartache never before shared, of memories too dark to easily discuss. Jada feared what he might reveal. Yet she wanted to help him carry the burden of a painful secret.

"I wish you would," she said.

"What if I'd rather not?"

"Your call, but I'd really like to know."

His attention drifted across the shadowed green for a long moment. "All right. Might as well." He drew a deep breath. "We were arguing. Bodi was four months pregnant."

"What were you arguing about?"

He splayed his palms, an act of contrition for sins she was certain he'd never committed. "Jada, I'm not going into the specifics tonight. I'm not ready." He winced. "I know you two were close, but there's some stuff I may never be able to share. Can you deal with that?"

"Sure." She pressed her palm to his cheek, wondered at the pain he seemed determined to hide. "I'll take whatever you're willing to give."

Philip rested his hand over hers, as if needing the comfort of her touch to proceed. "Like I said, we were arguing. Basically, an everyday event by that point in our marriage. There was never any telling what would set her off."

"I remember," she whispered. She recalled the first time Bodi stole cash at Gift of Garb. Jada had been in the store, sifting through the racks, when Penelope had confronted the teenager. Refusing to admit to the theft, Bodi let loose a stream of foul language. Then she'd pushed over a rack of clothes and stormed out.

"I was tired of the screaming, and walked out of the kitchen. Stupid move. Bodi came at me with a paring knife." He laughed derisively. "At least I had the sense to grab a towel before I drove to the hospital. The wound bled like crazy."

A clipped summation, and Jada was sickened by the telling. "She cut you deep enough to require stitches?"

"Oh yeah. Then she apologized for days. The only good thing that came out of it. At least I got a few nights of sleep before we started on the merry-go-round again."

A loud silence descended between them. Were there other times when Bodi attacked him? Were the secrets in his failed marriage so grave, he kept the memories locked deep inside his heart? She knew he was done talking about it. At least for now.

Steering her hand from his cheek, he kissed her lightly on the brow. "We should get back," he said. "Fancy will be home soon."

Chapter 11

In the dream, Millicent waited on the golden sands of Sweet Lake.

Tiny needlelike leaves pierced her feet. The pungent fragrance reached her nose—rosemary. She bent down to inspect the herb mixed in with the sand when a roar of wind reached her ears. A tornado cut a swath across the beach, wiping the clouds from the sky.

She stood calmly, as if the angry tower of air posed no danger to her—or to Penelope Riddle, standing twenty paces off in the surf. Penelope called out as she pointed at the churning waters of the lake. The tornado followed the same path, whipping across the lake with howling fury.

The scream of high winds jolted her from sleep. Swinging her feet to the floor, Millicent gulped down air. The oak floorboards were cold; a serene quiet enveloped the room. Through the window, the first threads of daylight fingered the treetops.

Twenty minutes later, she was dressed and glad to reach the inn's lobby. This early in the morning there wasn't a soul in sight, with the exception of the pretty brunette clacking on the keyboard behind the front desk. Outside, the first blush of dawn spread across the grounds.

Unable to calm herself, Millicent swallowed down the bitterness in her throat. A nightmare? Night terrors were the provenance of children. They weren't meant for an old woman with too much time on her hands, who'd spent too many days eating homemade puddings and cakes in the Wayfair's kitchen. Forbidding tornadoes notwithstanding, she ought to dream about her next physical—*that* was scary. Dr. Healy would read her the riot act for gaining more weight.

With a nod to the girl behind the front desk, Millicent strode toward the veranda. A healthy dose of fresh air would shake the dream from her blood.

Rosy light crept across the rocking chairs and wicker seating arrangements. Millicent's attention drifted to the charcoal shadows draping the veranda's farther reaches.

Glad for the seclusion, she chose a rocking chair deep in the shadows. Rocking slowly, she tried to sort herself out.

"Norah, you're a miracle worker." With wonder, Jada appraised the fabrics draped across every available space in Penelope's living room.

In each bundle, the Sirens had purchased two yards of cloth. The grand total was enough to make the perfect flower girl frock *and* a closetful of dress-up clothes for one excited girl. Gleaming satin in pale pink and rich purple, tulle covered with silver sparkles, chiffon in a rainbow of colors and georgette as shimmery as fairy wings—the selections placed before Fancy gave proof that the women in her life most assuredly viewed her as a big girl.

Fancy hefted the purple satin into her arms. "This one, Norah?"

"For the entire dress, or only the skirt?"

"Can I pick something else for the top part?" Fancy patted her chest.

The Siren toyed with a lock of her long silver hair, which she'd made distinctive with plum streaks. Deep in thought, she moved around the room considering one fabric after another.

Jada reached for the sparkling tulle and held it to Fancy's waist. "This would look pretty over the satin skirt," she suggested. "How about a neutral for the bodice?"

"What's neutral?" Fancy asked.

Approaching the couch, Norah tapped a polished finger against her crimson lips. "A neutral is a color that will *not* shout at the top of its lungs." With an appreciative glance at Jada, she picked up a bundle of satin in pale taupe. "This one. Fancy, do you agree?"

The first grader recoiled. "Dirt colors are for boys."

"Child, the color taupe is the backbone of a well-dressed woman's wardrobe. Now, wait. You haven't seen the best part." With a lion's grace, Norah prowled across the room. She paused by the stack of shoeboxes Penelope was setting out on the cut-out between the living room and the kitchen. "Which one is the Chanel? We'll start there. I dread how much time we'll spend prying the faux jewels from their settings."

Curious, Jada joined them. "Chanel?" Today, the Sirens were full of surprises.

Penelope removed the lid of the box she held. "This is Norah's fashion jewelry, from when she was a model. Most of the jewelry has been stored in her attic. She's letting Fancy add sparkle to the bodice of her dress."

"You'll destroy French costume jewelry to add glam to Fancy's outfit? It's too beautiful to destroy!"

Norah dipped her hand into the box. "Either we offer up Chanel on the altar of Fancy's obsession with glitz, or she'll pick lime green for the bodice. I will not have her traipsing up the aisle dressed like a cabaret singer from 1930s Paris. We'll add the jewels to the bodice when we sew the dress."

"Thank you, Norah!" Fancy hopped up and down. "May I put all the jewelry on the floor? Look through everything before I pick my favorites?"

Norah sighed heavily, but Jada caught the merriment in her eyes. "Fine, dear. Penelope and I will help you spread the necklaces out."

They were carrying the boxes to the center of the room when the front door slammed. Linnie waltzed through the kitchen, stopping short on the threshold to the living room.

"What's going on?" she asked Jada.

Seated on the floor, Norah and Penelope were handing off necklaces to the feverish child. With each pass, Fancy leapt up, accepted the gift, then scampered to the center of the rug. She'd already laid out ten necklaces in a haphazard row.

"Sifting through Chanel," Jada replied.

Linnie did a double take. "Like, the real deal from France? Or a knockoff?"

"The real deal. From Norah's modeling days."

"I love the Sirens. They always come through." Linnie noticed the coffee and the plate of shortbread cookies left out in the kitchen. Pouring two cups of coffee, she nodded toward the backyard. "Break time?"

"Definitely." Jada accepted the steaming cup. "I've been on my feet since dawn."

The backyard of the Riddle home resembled a whimsical haven for magical creatures. Stained glass butterflies rode above the pink, white, and yellow tulips wagging in the flower beds. Wind chimes sang out from tree limbs. Porcelain figurines—toads, chubby elves, a dragon, and even a large swan of cut glass—were tucked in among the pansies and the azaleas. Wedges of limestone painted in colorful designs nestled in the thick green grass.

Wending down the path, Linnie offered a playful glance. "How was last night?"

"You tell me." Jada slowed, took a sip of her coffee. "Did you talk to Fancy on her level?"

"I did my best. I doubt I'm anywhere near her favorite girlfriend, especially since you've already won the grand prize." Linnie gave her a small nudge, and Jada yelped as her coffee sloshed to the rim of her cup. "Stop stalling. Did you and Philip enjoy the alone time? I was afraid you'd veto the idea of dating him."

"I needed his assurance that, no matter what happens between us, my relationship with Fancy will stay on steady ground. She's never had a mother, and I've loved playing stand-in." Jada allowed her restless gaze to roam across the sunlit garden. "I also can't help but wonder if I . . ."

A sharp ache went through her as she broke off. Shame followed. Or guilt over the private code among women Jada feared she'd broken.

"Hey. What is it?" Linnie reached up, brushed a curl from her brow. Her touch eased the tension Jada was trying hard to manage. "What do you wonder about?"

"Bodi, and our friendship. By dating Philip . . . am I dishonoring her memory?"

"Jada—no. Absolutely not."

"Are you sure?" The ache squeezed her heart. Behaving honorably mattered to her—it always had.

Shaking her head, Linnie steered her onto the small stone bench tucked between the flowers. When they were seated, she said, "Listen, it's great you and Philip are dating. You aren't dishonoring Bodi by doing so. You've known each another forever, long before Bodi came into the picture. She's not the one he was supposed to be with. In fact, he's been crazy about you for a long time. Daniel clued me in. He says Philip has been searching for a way to ask you out. Like for years, Jada. He held off because he wasn't sure how you'd react to the idea."

"I *am* nervous."

"He's not a stranger. You know what you're getting into."

Beside the bench, a stand of pink tulips sparkled with dew. Brushing her fingers across the soft petals, Jada collected her thoughts. Yes, she understood—more so after the discovery she'd made last night.

With a close friend's sixth sense, Linnie rubbed her back. "Is there something else weighing on you? I'm getting the feeling there is."

With a nod in the affirmative, Jada set her coffee aside. "After dinner, we walked up to Sweet Lake Circle. Philip kissed me, and I noticed a small scar at the base of his neck."

"A scar? From what?"

"Bodi, during their marriage. Before Fancy was born. They had an argument, he walked away." Jada pressed her hand to her belly, sickened by the retelling. "She came at him with a knife. Philip drove himself to the hospital for stitches. Promise you won't tell."

"Bodi *attacked* him? We all knew she had issues with her temper, but not like this. Poor Philip. And of course, you know I'd never say anything."

"And poor Millicent." Frustration brimmed in Jada as she swiped the curls from her brow. "I'm sure she's Bodi's grandmother. Why else stay in Sweet Lake, and keep steering conversations back to seven years ago? She doesn't know if Bodi is dead or alive. And she's determined to track her down." She took a deep breath. "Linnie, I've grown to care about her. Millicent is prickly—but sweet at the most unexpected moments. She can never have Bodi again, but she can become part of Fancy's life. Why shouldn't she have the opportunity?"

"You're not telling her she has a great-granddaughter." Linnie regarded her with pity. She sighed. "Assuming she *is* Fancy's great-grandmother."

"How can I? Philip wasn't merely in a bad marriage—he was trapped in an abusive marriage. He's only capable of discussing Bodi in brief snatches. How can I ask him to allow Millicent to become part of Fancy's life? It'll only dredge up memories he wants to forget."

"And Fancy?"

"I love her, Linnie. No matter what happens between me and Philip, I want to do right by her."

"You will—you do."

"She's too young to understand she looks exactly like Bodi."

"Like a carbon copy."

Angry, Jada brushed away the welling tears. "She's aware she doesn't resemble the Ketterings, or carry a physical resemblance to anyone in her life. How can I hide from her the very thing she craves? What if Fancy has other relatives she resembles closely? Aunts and uncles with cornflower-blue eyes, or cousins with the same light-blonde hair?"

Jada made herself breathe. Willed away the tears before she crumbled.

Once her emotions were under control, she added, "What right do I have to pretend her other family doesn't exist?"

Chapter 12

The three new employees trailed behind Jada like attentive ducklings.

She'd already finished the tour of the kitchen, the main inn, and the south wing. Since both of the men were joining the waitstaff, Jada decided to end the tour in the Sunshine Room. Darrisha Ray, ten years older than the men and a new transplant from the city of Springboro, would begin at the front desk tomorrow.

At the restaurant's wall of glass, Darrisha surveyed the grounds. On the lawn, several families were playing an impromptu game of soccer. Mr. Uchida had dragged folding chairs out of storage; three older men and a middle-aged woman sat watching the game.

"I didn't expect this much activity for the first week in April," Darrisha remarked approvingly. Her résumé included posts with national hotels, and Jada was thrilled to hire her. "Are you always this busy in the spring?"

Jada smiled. "We're on the rebound. When Linnie's parents were in charge, we were usually eighty percent full by April. After they retired, bookings dropped severely. We're back on the upswing."

"You're doing something right."

"I can't take credit. Cat handles the marketing with the help of her husband, Ryan D'Angelo."

"I've met Ryan. He's with Adworks, right? His firm handled a campaign for my last employer."

"We're lucky to have his expertise. If you'd like an update on the ad campaigns scheduled for this year, Linnie will fill you in." Jada checked her watch. "Ready? She's waiting to help each of you complete the rest of your paperwork."

After depositing the new hires in Linnie's office, Jada checked in with the kitchen staff, and Mr. Uchida at the front desk. Then she hurried to the basement to check the Housekeeping staff on laundry duty. Most afternoons, she carved out time to make the rounds. It was a task Cat detested and Linnie, focused on her wedding, now overlooked.

Today the Wayfair hummed like a well-oiled machine. Jada welcomed a few minutes to spare.

Revelry from the impromptu soccer match carried across the grounds as she veered around the east face of the inn. Above her on the veranda, most of the rocking chairs were occupied. The guests were sipping tea and enjoying the lazy hours before dinner service would commence. Near the grassy perimeter where the lawn met the parking lot, a towheaded youth on Philip's crew mounted a riding mower.

Behind the ballroom, the men wore sweat-streaked faces. With the shipment of sandstone finally at the site, they were working double time to finish the patio. They were making great progress. Half of the stone was in place. Philip stood at the back of the site, leaning on a shovel.

Noticing her, he sauntered over. "What do you think?" There was no missing the pride in his voice.

"You're getting caught up fast."

He took her by the hand. "Come see what I picked up this morning."

On the lawn, several dozen azalea and boxwood plants sat on a plastic tarp. Near the back of the plant stock, a cluster of five-foot-tall fig trees rustled in the breeze.

"Nice, aren't they?" Philip scooted one of the fig trees closer for her inspection. "I was thinking about the ceremony arch we're building, where Linnie and my brother will marry."

"You've come up with a final design?" He'd been mulling it over for weeks.

"I'm using rustic branches to build the arch—I'm going for a natural look. What do you think about having the figs at each end of the arch?" When she nodded, pleased, he added, "Don't tell Linnie. I'd like to assemble the arch, then wow her with the results."

The enthusiasm rippling off him was contagious. "I won't breathe a word," she promised.

"Ready for the best part?"

Letting her go, he strode to the brick stairway winding up to the back entrance of the ballroom. At the bottom of the stairway, she spotted a cluster of plants hidden against the building. The row of climbing roses thick with green buds and deep-pink blooms shared space with smaller pots of white baby's breath.

Jada sighed with appreciation. "Philip, they're gorgeous. For the arch?"

"I'll wind the roses all the way up, then fill in with baby's breath. Moss too. I'm still waiting for the shipment to come in. Daniel picked out the roses—another surprise for Linnie." Dropping the subject, he glanced back at his men. Assured of their privacy, he looped an arm around her waist. "What time are you coming over tonight?"

She melted against him even as she quirked a brow. "I never said I *was* coming over tonight."

"You should. We'll watch a movie after Fancy goes to bed."

The expectancy in his eyes was appealing. "I'm planning on an early night," she said, brushing her lips across his. "Tomorrow Cat and I have our last appointment for alterations. I don't know why Cat made both of our appointments for the same time, at eleven. I have another cooking lesson first thing, then baking. I'm not sure how to squeeze it all in."

"No movie, then. I'll let you take off at nine o'clock. Should I order carryout, or will you settle for burgers and macaroni and cheese? Fancy informed me of the menu right before Norah picked her up."

Clearly, he wasn't taking no for an answer. "Don't count on me for dinner," she warned.

"You're skipping out on me and the munchkin?"

"I'm eating at my desk while plowing through paperwork. I'll stop by once I finish."

"Great. I won't keep you up past your bedtime." He gave her a lingering kiss, then started off. He'd only walked a few paces when he pivoted back around. "What's your take on a night at the orchestra? I was checking out tickets, for May. I'd take you on a real date sooner, but I have an arbor to build and best man commitments."

"In Cincinnati?"

"Penelope offered to watch Fancy while we're away. We'll stay the night in town." He caught her eyes narrowing, and rolled forward on his work boots. "In separate hotel rooms, Jada. I'm asking you out for a night on the town. I'm not jumping the gun."

The offer was romantic and surprising. "We'll talk about it tonight," she promised.

A real date, in Cincinnati. Strolling back around the inn, she went through a mental checklist of the dresses in her wardrobe. There weren't many, and she welcomed the excuse to shop for something new. Aside from the upcoming wedding, her life afforded precious few opportunities to dress up.

On a whim, Jada walked through the parking lot and down the rolling hill leading to the beach. Her worries regarding Millicent's possible connection to Fancy remained at the back of her mind. They weren't enough to blot out the anticipation flowing through her.

Caught up in the sweet reverie, she allowed her heart to move past the secret regrets she harbored about the past, and the shame that left a bitter taste in her mouth whenever she remembered the snow-blistered hills and Philip's late wife out in the blizzard, pounding on the truck's horn.

For a fleeting moment, she imagined the possibilities if her relationship with Philip blossomed fully.

"Whatever you're drinking, I'll have some."

The quip startled her. Jada snapped her head up.

On the empty beach, Millicent reclined near the water's edge. She'd plopped down in her standard tweed skirt and removed her sensible shoes. The frumpy blazer she usually wore lay in a sandy lump by her hip. Above her left ear, she'd tucked an emerald-green feather.

Amused, Jada tipped her head to the side. "Going for a new look?" Smiling, she motioned to the feather.

"I'm testing the waters. I ran into Silvia and Frances earlier. They invited me to tea." She studied Jada closely. "You're in a happy mood. Is a person of the male persuasion the source of your happiness?"

Glee danced across Millicent's features. No doubt the co-leaders of the Sirens had filled her in over tea, and she knew about Jada's new romance with Philip. "Millicent, why ask when you know the answer?"

"This is where I usually say 'I told you so.' Since you're not one of my doctoral students, I'll refrain." She patted the sand, waited until Jada sat. "Tell me. How are you planning to handle the new development with the little girl in the magician's cape?"

The friendly interest tugged at Jada's heart. No matter how briefly Fancy entered the conversation, Millicent was quite taken with the stories about the lemon-haired sprite. Possibly her great-granddaughter, a bright new leaf on her family tree—a child she might never meet. Philip would want nothing to do with Bodi's family.

The situation was brutally unfair.

Hiding the sense of resignation sifting through her, Jada slipped off her flats. "For now, I'll stick to my role of family friend." She plunged her feet into the soft sand. "I don't want Fancy racing to conclusions when I've just begun seeing her father."

"Sensible." Millicent's green eyes were quick and assessing. "I would imagine a relationship between two adults with a solid friendship has a good chance of success. And by all accounts, he's a man with strong fathering gifts. A good sign. He'll treat you well."

"He does."

Millicent glanced at her appraisingly. "How are *you* handling the new development?"

If prudence dictated the conversations regarding Fancy remain brief, Jada no longer felt the same compunction regarding her own life. Whatever the historian's true aim in coming to Sweet Lake, she meant well.

"The timing isn't great," she admitted. "Linnie's wedding is at the end of the month. I don't have lots of free time for dating. I need to keep my eye on helping Linnie through the biggest transition of her life, while ensuring the inn hums along while she settles in. She's been awfully preoccupied—not exactly a good thing with the tourist season commencing."

"You won't let her down. You're too considerate. You wouldn't know how."

The compliment stirred the regret Jada privately nursed. "I've had a few stumbles." The admission weighed heavily on her heart, and she burrowed her feet deeper into the sand.

Unbidden, the memory confronted her. The snow, falling in sheets. The panic gripping her as the sound of the ice cracking reached her ears.

Impulsively, Jada scanned the shoreline. She found the spot where she'd stood on that treacherous day, shivering against the wind's icy blasts, screaming out in warning, nearly blinded by the snow. The event so long ago, yet it seemed like yesterday. In all the years since, she'd never discussed those final moments—not with Philip, who'd lost so much; or Cat, who would've rocked Jada for hours as she unleashed the sorrow she'd kept buried for years. Not even with Linnie.

Running from the memory, she poked at the feather bobbing by Millicent's cheek. "My turn with the twenty questions," she said, desperate to turn the conversation. "Who flipped you to the bright side? Frances or Silvia?"

"Both of them, although they did mention that giving me a Siren feather was Penelope's idea. I guess she couldn't join us today because she's working in her shop." Millicent rolled her meaty shoulders with fizzy mirth. "Is there something in Sweet Lake's water? I find my friendships with the Sirens intoxicating."

"They *are* colorful." Jada rested her attention on a boat skimming the lake, the white sail flapping gently in the breeze. "Correct me if I'm wrong. I have the sense you don't have many women friends."

"Jada, I don't have many friends at all. What a terrible conclusion to reach in the last third of one's life. I was too busy getting ahead to get involved. When I *did* get involved later on, I managed to make a mess of my career in the process."

"Involved . . . you mean with your husband?" She was fairly mum on the specifics of her marriage, even during the longest baking lessons.

The question brought an impatient glance; Millicent seemed about to explain. She chuckled instead.

"What's funny?" Jada didn't like the impression she was the object of a joke.

"You, making assumptions about my marriage. Everyone does. Someday those assumptions will change." A silence followed the cryptic remark. Then she offered a smile composed of sadness, and the sort of regret Jada readily understood. "To answer your question, it wasn't my finest hour when I fell in love with a colleague's spouse. The gossip nearly destroyed my career. I began plotting out my retirement the year after we married. One of the many reasons I'm persona non grata at the University of Chicago."

"You broke up another professor's marriage?"

"Heavens, no. Their marriage was a hollow shell before I entered the picture. The rare times they attended functions together, you always found them arguing in a corner over their martinis. They had one child, a daughter. They never did agree on what to do."

"About the daughter?"

"It would be charitable to describe her behavior as problematic. Bipolar disorder, you see. There were so many treatment options. Not that we got far with any of them."

Millicent's voice had become ragged. Jada sensed she wanted the subject dropped.

Silently, she attempted to fit the pieces together. If Millicent was indeed the grandmother of Philip's late wife, was she implying a history of mental illness in Bodi's family? A history she confronted when she married Bodi's grandfather?

Was Millicent a *step*-grandmother—and Bodi's mother was bipolar? Jada's understanding of mental illness was limited, but she knew some disorders were inherited. Perhaps Bodi had also been bipolar, a disease she'd inherited from her mother.

In a lighter tone, Millicent said, "If I've forged one enduring friendship in my golden years, I've done just about everything to wreck it."

"You mean with the student living at your house?" Jada guessed.

Withdrawing the feather stuck in her hair, Millicent fingered the ivory shaft. "I really must stop referring to Vasily as a houseboy. When I get home, I'll do better. His parents live in Phoenix. He's probably formed an attachment out of loneliness."

"Or he enjoys your friendship," Jada countered. "You *are* likeable." For all her wit and intelligence, Millicent seemed incapable of believing anyone would enjoy her company.

"You really are too kind."

"Not at all." Jada got to her feet. It was time to get back.

"Are we still on for our lesson tomorrow?" Millicent asked. She gave an enigmatic smile. "I have a surprise."

"Seven o'clock sharp." Jada picked up her shoes and shook off the sand. "What's the surprise?"

"A recipe, which comes highly recommended. Interestingly enough, the recipe contains one of my favorite ingredients—for sentimental reasons."

"One of the Sirens gave you a recipe? Hey, if Silvia is the culprit, we won't have time tomorrow morning to whip up *tres leches*." The Mexican cake was an old standard in the Mendoza household. "Cat and I have a fitting in town later on, and I'll need to make headway on the inn's desserts before we leave for the appointment. I was hoping for something easier to bake with you—cookies, perhaps?"

"Perfect."

"You have a cookie recipe?"

"As the Sirens would instruct, let events unfold in their own sweet time." Millicent chuckled. "If I share the recipe now, I'll ruin the surprise."

Philip surveyed the stuffed animals and baby dolls abandoned on the floor. Usually at least two of the dolls escorted his daughter into dreamland, along with the fat teddy bear and the softly worn stuffed bunny she'd been dragging around since her toddler years. The bolts of fabric, which Penelope and Norah had neatly stacked when they'd brought Fancy home, were no longer on the dresser. A few chunks of cloth were strewn across the floor.

The rest were bundled in his daughter's arms.

"You're dragging that stuff to bed?"

Fancy balanced the stack against her chest. "Yes, Daddy." Wavering like a drunk, she zigzagged to the bed. "Just for tonight. My babies understand." One by one, she laid the colorful horde in a semicircle on the bed. Completing the design, she tucked a chunk of silvery fabric beside the pillow.

Scampering past him, she retrieved the fabric she'd dropped.

With consternation, he crossed his arms. "There's no more room on the bed. Where will you sleep?"

"Right in the middle," she assured him, climbing over the pillow. With painstaking care, she wiggled her way beneath the comforter. "Made it!"

"Kiddo, you're one shade from silly. Tomorrow night, let's return to our original programming and let your babies sleep in bed." He picked up a handful of toys, put them on her play table. "At the moment, your bedroom looks like the island of misfit toys."

"Penelope and Norah promised I can keep the pretty colors until they're ready."

"It's awfully nice of the Sirens to buy all this fabric and make you a bunch of new dress-up clothes."

"*And* my party dress."

"Wedding," Philip corrected.

Somewhere along the line, his daughter had transformed the upcoming nuptials into her coming-out party. He only hoped she wouldn't lobby to invite her peewee girlfriends.

Nearing, he studied the string of faux jewels she was winding around her wrist. "Is that a necklace?" When Penelope dropped her off with the fabric, he hadn't noticed jewelry in the bags.

"It's Chanel." Fancy shook her arm to make the jewels flash. Channeling a grownup voice, she added, "Elegant women *only* wear Chanel."

"According to whom—Norah?"

She flopped her arm to her side. "What does *elegant* mean?"

"It means you'd better hold off on marriage until a lawyer like Uncle Daniel gets down on bended knee."

After kissing her goodnight, he turned out the light. He was closing the door when she spoke again.

"Daddy?"

"What, sweet pea?"

"Why don't I look like anybody?"

The question made his heart overturn. "Does it matter?" he asked, hoping to skirt the matter quickly.

She didn't answer right away. She lifted a finger to draw imaginary pictures in the air, as if the endeavor might reveal secrets she'd never been told.

"You have dark hair, and Jada has dark skin," she said at last. "Uncle Daniel looks like you, and Grandma Kettering has your green eyes. Why am I different?"

It seemed best to skip her inclusion of Jada in the Kettering genetic pool, although her little-girl logic made him smile. "I don't know, Fancy," he lied, needing to protect her for as long as time would allow. "Half the girls in your first-grade class want your blonde hair and blue eyes. They're really different, and they make you beautiful. Don't you like being special?"

"I guess so." She reached for the silvery fabric, dragged it over her face. Hidden beneath, she blew out tiny breaths that made the fabric ripple. When she threw it off, she stared blankly at the ceiling. "Daddy?"

"What, sugarplum?"

"How many people am I allowed to love?"

An easier topic, and he leaned against the doorjamb. "Tell me this isn't about a boy. I'm not ready for that conversation."

"I don't like boys." On the pillow, she flopped her head toward him. "Except you and Uncle Daniel."

"And Gramps. He's flying in from Texas with Grandma for the wedding." She nodded, and he crossed his arms. "Fancy, you can love as many people as you'd like. There's no limit. In fact, it's a pretty good deal to love lots of people."

"Then I love Jada almost as much as I love you."

"You do?"

Wriggling her arm out from beneath the cover, Fancy scratched her wrist. She unwound the necklace and plunked it on the dresser. "Will you tell Jada we'll need her help, even after the wedding?" Sitting up, she looked at him fully. "I don't want her to go away."

Where the munchkin was headed with this, he wasn't sure. "What makes you think she will?" he asked.

"She never used to come around."

"Well, she *has* been trying to help us out—like Uncle Daniel used to do. He's busy now, setting up his new life with Aunt Linnie." The urge to come clean with his daughter grew strong. He'd love nothing more than to reveal his intention to keep Jada in their lives.

The desire quickly receded beneath more practical concerns. Nothing was settled. He'd only just begun to date Jada. It was premature to get his daughter's hopes up.

"I wouldn't worry too much, kiddo." Returning to the bed, he tousled her silky hair. When she rewarded him with a smile, he added, "Jada likes hanging around with us. Even if she doesn't always have time to stop over, you can see her at the inn. She likes when we stop in for dinner at the Sunshine Room."

"I like playing with her. We can't play at the inn."

At the wistful comment, he bent down to give her another kiss. "Get some sleep." He brushed the feathery strands of hair from her forehead. "I'll see you in the morning."

Philip closed the door with his emotions in flux. Everything might *not* work out. Fancy would be disappointed, but not as much as him. Then he ran toward a more optimistic thought. In many relationships, having a child from a previous marriage posed difficulties. A potential stepparent might not click with a child, delaying the option of deepening a commitment—or halting a romance altogether.

Gratitude whirled through him as he went out to the back deck. Among the blessings in his life was the natural, spontaneous affection Jada shared with his daughter. Fancy revolved around Jada like a planet circling the sun. Their daily interactions now formed a bond he prayed would never break.

Fancy loved Jada—and the feeling was mutual.

Stars winked in the night sky. Ridiculously, he searched for a shooting star, as he'd done long ago, when Penelope whispered magic in his ears, urging him to trust in the sorcery of his imagination and the untapped power to create a life big enough to contain his every dream.

The life he'd secured wasn't built on wishes. The world he inhabited was grounded in hapless error and foolish choices. But he'd done all right. Better than all right. From the bitter lessons he'd woven a life strong and secure. A world he dared to believe Jada would one day share with him and Fancy.

"Hey."

He turned. Jada stood on the threshold between the living room and the deck.

"Hey yourself." He smiled, adding, "You let yourself in." A good sign, in his opinion.

"Thought I shouldn't ring the doorbell. Fancy's in bed, right?"

"Falling asleep as we speak," he told her. "Are you hungry? There's a leftover burger and mac and cheese in the fridge."

Skirting the offer, she said, "Invite me over next Sunday, and I'll cook." She glanced toward the kitchen, as if conjuring a menu from the treasure trove of recipes she'd perfected. "What are your thoughts on curried chicken and rice, with peach pie for dessert? This morning we got in an unusually early shipment of Georgia peaches. Linnie won't mind if a handful go missing."

Curried chicken and peach pie were among his daughter's favorite dishes—and his.

"I'll help with cooking. Whatever you need." The idea of following Jada around the kitchen while she filled the air with mouthwatering scents was intensely appealing. "Want me to pick up the chicken?"

"I'll bring everything I need. Plan on seeing me in the afternoon. I'd come earlier, but I usually sleep in. My one day of luxury."

"Whenever you get here is fine."

"I'll send a text when I'm in the car." She looked at him expectantly, the light in her chestnut-colored eyes shifting.

Taking the cue, he advanced. She readily moved into his arms. He tempered his thoughts as he kissed her, allowing his hands to slide down her curves to her waist, doing his best not to allow the feel of her pliable skin undo his control. It didn't help matters when she arched close, her arms sliding up to rest on his shoulders, opening herself to him. When his heart began thundering in his ears, he broke off the kiss.

"You never told me if you want dinner." Giving in to the temptation, he dragged his teeth across the heated skin of her neck. She shivered with pleasure.

"I ate dinner at my desk."

"Right. I forgot. You mentioned paperwork when I saw you today." Her fingers crept toward his hairline, and he shuddered in response. Channeling a calm that belied the heat pouring through him, he asked, "Would you like a glass of wine?"

"Sure."

Letting her go took effort. She went outside, and the scrape of a wicker chair announced she'd chosen where to sit. He strode into the kitchen, found glasses. Pouring the wine, he concentrated on regulating his breathing.

When he returned outside, he found Jada slouched low in the chair, tapping a finger absently against her lips.

"What's the dilemma?" He handed her a glass. "You look stuck on something."

"I *am* stuck. Between work and all the preparations for the wedding, I haven't found time to give any thought to a gift."

He brought a chair close. "For Linnie and Daniel, or just Linnie? I'm not sure of the protocol for maid of honor. Or best man, come to think of it."

"I want to get something for them both."

"That's my plan."

"Have you bought something?"

"If I were confident they'd book a long honeymoon, I'd get something for the trip. New luggage, or gift cards for several nice dinners at the destination. My brother is aiming for Aruba, if he can get Linnie to come around." Philip took a sip of wine. "She won't commit to a real honeymoon until next autumn, when the Wayfair slows down. I hope it's not too late by then."

"Too late for what, Philip? Professional couples can't always coordinate a honeymoon right after the wedding. Not the perfect situation, but a woman with the controlling interest in a thriving inn *does* have responsibilities." She caught the mischief in his eyes. "Or do you know something I don't?"

Relishing her interest, Philip drew the moment out. He liked the way Jada hung her attention on him, her gaze warming as it wandered across his features. Setting his glass down, he took her hand. He brushed his lips across her fingers, and the faintest sigh drifted from her throat.

"I'm not sure I should tell you." He threaded his fingers through hers. She held tight, her thumb moving automatically, delivering tiny caresses. "One of those confidences between brothers. Besides, Linnie will tell you eventually. You *are* close."

"Philip, you're such a tease. Tell me!"

"Linnie went off the pill."

"Is she . . . ?"

"No news to report, not yet, but the decision has made my brother a little crazy—in a good way. Yesterday? I stopped by his office and found the goofiest surprise."

Slipping her hand from his, Jada caressed his jawline. Light, tentative caresses, but they were enough to intensify the hunger building inside him. If she kept it up, he was tossing out the playbook on proper dating etiquette. Was the first week too early for heavy necking, preferably without shirts? He remembered his daughter, sleeping inside, and drove the notion from his mind.

Grinning, Jada tapped him on the cheek. "C'mon, tell me," she prodded. "What did you find when you dropped by Daniel's office?"

"He was on his computer, tooling around on baby sites. Clothing, toys, cribs—he had four windows open on his iMac."

The description increased the emotion warming her gaze. "That's sweet," she murmured. "He's looking forward to becoming a father."

"I don't blame him. He wants to get started before he's staring down middle age."

"Good thing Cat and Ryan are talking about waiting a year or two." Tiny furrows appeared on the smooth brown skin between her dark brows. "If both of my business partners start the baby game at the same time, I'm not sure where that leaves me. Working seven days a week? Not what I have in mind."

"Jada, every problem that comes up isn't *your* problem."

"Says you."

"Says anyone with half a brain." It bothered him how she instinctively reached for the heaviest burden, a habit too well ingrained. Wishing to break it, he spelled out the obvious solution. "Granted, Linnie may want a shortened workweek after giving birth to her bundle of joy. But there's no reason she can't do part of the job from home after her maternity leave if she wants to. Same with Daniel. He's a lawyer, more than capable of handling some work from home. Trust me—a guy tooling around baby websites won't mind sharing diaper duty."

"Meaning I'm worrying about nothing?" She looked doe-eyed and fragile, as if she really wasn't sure.

He chuckled. "Recite after me: it's not my problem." He flicked her nose, like he'd do if Fancy did something silly. "Because it's not."

She held up a hand in surrender. "Okay, it's *not* my problem. You win."

"Don't forget the Sirens will insist on pitching in. Whenever Linnie starts a family, she'll have more than enough help."

"Two for two, Philip." Jada leaned closer, brushed a kiss across his mouth. "You're doing great."

"Do you want kids?"

The question slipped out before Philip checked himself. A blunder, and he hung his head. Even with his nonexistent dating experience as an adult, he knew to save the heavy stuff for later. Long enough to guarantee he didn't scare Jada away.

He stole a quick glance. A heady emotion swept through him.

Jada didn't look scared. In fact, she looked pleased.

"Yes, Philip," she said, lacing his name with affection, "I want kids. You had Daniel growing up—I'm an only child. I adore my parents, but they were starting to get old before I finished junior high. Sometimes they feel more like grandparents, this sweet older couple I pop in to check on several times each week, talking about their latest ailments, or bickering about what they should have for dinner if I haven't brought something over, which I usually do." She grinned into her wineglass, took a sip. "Dinner is usually at four p.m."

He liked Jada's parents. Sometimes he bumped into them at Gift of Garb. They held hands in public and were inseparable.

He'd never given much thought to what it had been like for Jada, growing up with older parents. They *were* closer in age to grandparents.

"I always felt like I had to be a self-starter, responsible—even more so now," she was saying. "I've been in a caretaking role with my parents ever since college. Not something most people expect to confront in early adulthood."

"I guess not." Daring himself to dream, he asked, "Best-case scenario, how many kids would you like?"

"Do you want the truth, or a diplomatic answer?"

"The truth, totally. Hit me with it."

Settling back in her chair, she seemed completely at ease. Her attention floated across the backyard, lifting to study the moon, fat and golden, rising above the trees.

"Three kids, minimum. Four, if pregnancy and long labors don't convince me otherwise. But I have a feeling I'll have easy pregnancies. Don't ask how I know, I just do."

"You *do* want a big family."

"Crazy, right?"

"Not crazy at all. Big families are great."

"And rare," she pointed out. "Raising a large brood doesn't come cheap. Food, clothing, sports fees, medical care, and let's not forget about college. Sometimes I doubt it's realistic to hope for a large family."

Count on Jada's pragmatism to get in the way of her dreams. "It's not unrealistic," he countered. "You budget, that's all. Teach your kids to share, and to expect more hand-me-downs than new clothes. As far as college, what's wrong with commuting? Or asking your children to save up for some expenses, *and* take out some loans?"

"There's nothing wrong with it. Pitching in teaches a child responsibility."

"Exactly."

She inhaled a deep breath, her features softening. "I hated being an only child. Linnie and Cat are the siblings I never had. What would my life have been like if we'd never become friends? I guess that's one of the reasons why I've always considered having a large family. I want my children to grow up knowing there's always someone they can trust, and love. Someone who'll stand by them no matter what."

"I want the same things."

"A large family?"

"Jada, no one wants to become a father before he's ready. But, yeah, I'd love for Fancy to have sibs. She'd love it too."

Sipping her wine, she cast a dubious glance over the rim. "Philip, there's a big difference between raising one child and a group of kids. The word 'chaos' comes to mind."

"Are you implying I can't deal with chaos? Man, you're way off base." He ran his hand across her tumbling curls, felt his chest warm as she brought her teasing gaze to his. "Pop quiz. Which one of us has dealt with a toothache, a birthday party, and two scraped knees in the same afternoon? The toothache wasn't Fancy's—and the girl's mother didn't stay for the party."

"Which birthday?"

"Last year, when Fancy turned five."

"All right, you win again. You've experienced chaos, the sort I'm still waiting to enjoy." She paused, a question dancing across her features. Evidently, she wasn't sure of the reception her curiosity would receive. He waggled his brows, urging her on, and she quietly said, "I know you're crazy about Fancy, but do you ever regret becoming a parent before your life was settled?"

The answer came easily. "No regrets," he said. "There's nothing better than knowing you mean everything to a child. You get to carry around their love even when you screw up and don't deserve it, even when you're stumbling to catch up as they vault through each stage of development. I've made so many dopey mistakes while parenting Fancy, but you know what? Kids don't keep score. As long as you protect them, encourage them, and keep the love coming, they never stop believing in you."

Straightening in her chair, she looked at him fully. "You do believe in family." Something shifted in her eyes.

"Family *is* everything. Don't you agree?"

"I do."

"All family," she clarified, "not just parents. I never had the benefit of aunts or uncles—my parents were only children too. I have dim memories of my paternal grandmother, not many. She died before I started school."

"Sure," he agreed slowly, unable to get a fix on what was upsetting her. "Kids benefit from the love they receive in an extended family. Look at Fancy. She's had Daniel in her life from the very beginning. My parents too, even if they are in Texas. When they visit, they spend most of their time with the munchkin. I'm grateful she has grandparents."

Doubt creased Jada's brow. Without warning, she rose. She walked to the edge of the deck, lowered her elbows to the wood railing. Confused, he nearly rose to join her.

A change in the air warded him off.

"We're not going into this now," she whispered, and he realized she wasn't talking to him. She was talking to herself, murmuring a vow to the shadows pooling in the yard. A pledge, a promise.

A secret.

One she believed he'd resist hearing. A truth too harsh for him to stomach.

Unmoored, Philip rose on unsteady legs. "Jada." He waited until she turned, her eyes unwilling to meet his. "Talk to me."

"I promised myself I wouldn't."

A bad response. "You promised to hold something back from me?" The sense of foreboding falling across his shoulders seemed darker than the shadows draped across the yard. "Why? Don't you trust me?"

"You don't understand. This isn't about trust. I *will* tell you, once I'm sure."

"Too late. Whatever it is, tell me now." He swallowed. "Please."

The soft plea dissolved the steel in her posture. He waited as she sank against the railing, her shoulders sagging, her hands suddenly alive with agitation, rubbing up and down her thighs as she marshaled her thoughts. She kept her attention planted on her feet, as if waiting for the strength she needed to arrive and carry her through.

"Are you sure?" she whispered.

With harsh, chilling clarity, he understood. He wasn't ready. Not even close.

"I'm positive," he said.

And so, she began.

Chapter 13

"We need to discuss Millicent," Jada said.

"The historian staying at the inn?" She nodded, and Philip added, "I've met her." When she paused to nervously lick her lips, he sat back down.

Leaning against the deck's railing, Jada searched for a safe route into a dangerous conversation. Philip deserved the facts. Unfortunately, there was nothing concrete to offer. Only supposition and theory, and the conviction that she understood the motivation that brought Millicent Earhardt to Sweet Lake. None of which mattered as Jada stiffened against the needling self-doubt.

Hadn't she assured Linnie and Cat that she wouldn't discuss this with Philip? Why delve in before her theories were grounded in fact, before she knew with absolute certainty why Millicent was in town?

Philip lowered his elbows to his knees, the gesture indicating his willingness to hear her out. He clasped his hands.

The outward pose didn't mask his unease, colliding with hers.

"You're giving Millicent baking lessons, right?" He tapped his foot, stopped.

"Several times each week. First thing in the morning, before I begin my normal workday."

"She's nice. She likes to stop by the work site, gauge our progress. We've shared a few words."

"She didn't come to the Wayfair on vacation."

"Why is she here?"

It seemed wise to start with the historian's initial behavior when she arrived. "From the beginning, Millicent asked a lot of questions about me, the past—almost like she was rattling items off a list. Most of all, she seems interested in what happened in my life seven years ago." Pausing, Jada regrouped. She didn't want to leave him confused by the telling. "Philip, I'm sure Millicent is related to your late wife. I can't prove it, not yet. But I'm positive."

The man deserved credit: he didn't rush to disagree. He didn't rise to his feet, to spout an objection. Weighing her words, Philip bowed his head. Somewhere in the darkness enveloping the backyard, an owl hooted.

When his eyes returned to hers, she understood his silence. Never in their long association had he known her to display poor judgment. She was too practical.

He was willing to hear her out.

"I'm also certain I've heard Millicent's name before," Jada said, despising the truth—despising the way the halting, stilted conversation hollowed out his gaze. "I can't remember when Bodi mentioned her. So many years have passed and my memory is hazy. But I'm positive she did. I walked in while they were talking on the phone, or right after they hung up."

"You're sure about this?" he asked, clearly hoping she wasn't.

She nodded. "I asked Bodi who she was talking to . . . or I heard her say Millicent's name *while* they were talking." She crossed her arms, frustrated with her inability to recall the specifics. "I've spent weeks trying to dredge up the exact conversation. I can't. At the time, it didn't seem important. We all knew Bodi hated discussing her life before she came to Sweet Lake."

Philip grunted. "She refused to discuss the past. Believe me, I tried to get her to talk, especially after we were married."

"Like everyone else, I assumed her parents were abusive, and had kicked her out of the house right after she finished high school. Reason enough to avoid the discussion."

"That's pretty much what she implied." His eyes dulled with unease. "Millicent is in her sixties. You're saying she's Bodi's grandmother?"

"Well, step-grandmother. I'm sure she's married to Bodi's grandfather."

Jada paused again, her mind turning. It occurred to her that Millicent never mentioned her husband directly. She offered nebulous threads about her marriage and the therapy sessions her spouse continued to need.

Dismissing the observation, she got back on track. "Millicent's husband—Bodi's grandfather—was seriously injured in a car accident. I have the impression the accident happened around the same time Bodi came to Sweet Lake. He's in a wheelchair. I believe Millicent came to Sweet Lake alone because it's difficult for him to travel."

"Assuming I buy any of this—where are Bodi's parents?"

"I'm not sure about her father. From what Millicent has described, Bodi's mother is bipolar."

Philip unclasped his hands. "When I found out Bodi was pregnant, and convinced her we should marry"—he fell back in his chair, his face pale—"Frances showed up at my apartment. Penelope was with her. It was pretty late, around ten o'clock."

Neither of the women were night owls. "What did they want?"

"To lend advice about Bodi, since they knew I intended to go through with the marriage. They felt she needed counseling. She'd been in town for several months by then, long enough for most of the Sirens to have witnessed her temper tantrums and mood swings. Frances offered to pay for therapy, if I could get Bodi on board with the idea. I couldn't."

Drawn by the sorrow etching his features, Jada returned to her chair. "They thought Bodi was bipolar," she guessed. Frances understood a great deal about mental health issues. Her sister—Cat's mother-in-law—suffered from depression. Julia D'Angelo lived with Frances, and continued to meet with a therapist to help her through the lows.

Philip said, "Some mental health disorders run in families. If Bodi's mother was bipolar . . ." His voice drifted away.

Quickly, Jada said, "While it's true many traits are inherited, not everyone in a family inherits the gene. You don't have to worry about Fancy. She's a perfectly well-adjusted child. Yes, she bears an uncanny physical resemblance to Bodi, even if she hasn't noticed yet. She will, once she's older and becomes more interested in studying the few photos of Bodi you have. Still, she's got a lot of you in her."

"What about Bodi's grandfather?" he asked, unwilling to accept the reassurance she offered. "Does he have mental health issues?"

"I don't know. Millicent rarely talks about him. She's more interested in gleaning the details of my life. Like she's trying to find traces of Bodi in the story."

"Which makes sense. Bodi never brought up her parents, and I assumed they didn't give a damn about her. That's certainly the impression she gave. She always said she didn't have a family."

"She did."

"Well, maybe she *did* have grandparents who cared about her. And if she talked to them from time to time, she'd mention you. She sure as hell wouldn't mention me. We were practically strangers. I was the latest of her one-night stands, the dumb guy who knocked her up."

"Philip—"

He lifted his hand, silencing her. "Let me get this out."

Anger creased his face. Pain followed. The emotion was stark, tangible, and she winced.

Miraculously, Philip reined in the emotion. "I didn't intend to go into this until we were further in our relationship," he explained, his voice flat. "Heck, I was hoping never to bring it up. I need to explain now. Once I do, you'll understand my decision." He dragged tense fingers through his hair. "At least I hope you will."

On the small table between them, she noticed her forgotten wine. "Go on." She drank the rest.

Following suit, Philip drained his glass. "After I married Bodi, I knew I had to step up my game on the work front." He set the glass down with a bang. "New wife, baby on the way—I had such a crappy work history, I had to turn things around. I took every odd job I could find, worked crazy hours."

"I remember." He wouldn't establish his own landscaping company until after Bodi's death, but Jada recalled how he cobbled together a series of part-time jobs. "Isn't that when you took the delivery job with the trucking company, the one outside Cincinnati?"

"Part-time, second shift. Short hauls between Cincinnati and small towns in southern Ohio. Usually I got home around one a.m. The apartment always looked like a tornado had blown through, and I'd find Bodi conked out. Most days, I'd leave for my next part-time job before she woke up."

"You were avoiding her."

"We were avoiding each other. Jada, we'd only had that one night together. Six weeks later, she was back on my doorstep—pregnant."

The past accosted Philip. The memories carried him back to the day he sent his life into a tailspin.

With brutal clarity, he recalled the rattrap he'd rented on the north end of town after dropping out of college yet again. Unlike Daniel, with his impressive GPA and focus on law school, Philip never settled his feet on solid ground. His parents grew tired of his aimless pursuits, the partying and the dead-end jobs, the sleeping in late and the series of short-term girlfriends. If he'd had anything in common with Bodi— and Philip shuddered at the prospect they'd shared *any* traits—physical attractiveness was their common blessing.

It was also their shared curse.

Throughout his youth, Philip came to rely on his raw sexuality. At an age when other young men cultivated their minds, he learned to maneuver through schoolwork by convincing the smartest girls to help him with his studies. He steered into the emotional center of his girl-friends' lives with his long-limbed, animal grace. There seemed nothing he couldn't get for free if he sauntered into a room with his thousand-watt smile.

Why his parents put up with his behavior for so long was impossible to tell. After his twenty-fourth birthday came and went, they announced he should get his own place. The threat was meant to scare him back into finishing his studies at Ohio State.

A poor gamble. Cocky and proud, he moved out the same week.

He was only living in the apartment for a few months when Bodi found him on the front stoop one evening, working through a bottle of cheap whiskey. The rent was late again. Philip needed groceries, but his car insurance was also due. The search for a second job wasn't going well. Most of the shop owners in town knew about his reputation as a party animal and a slacker on the job. All of which seemed reason enough to stop by the liquor store to drown his worries in booze.

Without seeking permission, Bodi took the whiskey from his fist and sat down beside him.

The anger Philip wore like a coat of armor to hide his self-doubt—misdirected fury at his parents for throwing him out, but also rage at himself for screwing up with frustrating consistency—all the negative emotions sabotaged him. Bodi tipped her head back to take a long swig from the bottle, and heat pooled in his thighs. The soft skin of her neck was riveting. Her lemon-colored hair whipped around her arresting face like a lure. When she caught his blunt appraisal, she lowered the bottle. Holding his gaze like a challenge, she glided the tip of her tongue across her lower lip.

He should've backed off. A more responsible man would've understood how frustration could morph into desire. Then again, a more responsible man wouldn't have dug his life into a hole in the first place.

Another wave of pain rolled through his expression, and Jada pressed her hand to his thigh. "I wish . . ." She stopped, and her heart clenched. That Bodi had never scarred his life? That he'd fathered his daughter from a distance, and had never married?

Reading her expression, he sighed. "Jada, I really meant what I said," he confided. "I never regretted marrying Bodi. If I hadn't talked her into it, she would've had an abortion. She only went through with the pregnancy because I promised to take care of the baby."

The disclosure threatened to halt the steady beat of her heart. Bodi would've aborted Fancy? Despair welled up so quickly, Jada pressed her fist to her mouth.

In response, he took her fingers and held them in a painful grip. "Don't," he said gruffly. Bitter tears gleamed in his eyes. "Let me get this out. If you fall apart, I will too. Let me finish."

She gave a shaky nod.

"One night, on the second-shift job, I was on a route near Sweet Lake. I was really under the weather, running a fever. After I made the delivery, I figured I'd head home, grab an hour of sleep before making the drive back to Cincinnati." He let her hand go, pressed his palms to his knees. "I got into the apartment around ten o'clock that night."

The ragged breath he took made her skin clammy. He looked beaten, a man whose dignity lay in tatters. Jada squeezed her eyes shut.

"Bodi was almost five months pregnant," he continued in a low, monotone voice. "She was really pissed off because the pregnancy was beginning to show—she'd been in one of her dark moods for over a week. I walked in and found her with a guy she'd picked up in a bar somewhere outside town. I'd never seen him before. They were in my bed, going at it, totally into what they were doing. Seeing them . . . I was shell-shocked. Really stunned. I don't know how long I stood in the doorway before they noticed me."

"Philip, I'm so sorry."

"I don't want your pity." He stood suddenly, walked to the railing. Facing the night, he added, "Jada, I'm telling you because you need to understand. Everything Bodi did to me? It's in the past. It's over. Everything I went through was worth it, because I have Fancy. I never forget to thank God for giving her to me. Every morning, first thing. My first prayer of the day. She's healthy, and perfect, and beautiful."

"What *do* you want me to understand?"

Pivoting, he regarded her.

"I buried Fancy's mother a long time ago. She stays buried—her family does too. Lie to Millicent if you must. Pretend you've never heard of Bodi. I forbid you to tell her that Bodi married and had a child." A muscle twitched in his jaw. "I *will* protect my daughter. Fancy will never meet a relative from the wrong side of her family."

Chapter 14

Reaching the lobby at a buoyant stride, Millicent caught the tantalizing scent in the air.

Cinnamon. Warm and sweet, wafting from the kitchen.

Apparently Jada was at work earlier than usual, crafting a new batch of confections for the inn's guests. A good sign, Millicent decided. She smoothed her fingers across the recipe card tucked in the pocket of her sweater. The recipe Penelope had suggested she bake with Jada.

The strategy was simple. As they set about measuring sugar and sifting flour, Millicent would pose the questions she'd been hungering to ask. No longer would she delay.

Expectancy quickened her stride. After more than seven years, she'd finally have answers. The quest would reveal a phone number, or a street address. With the information Jada provided, she'd repair her shattered family at last.

Activity hummed in the spacious kitchen. The chef and his assistant were setting out a bowl of eggs and a platter of breakfast meats. They conversed in low tones in front of the built-in griddle abutting the six-burner stove. Behind them, three waitresses shared coffee and murmured conversation in preparation for their shifts in the Sunshine Room. At the opposite end of the kitchen, away from the others, Jada drizzled icing over a sheet of freshly baked cinnamon buns. Bent over her task, she appeared lost in concentration.

Hope carried Millicent across the room.

⟲

Pausing in her task, Jada padded cautious fingers around the burn at the base of her thumb. On the smooth curve of brown skin, the red welt throbbed as she affixed a bandage. The injury would hinder progress with yeast breads that required kneading and cakes waiting to be iced. Yet another reason why she ought to throw in the towel and return home for more rest.

Dismissing the idea, she spooned the last of the icing onto the buns.

After last night's conversation with Philip, she'd spent bleak hours pacing in her apartment. Sleep came in short snatches. When the first glimmer of daylight crept in beneath the drapes, she gave up all pretense of sleep and grabbed a quick shower.

From behind her, she heard Millicent say, "Oh, I do hope we're allowed to sneak into the cinnamon buns before the waitresses carry them off to the Sunshine Room."

"Of course." Jada reached for a knife, cut two doughy squares. Depositing them on a plate, she asked, "Would you like coffee before we begin? I've just made a new pot."

"That would be lovely. Black, please."

The retired historian looked happy this morning, her green eyes bright and alert. For once, she'd dispensed with the stodgy blazers that were the backbone of her wardrobe. She'd chosen a nubby sweater instead, in a bold azure hue. The typical brown slacks were traded in for white jeans.

Jada returned from the coffee station with a steaming cup. "Look at you. Dressing down today?"

"I'm going for a relaxed look."

"It suits you."

"Does it? I suppose I'm turning over a new leaf." With a disapproving glance, she poked at the bandanna hastily tied around Jada's unkempt curls. "Did you pull an all-nighter? You look like a doctoral student who's been up until the wee hours preparing to defend a dissertation."

"I dressed in a hurry." Frustration and resignation had compelled her to grab clothes at random once she'd decided to start the workday early.

"I'd ask if you were up late tending to a sick child, but you're single."

"I didn't get much sleep," she admitted.

Revealing the contents of last night's discussion was off-limits. The observation brought a sudden twinge of guilt. Even if Millicent did reveal a family connection to Philip's late wife, the conversation would lead nowhere. Philip expected Jada to lie on his behalf. He considered it necessary to protect Fancy.

Was the historian related to Bodi? In her bones, Jada already knew the answer. Which led her back to the dilemma that had kept her awake for most of the night: Which claim took precedence? Philip's desire to bar his late wife's family from any contact with Fancy? Or Millicent's right to lavish affection on a small child, the newest member of her family line?

Learning of Bodi's death would come as a terrible blow. Discovering she'd left behind an engaging, beautiful child would provide a salve for Millicent's heart.

Millicent eyed her with concern. "Why *are* you running on fumes?" she asked pointedly. "Is one of your parents ill?"

"My parents are fine. Dad's a little cranky after a visit to the dentist— par for the course. He hates going to the dentist."

"I don't blame him. The moment a dental drill starts whirring, I get heart palpitations."

"Me too."

"Are you coming down with a bug?"

Calling to the sous-chef, Jada handed off the sheet of cinnamon buns. After the woman walked away, she confided, "I had a difficult conversation with a friend. We don't see eye to eye on a particular subject."

"You'd like to persuade your friend to agree with your point of view?"

"It's not possible."

"With enough perseverance, anything is possible. People become adamant out of fear. The more they're frightened, the more they stick to their guns. You're convinced your position is the correct one?"

Receiving advice from the woman who was the source of the quarrel seemed a ridiculous irony. "I'm sure it is," Jada murmured, touched by Millicent's eagerness to help.

"Well, then." An air of authority lifted her chin. It was easy then to glimpse her as she'd once been, a professor holding court in front of a classroom of students, generously imparting her wisdom to the next generation. "Use calm logic to state your case. Don't get emotional. People rush to fear and hate, or other low emotions, in an instinctual way. Elevate the debate by stating the facts dispassionately. Once you've stated your case, allow your friend time to consider the merits of your argument."

"I'll try," Jada promised, although she didn't hold out much hope.

Philip wouldn't revise his opinion. The scars from his marriage ran too deep.

"I'm rooting for you." Dismissing the subject, Millicent gave her another thorough—and thoroughly kind—appraisal. "Young lady, you do look exhausted. Should we reschedule?"

The suggestion was tempting. Without a baking lesson hampering the morning schedule, there was a chance of finishing in the kitchen soon. She still had the dress fitting with Cat at eleven this morning, and, later in the afternoon, Penelope and Norah expected her to stop by Penelope's house. They'd finished sewing the flower girl dress. Today

Fancy would receive a last fitting to adjust the hem. Linnie was also going over.

Somewhere in between all the tasks that would occupy her day, Jada had hoped for a few minutes of downtime in her office. Dozing behind her desk held a strong allure—but it was a fantasy she quickly dismissed.

A fizzy atmosphere snapped around Millicent. Already she'd polished off the two cinnamon buns like an antsy child itching to race outside to play. The baking lesson, which provided her with ample time to sift through Jada's past, seemed the highlight of her day. It was cruel to steal the time away from her.

"Don't you have a recipe you'd like to prepare, something one of the Sirens gave you?" Jada asked. There was a good chance the Sirens had divined the historian's amateur baking skills and offered a simple recipe.

"You're sure we should proceed?"

"Absolutely."

Millicent produced the recipe card. "I would like to give this a whirl. It's unusual. Do you have fresh rosemary on hand?"

Rosemary.

Jada stilled, then found her voice. "We use the herb in several dishes—standard fare on the Sunshine Room's dinner menu."

"We'll need one tablespoon, finely minced, for the batter."

"May I see the recipe? If this is an Italian yeast bread, I'm afraid we don't have time to make it this morning."

Millicent laughed. "I wouldn't dream of trying a yeast bread. This is much simpler."

She placed the recipe on the counter between them. Jada scanned Penelope's familiar cursive streaming across the card stock. She gave a soft gasp of surprise.

Rosemary Butter Cookies.

During the Christmas season, Penelope made the cookies in large batches. She arranged them in a swirling pattern inside hand-decorated tins she gave out as holiday gifts. Everyone from the staff at the local post office where her son Ozzie worked to many of the longtime employees at the Wayfair, like Mr. Uchida, received a tin. The recipe was a Riddle family tradition, handed down through the generations. Jada had only made the recipe once—on a day she remembered vividly.

Emotion spilled through her as she picked up the card.

"What is it?" Slowly, Millicent set down her coffee mug. "Is something wrong? I can't tell if you're ready to laugh or cry."

Jada blinked away the tears. "I'm surprised, that's all." She gave a watery smile.

"What's surprising about a cookie recipe?"

"Penelope rarely shares the recipe. Frances is the only one of the Sirens with a copy. She lobbied for years before receiving it."

"How intriguing."

"According to Penelope, one of her ancestors brought the recipe from England in the sixteen hundreds, on a ship bound for the colonies. Not on the *Mayflower*, but soon after. On a ship named the *Fortune*, I think."

"Good heavens. I had no idea Penelope gave me something dear to her heart."

"When *did* she give you the recipe?"

"A few days ago. We were in Gift of Garb, chatting."

Jada wasn't aware she'd left the inn's grounds since arriving in late March. "You visited the consignment shop?"

"I was feeling stir-crazy and went for a walk. I didn't stay in her store long. I was preparing to leave when Penelope mentioned there was something she wanted to share with me."

"Consider it an honor." Jada chuckled. "Don't tell the Sirens you have the recipe. They'll hound you for a copy."

"You've never made a batch?"

Pulling herself together, Jada framed an explanation that wouldn't reveal too many details. "I've made the cookies once before, with a teenager who worked at Penelope's shop. She'd hurt Penelope's feelings and wanted to bake an apology gift. I doubt Penelope was aware the girl had copied down the recipe."

Lost in the memory, Jada recalled Bodi shifting from foot to foot beside the counter, in nearly the exact spot where Millicent now stood. Her lemon-colored hair was pulled back in a loose ponytail, her arresting blue eyes pooling with tears—depression swamped her whenever she regretted a wrong she'd inflicted. How she'd carefully shaped each cookie, placing it on the baking sheet with her spine curving beneath the weight of her remorse. A halting litany rose from her lips: Bodi couldn't explain why she kept stealing from the cash register.

As they mixed the cookie dough, Jada had felt a sisterly connection, as if her reassurances could turn Bodi's life around. Working together in the sweet-smelling kitchen, she'd actually believed her affection held the power to heal the psychic wounds Bodi carried.

Millicent was saying, "Penelope mentioned the troubled kids she likes to hire. An admirable pursuit. We need more adults willing to step in whenever a young person strays from the path."

Remembering Bodi's tear-stained face, Jada said, "When we were baking the first batch of cookies for the apology gift . . . the girl admitted she could never decide if she loved or hated rosemary. It *is* an unusual ingredient for cookies."

"I'm not indecisive. I can't wait until the first batch comes out of the oven."

"You like rosemary?"

The question floated between them, unbound. Then a secret agony, blended with the most exquisite joy, crept across Millicent's features.

Beneath the nubby fabric of her sweater, a gold chain glimmered. Lifting the necklace out from its hiding place, Millicent stroked the oval pendant dangling from the chain. Large and heavy, the pendant was composed of thick gold. It was valuable and clearly cherished.

She held the pendant out for Jada's inspection. Drawing close, Jada studied the fine detail.

Stamped into the gold was a familiar image. A sprig of rosemary, the spiky leaves etched with impressive skill. The herb Bodi, less than a year before her death, wasn't sure if she loved or despised. The same rich green herb Penelope tucked inside a sachet, as if to provide Jada with a talisman to resolve a burden from the past.

Astonishment swept through Jada. "I don't need to guess your favorite herb." She chuckled.

"No, you don't." Reverently, Millicent caressed the grooves etched into the gold. She returned the pendant to its hiding place. "I love rosemary."

Devotion softened the sweet declaration. It hinted at a deeper meaning than mere enjoyment of a pungent herb used in savory dishes—or the odd cookie recipe. But the historian did not elaborate. Instead, she picked up the recipe to review the ingredient list.

Following her cue, Jada collected everything they needed, including a handful of fresh rosemary and a pound of butter. For several minutes, they worked in companionable silence. When the timer dinged, announcing the first batch was ready, Millicent spoke again.

"Jada, I want to tell you something." A stark note colored the words. "And ask something as well."

"All right."

"I lost someone like the teenagers Penelope works so hard to help. A young woman, barely out of high school. She ran away. I loved her very much. I've spent years following a wretched number of false leads. I still haven't found her."

With jerky movements, Jada reached for the spatula. "When did she run away?" A sickening wave of anxiety rolled through her. She already knew the answer.

"A little over seven years ago."

Millicent hesitated, her eyes skittering across Jada's face. She appeared to be waiting for Jada to pick up the story.

When Jada remained quiet, the historian continued in a nervous rush. "At first, she'd pick up if I left a dozen messages on her cell phone. Our conversations never lasted long, but I got the impression she moved from one city to another—at first. She had enough money to last a week or two. How she managed afterward, I have no idea."

So Bodi was originally from Chicago. Had her grandfather and Millicent cared for her? Were Bodi's parents totally out of the picture? Struggling beneath the questions swirling through her, Jada walked to the oven. Numbly, she removed the first sheet of cookies.

When it became obvious her voice had deserted her, Millicent added, "Two months after she left Chicago, she cut off contact. Afterward, I began hiring detectives to search for her whereabouts. There were years when I suspended the search, after growing tired of the disappointment. Then I'd start again."

The scents of butter and sugar perfumed the air. The cookies slid off the sheet easily. But the slight tremor in Jada's knees was traveling swiftly past her ribcage and into her arms. A cookie slid off the spatula. It broke in pieces at her feet.

She'd begun to pick up the pieces when Millicent took her hand firmly. Their eyes met.

"I hired the latest detective in February," the historian continued. "He found several news items about the Wayfair. I doubt I would have stumbled across this place otherwise—but everything fits. She didn't leave many clues once she broke off contact, nothing specific about where she'd gone. She *did* mention landing in a small Midwestern town. She struck up a friendship with a young woman who worked at a country inn. She wouldn't share the name of the town." The conversation was affecting Millicent too, and she planted a steadying hand on the counter before adding, "Jada, her name was Bodi Wagner. Bodi Elizabeth Wagner. Do you know her?"

Pausing, she waited for Jada to fill in the rest. On the other side of the center island, a waiter hummed quietly. He filled a row of glasses with orange juice.

Dizzy, Jada couldn't draw a breath.

Frustration welled up on Millicent's face. "The woman Bodi met at the country inn—she was African American. A pastry chef named Jada, in her twenties at the time. I never learned her surname. Bodi wouldn't reveal it." She cut off, gulped down air.

A perilous silence descended between them. A waitress swept into the room with a handful of breakfast orders. Bacon sizzled on the grill as the cook took the orders from her fist.

Millicent's face turned stony. "I believe you know the rest." She clasped Jada's wrist. "And I'm begging you. Will you please tell me what you know?"

Chapter 15

"It's okay, Norah. Jada will help me."

Taking care not to prick her fingers on stray needles protruding out of the cloth, Fancy balanced the pincushion on her palms. With dainty steps, she moved past the sewing machine and stacks of fabric dominating one end of Penelope's living room. The dress swished appealingly as she approached. From the kitchen, the rattle of plates announced that Penelope and Linnie were nearly finished preparing dinner.

Setting her iced tea aside, Jada sat on the floor to complete the task of pinning the two-tier hem. Despite her sorrow over the encounter with Millicent that morning, she managed to put on a cheery front. A necessary precaution. Like most children, Fancy was finely tuned to the emotions of the adults around her.

Jada tacked a smile on her lips as she carefully pinned the hem. The bottom layer of purple satin fell in a bell-shaped pattern to Fancy's ankles. Stiff crinoline underneath gave volume. Over the satin, Norah had sewn a layer of shimmering tulle in a scalloped design. The bodice of pale taupe and an oversize bow in back provided elegant touches. The final design was a gown befitting a princess.

Jada sent the Siren an appreciative glance. "Norah, you've outdone yourself. I had no idea you were such a talented seamstress. After you quit walking the New York runways, why didn't you pursue a career in fashion design?"

From the kitchen, Linnie shouted, "I've been wondering the same thing. If someone had let me in on the secret, I would've asked Norah to design my wedding gown."

"A bridal gown is more than I can handle," Norah called back to Linnie. Settling on the couch, she told Jada, "I didn't pursue a career because my first husband swept me off my feet. Incredible timing—he waltzed into my life right after I quit modeling."

"He didn't want you to work?"

"Doubtful he would've cared either way. He was in international banking. We spent much of our time jetting to Europe and Asia."

"I wasn't aware you've traveled the world." Jada was glad for an uplifting stroll through Norah's fascinating past. A better choice than silently ruing the way she'd let Millicent down. "How did you end up in Sweet Lake?"

"Husband number four. He wanted to leave the rat race behind and retire in the country."

Fancy wrinkled her nose. "You sure like a lot of boys." At the tender age of six, she made no attempt to hide her disapproval.

Norah waved off the censure. "One day soon you'll revise your opinion regarding boys. When you do, I shall remind you of a time when you found them all despicable—except your father and Uncle Daniel. You will not be amused when I remind you."

"I hate boys."

"A passing phase. One day, you'll find a boy you can't live without."

Lifting her shoulders to her ears, Fancy channeled her singsong voice. "I don't think so."

Grinning, Jada instructed her to hold still. She started pinning up the hem for the satin layer. "We still have to discuss your shoes for the wedding," she reminded Fancy. "We can't wait forever."

"Why can't I wear my purple sandals? I love them."

"Linnie bought three new pairs of shoes for you to choose from. Once you decide, she'll return the others to the store." The taupe ballerina slippers were Jada's favorite, but she knew not to interfere with a big-girl decision. "You promised to pick shoes this week. Forget about the sandals, and anything else from your dress-up wardrobe. You must pick one of the pairs of new shoes for the wedding."

On a sigh, the child nodded. "Okay."

The ready agreement caught Jada off guard. Unsure if she'd heard right, she continued pinning up the hem.

As she worked, Fancy toyed with the tight curls tumbling across Jada's forehead. Delicate fingers trailed across her crown with the curiosity of a blind man learning braille. Whenever they were together, the child found ways to make a physical connection.

"Which shoes do you like best?" Fancy asked her.

"I was about to ask you the same question."

"You first."

The invitation to lend an opinion was heartwarming. Eager to comply, Jada smoothed her palm across the soft bodice of the dress. The bodice would soon receive added glam once the Sirens hand-sewed Chanel faux jewels to the fabric.

"I love the taupe slippers. They're a perfect match for the top part of your dress. And they're elegant." Prepared to be shot down by an independent little girl, she added, "The pink shoes are nice too, even though they're more casual. So are the silver pumps, but I'm worried about you walking around in heels—even teeny-tiny heels."

"I don't like the silver ones," Fancy confided. "I like the color pink. I like it a lot."

"I know you do, girlfriend."

On the couch, Norah swirled impatient fingers through the air. "May the angels equip us all with survival skills when Fancy prepares for her first high school prom. Brain surgery is easier than getting her to settle on an outfit. Jada, I'll give you points for patience. Get the child to decide, and I'll spring for the champagne—and help you drink it."

"What's champagne?" Fancy asked her.

"The perfect reward for women who've spent too much time kow-towing to an obstinate first grader."

"What's obstinate?"

"You, my dear. And don't ask for the definition of kowtow—I'm not a dictionary." From the end table, Norah snatched up a magazine to fan away her agitation. The attempt didn't appear successful. "If not for Jada's patience with you, most of the Sirens would've pulled out their hair by now. I know I would have."

The remark put the light of battle in Fancy's gaze. "Jada's patient because she loves me." She gave Jada's bent head a few benevolent pats, as if she'd located her favorite puppy in the pet store. Then she announced, "I've decided, Jada. I'll wear the shoes you like."

"You will?"

"Yep."

"No games, kiddo. You're absolutely sure?"

"Yes, yes, yes."

Careful to hide her delight, Jada finished pinning the satin. She began working on the shimmering tulle. "Hey, I have an idea. Why don't we curl your hair for Linnie's big day, and pull some of it back from your face?" If Fancy was experiencing the first pliable mood of her young life, it seemed a waste not to play it to greater advantage. "I'll bet Norah will sew a smaller bow to match the one on the back of your dress. You can wear it in your hair."

Tossing down the magazine, Norah clapped her hands. "A splendid idea! A matching bow in her hair will be perfect. Fancy, would you like to visit the beauty salon on the morning of the wedding? You can go with Jada, Linnie, and Cat. They've already scheduled their appointments."

The suggestion sent Fancy's attention back to Jada. "Can we put on our dresses at my house after the salon? Let's get ready with Daddy."

The ceremony was scheduled to begin at one o'clock, on the new patio behind the inn's ballroom. Jada had planned to dress at Cat's new home on Highland Avenue. They'd have ample room to help Linnie with her gown and makeup.

"Why don't I take you back with me to Cat's house?" She finished pinning the tulle layer, and helped Fancy step out of the dress. "I'm sure your daddy won't mind. He can meet us at the Wayfair."

"I have to dress up at home. My babies want to watch."

On the day of the wedding, there wouldn't be time to drag all of Fancy's baby dolls and stuffed animals across town. "They'll understand if you get ready at Cat's house. We'll take a picture. You can show it to them later."

"But I *promised* them. Why can't we get ready at my house?"

"Sweetie, I'm the maid of honor." Jada reached for the child's play clothes, helped her shrug the T-shirt over her head. "It's my job to help Linnie on her wedding day."

"Why isn't it your job to help me and Daddy? We need you too."

Appearing in the doorway, Philip said, "Fancy, she's given you an answer. Stop badgering her."

Padding her hand beneath the coffee table, Jada located his daughter's tennis shoes. She'd assumed Philip wasn't joining them for the light dinner. In a best-case scenario, she'd hoped to leave before he arrived to collect Fancy. They hadn't spoken since last night. Throughout the day, Philip and his men had completed the installation of the sandstone for the patio, and then began planting boxwood around the perimeter. Given the demands of his schedule, she'd had no trouble avoiding him.

With an indecisive step, he started toward her. The cool glance she sent brought him to a halt.

"I'm early," he told her.

"By an hour." Rising from the floor, Jada plunked into a chair.

"Should I come back later?"

"Maybe you should."

Hurt sifted through his features. "You're asking me to leave?"

The pointed question threw all eyes on her. Pinpricks of embarrassment tingled across her face.

She guided Fancy into her lap. "Philip, I'm not in charge of your schedule," she said. "Do whatever you like."

"Fine. I'm going."

"Okay."

Planting his feet, he crossed his arms. "I have a better idea." He leaned against the doorjamb. "Why don't we take a walk?"

A wary silence thickened the air. Norah, frowning at the interchange, reached for the magazine. She resumed fanning herself, as if her exertions were capable of warming the chilly atmosphere.

From the kitchen, Linnie shouted, "Philip, are you joining us for dinner? We're having sandwiches and fruit salad."

"No, thanks."

"We have more than enough food."

"I'll pass, Linnie," he shouted. Then he frowned at Jada, who was guiding his daughter's right foot into the tennis shoe and knotting the strings.

"Too tight!" Fancy protested. She fumbled with the strings, loosening them. Satisfied, she pointed her left foot, allowing Jada to slide the shoe on.

Penelope appeared in the doorway. "Philip, stay for dinner. You've been working all day, and—oh!" She pressed a hand to her generous bosom. "What's going on in here? The vibrations are all wrong."

Fancy, predictably charmed by Penelope's mystical leanings, hopped down from Jada's lap. Scrunching up her face, she did her best to channel adult distaste. "The room felt happy before Daddy came in," she informed the quivering Siren. Then she aimed an accusing finger at Jada. "She started it."

"She did? What happened?"

"Daddy was being nice. She's acting like he's a rowdy boy." Fancy wagged her finger at Jada. "Mind your manners."

Humiliation brought Jada to her feet. "Fancy, you're imagining things," she said with fading dignity.

Philip gave her a mulish look. "No, she's not."

Slapping down the magazine, Norah regarded Penelope. "Lover's quarrel," Norah told her. "I'd sit and watch the fireworks, but it's been a long day."

"What's a quarrel?" Fancy asked her.

"Come, child." The elegant Siren took her by the hand. "I'll consider it my lucky day that you didn't ask the definition of the other word."

"Can I have chocolate milk with dinner? Penelope always has chocolate milk."

"You may have two glasses if you're good."

Norah and Fancy went out. Penelope scurried to catch up.

They left behind an uncomfortable silence Jada hesitated to break. Debating with Philip over the merits of his stance regarding Millicent was *not* a sensible move. The discussion wasn't proper fare to dish out in Penelope's living room. Philip wasn't aware of the morning's conversation in the kitchen, when the historian confirmed she was searching for Bodi.

Filling him in was not a task Jada wished to undertake.

Chapter 16

There were rules a smart man never broke. Don't leave the toilet seat up. Walk away from the guy downing too many beers at the bar and looking for a brawl. Never insult another man's wife, or his mother.

If a woman is fuming, give her a wide berth. The gentler sex wasn't gentle when their dander was up. If the woman is your girlfriend, pray to God she'll calm down—eventually.

"Can we take a walk?" He motioned toward the door.

"I'm not ready to talk." She hit him with the death-stare.

"C'mon, Jada. We could both use some air."

Thankfully, the suggestion put her in motion. She swept past him. A good deal, since her death-stare was making him jumpy.

It was also making him defensive.

Cutting across the grass, Jada threw him a glance from over her shoulder. She began to say something. Then she checked herself and kept moving.

Catching up, he matched her strides. When she looked away, presumably still unprepared to hash this out, he said, "Listen, I don't want to fight. Couples don't always agree. I'm sorry we have differing viewpoints. Can you at least try to understand why I'm protective about who enters Fancy's life? She's my kid, Jada. I'm trying to be a good father."

"You'd do a better job if you kept an open mind."

"About Millicent?"

"Yes, Philip. You've only spoken with her a few times. I've had the opportunity to get to know her. She doesn't pose a threat to Fancy."

"Can we go into this once we're sure of her motives?" A delaying tactic wasn't admirable, but he couldn't think of a better way to defuse the situation.

The suggestion brought Jada to a halt. "I *am* sure. She asked me this morning. I spent the rest of the day hiding out in my office, making sure I didn't run into her again. If you're interested, I feel terrible about lying to her. She deserves better."

Fear rolled through him, chilling his skin. "What did she ask you?"

"If Bodi came to Sweet Lake."

"Then she *is* Bodi's grandmother?" At some level, he'd managed to convince himself that Jada's theories were ludicrous. A foolish gambit.

"I shut down the conversation before Millicent had a chance to explain. She didn't marry until middle age. Best guess, she fell in love with Bodi's grandfather while they were both teaching at the University of Chicago."

The fear crawling over him brought out his fighting spirits. "I'm lost here," he admitted, unable to temper the harshness in his voice. "How did you 'shut down' the conversation?"

"By faking a problem in the laundry requiring my immediate attention. I said I'd never heard of Bodi Wagner, and just left her standing there in the kitchen, devastated." Jada's dark eyes flashed. "What does it matter? Whoever she was to Bodi, she really cares about finding her. Millicent has been hiring detectives since Bodi ran away from Chicago. She's been looking for a baker named Jada ever since."

"Slow down. Millicent hired a PI to look for you?"

The fire went out of Jada's eyes so quickly, his heart seized. "They didn't have much else to go on," she said in a hollow voice. "Bodi did tell Millicent about a black woman she'd become friends with. Then the calls stopped."

In turmoil, Jada wound her arms around her waist. Regrets that were never hers to carry bent her spine with the weight of her despair. She looked like a woman preparing to walk into gale-force winds.

He wanted to pull her close but knew better. What right did he have to offer comfort, when his actions were the reason for her sorrow?

"Jada, how long were they in contact after Bodi left Chicago?"

"A month or two, I guess. Then Bodi stopped picking up Millicent's calls."

Sick-hearted, Philip stared at his feet. A matter of a few short weeks. A month, maybe two. Long enough for Bodi to run out of money and to try her hand at purse-snatching in Columbus—and to receive Penelope's invitation to come back with her to Sweet Lake.

Long enough for a troubled eighteen-year-old to show up on his doorstep and change the trajectory of her life. And his.

Did Bodi stop calling home once she became pregnant? Numbly, Philip scraped the hair from his brow. Was she too embarrassed to tell her grandmother or great-aunt—or whoever Millicent *was* to her—she'd become a pregnant runaway? It was feasible Bodi took off from Chicago on a whim. He bore full responsibility for barring her from returning to the life she'd known.

A life that, on the surface, seemed nothing like the abusive past she'd described during their short marriage. There were too many pieces to the puzzle. None of them fit.

"I don't get it. Millicent is a wealthy, retired college prof. Who abused Bodi?" He kicked a stone from the sidewalk, frustrated by his inability to figure it out. "She *was* abused—I'm sure of it. I saw the proof with my own eyes. You remember, right?"

It came as a relief when doubt creased Jada's brow. "Yeah," she murmured. "I remember. Something isn't right. The cut on Bodi's face when she first got to town, and the bruises. Someone had beaten her."

"Exactly what she implied when I tried to get the details from her." He recalled the welts marring Bodi's angelic face, the purpling bruises scattered across her left shoulder. Other bruises on her ribcage.

Jada asked, "Did Bodi lie to us?"

"Hard to tell, but it's not like she could fake the abuse. We saw the damage for ourselves." Yet another reason not to get his six-year-old daughter mixed up in this. Millicent was a decent woman. Everything about her indicated a stable personality. But what of Bodi's parents? If he gave Millicent permission to become part of Fancy's life, how to keep the less-stable elements at bay?

A conclusion that must've become transparent. Jada lowered her arms listlessly to her sides.

"Well, I did what you asked," she told him. "I pretended I'd never heard of Bodi Wagner. It just about broke Millicent. All those years searching, and for what?" She regarded the shadows lengthening across the street. "I'll never forgive myself for what I've done to her."

"Jada, I'm sorry. I never meant to put you in a bind. I just can't . . ."

The words drifted into a miserable silence. Philip refused to bend. Doing so would put Fancy at risk. It would bring her into contact with the people who'd beaten her mother, who'd given Bodi ample reason to run away from Chicago.

Protecting his daughter came at a terrible cost. He'd lose the only woman he'd ever loved. By forcing Jada into an untenable position, he'd lose her.

Turning away, she said, "Fancy will be wondering where you are. We should get back."

~♥~

After they returned to Penelope's house, Jada insisted Philip go in for dinner. She had no intention of joining him. The hurt feelings colliding between them were nearly tangible and might upset Fancy.

The others were already seated at the table, digging into their sandwiches as the conversation swirled. On the fly, Jada invented a problem at the inn demanding her attention.

The falsehood brought her favorite six-year-old scampering across the kitchen. "You *can't* go," Fancy implored her. Leaning into Jada's thighs, she faked a crestfallen expression that didn't reach her eyes. With all the attention being lavished on her, not to mention the promise of new dress-up clothes after Norah and Penelope completed the flower girl dress, Fancy remained in an ebullient mood.

"I'll see you tomorrow," Jada promised her. She regarded Linnie. "Why don't we take Fancy out for ice cream after you return the shoes to the store in Fairfield? Your amazing flower girl has made a selection. We should celebrate."

Linnie nearly spit out a bite of chicken salad. "She did? She made a decision?"

"She's going with the taupe ballerina slippers."

Fancy bounced on the balls of her feet. "Because Jada likes them."

"I do too. The taupe slippers are my favorite!" Linnie fell back in her chair with a sigh. "Another item off my list. We *will* celebrate. I'll spring for the ice cream."

Jada looked at Philip, lingering by the counter. "Mind if I pick Fancy up from school tomorrow? I'll bring her home at dinnertime."

The subtext of the query sent a pained expression through his gaze: a disagreement between adults shouldn't affect a child. Nothing they'd discussed regarding Millicent would put Jada's affection for his daughter at risk.

"Sounds great," he murmured.

Giving Fancy one last kiss, she hurried to her car.

The prospect of spending the night alone held no appeal. Darkness had fallen across the sleepy town, and Jada drove slowly through Sweet Lake Circle. Out of habit, she called to check in with her parents. They were happily watching the nightly news and planned an early bedtime.

Hanging up, she drove up the hill leading away from town and to the Wayfair. She felt out of sorts, too wound up for anything but a good hour shuffling through paperwork.

The warm April night had lured many of the guests out to the rocking chairs on the veranda. Two boys were playing checkers on the floor by the stairwell, their heads bent with concentration. Nervously, Jada scanned the adults lingering nearby. Millicent spent some nights outdoors, chatting with the other guests.

But not tonight.

At the front desk, the new hire Darrisha Ray was taking over for Mr. Uchida. He stepped away from the desk as Jada entered.

"Jada, do you have a moment?" With a frown, he led her to a corner of the lobby.

"What is it?" she asked.

"Mrs. Earhardt." A couple walked past, and he lowered his voice. "She canceled the remainder of her reservation. I've checked with the staff, and no one is sure why. Did something happen to upset her?"

"Yes, actually." Jada's stomach lurched. "Don't worry. I'll take care of it."

She started toward the south wing's stairwell with no idea how to remedy the situation. Apologize to Millicent? For a fleeting second, she considered running afoul of Philip's decision and telling the historian everything. Scatter the truth at Millicent's feet like priceless jewels she craved. Jada would admit she'd lied. Find the courage to explain about Bodi's death. Then she'd salvage Millicent's broken heart by explaining about the child Bodi had left behind.

"Jada, hold on."

As she pivoted to regard him, Mr. Uchida lifted his palms with regret. "You're too late," he said. "She's already checked out."

Chapter 17

"Who's ready for a refill?" Silvia raised a pitcher of her famous mojitos.

Along with fourteen other members of the Sweet Lake Sirens, she'd converged upon Frances's beautifully appointed colonial to wrap gifts for the bridal shower. From the kitchen, spurts of giddy conversation drifted in as several of the women riffled through wrapping paper and ribbons at the kitchen table. In the large, rectangular living room, a small group sat at a card table at the opposite end of the wet bar, surrounded by yet more ribbons and bows and decorative rolls of paper.

Under normal circumstances, Jada would question the timing for the shower—one short week before the wedding. In this case, she concluded the Sirens had used brilliant timing in convincing Linnie to allow them to host the shower on the Saturday before her wedding day. With only seven days between the events, the bride-to-be was kept busy with last-minute preparations. There was no time left over to nurse her usual second thoughts.

Although they weren't Sirens, Jada and Cat were both pleased to attend the impromptu party.

Cat slid her glass toward her mother. "Mami, I'll take a refill." With misgiving, she appraised Jada seated on the barstool beside hers. "Drink up. You look like you need it."

Feeling out of sorts, Jada swiveled the barstool from side to side. "I'm not in the mood to drink."

Over the last days, most of the time she'd felt like crying. For Linnie's sake, she'd donned a mask of cheer as they worked out the last-minute details for the ceremony and Linnie waxed rhapsodic about her imminent marriage. Despite all her fears and worries, she was looking forward to her new life with Daniel.

Cat asked, "Are you still dodging Philip?"

"It's more accurate to say I'm keeping my distance."

"Meaning you're no longer enjoying cozy evenings with him and Fancy?"

"No cozy dinners. I *have* been seeing Fancy, mostly when she's done with school for the day."

"Is it a good strategy to avoid Philip?" A hint of censure came across in the remark.

Several of the Sirens approached the bar, and Jada leaned close for privacy. "I don't know what to do," she admitted. "I understand his position, but I'm angry—at him, but mostly at myself. During her stay at the Wayfair, Millicent showed me nothing but kindness. I rewarded her by lying."

Following her cue, Cat dropped her voice to a whisper. "Stop beating yourself up. It wasn't your call. What were you supposed to do?"

"Gosh, I don't know," she replied acidly. "Tell the truth? Millicent checked out of the Wayfair without even saying goodbye. Imagine how she felt. All her hopes dashed, after years of searching for Bodi. Her heart broken because I didn't have the guts to play the honesty card."

"You didn't have a choice."

"We always have a choice about how we treat people."

"Jada, be fair. Philip doesn't want anyone from Bodi's family involved with Fancy. Plain and simple. Do you blame him?"

Sorrow tightened Jada's throat. "I don't blame him," she replied, "but he's wrong."

"Don't judge him too harshly. He's doing what he believes is best to protect Fancy." Cat pushed the mojito toward her. She flicked the tight curls spilling across Jada's forehead. "You've been blue for days, and we should be celebrating. We'll enjoy watching Linnie open all her shower gifts on Saturday, and we're totally obligated to send out nothing but happy vibes during her wedding week."

"Happy vibes. Got it." Jada gave the thumbs-up, even though she felt absolutely dismal.

Cat gave her a quick hug, then said, "I feel bad too, you know. Millicent seemed like a nice lady. She would've made a wonderful addition to Fancy's life. But you have to respect Philip's wishes."

Murmuring in agreement, Jada took a sip of the lime-infused rum. In the five days since Millicent's departure, she'd tried to square Philip's decision with her own beliefs. An impossibility. It wasn't fair to dismiss one side of the family under any circumstances. An active, extended family gave a child a rich soil in which to flourish. Remove some of those relatives and you sheared off the roots a child needed to thrive. Yet despite her conviction, Jada still wondered: If put in Philip's shoes, would she have reacted differently to Millicent's arrival? Claiming the moral high ground was easy when she didn't have a child to protect.

Even now, she doubted there was a simple way to heal the breach with Philip. If they couldn't agree on a fundamental issue like family, what chance did their relationship have long-term?

After Silvia refilled glasses, she produced a second pitcher of mojitos from the small refrigerator beneath the bar. Setting it down, she cast an attentive glance toward her daughter.

"What are you girls whispering about?" she asked Cat.

"Jada's problems with Philip," Cat swiftly supplied. Jada whacked her on the arm, although she wasn't sure why she bothered. Cat shared just about everything with her mother.

When curiosity brought Silvia nearer, Jada held up her hand. "Silvia, please. I don't want to go into it."

"And why not? My daughter isn't your only friend here."

"I still don't want to talk about it."

"There's no gain in brooding."

"There's no loss either. My life, my problems." Jada shot a desperate glance at the card table, still crowded with Sirens. "Are they nearly finished? I have to wrap my shower gifts." Bent on escape, she got off the barstool.

Surprise froze her like a burglar caught in the act.

Three of the Sirens were standing behind her. Frances, Penelope, and Ruth formed a wall of matronly concern.

At least Frances and Penelope looked soft-eyed and sympathetic—they'd evidently listened in on a private conversation. Ruth, who'd moved up from mojitos to straight whiskey, simmered with ill-concealed impatience. She tossed back her shot of Jack Daniel's.

"I've had enough." Her white braids danced as she whirled around. She planted her fiery regard on Frances, then Silvia. "You're the co-leaders of our merry bunch. Call a vote immediately."

Frances pressed a palm to her brow. "This *has* gone too far."

"Get a grip, Frances. I'm within my rights to call for a vote."

"Ruth, please. The night is young. Let's discuss this after Jada and Cat depart."

Cat raised her glass. "We're not going anywhere." There wasn't much she enjoyed more than the random altercation between the Sirens. With glee, she elbowed Jada. "We're staying, right?"

In a jumpy arc, Jada bounced her attention across the room. "Should we leave?" A strange tension bloomed in the air. Heading for the hills didn't strike her as a bad idea.

Ruth stomped her foot. "Jada, don't move a muscle. Can't you see I'm rescuing you from a fine pickle? You can thank me later."

"Thank you—for what?"

Jada's query sank beneath the toxic atmosphere.

Squaring her shoulders, Ruth turned to the room at large. "Is everyone listening?" She looked pointedly at Tilda, slurping her third mojito at the card table. "If you're already drunk, I expect you to listen anyway."

She paused dramatically, her wrinkles collapsing in an expression of determination. "I hereby invoke the Virtues of Kindness clause."

Gasps rose across the room. Tilda drained her glass, and Penelope whimpered. Silvia pounded the wet bar's counter. She looked ready to take the granite tiles outside and give them a good thrashing.

Cat's eyes widened.

Leaning toward her, Jada asked, "What's Ruth talking about?"

At the question, Silvia thumped the counter again.

Then she shook off her ire long enough to pat her daughter's hand. "Close your mouth, or you'll catch flies."

Cat's jaw snapped shut. "Yes, Mami."

Silvia placed her steely regard on Jada. "Cat doesn't know much about the clause or the contract," she said. "And don't ask for the details—I can't reveal our secrets. The Siren code is kept under wraps, known only to our comrades. Every woman signs the contract when she's inducted into the group. She's then sworn to secrecy." With emphasis, she added, "I will say The Virtues of Kindness proviso is an important section of our contract. It is only invoked in dire circumstances."

"And I'm invoking it," Ruth growled. Swinging around the side of the bar, she took down the bottle of whiskey. "I'm all for keeping our meddling to a minimum. It's best to let events take their natural course, but this here is a dire situation. I'm not spending another decade watching Philip pine away for Little Miss Ethical because the rest of you fools don't know when it's time to take action."

Nervously, Jada plucked at her head. "Wait. You're talking about *me*?"

Ruth bared her false teeth. "What? You're going to stand there and deny you're Miss Goody Two-shoes?"

"Hey!"

"Girl, if you ever get out of your own way and get hitched, don't make Philip crazy with your ethics. Who wants to crawl into bed with King Solomon every night? And stop playing with your 'fro. Keep fussing with your curls, and I'll be calling you Jimi Hendrix until hell freezes. I swear I won't let up either."

Jada dropped her twitchy fingers to her side.

Satisfied, Ruth turned to the others. She raised an angry fist. "Let's vote!"

The hearty call to action brought women streaming in from the kitchen. On the couch, Norah and several others shifted nervously. Jada was still trying to make sense of the proceedings when she realized all eyes were on Penelope, quivering silently beside Frances and wringing her hands. And Penelope?

Her attention was stuck like glue on Jada.

Their gazes volleyed back and forth, one confused and one contrite, as the room quieted. The only sound was the clink of the whiskey bottle as it met the rim of Ruth's shot glass.

As the silence lengthened, the skin on Penelope's cheeks grew splotchy. She made a valiant attempt to form words. The helpless contorting of her lips was heartbreaking to behold. She appeared beyond speech, too upset for logical thought. Her bosom quivering, she took unsteady steps toward Jada.

"I should've told you right away." She pushed her eyeglasses up her perspiring nose. "I know that now. I didn't know at the time. I thought it was better to let events unfold on their own."

Ruth threw back her shot. Then she belched. "Hells bells, Penelope. Stop beating around the bush. Tell her. If you don't, then we *are* voting."

A sensation of vertigo caught Jada unawares. Grappling with the sensation, she tried to steady herself. Whatever injury Penelope believed she'd caused, it was major. A bizarre conclusion, all things considered. She went to extreme lengths never to cause harm.

"It's okay, Penelope," Jada murmured in the soothing tone she used whenever Fancy was hurt or frightened. A mother's tone, replete with love and forgiveness. She drew Penelope into a reassuring hug. They clung together for a moment, rocking. When the Siren appeared calmer, Jada asked, "What do you need to tell me?"

From where she'd pressed her face to Jada's shoulder, the Siren muffled, "Millicent's necklace, the one with the image of rosemary etched into the pendant? The minute she showed it to me, I knew."

"She mentioned you liked the necklace during one of our baking lessons."

Withdrawing from the embrace, Penelope found an inner reserve of strength. "Jada, you don't understand," she said slowly. "When Millicent showed me the necklace, I *knew*. I made the connection."

"What connection?"

"Remember when Bodi first came to Sweet Lake, and moved into my house? She had a necklace just like Millicent's."

Jada stared at her, wide-eyed. "You're sure?" She searched her memory in vain. She couldn't recall Bodi having jewelry remotely like Millicent's valuable gold necklace.

Clearing up the mystery, Penelope said, "Not long after Bodi moved into my spare bedroom, she threw the necklace away. I was changing the sheets in the room and found it in the garbage. Pure gold, with such a lovely pendant. I couldn't imagine why she threw away something so beautiful."

"Did she explain?"

"She wouldn't talk about it." Penelope worked her hands with nervous movements. "After she married Philip, I tried to give it back. She told me to throw the necklace away because she'd decided she hated rosemary."

Adrift, Jada said, "Millicent loves rosemary."

"I know. She told me the day we had tea on the veranda."

Hesitating, Penelope scanned the women behind her. From the Sirens crowding near, someone handed over her purple leather purse. Murmuring thanks, Penelope clicked open the bag. She withdrew a long golden chain. The thick pendant swung gently as she deposited the necklace in Jada's outstretched hand.

"Look on the back of the pendant," she instructed.

Hesitating, Jada thumbed the cool metal. Turning the pendant over, she read the inscription.

To Bodi. With love, M

Her breath caught in her throat. The inscription was personal, heartfelt—more proof Millicent had been central to Bodi's life. She'd cared enough to give the teenager a necklace worth thousands.

Penelope continued, "That first weekend, when the Sirens invited Millicent to join us for tea? Once I saw the necklace, I remembered everything I'd forgotten. Bodi, locking herself in my guest bedroom and talking on the phone. Later, all the calls she wouldn't pick up. And the name of the woman calling her—Millicent. I wish I'd remembered the name sooner." She shook her head, clearly annoyed by her faulty memory. "That's when I remembered Millicent was friends with Bodi."

"A friend or a relative?" Jada asked her. "Please try to remember. It's important."

"Aren't friends also relatives?" Penelope replied in her typically enigmatic way. She regarded the other women, listening avidly to the exchange. "Everyone here is part of my family."

Jada sank back onto her barstool. "Why didn't you explain right away? You could've saved me weeks of digging around in the dark. Do you have any idea how much time I've spent trying to sort out Millicent's relationship to Bodi?"

"Oh, I couldn't intervene. You needed to discover the truth for yourself."

The comment brought to mind a benevolent witch and ruby slippers. "I wish you'd clued me in right from the start," Jada said. "If I'd handled things differently with Philip, gone to him with solid proof . . . I don't know. Perhaps he wouldn't have reacted negatively. All I gave him were theories and supposition."

Distress shivered across Penelope's double chins. Beside her, Frances bent her silvered head to whisper in her ear. The words seemed a tonic. Penelope released a sigh of relief.

When she withdrew to the couch, Frances took up the gauntlet. "Now I have a question for you." She rested a gentle hand on Jada's shoulder. "Why have you never spoken of Bodi's death? You've kept the experience bottled up for too long. Those last minutes, when you followed her out in the snowstorm—"

Nausea and sudden anger pulled Jada back to her feet. "Frances, I'm not rehashing the worst mistake of my life."

"Mistake? How can you draw such a wrongheaded conclusion?"

The effort to disagree took more energy than Jada possessed. Naturally, Frances would exonerate her of any wrongdoing. They all did. Self-reproach put bile in Jada's throat.

They were wrong.

Frances lowered her hand, her expression soft. "Child, you must share Bodi's last minutes with us. Don't you understand? You guard the memory jealously. The past won't stop tormenting you until you release the pain into our safekeeping."

A shard of grief pierced Jada. Quick, and without mercy. "You're asking too much of me. I can't share those last minutes. Frances, I can't." The memory threatened to overtake her—the wind howling, and her bellowing, frantic voice reduced to tatters. In a habit long perfected, she willed the memory away.

Cat, the daughter of a Siren, seemed to understand what Jada failed to grasp. Taking Jada's hands, she gently squeezed her fingers. Glancing at Penelope seated on the couch, she said, "You wanted Jada to become friends with Millicent, so they could heal together?"

Penelope nodded. "They both loved Bodi in their own way. I thought once Jada discovered why Millicent was in Sweet Lake, she'd tell her everything. She'd talk about Bodi's death . . . and give Millicent comfort, once she told her about Fancy."

Jada withdrew her icy fingers from Cat's grasp. "I never got the chance," she admitted. "Philip nixed the idea of telling Millicent anything."

Penelope sighed. "You told him too soon. Before events unfolded properly."

Frances's eyes grew sharp. "*Is* she Bodi's grandmother? There's been some debate regarding their relationship."

"I'm not sure, Frances. I never gave Millicent the opportunity to explain."

Penelope said, "It doesn't matter. Millicent cared about Bodi. Nothing else is important."

"She did," Jada agreed. She thought of something else. "Penelope, the sachet you gave me, in March—how did you know to put rosemary inside?"

"Why, every time a Siren dreamt about you, rosemary appeared in the dream."

"Talk about a strange coincidence." Jada had never been entirely sure the dreams weren't an invention by the Sirens—a convenient excuse to meddle in her life. Dismissing the thought, she added, "What *is* the significance? It's strange for anyone to have a strong opinion about a common herb. Why did Bodi hate rosemary, yet Millicent loves it?"

Behind the bar, Silvia drummed her fingers. "Jada, there isn't a Siren in this room who wouldn't like to solve that puzzle."

"Help me out here, little brother. Do you want advice on dealing with Fancy's potential relatives, or patching up your relationship with Jada?"

Seated behind the desk in his office, Daniel Kettering waited patiently. Broad-shouldered, with sandy-brown hair, Daniel was the only legal counsel in a thirty-mile radius. He was also Philip's most trusted friend.

"Both," Philip admitted, pacing a tight circle before the desk.

"Things are still frosty between you and Jada?"

"She's fine when I see her. Polite, if distant. Like we're back in friend territory."

"Then things *have* cooled off."

Philip stopped moving long enough to send his brother a frustrated glance.

"What did you expect?" Smoothly, Daniel stated the facts. "Jada shared her suspicions regarding Mrs. Earhardt. You made it plain you'd have no contact with Bodi's relatives. You gave her no choice but to lie. How did you want Jada to handle the situation when Mrs. Earhardt *did* ask about her acquaintance with Bodi?"

Miserable, Philip resumed pacing. There was no sidestepping the facts. He'd put Jada in an untenable situation. He'd given no thought to how difficult it was for a woman of her caliber to use subterfuge to comply with his wishes. The only consideration? His need to protect Fancy—and his injured pride. Sharing the blistering memory of Bodi's infidelity had scraped his ego raw. Ashamed, he recalled what he'd told Jada.

Lie to Millicent if you must. Pretend you've never heard of Bodi. I forbid you to tell her that Bodi married and had a child.

His heart lurched. "I've really screwed up. I made it clear to Jada she couldn't mention Fancy." He grimaced. "I made her lie to Millicent."

"Not your best move."

"Not even close."

"Are you reconsidering your position?" When his nervous gaze lifted, Daniel added, "Ohio law allows for visitation by grandparents and other extended relatives. For argument's sake, let's assume Mrs. Earhardt is Fancy's great-grandmother. She's within her rights to petition the court for visitation. This doesn't mean a judge won't take into consideration other relevant factors—including your concerns as Fancy's sole surviving parent."

"What about Bodi's parents, wherever they are?" To Philip's mind, they posed the real problem. Just thinking about them washed apprehension through him. "Bodi wasn't in good shape when she came to Sweet Lake. A gash on her forehead, bruises on her shoulders and rib cage—someone had beaten her. She implied it was her parents. Jada will back me up on this. She also had the impression Bodi's parents were abusive."

"Did Bodi tell you directly she'd been abused by her parents?"

Philip searched his memories, an unpleasant task. Thinking about those years left him sick-hearted and queasy. "Not directly. She'd insinuate, mostly. Didn't matter—she knew the conclusion I'd draw." He came to a standstill. "During one of their baking lessons, Millicent told Jada she didn't marry until middle age. She mentioned a stepdaughter with mental health issues. Bipolar disorder."

"The stepdaughter is Bodi's mother?"

"It seems likely, right?"

Daniel chewed this around for a moment. Then he asked, "Where is Bodi's father?"

"I have no idea. I can't even tell you if Bodi's parents are together. Millicent never mentioned the father."

Daniel fell into a contemplative silence to weigh the information in his levelheaded way. As he did, Philip's love for him shook past the worry he harbored about protecting Fancy from unknown elements—from unstable relatives who might possess more than a passing similarity to the mother Fancy had never known. Throughout Philip's life, he'd always relied on his big brother. He couldn't recall a time when Daniel's quiet protection wasn't available to him. The awareness rolled gratitude through him so quickly, his eyes watered.

His brother wouldn't fail him now.

"First off," Daniel said, organizing his thoughts, "I see no reason why the courts won't grant Mrs. Earhardt and her husband visitation. She's a retired college professor and, to all outward appearances, an upstanding woman. For argument's sake, let's assume her husband *is* Bodi's grandfather—and Fancy's direct blood relative. Assuming his daughter, the one with mental health issues, is Bodi's mother, her rights as Fancy's grandmother are well protected." Daniel rubbed his jaw, his expression growing taut. "You need to understand, Philip. Once the courts grant Mrs. Earhardt visitation, they won't be inclined to refuse Fancy's grandmother those same rights. Not even if the woman's mental health struggles are well documented."

"Even if she raised Bodi in an abusive household?"

"Supposition. Where's the proof?"

"Daniel, I *saw* the proof—the gash on Bodi's forehead, the bruises."

"You documented this abuse?"

Philip bristled. "Right. I asked Bodi to hold still while I grabbed my phone and took a picture."

"Calm down. I'm merely asking."

Philip resumed pacing. "You know what she was like. Moody, argumentative—I had enough trouble convincing her that we ought to marry. Hell, she blew up when I broached the subject. She would've gone through with the abortion, you know. She'd already made the appointment when she dropped by my apartment to announce she was pregnant. Like I'd gladly drive her to the clinic to undo the mess we'd made of our lives." He swiped at his eyes. "She never wanted Fancy. She bitched and complained all through the pregnancy."

A fraught period in his life, and the comment stamped pity in Daniel's eyes. No, it wasn't necessary to remind Daniel. On the night when Philip learned of the pregnancy, Daniel stayed up until morning sent ribbons of light beneath the curtains of Philip's apartment, convincing a troubled girl he didn't know to choose marriage. Back then Daniel was nearing his thirties—a level, patient man with an unspoken passion for Linnie Wayfair and the life he hoped they'd one day share. He'd make a good father, the best kind.

During Bodi's arduous, twenty-hour labor, he never left Philip's side. When the nurses swaddled Fancy, red-cheeked and squalling, in a soft pink blanket, Daniel readily took the fragile bundle and stepped away from the bed where Bodi lay in sullen gloom, refusing to look at her child. Rooted in a corner of the hospital room, Philip scrambled to comprehend the radical change sweeping into his life. The onerous responsibilities that lay ahead with an unpredictable wife. A baby to love and protect, and somehow support. The future terrified him.

Daniel gave him a loving glance as he strode into the corridor, humming sweet nothings to the infant cradled to his chest.

In the following months, everything Philip learned about fatherhood came through his brother's gentle example.

Breaking into his thoughts, Daniel said, "Should I contact Mrs. Earhardt? Given the circumstances, I'm sure Linnie will share her number."

"Let me think about it."

"What about Jada? I suggest you find a way to gain her forgiveness. Let this go too long, and it'll only get harder."

"I'm not sure how to patch things up." Philip lifted his head, embarrassed. "I'm sorry to dump all this on you one week before your wedding. Like you need a downer right before getting your life on track."

Daniel grinned. "Get your story straight. My life has always been on track." His eyes softened. "Your life will get there too. Give it time."

An optimistic conclusion, one Philip couldn't imagine. If he found a way to turn things around with Jada, he'd revise his opinion.

Steering the conversation to happier topics, Daniel said, "Linnie wheedled the surprise about the honeymoon out of me."

"Is she still griping about taking time off from work?"

"I'm not listening." Triumph glossed Daniel's features. "She *did* go shopping for beachwear. She also dragged a suitcase down from the attic. A waste of time—several of the Sirens pooled their cash for new luggage. The bridal shower starts at one o'clock tomorrow."

"I know. Penelope is picking up Fancy."

"They invited the munchkin?"

"It's more accurate to say Fancy announced her interest in going." According to Penelope, his daughter had been lobbying for days. Attending a bridal shower with a bunch of women represented another item on Fancy's list of big-girl achievements.

"Why not drop by the inn tomorrow and talk to Jada?" Daniel suggested. "Tell her you're still on the fence about contacting Millicent, but *are* giving the idea serious thought. She may be less frosty once she's aware you're considering bringing Millicent into Fancy's life. And don't forget to apologize to Jada for putting her in a bad situation." He sent a warning glance. "Actually, I'd start with the apology."

The suggestion held merit. "What's your opinion on groveling? Think it'll make Jada budge?"

Daniel chuckled. "Don't worry about groveling—unless you can't get her to thaw."

Chapter 18

A funereal gloom hung over the mansion.

All we're missing are white lilies and matrons in black, Vasily Pruszynski mused, slapping the book shut.

Since Millicent's return from Ohio, Vasily felt like the sole occupant of the grand house. No longer did he confine the studies for his dissertation to his private quarters in the basement. The deserted living room was nearly large enough to land a small aircraft; the neglected library was comparable in length to a bowling lane. If the mansion's unhappy couple chose to avoid each other and the bulk of their luxurious nest, he saw no reason not to branch out. Today he'd given the dining room a whirl, commandeering the mahogany table with dog-eared books, his laptop, and several notepads filled with his indecipherable scrawl.

In the foyer, the housekeeper muttered in Spanish as she yanked her coat on. The broad-faced woman had dusted every room on the first floor, and then spent a good hour in the kitchen dealing with the plates Millicent left heaped in the sink, and the greasy pans crowding the stove. The housekeeper was still rattled by her experience outside the master suite upstairs. Around one o'clock, when she'd foolishly steered the vacuum toward the suite, the foul-tempered occupant had thrown open the door to deliver a verbal lashing that sent the poor woman scurrying to the stairwell.

Outside, the landscapers were finishing up, laying mulch on the sleeping flower beds. They'd surrendered the gardens at the back of the estate after Millicent ran them off.

Pushing away his research, Vasily tapped his pen against his teeth. The idea, stealthy and rewarding, took shape yet again. He'd been mulling it over for days. Was it madness to intervene? Tossing the pen down, he flipped open his laptop.

Navigating to the American Airlines site, he located the flight and punched in the reservations. Satisfied with the bold move, he grabbed his coat and went to find Millicent.

With the last of Chicago's winter gone, the grey scenery was entering the time of year Vasily thought of as "mud season." Slogging across the sodden ground, he yearned for Arizona's purple-streaked sunsets and blistering heat.

At the south end of the garden, Millicent wielded loppers with the ungainly movements of a woman who knew exactly zip about gardening.

He groaned as she swung the loppers to shoulder height and took aim at a sleeping cherry tree. The implement seized a defenseless branch.

"Millicent, those pruners are sharp as knives. Are you trying to draw blood?"

She got the tool into position, sheared through the branch. "Trees don't bleed, you simpleton."

"I was talking about you."

"Go inside, Vasily. I'm blowing off steam. Some people drink when they're upset. I thought I'd garden."

The branch flopped to the ground. On a growl, she swung the loppers back into the tree. Colorful oaths sprang from her lips as the tree fought back, tugging at the implement and nearly pulling her off her feet.

With long strides, Vasily came across the grass. They tussled like energetic schoolboys, and he finally wrenched the loppers away. Fury rolled off her as she craned her neck to glare at him.

He tossed the implement down. "I need to talk to you. Now. Before you hack off your leg or deforest the grounds."

"Then talk."

"It's been five days. You've done nothing but sulk like a great beast with a thorn stuck in its paw. When you're not sniping at me, you're picking fights with the only person who loves you—and I'm *not* referring to myself." Leaning forward, he assessed the mud spattered across her brow. A glob of muck inched toward her eyebrows. With the sleeve of his coat, he took a hasty swipe, adding, "Enough is enough."

"How do you expect me to react? It's over. I need to sort myself out."

A shovel angled out of the nearest flower bed. A garden bed, he realized, she'd gone through like a vicious mole. Dormant rose bushes were clawed from the ground, leaving behind a series of muddy holes. Across the lawn, she'd thrown the roses in a crazy arc.

Yanking the shovel free, he gestured at the holes. "What's this? Digging your way to China?"

"I'm rearranging."

"This isn't furniture, Millicent. It's plant stock. Did you intend to transplant *after* you destroyed the entire bed?"

In response, she picked up the loppers and tossed them into the wheelbarrow. "I'm asking you nicely," she said from between her teeth. "Go away. Let me deal with this in my own way."

"You're not dealing with anything. You're giving up."

"Oh, and you have a better idea?"

"I do, in fact. Return to the Wayfair. Reason with Jada."

"You aren't serious. She informed me quite plainly she's never heard of Bodi."

"And you didn't believe her," Vasily reminded her. "You said so after you flew home. You dropped your bags in the foyer, let me pour you a drink, and shared your conclusions. You were positive she lied, although you didn't know why."

"I'm still sure."

"Precisely why you must go back."

"Vasily, what do you expect me to do? Jada Brooks is a pastry chef, not a felon. I can't interrogate her."

"She may have lied out of fear. Or to protect something. Or someone—perhaps Bodi doesn't want to be found. If she keeps in touch with Jada, she may have asked her to lie."

The hypothesis ejected a small, sputtering sound from her lips. Stalking across the grass, Millicent grabbed up a rose bush. "You're grasping at straws." She flung the plant into the wheelbarrow. "It's over, Vasily. There's nothing more I can do."

"I can't help but wonder. Are you *glad* there's nothing else you can do? We're both convinced you've found the trail. You got close, then you ran away. Like you ran away from a stellar career when your love affair became common knowledge at the university. Isn't *that* the reason you retired?"

The muscles in her throat worked. "I don't like your implication," she growled.

"You won't like this either. You're scared, Millicent. You hide in the country on your fabulous estate because your colleagues have discovered what you are, and you're ashamed. You've bought into their stupid, poisonous conventions and you've let them cripple you." He swung his attention to a window on the second floor of the house, to the soft glow emanating from the master suite. When her eyes followed his on a painful trajectory, he added, "You've let those conventions cripple you both."

Tortured, she balled her fists. "How dare you tell me how I feel?"

His heart went out to her. Shivering in the frigid air with her eyes wavering and her pride no more substantial than mist. But he didn't let up.

"Are you afraid once you find Bodi, she won't accept your marriage?" he demanded, needing to steer her battered heart to reason.

"Millicent, she was a kid when she ran off. I doubt she remembers any of the hurtful remarks she flung at you after the car accident."

Mention of the accident snuffed out her fury. Millicent pressed her eyes shut. She tipped her face down with the resignation of a woman praying over the dead remains of her once-beautiful life. She looked beaten and resigned, an old woman pushed beyond her reserves. Beyond her ability to forgive an unforgiving world.

On impulse, Vasily reached for her. He'd meant to lead her to reason, not tax her aging heart.

Warding him off, she scooped up another rose bush. "I have no idea how Bodi will react if we find her." She hesitated long enough for pride to rearrange the sorrow on her face. "Which doesn't change the facts. I can't force Jada to reveal her whereabouts. It's clear she won't."

"With enough persuasion, Jada will crack. I'm sure of it."

She gave him a look that implied he was a dunce. "Poor boy," she murmured. "You've been hanging around with me for too long. I've infected you with the malignant disease. Forgive me. I had no idea it was contagious."

"Hope isn't a disease. It's ennobling."

"You'll feel differently once life bangs you around enough." She dropped the plant into the wheelbarrow. Then she rubbed her palms across her face with plaintive strokes, as if the gesture might erase the folly of her wasted dreams. When she regarded him again, the surrender hollowing out her eyes filled him with pity. "Find a cure, young man. Hope only brings disappointment. Which is why I'm giving up."

"No, you're not." He rocked back on his heels. "I won't let you."

She laughed derisively. "As if you can stop me."

"I've taken matters into my own competent hands." He offered a smile forged of steel. "I'm serious."

The wind caught her grey-streaked hair, throwing the locks skyward. She resembled a porcupine cornered in a homeowner's garage.

"Vasily, what have you done?"

"American Airlines flight 1873 to Cincinnati," he rapped out. "Three tickets."

When her jaw loosened at the audacity of his plan, he allowed himself a silent cheer of victory. *Bravo, me.*

"*Three* tickets?" Millicent sputtered. "You bought three tickets? We're all going?"

"We must arrive at O'Hare tomorrow by six a.m. Dragging a wheelchair and its foul-tempered occupant through security won't be the highlight of my day. I'll manage."

When she began to object, he sent her a thunderous glance. Amazingly, she clamped her mouth shut. The closest he'd ever get to witnessing Millicent surrender on any field of battle.

He didn't waste the moment, saying, "I suggest you throw clothes into a suitcase for yourself and the dour specter who's now *only* taking meals in the master suite. A master suite, I might add, you haven't visited in days. There's no glory in sleeping on the living room couch like an errant spouse. Where's your pride?"

She snorted. "Gone and buried in Sweet Lake."

"We'll resurrect it from an undeserving grave."

"And how will we manage that fine miracle?"

Sloshing past her on the muddy ground, Vasily took possession of the wheelbarrow. The wind kicked up, a chilling blast. It carried off the small, weak query she'd tossed out.

But not before he detected the undertone in her voice, the glimmering current swimming beneath her words.

Hope. The rare, raw material from which Millicent was created.

Wheeling forward, he paused by the mudroom door. "Are you coming, or not?" he asked.

Chapter 19

The lively chatter of sixty-plus women resounded through the ballroom. On the dais, Linnie sat amidst a circle of unopened presents. Frances and Silvia were on either side of the happy bride-to-be, handing her gifts and dispensing with mounds of crumpled wrapping paper.

Below the dais, Fancy skipped down the row of tables brimming with treats. Jada watched with mild amusement as the child filled her plate with grapes, petits fours, cucumber sandwiches, and a variety of cheeses. Nearing the middle of the fabulous spread, Fancy reached for the tray of barbecued drumsticks. She stopped abruptly to frown at her groaning plate.

Jada approached. "You're allowed to come back for seconds, kiddo."

The suggestion seemed unwelcome. "Can I put something back?" Fancy licked her lips.

"Once you pick something, it stays on your plate."

"What a dumb rule."

"Big girls don't put food back. It's not polite."

Fancy surveyed the roomful of women, her pretty frock rustling softly around her knees. "What if they eat everything before I have seconds?"

"Are you kidding? With this much food, everyone will take leftovers home tonight—you included." Relenting, Jada reached for a second plate. Barbecue was at the top of Fancy's most-loved foods. "How many drumsticks would you like?"

"Four, please."

Jada put the chicken on the plate. She steered Fancy to a table by the large casement windows to the right of the dais.

The table overlooked the new patio one story below, where the wedding would take place next Saturday. All the boxwoods were now planted around the large sandstone pavers. Oval beds of pink-blossoming azaleas decorated each corner of the patio. The arbor stood at one end of the patio, awaiting Philip's last touches. Like everyone else, Jada now checked the weather forecast daily. So far, so good: the seven-day forecast called for temps in the seventies and sunny skies with little chance of rain.

At the table, Cat was deep in conversation with several of the women who'd graduated from Sweet Lake High the same year. The shower provided the perfect opportunity to catch up, especially with friends who'd moved away from Sweet Lake.

Cat slid out the chair beside hers and smiled as Fancy sat down. Then she eyed the child's overstuffed plate. "Whoa. Fancy, you're allowed to get seconds. The food isn't going anywhere. The party is just getting started."

Fancy plunked the plate down. "Yes, yes, yes. Jada told me."

"Did she also mention how pretty you look?"

"I certainly did," Jada said. The tulle ballerina dress in shimmering layers of shell pink was Philip's most recent find at Gift of Garb. To finish off the outfit, he'd also sprung for three barrettes with rhinestones and rosebuds, which he'd affixed to his daughter's light-blonde hair.

While the other women at the table murmured in agreement, Jada told Cat, "I'll be back in thirty."

"No problem. I'm happy to hang out with the munchkin."

Fancy was polishing off her second drumstick as Jada tucked a napkin into the collar of her dress. "I'll see you soon. Have fun with Cat and her friends."

"Come back fast, okay?"

"Will do." Jada did a double take and grabbed the napkin by Cat's finished plate. She patted away the barbecue sauce rimming Fancy's mouth. "I'll hurry, promise."

Slipping out, Jada went to the front desk to scan the reservation list. The Wayfair was enjoying a busy Saturday, with eighty percent of the main inn booked for the weekend. Half of the suites in the south wing were also booked—an unexpected bonus. Although the lake wasn't yet warm enough for swimming, guests trooped past in casual attire and sandals, to take in the sun and enjoy boat rides on Sweet Lake.

Behind the front desk, Mr. Uchida said, "We had two last-minute bookings, one for a suite in the south wing, and the other for the main building." His fingers flying across the keyboard, he peered at the computer screen. "The guests are scheduled to arrive any minute."

"Has anyone called in sick?" Some of the employees were trading around a spring head cold.

"Relax. Everyone is here."

"Color me happy. I was afraid I'd need to bail out the Housekeeping staff in the laundry room."

Mr. Uchida chuckled. "You're off the hook."

Relieved, she strode to her office. The bridal shower was proceeding nicely. With Fancy happily pigging out, she suffered minimal guilt as she dug through the paperwork on her desk. Once Linnie departed for her honeymoon in Aruba, responsibility for managing the inn would fall on Jada's shoulders. Keen to do a good job, she reviewed the to-do list she'd requested Linnie draw up.

She was reading the fourth point on the list when she noticed Philip in the doorway. He pulled away from the doorjamb. She had no idea how long he'd been standing there.

"Got a sec?" he asked. He seemed unsure if he should enter.

He looked more delectable than the treats his daughter was plowing through in the ballroom. As usual, he needed a haircut. She loved the way a lock of glossy, overlong hair fell across his wide brow. On weekends, he often skipped shaving—and he'd done so today. The shadow on his strong chin gave him a rakish look. Yearning wove through her as she composed her features.

"Come in." The cool invitation belied the warmth cascading through her.

Philip left the door open. He gave a cursory glance at the chairs arranged before the desk, but remained standing.

"I talked to Daniel." He caught her wavering gaze. "I didn't go to him for advice as a way to patch things up with you. I'm not interested in scoring brownie points."

"Good to know." She wasn't sure where he was going with this.

"Don't get me wrong. I *do* want to get back to where we were. There's nothing I want more. I miss you, Jada."

"I miss you too," she admitted, and her heart moved into her throat.

"You do?" He released a soft, ragged expulsion of air. "I wasn't sure how you felt, other than pissed off at me."

"I'm not angry. Disappointed is more like it."

"With me?"

"With everything. The way I dropped the news on your head, and the way you reacted. Philip, I didn't want to begin dating and have a disagreement ruin everything. We were just starting out."

"We're still together. Nothing has changed. At least not for me it hasn't."

A question lay hidden beneath the remark. He wanted to know if their relationship was ongoing. If there was a way to forget their recent differences and continue on. She thought of Millicent, and the countless times she was tempted to pick up the phone this week. To ask

Millicent how she was doing. To mention how much she'd enjoyed her stay at the Wayfair, and giving the baking lessons.

Out of respect for Philip's wishes, she never made the call.

"What did you discuss with Daniel?" she asked.

"The pros and cons of telling Millicent."

"About Fancy?" Her eyes widened. "You're reconsidering?"

"Yeah, I am."

She regarded him warily, not trusting her ears.

When she remained silent, he said, "There's a lot to consider, including whether I should steal a page from Millicent's playbook and hire a detective. I'm batting around the idea. It would sure be easier to decide what to do if I understood her relationship to my daughter." A muscle twitched in his jaw. "There's a lot to consider. From what I understand, once Millicent learns about Fancy, I've opened the door to all comers."

Anxiety darted through her. "Including Bodi's parents."

"Which scares me. Hell, I feel sick just considering it."

The concern was understandable. "Bodi's parents were abusive. We both saw the proof when she first came to Sweet Lake. All those bruises, and the gash on her forehead. Can't you . . . I don't know. Exclude them?"

"Not if Ohio law has anything to say about it. Grandparents have visitation rights, Jada. Once they learn about Fancy, they can drag me to court if I try to stop them from seeing her. According to Daniel, they have an even stronger case for visitation because their daughter— Bodi—is deceased. Her death kept them from knowing about their granddaughter."

The explanation seemed unfair. "That doesn't change the facts," Jada replied, with heat. "If they were lousy parents, they shouldn't be allowed anywhere near Fancy. Can't you ask a judge to keep them away?"

"There's no way to back up an abuse claim. Daniel believes the court may agree to supervised visitation. We wouldn't cite abuse as the reason. Fancy's unfamiliarity with her mother's side of the family might represent enough grounds."

"Who supervises the visits?" This was unknown terrain, and she suddenly felt queasy.

"The court would assign a social worker to sit in whenever Fancy's grandparents are with her. They won't like the restriction. No grandparent would." His features tensed. "At some point, the court will end supervision and give Fancy's grandparents full access. Essentially, I'll navigate on my own regarding how to handle the visits."

"How do you feel about that?" she asked doubtfully.

Philip never received the opportunity to reply. Daisy from Housekeeping burst into the office.

"Jada, you've got to see him!" Noticing Philip, the young maid scudded to a halt. "Oops—I thought you were alone." She gave a tentative wave. "Hi, Philip."

He nodded in greeting as two other women from Housekeeping raced inside. Young like Daisy, they were giggling as they failed to catch their breath.

Jada gave them a warning look. Then she turned back to Daisy. "What is it?" She didn't need a major calamity.

Daisy gestured toward the corridor, and the lobby beyond. "The actor, Liam Hemsworth? I swear, his brother is checking in." She shivered with excitement. "Mr. Uchida just handed the guy his room key, south wing. You've got to see him!"

Jada bounced a thumb toward the corridor. "No fraternizing with the guests," she ordered. Philip regarded her with devilish amusement. Tamping down the pleasure his attention darted into her belly, she focused on the maids. "I don't care if the guy's drop-dead gorgeous. Steer clear of him."

Daisy thrust out her lower lip. "I'm sorry I told you."

"I'm sorry I'm considering sending you home without pay. Don't push your luck." Jada began to order them out when a more worrisome thought intruded. Pecking on her keyboard, she located the employee file. "Is Benny working today?"

Catching on, Daisy said, "Not fair. Benny's assigned to clean the common areas in the main building." She regarded her crestfallen friends. "The south wing is *our* responsibility."

"Not today it isn't." Jada read through the file with relief. Benny was scheduled all weekend. In a pinch, the bashful employee could handle the south wing. "Here's the deal: Benny will service the room. Daisy, trot back to Mr. Uchida's desk. I need the guest's name."

A man strode in from the corridor. "Don't bother fetching the name," he announced. He stepped past the maids and Philip. "I'm Vasily Pruszynski."

His appearance threw the room into silence. Even Daisy and her friends were speechless.

Shock held Jada transfixed. Vasily—the doctoral student. Millicent's resident houseboy, the young man living at her estate.

He's flown in from Chicago to speak with me?

She doubted Millicent was aware of his bold actions.

Philip, his expression darkening, shooed the maids out.

Chapter 20

A dangerous male energy crackled through the office. The men regarded each other warily, like combatants drawn into a battle neither had foreseen. Vasily—younger than Philip by nearly a decade—was the first to regain his bearings. Sliding his attention away from the man gauging him with unmistakable disdain, he looked to the desk where Jada breathlessly waited.

"Would you mind if Mr. Kettering leaves for a moment?" Vasily said. "I need to speak with you privately."

Surprise lifted Philip's brows. "How do you know who I am?"

The harsh query made no dent in his opponent's composure. "Philip Kettering, owner of Unity Design, a small-but-thriving landscaping business. If memory serves, you have a child. A daughter in primary school." Vasily arched an elegant brow. "Should I continue?"

"Not unless you'd like to swallow your teeth."

"You're threatening me?"

"You catch on fast. What gives you the right to pry into my life?"

"And Jada's," Vasily supplied, foolishly goading him on. He was young, but he wasn't lacking in confidence. "The prying was a necessity, given the circumstances. If you allow me a moment to talk with her alone, she'll explain after I fill her in."

"Like hell—"

Rising swiftly, Jada came around the desk. She planted herself between the men.

"Calm down, both of you. No one is drawing blood in my office." After they stepped back, giving each other space, she closed the door to assure their privacy. Then she swung her attention to Vasily. "Philip isn't going anywhere. This concerns him too."

Now it was Vasily's turn to register surprise. He rolled back on his heels, clearly impressed with the steel in her voice.

"The lady's prerogative, of course." He didn't appear prepared to argue the point.

Without awaiting an invitation, he settled into one of the chairs arranged before the desk. Philip took the other chair and dragged it to the side of Jada's desk.

She was about to question his actions when he wheeled her chair away from the computer, positioning it close to his. There was no mistaking his intention to protect her, and she expelled the anxious breath locked in her lungs. Once she seated herself, he took her hand.

With interest, Vasily watched the interplay. "I won the bet, you know." He appeared to lower his defenses as his expression warmed. "Initially there was some debate regarding whether you were dating, or just friends. The report from the detective Millicent hired was short on details about your relationship. She wasn't sure until she came here. I had my suspicions all along."

Philip held his opponent with a level stare. "We're dating." His clasp on Jada's fingers tightened.

"Then I suppose this *does* concern you."

The observation met with a chilly silence, and the tension inside Jada increased. Vasily assumed Philip's only interest was in protecting her. She knew Philip had no intention of revealing the other reason the events concerned him—his daughter.

Jada said, "I can't imagine Millicent is happy about you coming here. Does she know?"

"Actually, she does." Vasily gave her a cryptic smile.

"Why *are* you here?"

"To get you to see reason." Leaning on the armrest, Vasily rested his chin on his knuckles. "Jada, I want to be fair. From everything Millicent has described, you're a good person. It's hard to know what she expected when she came to Sweet Lake. Not to become friends with the woman she was investigating, I'll wager. You deserve an explanation. She *did* come here under false pretenses."

Silently, Jada agreed. How much simpler it would've been if Millicent was truthful from the outset. "Why didn't she explain the true reason for her visit to Sweet Lake immediately?"

"I'm sure she wanted to explain. Hard experience taught her not to reveal her true intentions—or her identity—when embarking on a fishing expedition. Not at the outset."

"Why not?"

"The year before she hired me? A private detective gave her a lead on a cook named Jada working at a B&B near Indianapolis. Not a pastry chef. Millicent didn't care. She felt the lead was worth checking out."

Jada wondered how many trips Millicent took in search of Bodi. After the first fruitless journeys, most people would've given up. They wouldn't spend the better part of a decade scouring the country for African American pastry chefs named Jada. Millicent's endurance was admirable.

"Why didn't Millicent have the PI check out the lead?" she asked. "Why go to Indianapolis herself?"

Vasily regarded her with disbelief. "You know the reason," he remarked dryly. When she inhaled quickly, the truth dawning, he added, "Millicent has the impression most of us are simpletons. She only trusted the PI to find leads."

"And she insisted on checking out each one personally?"

Vasily nodded. "The cook at the B&B? The PI did sloppy work on her background. She'd recently finished a stint in prison, a significant fact the detective missed. When informed she'd been located with the help of a detective, the ex-con pulled out a gun." When Jada gasped, he added, "Millicent wasn't hurt. She did leave in a hurry. After that, she kept her real motivations under wraps whenever looking into the latest Jada."

Philip, silent until now, shifted uneasily in his chair. "Clear something up for me. What is Millicent's relationship to Bodi Wagner? I'm tired of guessing."

Mention of Bodi filled the air with sizzling electricity. Vasily looked up sharply. "Is Bodi here?"

Anticipation sparked on his features. He swiveled in his chair, seemed about to leap to his feet. His reaction was heartbreaking to behold, as if the missing girl would miraculously appear.

Philip lifted a hand in warning. "We're not discussing Bodi until I get some answers."

"Who are you to call the shots?"

"Pal, you're starting to piss me off. Answer the question."

Fearful they'd come to blows, Jada rose. She approached their young visitor, who'd flung his attention back to the door, his expression flowering with the most terrible example of hope. Millicent's quest to find Bodi wasn't a sole effort. The outcome mattered greatly to the young man in her employ.

"Please, Vasily." She rested her palm on his shoulder. "Explain Millicent's connection to Bodi. It's important. I'll tell you everything once you do."

He flinched, his attention drawn to the hand settled on his shoulder. His eyes lifted to hers. He seemed astonished by the way she'd broken the physical boundary between them to speak with the lilting affection of a mother calming an overexcited child.

The confidence drained from his handsome features. Tapping his foot, he became fidgety, like a schoolboy confronted with wrongdoing.

Has Millicent sent him to Sweet Lake seeking answers, without thinking he'd need to volunteer any in return? Jada wondered if he'd earn his employer's displeasure by revealing too much.

With bated breath, she waited as he quietly weighed the merits of speaking candidly or remaining silent.

At last he came to a decision. "Millicent is Bodi's stepmother," he said.

Confusion sank Jada back into the chair. *Her stepmother?*

Millicent was well into her sixties. Bodi was nineteen at the time of her death. The math didn't add up.

A conclusion Philip shared. "She's married to Bodi's father? She must be a lot older."

"She *is* a lot older," Vasily agreed, "by nearly twenty years. Millicent isn't married to Bodi's father. She's married to Bodi's mother." He paused to gauge their reaction. Pleasure creased his features when they merely stared at him, eager to hear more. "They were married during Bodi's senior year of high school."

Philip scraped the hair from his brow. "Man, I didn't see that coming."

"Most people don't," Vasily replied smoothly. Sadness tensed his features. "Bodi ran away a few months after the wedding. Not because of the marriage—she loved Millicent, although they fought like cats and dogs. She ran off right after the accident."

"What accident?" Philip dropped his hand to his lap.

"Wait. I assumed Jada told you."

Philip regarded Jada with confusion. "Did you tell me about an accident? I'm having trouble keeping up."

Deep in her own thoughts, Jada reached for the fragrant sachet she'd left beneath her desk lamp. Fingering the soft cloth, she recalled Penelope's gentle words as she presented the simple gift. *Keep this with you. It will help resolve the burden.* Then she envisioned Bodi, her arms pebbled with flour as she mixed the dough. *Love or hate—I never can decide how I feel about rosemary.* Next Jada's thoughts flowed to Millicent, the mystery in the historian's gaze blending with unmistakable devotion as she uttered the simple pronouncement. *I love rosemary.*

The historian hadn't meant a sharp-scented herb, the ingredient in a recipe handed down through the generations by Penelope's ancestors. She'd meant something different. Something infinitely more important.

Millicent was referring to a person. A woman, Jada decided, she hoped very much to meet.

"Bodi's mother . . . ," she said to Vasily. "Her name is Rosemary."

He nodded. "Rosemary Wagner-Earhardt."

"Bodi didn't get along with her?"

"Not from what I understand. I came into Millicent's employ after her stepdaughter ran away. Rosemary and her ex-husband had difficulty controlling Bodi. The highs and lows, her provocative behavior with boys at school—from what Millicent has described, they viewed Bodi as a constant challenge. They divorced when she entered high school. The only person able to get Bodi to stay on medication for any length of time was Millicent. Bodi hated taking meds."

The story was immensely sad. "When did her parents learn she was bipolar?" Jada asked. The question took Vasily aback, and she assured him, "Millicent never mentioned Bodi directly. During one of our baking lessons, she *did* say her stepdaughter was bipolar. I thought she was talking about Bodi's mother."

"Given Millicent's age, I can see why you came to the wrong conclusion." Vasily hesitated. "I believe the first psychiatrist that worked with Bodi gave the diagnosis. She was in junior high. Seventh grade, I believe."

Jada blinked. First psychiatrist . . . meaning there were many? Overwhelmed, she tried to digest all she'd been told. Philip's late wife hadn't been merely a teenager with a mercurial personality. She'd suffered from an untreated disease.

A *treatable* disease.

How long was Bodi off her medication when Penelope first met her in Columbus? Heartsick, Jada wished she'd possessed these facts years ago. If she'd known, she would've encouraged Bodi to seek treatment. She wouldn't have let up until she did.

At the door, a spirited rapping commenced. The sharp sounds drew Jada from her thoughts.

Millicent strode inside.

With confusion, she swung her attention across their heads, still bent close in discussion, before fixing Vasily with a look of fury. "Vasily, I've had about enough of your help to last a lifetime. I told you to fetch Jada, not interrogate her on my behalf." Puffing out a raspy breath, she pivoted to shut the door. "How difficult is it to follow a simple order? You could've at least sent a text and explained the delay."

Vasily eased his tall frame from the chair. "I couldn't send a text." He didn't seem the least perturbed by the outburst.

"Of all the stupid excuses—why in blazes not?"

"Your better half forgot to pack her smartphone, and you lost yours in O'Hare, remember? When you were bickering with Rosemary in the food court?"

"How can anyone remember to bring matching shoes for every outfit, yet forget to drop a phone into her purse? And stop exaggerating. We were conducting a lively debate in the food court."

"You were bickering."

She flapped her arms at her hips. "What if we were? I'll never understand why she cares for sushi. The sight of raw fish is nauseating." Her attention wove back to Jada, and injured pride shifted through her eyes. "Hello, dear. I suppose you're already aware that we need to talk."

Jada, reeling at the turn of events, joined them by the door. "Why didn't you let me know you were flying in?" she asked, taking care to keep her voice steady. She'd hurt Millicent by lying to her. Now she'd wound her more deeply once the truth about Bodi was revealed. "Rosemary is here with you?"

"She's out back, enjoying the new patio. Told me to take my good sweet time finding you because I'm making her nervous, as if she's not feeling just as—" Millicent cut off. "Vasily told you about Rosemary?"

"He did."

Millicent shrank back. "What else is going on in here?"

Something childlike and plaintive came across in the query. Jada's heart went out to her. The desire to shelter the historian through this most difficult storm sprinted past her apprehension regarding the bleak conversation to come.

She pressed a steadying palm to Millicent's arm. "We've been discussing your stepdaughter," she remarked slowly. "I met Bodi when she first came to Sweet Lake seven years ago. She was my friend."

A stuttering breath escaped Millicent. "When I asked, that day in the kitchen, why did you lie?"

"I'm so sorry. I didn't want to deceive you. I hope you can forgive me."

"Tell me why you did."

The chair creaked as Philip came to his feet. "Millicent, she was only doing what I'd asked. I'm the one who owes you an apology."

"You do? I'd certainly like to know why."

"We'll get to that soon." Miserable, he compressed his lips. Then he said, "There's a lot we need to explain. Would you like Vasily to go out and get Rosemary? She'll want to hear this too."

At the gravity in his voice, Millicent's fingers twitched with the palsy that stormed across her great dignity whenever distress consumed her. A tremor shook her left arm. On instinct, Jada took her hand. Their gazes meshed, one rife with sympathy, the other dark with fear. Beneath the fear, gratitude flickered in Millicent's eyes.

Withdrawing from Jada's hold, she lifted her head like a banner. Her jaw set, she strode to the chair vacated by her doctoral student.

"Let's get started. Philip, Jada—sit down." Lowering herself, she managed to rein in the palsy as she gripped the armrests. "I'd rather hear the details before we involve my wife. Rosemary is perfectly content on the patio for now. She's enjoying the beautiful weather." To Vasily, she added, "The lobby is a madhouse with people running in and out. If anyone comes looking for Jada, send them away."

With a nod, he leaned against the door.

Chapter 21

Millicent wasted no time getting started.

She directed her first question to Jada. "You met my stepdaughter seven years ago? What brought her to Sweet Lake?"

"She came at Penelope's invitation." Anxiety trundled up from Jada's gut. Philip took her hand, and she was glad for his support. She gave Millicent a brief explanation of Bodi's attempt at purse snatching and her agreement to come to the town. Wrapping up, she added, "You've met Penelope, so you know what I mean. Bodi wasn't very trusting, but she was persuaded to try starting over in Sweet Lake."

"She lived at Penelope's house?"

"In the guest bedroom."

"I suppose she also worked at Gift of Garb." When Jada nodded, Millicent sank back in her chair. "Why didn't I sort this out for myself? I wonder if Penelope was trying to tell me—she did go into quite a bit of detail about why she likes to help troubled kids. Bodi is certainly one of those. Well, she was back then. I hope she's changed, or at least gone back on her medication."

The moisture fled Jada's throat. "We didn't know she was bipolar," she said, dreading the next question Millicent was sure to pose.

"Of course you didn't. Bodi refused to believe there was anything wrong. She refused to believe she was bipolar."

Breaking in, Philip said, "I'm still confused about something. From what Vasily told us, Bodi was raised in a loving home. When she first came to Sweet Lake, she looked like she'd been beaten."

Millicent studied him closely. "You're also friends with my stepdaughter?" When he dropped his eyes, she looked back to Jada. "Is she still here? After all this time? Now, I don't care what nonsense she's trumped up about me or her mother—or Rosemary's ex-husband, for that matter. Bodi's childhood wasn't perfect, but she was most assuredly loved. I insist you take me to her immediately. We'll leave Rosemary in the dark until I've had the opportunity to hash this out. Even if Bodi isn't willing to speak to her mother, let me attempt to reason with her."

Philip pulled Jada's hand into his lap. She sensed the turmoil churning inside him.

There was still so much to share. A heartbreaking task.

Sparing them both the anguish for a moment, Philip said, "I won't ask anything else, Millicent. Just walk me through why Bodi was in such bad shape."

The injury in his voice lifted the historian's chin. It was clear she was aware his reason for asking, still hidden, was important.

"You first met her seven years ago?"

"That's right."

Some of the fire went out of Millicent's gaze. "My guess? Her injuries weren't healed, the ones from the car accident. Bodi was driving. I was in the passenger seat, Rosemary in back."

"Rosemary wasn't wearing a seatbelt," Jada guessed, and her stomach clenched. So much of the truth had been staring her in the face, but she'd never put the pieces together. "When you told me about the accident during one of our baking lessons . . . I thought you were behind the wheel."

"Bodi was driving." Millicent bowed her head, stared absently at her feet. "We were arguing about her medication. She'd gone off it again. I was trying to persuade her to go back on." She looked up, grim-faced. "Rosemary will tell you the icy roads were to blame. I'm not so sure. I've always wondered if Bodi purposely drove into the tree. Her airbag deployed. Mine did too. We were pretty banged up, but nothing life-threatening."

Jada's blood turned cold. "And Rosemary?"

"She was"—Millicent's voice broke—"thrown from the car."

In the deafening quiet, pain shuddered up her back. Her complexion went grey. Shutting her eyes, she gripped the armrests of her chair. The sight of her undoing, her tangible despair, blurred Jada's vision. She flinched when Philip reached over and tenderly swiped the tears from her cheeks.

Once Millicent pulled herself together, she finished the story in a dull monotone. "Rosemary was paralyzed from the waist down. She experiences brutal pain in her back and shoulders—physical therapy twice a week helps. She still agrees to the sessions, all these years later. She would've put herself into an early grave if I weren't so damn stubborn. She's only forty-seven, you know. Still beautiful, and equally stubborn." Millicent chuckled then, her face now bleached of color. "It's the one thing we have in common. The stubborn streak."

The story finished, Millicent struggled out of her chair. She looked exhausted from the telling, too spent to realize they'd never given her a satisfactory explanation about Bodi's whereabouts. Agony stole through Jada at the sight of the proud woman waving Vasily back as he tried to approach; this bright, strong-willed soul reduced so cruelly by the story she had shared.

Philip rose too. With the smallest gesture, he telegraphed for Jada to stay where she was. She pitied him. The task he'd set for himself was difficult.

Brutal, really. Philip despised venturing back into the darkest memories of his past. He would do so now out of a sense of obligation.

Millicent looked to him expectantly.

Relief warmed Jada's chilled heart. Philip would take it from here.

Chapter 22

Millicent and Philip spoke in low voices.

Face-to-face, they each studied the floor as Philip began, his arms crossed as he ventured into the story. Vasily stepped to the window behind Jada's desk, and stood with his feet planted wide apart. He leaned into the sunlight as if the golden waterfall of light could wash away the awful snippets of conversation reaching his ears. Jada, much nearer to the conversation, sat rigidly.

Millicent looked up sharply, her eyes glinting with shock. From her reaction, Jada knew Philip had reached the tragic ending on the ice-glazed lake.

"She fell through?" Millicent asked weakly. "There was no one to stop her?"

"There wasn't time," Philip said.

An evasion, and the historian frowned. "Was Bodi alone, or not?"

"Jada followed her." A protective note rimmed Philip's voice. "There wasn't anything she could do."

The thin assurance trembled distress up Millicent's stout frame. She pivoted toward Jada. "You . . . stood there and watched her die? If Bodi was your friend, you must've had some idea of the demons she battled. Why did you just stand there?"

The accusation struck like a blow. Unprepared, Jada covered her face with her hands.

"Millicent, don't," Philip said. "She couldn't get to Bodi in time. Don't you think she tried? No one could have done more."

There was no dignity in hiding behind her eyelids like a child. Jada lowered her hands to her lap.

"Millicent, I will tell you everything, and answer all your questions," she whispered. Her heart was a stone in her chest, but it was a relief, a small and horrible consolation, not to feel anything at all. "Later today, when we have an opportunity to speak alone with Rosemary, we'll cover everything. I imagine she'll insist on hearing the worst details. Philip doesn't know all of it—I've never spoken about Bodi's last minutes with my friends. It's very difficult for me." On shaky legs, she joined them. Millicent was leaning against the wall, clearly overcome by the story. Jada waited until her eyes lifted before adding, "There's more. Something else we need to tell you."

"Something *I* need to tell you," Philip put in. Grappling with his composure, he shoved his fists into the pockets of his jeans. "Millicent, I was married to Bodi."

The announcement put blotchy patches of color on the historian's cheeks. She stared blankly for a long moment before her eyes cleared.

"You were married to my stepdaughter?" The disclosure taxed her overburdened mind. She blinked rapidly, her chest heaving as she tried to regulate her breathing. Then she gasped. "Your daughter, Fancy. You're mean she's . . . ?"

"Bodi's daughter," Philip supplied.

"Rosemary has a granddaughter?"

"You do too." Easing the smartphone from his pocket, Philip showed their stunned guest the image on the lock screen.

Jada knew the picture well: Fancy beaming at the camera in a hot pink dress-up gown and purple magician's cape.

"Jada has shared a few delightful stories about Fancy. I have wondered what she looks like." Shock appeared to have loosened Millicent's tongue, and her hand shook as she accepted the phone. "Good heavens. I don't believe this. Philip, she's extraordinary."

"Thanks."

"Vasily, come look. Three generations stamped from one mold. I've never seen anything like it." When he sauntered over, she held out phone to allow him a quick peek. "Remarkable, don't you think?"

"Quite," he murmured, giving the phone a cursory glance before regarding her closely. He seemed to weigh the shock of the unfolding events against her ability to manage them.

Yet he made no attempt to assist her as tears quickly filled her eyes. They brimmed over as she traced a finger around the image on the lock screen. "For goodness' sake, you could knock me over with a feather. What an absolutely beautiful child. She's Bodi's spitting image—and Rosemary's."

Philip's brows lifted. "I wasn't aware Bodi resembled her mother."

"No, you couldn't have been. Not if she made her family out to be something less than it was." A portion of Millicent's natural vigor returned as she navigated to the camera roll. Eagerly she spun through photos of her granddaughter. "Young man, I'm sorry to point out the obvious. There's absolutely none of your likeness in Fancy at all."

"Oh, she's mine all right. Personality-wise, at least. Dreamy, persistent—"

"Silly, charming," Jada broke in. She stroked Philip's arm. It was the first time she'd reached for him since their argument at his house. The simple affection lured his eyes to hers, and the private moment they shared spun something good through her chest. Remembering their guests, she added, "Fancy is *all* Kettering on the personality front."

"I can't wait to meet her." Catching herself, Millicent sobered. She dragged a palm across the moisture glistening on her face. "I'm not sure how to tell Rosemary the other news. She'll be inconsolable. Her daughter, gone." Handing back the phone, she wove a slow path to Jada's desk. "How do I proceed?" she murmured to herself. "Wait to mention Fancy? There's no reason we can't stay in Sweet Lake for several days. Perhaps Rosemary should learn about losing Bodi today. Should I tell her about Fancy tomorrow?"

The sorrow she'd managed to put at bay again blistered her expression with pain. Jada resisted the urge to go to her. The sharing of grief and then joy was a private matter. However Millicent wanted this handled, it was best to do whatever she asked.

Coming to a decision, she marched back across the office. "All of you—stay here," she ordered. "I'll bring Rosemary inside. The news about Fancy can wait several hours, but she'll never forgive me if I don't tell her about Bodi immediately." She turned to Jada. "We'll play this by ear. Let me give Rosemary the basics privately. Afterward, I'll let you know when we're prepared for you to join us. She'll demand to hear the rest. In an hour or so."

She marched out. The door slammed shut behind her.

Jada pressed a hand to her stomach. "Philip, we didn't tell her that Fancy is here." Given the difficult events, her insides were a coil of knots.

"At the inn?" Vasily looked from one to the other. "Where?"

"In the ballroom," Jada told him.

Philip brushed past. "I'll grab her, take her home. Millicent is right—it's better for Rosemary to hear about Bodi first. Let's tell her about Fancy tonight or wait until tomorrow."

Jada grabbed his arm, stopping him. "Philip, no. If you cart her away from Linnie's bridal shower, she'll be heartbroken. She's having so much fun. Why upset her right before we're about to turn her world upside down? This isn't just about Rosemary and how she'll deal with the news. This affects Fancy too."

"I hadn't thought of that."

"Come on." She hurried into the corridor. The men fell in line behind her. From over her shoulder, she told Philip, "Let's introduce ourselves and help get Rosemary off the patio. There's no need to tell her or Millicent that Fancy's nearby. We'll get them settled in their suite upstairs."

"Then what?" Philip asked.

"I'll ask Cat to keep Fancy occupied. In an hour or so, go in and take her home. She won't like leaving early, but at least she will have stayed for most of the party."

"Jada, she also won't like that you didn't return to the party. She was really looking forward to hanging out with you."

"I know." Jada sighed.

Vasily held up his hand like an eager student.

"One question," he said, and his lighthearted tone broke the tension for a blissful moment. "I'm dying to meet Rosemary's look-alike. Can I go with Philip when he crashes the party?"

Feeling weightless with apprehension, Jada clasped the hand Philip offered. He looked equally shell-shocked as they led Vasily back to the lobby. Two girls, apparently coming in from the lake, were battling over a pail of sand they'd dug from the beach. At the front desk, a silver-haired couple was checking in. Voices carried from the veranda. They mixed with a celebratory cheer emanating from the ballroom, where Linnie's bridal shower was in full swing.

Philip took the lead; their young friend trailed behind. To Jada, he whispered, "Who's watching Fancy?"

"I left her at a table with Cat."

"Where are they sitting?"

She gave his fingers a reassuring squeeze. "Don't ask. You really don't want to know."

"If Fancy is anywhere near the windows, she may see Rosemary." The crow's feet at the corners of his eyes deepened with worry. "Geez, how do I introduce my kid to her look-alike grandmother? Not to mention her other grandmother?"

"Don't worry about it now. Let's just get Rosemary through the worst news she'll ever receive."

"I have a funny feeling this won't hold until tomorrow."

She knew what he meant. Despite Millicent's desire to control the course of events, life had a way of playing out as it chose. Jada sighed. She'd left Fancy near the windows overlooking the patio. On the plus side, Philip's daughter was unfamiliar with Millicent. However, if any of the Sirens were at the table with Fancy and Cat, it would take them no time at all to notice the historian wandering around the patio one story below. Jada doubted they'd resist hurrying out the ballroom's back door to invite her to join the festivities.

Philip quickened his pace around the side of the inn, taking the pavement with swift strides she had trouble matching. At the back corner of the ballroom, the pavement met the grass. On the sloping lawn curving downward to the patio, deep ruts cut through to the soil.

Jada was trying to make sense of the ruts when Philip pulled her to a stop.

Below them, near the arbor he'd built, Millicent was talking to a woman in a wheelchair. Millicent's hands gestured in the air, no doubt to describe the greenery and the flowers Philip would use to dress the arbor. The lavender scarf tied at Rosemary's chin glimmered in the sunlight. Listening avidly, she lifted her head.

As she did, a startled gasp broke from Jada's mouth. Rosemary Wagner-Earhardt possessed the arrestingly beautiful face of a woman in her prime.

A nearly exact replica of Bodi's face, Jada thought with a start. *And Fancy's.*

Vasily brushed past them. "Get moving, soldiers. Millicent will be peeved we didn't follow her orders, but if we delay much longer, the gig is up."

Millicent continued to gesture as he took the hill with long strides, the movement catching her attention and swiveling her around. She squinted, her gaze finding Jada and Philip still rooted on the knoll. With a look of consternation, Millicent dropped her hands to her sides.

When she did, she grazed her wife's head. Laughing, Rosemary batted her away. As she rolled the wheelchair back an inch, the scarf tied beneath her chin loosened.

The breeze, conspiring to reveal her secret, rippled across the fabric. A strong gust completed the undertaking, blowing the silky material from her head. Suddenly the scarf was aloft, bounding skyward like a kite toying with the air currents. Vasily took off after it, leaping over the boxwood surrounding the patio to play catch-me-if-you-can across the grass.

His vain attempts at capture went unnoticed. Philip whispered unintelligible words. At precisely the same instant, Jada's brows lifted. Rosemary's hair—a silky, streaming ribbon—was a rare lemon hue.

"Jada, look." With jerky movements, Philip pointed to the ballroom, zeroing in on the last window. "There."

Obeying the command, Jada looked past the arbor and the steps ascending to the back entrance. She looked all the way to the last window, the one nearest the door leading down to the woman in the wheelchair.

Fancy.

Pressing her small hands to the glass, she locked her attention on the woman seated in a corona of light as clear and bright as her hair.

Chapter 23

Fancy disappeared from the window. Hurrying onto the patio with Philip, Jada heard the squeak of the ballroom door.

Philip did too. He began sprinting past, to ascend the stairs and escort his daughter into the breathless group waiting for her below. A garbled command from Millicent arrested his feet. She knew as he did—just as Vasily knew, ambling across the grass to join them, and Jada, covering the fierce beating of her heart with her palm—what would come next.

Rosemary did not.

She cast a curious glance across the people crowding around her wheelchair. And why not? She couldn't possibly comprehend the momentous change sweeping into her life.

The door creaked shut. Fancy wavered at the top of the steps. But only for a moment.

If love was a golden cord, the starstruck child clasped one end and let it guide her down the steps to the woman in the wheelchair. A dizzying array of emotion darted through Rosemary's cornflower-blue eyes as her granddaughter neared—shock, wonder, disbelief. Then joy clearer than the April sky as Fancy paused several paces away.

They were twin moons revolving around each other in an orbit that excluded everyone else. A cry of wonder burst from Rosemary. Her reaction, pure and unrestrained, widened Fancy's eyes. She trotted forward in her pink party dress, hurrying now to the woman opening her arms wide to receive her.

Fancy—with nothing but the glowing invitation of the selfsame blue eyes that were locked on hers—approached the heavy steel wheelchair with curiosity and not a trace of apprehension. Then she stopped again. She was mesmerized by the breeze toying with Rosemary's hair, fanning it out around her shoulders and her pale features. But only for the space of time one heartbeat needs to merge into the next.

She climbed into Rosemary's lap.

"You're my twin." Fancy caught a dancing strand, tucked it behind Rosemary's ear.

"Actually, you're *my* twin," Rosemary told her with admirable calm. "I'm older than you."

"I look just like you."

"You do."

"I don't look like anybody." Fancy went nose to nose with the woman holding her tightly. She blinked rapidly, fluttering her lashes against Rosemary's. "Our eyes are the same blue."

Millicent, standing behind them, began to sway. Vasily darted to her side. When he slung an arm across her shoulders, she sank against him.

The dam holding in Rosemary's emotions broke without warning. Through tears, she touched Fancy's arms and her lips, the downy curve of her cheek and the slender length of her thigh, hidden beneath the party dress. She looked up at the others. Her voice rife with emotion, she said, "I would very much like someone to explain who this child is."

Philip knelt beside her chair. "This is Fancy, my daughter."

"Your . . . I don't understand."

He took Fancy's chin, and her eyes delved into his. "Fancy, this is your grandmother. Her name is Rosemary."

A child's world is a simple place, and Fancy accepted the news with a nod. "What about Grammy in Texas?"

The question furrowed her father's brows. Jada knew what Fancy meant.

When she approached, Fancy hopped down from her perch. Something about the proceedings had begun to unnerve her. She clambered into Jada's arms.

"Grammy in Texas is still your grandmother," Jada assured her, and Fancy's legs tightened around her waist in response. She steered the child's head to her shoulder. "No one is being replaced. You now have Grammy, Grandmother Rosemary—and Millicent."

"I have *three* grandmothers?"

"You do."

"Like Flora, Fauna, and Merryweather?"

Sleeping Beauty's fairy godmothers weren't an exact fit, but Jada saw no reason to quibble. "That's right."

Fancy released a breathy sigh. "That's a lot."

Any child would need time to process the discovery, and instinct carried Jada farther away from the others. She stood rocking Fancy until she relaxed. Then Jada inhaled sharply. The scent of barbecue sauce was heavy on Fancy's skin.

A brown streak of sauce formed a thin line on her temple. "Did you get enough drumsticks?" Licking her fingers, Jada used the moisture to rub the streak away.

"I guess I'm not allowed to have more." Evidently Fancy recalled their conversation about polite serving portions. "I ate four drumsticks."

"Would you like more?" There was no question about it: Fancy *was* Philip's child. She'd inherited his barbecue lust.

"Can I?"

"Why not? Run inside and get another drumstick. Get two. You can eat out here and visit with your new grandmothers. We'll go back to the party in a little while."

"Will you dance with me? Cat said she brought boogie-woogie music. She said she'll turn on the music after Linnie opens her presents."

Boogie-woogie music? The silly description sounded exactly like Cat. "We'll dance together for as long as you want," Jada promised.

Delighted, Fancy squirmed out of her arms. She was halfway up the stairs when she stopped. She trotted back down.

At a tentative pace, she returned to the wheelchair. "Would you like some chicken?" she asked Rosemary. Clasping the armrests, she leaned close, whispering, "I'll get you two because we're twins."

When Rosemary gave her a watery smile, Fancy dashed up the steps.

Determined to finish her latest art project, Fancy raced from the dais with another discarded bow. More ribbons and bows already covered the dark hair cascading past Cat's shoulders than Jada cared to count.

Late-afternoon light slanted through the ballroom windows. Most of the partygoers were gone, with the exception of Frances and Silvia. The co-leaders of the Sirens were helping the Housekeeping staff clear the buffet table. They'd wisely left the heaps of wrapping paper scattered across the dais where Linnie continued to stack shower gifts. No one planned to clean up the wrapping paper until Fancy tired of the pretty-pretty game.

Fancy pressed the latest bow to Cat's head. After she ran back to the dais, Cat resumed the conversation.

"They're still in their suite?" she asked Jada.

"Millicent is unpacking, I guess," Jada replied. "According to Vasily, Rosemary needed a nap. This afternoon was awfully hard on her."

Worry inked Cat's eyes. "She'll want details, all the stuff you refuse to share even with me and Linnie. How do you feel about that?"

"Scared, I guess. I can't talk about Bodi's death without reliving those moments. Every stark detail."

"Should I go with you? For moral support?"

"I'll muddle through on my own, but thanks."

Giggling erupted on the dais. Sorting through the heaps of wrapping paper, Fancy looked like a kid about to leap into a pile of autumn leaves. Helping her, Linnie found a large yellow bow and a length of pink ribbon. Together they returned to the table.

Linnie dropped the bow into Fancy's waiting palm. "Cat needs something pretty on her forehead." She gave the first grader an encouraging push.

"Hold still." Fancy pressed the bow to her victim's brow.

Cat scowled. "Thanks, Linnie."

"Anytime."

Fancy ran off to collect more supplies. Frances and Silvia called to her. They began pointing at the leftovers, platters stuffed with untouched appetizers, cheesecake slices, Jada's delectable brownies—and an oval platter half-filled with the barbecue drumsticks Fancy adored. The co-leaders of the Sirens planned to send the child home with several days' worth of food.

Linnie made good use of the privacy. "About tonight," she said, scooting her chair close to Jada's, "you don't have to do this alone. I've already talked to Daniel. He'll take all the shower gifts home. I'm sticking around. There's no need for you to speak with Rosemary alone."

Cat said, "Too late. I've already offered. Jada wants to do this solo."

"I do," Jada agreed. "I appreciate both of you offering, really."

Her phone vibrated, drawing the conversation to a close. Scanning the text, she excused herself.

In the lobby, Millicent paced beneath the watchful eye of Mr. Uchida, who sat behind the front desk. When Jada appeared, the historian looked relieved.

"I wasn't expecting to see you this soon," Jada admitted. "Is everything all right?"

"Yes. Well, I guess." Millicent rubbed her palms together. She attempted a cheery expression. "The suite is lovely, by the way. The view of the lake from the bay window is breathtaking. I dozed off in one of the easy chairs."

"Did you finish unpacking?"

"Right after we got to the suite. Rosemary insisted—she's never comfortable until everything is neat and tidy." Millicent paused abruptly. Then she motioned Jada toward the privacy of the seating area to the right of the lobby. Growing somber, she asked, "Would you mind if we accelerated the schedule? This afternoon instead of tonight? Rosemary has woken from her nap. I was hoping she'd sleep longer— travel is hard for her, and it *has* been a long day—but she's becoming insistent."

"She wants to talk now?" The nerves Jada had managed to keep at bay spilled through her in an icy rush.

"If it's not an imposition." Angling her neck, Millicent peered toward the corridor on the opposite side of the lobby that led into the ballroom. "Is the bridal shower finished?"

"They're cleaning up now."

"Did Linnie receive everything on her wish list?"

"And more. It will take Daniel several trips to haul the bounty to their house. I'd ask Philip to help, but he went into town. His men are finishing a new landscape installation on Highland Avenue."

The historian's eyes were overly bright as she bobbed her head with interest. "Would Daniel like help ferrying the packages? Vasily has the rental car. He's been roaming the grounds, bored out of his mind. Being stuck in the country with two fussy women is testing the limits of his endurance."

"I'm sure Daniel would love the help." Jada sent him a text.

It occurred to her that Millicent was drawing out the conversation to avoid the impending discussion. Was she more fearful of the dreadful facts awaiting her, or the effect they would have on Rosemary? Sympathy for her bounded past Jada's apprehension.

"Why don't we talk in your suite?" When Millicent bobbed her head once more, Jada offered her most encouraging smile. "It's nearly dinnertime," she said, alighting on the perfect way to allay the historian's nerves. "Would you mind helping me pull together a few snacks? You and Rosemary must both be starving."

"Why, thank you. What a lovely suggestion."

They went into the kitchen. Jada filled a tray with cheese, crackers, a dish of shrimp salad, and large handfuls of red grapes. Then she added three goblets and two bottles of Chablis. Millicent went to hoist the tray, a ridiculous idea. The palsy that invaded her hands at unpredictable moments trembled through her fingers. Gently moving her aside, Jada picked up the tray and led her to the lobby elevator.

In the suite, the king-size bed was neatly made, the luggage presumably tucked inside the closet. One of the largest suites in the main section of the Wayfair, the room featured an oversize bay window in the sitting area. The wheelchair stood vacant near the dresser. On one of the leather club chairs by the window, Rosemary waited for them. Hands folded, she was the vision of tranquil seas.

A fortunate discovery since her spouse was nervous enough for them both. Millicent walked to the other club chair, her features tense. She looked unprepared for the difficult conversation ahead.

Jada lowered the groaning tray to the coffee table.

Rosemary gasped, her attention tripping across the food. "Jada, you're too kind." Gratitude washed through her blue eyes. "Room service, from the sweetest pastry chef I've ever met. Actually, the *only* one I've ever met."

"It's the least I can do." Jada uncorked the wine. "Can I tempt you?"

Intervening, Millicent took the bottle. "There's no temptation necessary." She filled the goblets and handed Rosemary a glass. "Jada, you're joining us. We all need a drink."

"Of course—thanks."

A folding chair was stationed beside the coffee table. Had Mr. Uchida brought it upstairs? Jada made a mental note to thank him later.

They sipped their wine in the lingering quiet. From the window, guests were visible one story below, wending toward the inn through the crimson-colored light.

Rosemary broke the silence. "Philip asked if we'd like to come over tomorrow," she told Jada. "Such a nice invitation. I'm looking forward to seeing where Fancy lives."

A kind gesture—Philip hadn't mentioned the offer in the text he'd sent. "I hope you have a good memory," Jada confided, smiling. "You'll need it once Fancy drags you into her bedroom."

"Why?"

"She'll expect you to memorize the name of all her baby dolls and stuffed animals. She'll also try to interest you in watching a fashion show. Prepare for her to suggest she try on *all* the dress-up clothes for your viewing pleasure."

"Oh, I'd like that!" Pausing, Rosemary noticed the moisture gathering in her partner's eyes. She patted Millicent's knee. "Do you need a tissue?"

The gentle offer struck Millicent like a rebuke. "Don't start pestering me," she replied, snatching up a plate. She reached for a handful of grapes. She fanned out several crackers, did a poor job scooping shrimp salad on top. "It's my job to pester *you*. I'm quite good at it."

"There's nothing good about your behavior when you nag."

Millicent popped a grape into her mouth. "I'm thrilled the nap put you in a feisty mood, Rosemary. Nothing makes my day like when you're brimming with piss and vinegar." With a grunt, she settled back with her plate. "Now, leave me alone. Talk to Jada."

The affectionate squabble was a bright note Jada sorely needed. "I'm sorry you didn't have more time with Fancy today," she said to Rosemary.

"Oh, it's fine! How could I interest my granddaughter in a long conversation with a party underway? No, it was much better for her to enjoy the festivities." Rosemary trailed a thoughtful finger around the rim of her glass. "After you took Fancy back inside, one of the women attending the party came outside to visit with us."

"Penelope," Millicent garbled. In her state of high anxiety, she was finishing her plate in record time. "We had a nice chat."

"About you," Rosemary softly added. "Penelope said you were the only real friend my daughter made in Sweet Lake. The only one who was patient with Bodi even when she behaved badly." When she paused, a light feathering of grief centered between her brows. "She also mentioned that you went with Philip to identify the body. That he was so upset, the police chief suggested you help him through the ordeal."

Jada's stomach pitched. "Daniel went with us." She steadied herself. "He's Philip's brother."

Her eyes misting, Rosemary nodded. "Bodi didn't have many friends growing up. Her behavior was hard for her schoolmates to understand. The stealing didn't help. I can't remember a time when she wasn't rifling through the other children's book bags at school. Those were the easy years, I suppose."

"What do you mean?" Jada asked.

"You were acquainted with Bodi. She was beautiful, yes?"

"Very." *Like you,* Jada nearly added. The sorrow canvassing Rosemary's face silenced her.

"My daughter's beauty came at a cost. I was so foolish." Rosemary took a long sip of her wine. "Bodi was still in eighth grade when she became sexually active. I had no idea. None whatsoever. It's horrible to consider that she initiated many of those encounters."

Jada's stomach pitched. "How do you know?"

"Her second year of high school, the mother of one of Bodi's classmates took me aside. After a PTA meeting." A sigh escaped Rosemary's lips. "She'd found a dozen photographs of Bodi on her son's phone.

Awful pictures, taken of Bodi with two of the boys on the high school football team."

The disclosure sickened Jada. "I wish—" She broke off.

She wasn't sure what she wished. Mostly, she decided, she wished the sorrow in Rosemary's eyes wasn't melding with a quiet expectancy as she pursed her lips, drawing silently on an inner core of strength. She was ready now, it seemed, for the conversation that would lead them back to a brutal day in March, and the dark secrets waiting there.

Rosemary set down her glass. "Should we get started?" She rested a hand on Millicent's wrist.

Her heart beating in her throat, Jada nodded in assent.

Then she led them into the past.

Chapter 24

The Wayfair Inn, six years ago

Veins of ice spread across the windowpane.

Plugging in the coffee pot, Jada mentally ticked through the employees who'd already called in due to the snowstorm. A paltry list since most of the staff had been let go last autumn. The absences represented a minor inconvenience. Only five rooms at the Wayfair were presently occupied—an unlucky couple from Dayton and four businessmen, all of whom were staying put until the vicious weather broke. The March snowstorm barreling down from Canada had already brought most of Ohio to a standstill.

Fortunately, Mr. Uchida had made it in, along with three others with four-wheel drive vehicles or trucks capable of negotiating the whiteout conditions. As the coffee brewed, Jada squinted, looking past the ice crawling across the window. The rolling hills resembled a moonscape as layer upon layer of snowfall erased the landscape's familiar contours.

Brows puckering, she leaned closer. The yellowish glow of headlights cut through the curtain of white.

"The snow plow service," Mr. Uchida informed her when she strode into the lobby.

"Shouldn't they wait until the storm lets up?"

"Mr. Curcio will send someone back again at noon. We'll have another foot by then."

"Thank you, Mr. Curcio," Jada murmured, approaching the glass door that led out to the veranda. In the parking lot beyond the sloping entry and the snow-laden walkway, the blade on the Dodge Ram sliced neat paths through the three-foot drifts.

Mr. Uchida smiled. "Guess he's serious about keeping his promise to Linnie's father."

"I guess so."

Like everyone else, the owner of Curcio Landscapes had been upset last year when a stroke forced Linnie's father to hand over management of the inn to her. Once Treat Wayfair and his wife left for an early retirement in Florida, the whispered talk in Sweet Lake grew like a groundswell. Jada did her best to ignore the gossip about the Wayfair going under because Treat Wayfair's daughter couldn't save the inn from its death spiral. Outside of Jada and Cat—and the Sirens—few towns-people held out hope for Linnie's chances.

Banishing the thought, Jada pressed her fingers to the glass. "Mr. Curcio didn't send out Lance Treadwell, did he? All he does is flirt with me or Cat. He's given up on Linnie. She told him it's disgust-ing how he smells like grilled onions all the time." Linnie had actually spritzed air freshener in the hulking youth's direction while making the pronouncement.

"You ought to give Lance a break." Mr. Uchida shook his head with bemusement. "He's not interested in your girlfriends, Jada. He's been searching for a way to ask *you* out."

"Not happening."

"A girl your age shouldn't work seven days a week. Let him take you out to dinner."

"I don't have time to date. Even if I did, Lance isn't the type of guy I'd consider."

Christine Nolfi

Mr. Uchida gazed at her steadily. The sympathy he made no attempt to hide sent a prickly discomfort across her skin. There wasn't much he missed. Jada suffered the uneasy sensation he was holding back advice he sorely wanted to give.

Instead, he nodded toward the parking lot and the truck sliding to a halt. "Mr. Curcio sent Philip out to plow."

The news jolted her. "In this weather? The whole state of Ohio looks like the frozen tundra. He should be home with his wife and the baby."

"Jada, he's got a lot on his shoulders now. He needs the money."

"He's already working two jobs." She'd never cared much for Philip's cocky ways in high school, but the fix he'd put himself in would make any decent woman revise her opinion. "The rest of the time, he's taking care of the baby."

The sympathy in Mr. Uchida's eyes turned to worry. "Sad how Bodi still hasn't taken to Fancy. It's been two months."

Not sad, Jada mused. *Frightening.*

She'd never before witnessed a new mother less interested in her newborn. "Bodi just needs time," she offered. The words sounded false, even to her ears.

They both fell silent as Philip wended his way through the snowdrifts and clomped up the steps to the veranda. Rubbing his red-knuckled hands, he paused to stomp the snow from his boots. Spotting Jada, he grinned.

Behind her, Mr. Uchida made a weary sound. His disapproval was incapable of dispelling the swift joy arcing through her. Philip came inside, his eyes focused on her like a beacon.

Frigid air streamed in, and he slammed the door shut. Philip made no effort to hide his pleasure at finding her waiting for him in the lobby.

"Hey," he murmured.

"Hey yourself."

Mr. Uchida was still watching them, and Jada donned a business-like expression. "Have you eaten? I'm happy to whip something up."

"No time. I have to head back, plow Sweet Lake Circle. Mr. Curcio took care of it at dawn. I'm sure it's buried again."

"Want an egg sandwich for the road?"

"You don't mind?"

"Not a problem, really."

As he followed her into the kitchen, Jada smiled at the irony of the situation. When they were younger, she viewed Philip as the flakiest guy at Sweet Lake High. They weren't exactly friends now, but she'd begun revising her opinion. Thanks to her friendship with Bodi, she was happy to help them both out whenever possible—especially now that they had a baby to care for.

Like countless times before, she failed to pinpoint when her feelings toward him had begun to soften. When he became chivalrous, marrying Bodi after learning she was pregnant? Jada had listened in stunned silence when Bodi shared the embarrassing details of the one-night stand, and how Philip announced his intention to do the right thing. Or was it during her first visit to his apartment after he brought his new family home from the hospital?

She had found him diapering the baby on the kitchen table, of all places. His large frame was bent over his daughter while he cooed like a lovesick hen and covered her tiny, wagging arms with sloppy kisses. The earthy delight glowing on his features, the careful movements of his callused hands as he gently turned the baby, slipping the diaper underneath her pink bottom before pausing to brush kisses across her downy head—his devotion to the fragile life cradled in his palms captivated Jada. Time slipped its normal rhythm, unspooling as she watched, her throat tight with emotion. It seemed cruel to break the spell binding Philip to his daughter, and so she had retreated to the living room. On the couch, Bodi stewed in front of the TV. The sweet babble drifting in from the kitchen had set her features with bubbling fury.

Philip pulled her from the reverie, asking, "Where are your partners in crime? Sleeping in?"

"Linnie and Cat are in the south wing, dealing with the window." Jada found a skillet, set it on the burner. "When the wind starting kicking up, around four o'clock? A tree limb came through."

"It broke a window?"

"Scared the crap out of us. We were all huddled in Linnie's suite—the heating in the south wing doesn't work too well. Anyway, we heard a loud crash at the other end of the corridor. We didn't have the guts to investigate until dawn."

"How did you deal with it?"

"We dug around the basement, found some plywood. Linnie and Cat are nailing it in place. They're doing an awful job, but who cares? The south wing is in such bad repair, I can't imagine we'll ever scrounge up the cash to refurbish the suites."

Philip noticed the patches of snow dripping off his coat. "Should I go up to help?" He grabbed a dish towel, began mopping up the puddles surrounding his feet.

"Don't bother. They're almost finished." She tossed a pat of butter into the pan. "How's Bodi?"

"Pissed, mostly. I've been leaving my truck on a quarter tank. If I don't, she goes on joyrides with the baby."

"She does? Philip, it's freezing outside." Jada made a mental note to discuss the situation with Bodi. The temperamental new mother might accept advice more easily from a friend. "If you want my opinion, she shouldn't take Fancy out until spring. The weather's just too cold."

He smiled grimly. "Exactly why I leave the tank a quarter filled."

"Wait a second. You mean you leave your truck with Bodi every morning?" Reaching for the eggs, she frowned at him. "How do you get to work?"

The eggs sizzled in the pan, and he licked his lips. "Dumb question," he joked. Then he shrugged. "I'll say one thing for Mr. Curcio.

The heat works like a dream in the trucks he has us use to plow the streets."

She read between the lines. "You *walk* to work? You walked *today*—in a blizzard?" It was a good three miles from his apartment to Curcio Landscaping on Ridge Street.

He shrugged, the injured pride heavy on his features. Letting it go, Jada made small talk until she'd slid the eggs from the pan and stacked them on thick slices of bread. With misgiving, she noted the dark patches of exhaustion forming half-moons beneath his eyes. When she returned to the fridge to grab an orange and two apples, he glanced at her with gratitude.

With murmured thanks, he strode from the kitchen to resume his workday in town. The roar of an engine announced his departure. From the kitchen window, she watched the storm swallow the glowing taillights as he wended slowly down the hill.

Returning to work, she began organizing breakfast for the few guests staying at the inn, planning to serve them whenever they shuffled downstairs. Seeing no reason to hurry, she took her time with the chore. If they all decided to sleep until noon, she couldn't blame them. The snow was coming down now in heavier sheets, a wall of frigid weather.

A shrill blaring cracked the silence.

Following the ear-shattering noise, Jada raced to the lobby. Halfway up the stairwell one of the guests, rattled awake, was cinching on his robe. The businessman from Cleveland flinched as the blaring started again.

Jada hurried to Mr. Uchida. He was already at the front door, peering out, trying to see anything through the blinding snow. The wind shifted, and the curling cyclones of white parted for the slice of a second. Jada gasped. In the parking lot, beneath the fast-falling snow, a truck swerved wildly. It barely missed one of the snowbanks edging the newly plowed asphalt. Then the driver hit the horn again.

"Mr. Uchida—I need your coat." She pushed him toward the front desk. "Hurry! There isn't time to run back to the kitchen for mine."

He lobbed the heavy parka at her. Jada was still zipping up the front as she carefully negotiated the snow-packed steps. Trudging at a fast clip, she plowed through the icy drifts, blinking rapidly as the sky pelted her with snowflakes. She recognized the make and model: Philip's truck.

Bodi was behind the wheel.

The tires squealed as she hit the gas and carved a donut on the frozen parking lot. Catching sight of Jada, she let up on the horn. The Ford pickup skidded to a halt.

Bodi flung open the driver-side door and jumped out. "I thought you were my friend, Jada!"

She wasn't dressed for the weather. Jeans, sweatshirt—at least she'd had the sense to wear boots. She seemed impervious to the cold blasting against her petite body. Wild fury lit her brilliantly blue eyes.

Jada began to approach, felt the snow crunch beneath her shoes. She stopped abruptly when Bodi scrambled farther away. "Bodi, come inside."

"Go screw yourself. I know what's going on between you and my husband." The furious girl spun on her heel. She appraised the plowed section of the parking lot. "Philip was here, wasn't he?"

Frustrated, Jada swatted at the snowflakes clinging to her face. She was tired of Bodi's weird accusations. Since giving birth to Fancy, the mercurial girl had become moodier, nearly paranoid.

"Bodi, there's nothing going on," Jada assured her.

"Maybe not on your end. But just wait. Someday, you'll feel differently about Philip."

"Stop this. You're being ridiculous."

"Oh yeah? Wake up, Jada." Bodi's lips curled with disdain. "Anytime you need something, Philip always volunteers. Lance Treadwell was supposed to plow the Wayfair this morning, not my husband. They swapped jobs. I'm sure Philip was dying to come out to see you."

There was no telling if the accusation held merit. Jada had no idea how Mr. Curcio assigned jobs. "Come inside," she begged the shivering girl. "I'll make hot chocolate. You love hot chocolate."

"I'm nineteen, Jada. Don't talk to me like I'm a kid."

"Bodi, your lips are turning blue. Come inside. I'll make you something to eat."

"Did you make him breakfast? Ask him to stop back for lunch?"

The comment bounced off Jada as a question seized her mind. Her fearful gaze shot to the truck.

"Bodi, where's the baby?" The passenger seat was empty. No car seat, no infant buckled inside. Anger cut through her terror. "My God, did you leave her alone at the apartment? Where is she?"

Mention of the infant Bodi refused to love sent her attention to the fierce swells of white rippling away from the parking lot and toward the lake. She gripped her skull. "What am I doing here?" she screamed.

"It's okay. Please, let's go inside—"

"I'm sick of being trapped in a dirty apartment. All the kid does is bawl nonstop and make me clean up her messes. Why doesn't she clean up her own messes? Look at me." The wind whipped around her as she shoved up her sweatshirt to reveal the loose roll of flesh on her belly. "I want my body back. I don't want to look like an old lady. I'm only nineteen." Her eyes blazed. "Look what she's done to me."

What happened next seemed out of a nightmare.

Bodi sprinted past the truck. Large snowdrifts covered the steep hill leading to the lake, but she plowed through them with astonishing speed. The ribbons of her blonde hair fanned out behind her as she raced downward. She was making the trek quickly, moving in and out of sight as sheets of white fell from the sky.

Indecision gripped Jada. She flung her attention back to the inn. It would take only a moment to run back inside and call the police. Someone needed to get to the apartment, where a two-month-old had been left alone.

During all the years that would follow, Jada picked at the memory of her hesitation like a wound she wished to make fester and burn. Were those wasted seconds all that stood between a depressed young mother and a frigid lake waiting to engulf her?

Jada raced down the hill.

Unlike Bodi, who was equipped with heavy boots, Jada wore only tennis shoes. The thin soles refused to grip the icy ground. She fell repeatedly. Grappling to follow the path Bodi had carved in the snow-drifts was difficult, and she lost her balance again. Slipping and sliding her way to the lake, Jada cried out for Bodi to stop.

Ice crusted on Jada's lashes as she crawled onto the beach. The wind was stronger here, a howling menace whipping across the open ground, shearing the snow from the sand and tumbling it toward the dark wall of the forest. Jada winced as the taste of iron coated her tongue. A droplet of blood splatted on the icy ground between her fists. She found a cut throbbing on her lips that she quickly dismissed. Scrambling to her feet, she batted against the curtain of white obliterating her sight.

The lake was a sea of glass. In the dim morning light, mounds of snow carved a wavy pattern across the sheet of ice, hiding the tumbling waters beneath. Earlier in the week, some of the boys in town had turned the section of the lake near the beach into a skating rink. Jada spotted the hash marks from their skates etched into the glassy surface. Linnie had driven the boys off with a speech about how the ice might not hold, then she'd planted a sign warning everyone to keep off the ice. The water below was barely above freezing, cold enough for hypothermia to bring death in minutes.

When Jada finally caught sight of Bodi, she screamed with a fury that scraped her throat raw. Cold, animal panic gripped her.

Bodi was out on the lake, walking smoothly, purposefully, with her arms flung out for balance.

"No, no! Bodi—come back!"

The hoarse plea went unheeded. Jada's teeth chattered as she toed the ice. Go out after her? If she allowed Bodi to walk much farther, the ice would give way. She'd plunge to her death.

A litany of prayer accompanied Jada as she took the first step.

Mother Mary, protect me.

The rubber sole of her right shoe began to slip, and she made the terrifying decision to pull it off. She flung off her other shoe, glad when her thick socks gripped the ice.

Heavenly Father, please don't let me die.

Cold pierced her feet with pain so deep it felt like fire.

Four steps, then five. She clenched her teeth. She pushed away the awareness that she was much taller than the girl bobbing in and out of view. And heavier, by at least twenty pounds. Tight to her breast, Jada held the hope she would reach Bodi in time.

When the ice gave way, the shock of freezing water was a surgeon's knife. Precise, deep, a torturous assault.

Water poured down Jada's throat. Gagging, she clawed at the chunks of ice colliding with her shoulders and scraping against her face. She was like a child plunged down a well, with no way to safety. Flailing wildly, she grabbed vainly for purchase as the ice broke off in large chunks. She went under a second time, her energy fading in the bone-chilling water, her knees scraping the lake bed below. Pain scattered across her skin. She came up again with a sharp, guttural roar bellowing from her throat as the current pushed her closer to shore, pushed her through a seam in the ice to shallow water, allowing her to plant her feet.

With the last of her strength, she struggled to heave herself upright. When she did, Jada sloshed back to the safety of the beach.

Only to hear the crisp, killing sound of ice cracking out on the lake.

Chapter 25

Following the dim glow of her phone, Jada tiptoed around the side of the house. Crickets chirped in the velvety blackness draping the yard.

She settled on the deck's top step, inhaled sharply. The air smelled sweetly of mown grass. Clouds floated across the waxing moon, gently drifting boats skimming the universe. A whole fleet drifted by before she sent the text.

The light blinked on. The sliding glass door swished open.

Philip joined her on the top step. "I wasn't expecting to see you tonight," he said, the pleasure thick in his voice.

She plucked at the bathrobe pulled loosely across his chest. "Turning in soon?" He usually stayed up late on Saturday night.

"Yeah. Planning to wake the munchkin early, get her to help me tear through the house. Millicent and Rosemary are coming over. I don't want to leave the impression I'm raising their granddaughter in chaos central."

"Philip, they know you're a single father juggling a lot. Run the vacuum through the living room, and leave it at that."

"Nope. Come morning, Fancy and I are in the marines. Polishing every buckle, making the place gleam. Her grandmothers deserve nothing less."

"I'll come over and help." She bumped her shoulder against his. "But you get bathroom duty. I haven't been around lately to help Fancy with 'bathtub time.' I'm guessing the tub is covered in grime."

"I'm not enlisting you. Come over, but only to hang out. It'll be fun watching the munchkin wow Rosemary and Millicent with a fashion show. My nutty kid started organizing costumes before she climbed into bed." Dropping the subject, he drew a protective arm around her. "How did it go?"

The affection he offered melted the tension pinging through her. Jada relaxed against him. She rested her hand on his thigh, glad for his quiet strength. He wouldn't push for details she didn't have the stomach to share.

"It was hard, and kind of surprising. Rosemary kept herself together, even when I got to the awful parts. Millicent . . . not so much. She was sobbing when I finished."

"Funny how you never really know what goes on in a friend's marriage," Philip said. "I had Millicent pegged as the strong one."

"She is, in some respects. With Rosemary's physical needs, obviously. The personal stuff? Rosemary is an awfully strong woman."

"I guess she's had to be."

They drew silent. Philip's hand wove gently across her back. The caresses gave Jada the courage she needed.

At last, she looked at him. "I'm not ready to go into the details with you," she admitted, "although I will at some point. I should've told you everything a long time ago. But there *is* something I need to tell you now." Her lips were suddenly dry. A new wave of tension shuttled through her.

He palmed the curls from her cheek. "Sure," he murmured. "I'm listening."

"The day Bodi died, when she came to the inn? She was livid. Really furious." Shame and self-loathing made Jada shut her eyes tightly. "She was furious at me. Laying on the horn in the parking lot. When I came out, she really tore into me."

The revelation shuddered distress through Philip's chest. "She did?" He met her eyes with a look of concern. "I've always assumed she went up to the inn looking for me. Pissed off about something I did, looking for an argument." He drew in an unsteady breath. "I don't know why she confronted you, Jada. It never should've happened."

"I've been haunted by what she said—especially lately. Philip, she thought you were attracted to me, which didn't make any sense at the time. But the way she raged at me . . . I don't know. It's almost like she knew. Like she had a premonition."

"A premonition of what?"

"That someday I'd betray her memory by falling in love with you. Totally, completely, head over heels. I've been in love with you for months, nearly from the beginning, when Linnie asked me to start coming over to help you out." Jada gave a watery laugh, which struck her as horribly inappropriate. Her heart felt cleaved in two at the wrongs she'd inflicted on his wife. "Bodi was my friend. I couldn't save her on the lake, and I'm a strong swimmer—I should've been able to get to her in time. Now I've betrayed her again. I'm in love with her husband. I can't rid myself of the guilt. Don't tell me none of this makes sense. What my head knows doesn't match up with what my heart feels."

"Hold on. You're in love with me?" Disbelief colored Philip's voice. He lifted his palms to his face, scrubbed hard. When he came up for air, her stomach clenched. He looked angry. "Why didn't you tell me?"

"Philip, I cared about Bodi," she shot back. She couldn't believe he'd asked. "She looked up to me like a big sister. She was my friend. It doesn't matter if the two of you only got together because of Fancy."

"No," he said firmly. "Before Millicent came to Sweet Lake and I screwed everything up. Why didn't you tell me how you feel?"

"I wanted to, Philip. I couldn't." In turmoil, she studied the night sky.

The crickets broke off their singing. The silence they left behind was full and rich. A cloud slipped over the moon, sleek as a schooner, and drifted into a velvety sea.

Philip took her chin, gently steered her eyes to his. "Jada." He said her name firmly. A remarkable achievement since his expression was fluid. "The way we feel about each doesn't betray my late wife or her memory."

"But Philip—"

"No. You need to let this go. Bodi killed herself. She had a lot of problems. She'd gone off her meds. We didn't even know she *needed* medication. You aren't to blame."

Tears blurred her vision. "That's not how it feels. How it's ever felt."

"Take comfort in what she left behind. Bodi isn't gone. She lives on in Fancy."

It was a beautiful thought, and Jada clung to it. "She does."

Philip brushed the tears from her eyes. "I love you." He paused long enough for the words to sink in. "I always have."

He kissed her then, slow and sweet. His lips carried a thousand ardent messages. They flowed through Jada like a river, washing her clean.

In the darkness, the crickets began to sing.

Chapter 26

A toy was *not* part of the deal.

Smoothing the last fold in Linnie's veil, Jada excused herself. The wedding would begin in fifteen minutes. The entire wedding party was milling around the ballroom, preparing to walk down to the patio. With an outdoor ceremony, hiding the bride wasn't an option; they would assemble behind the rows of chairs where the guests waited. Then they'd proceed up the aisle to the greenery-festooned arbor Philip had built.

At the clack of Jada's heels nearing the table, guilt flashed through Fancy's eyes. The child whipped the toy behind her back. A gift from Millicent and Rosemary, Jada presumed. They'd spent the entire week lavishing gifts on their new granddaughter.

Jada patted the wicker basket she'd left on the table. "Fancy, you're tossing out rose petals, remember? You'll need both hands. One to hold the basket, and the other to throw the petals. Whatever you're hiding behind your back, please leave it here. You can play with it after the ceremony."

"Why can't I bring my toy?" Fancy thrust out her lower lip. "I'm a fairy godmother today."

"Do you have time to grow a third arm?" Jada channeled the child's singsong voice. "I don't think so." Outside, the first chords from the harpist shivered through the air.

"I don't need three arms. I do fine with two."

"You're silly. Granted, you're awfully pretty in your dress, but that doesn't make you less of a cuckoo bird." Jada picked up the basket. "Watch. You'll need both hands."

She demonstrated a gentle throwing motion. Best-case scenario, Fancy would let the petals flutter to the ground. Or she'd hurl big handfuls at the guests. The excitement of being center stage for thirty seconds might go to her head. There really was no telling.

Finishing the demonstration, Jada returned the basket to the table. "Okay, now show me how you'll pull this off if you're also holding a toy."

"You want me to practice?"

"Not really. I want you to leave *all* toys in the ballroom. Please, sweetie. The wedding is about to begin."

Philip approached, brushed a kiss across Jada's cheek. "Problems?" He looked dreamy in the black tux as he regarded her and then his daughter.

Jada sent a frustrated hand toward her head. She stopped, remembering the baby's breath twined in her curls. The sprays of tiny flowers were pretty. They were also irritating her scalp in the most vicious way. Not that she'd consider uttering a complaint. Linnie Wayfair was in an incredibly serene mood. No last-minute worrying, no fretting— which meant Jada was out serious cash. She'd lost the wager with Cat, Mr. Uchida, and nearly half of the Sirens. They'd all taken the bet, confident Linnie would greet her wedding day in a state of bliss.

To Philip, Jada said, "Check out whatever your daughter is hiding behind her back."

He glanced at Daniel, standing at one of the ballroom windows. "We don't have time for this," he muttered, bending toward his daughter. "What are you hiding, sugarplum?"

"My new present. Penelope helped Grandma Rosemary make it for me. Millicent helped too."

"They made something for you? Can't you play with it *after* the wedding?"

Fancy shifted on her feet, and the foamy yards of her gown swayed. "I'm a fairy godmother today." She gave her father a stubborn look. Evidently, she was already deep into her imaginative play. "I'll make wishes on everyone. I'm good at making wishes, and I know what I'm doing. I'll make them when I walk up."

"When you walk up the aisle?" Jada asked, touched by the child's intention.

Fancy nodded. "Wishes are more important than rose petals."

To emphasize the point, she drew the wand from behind her back. With big-girl authority, she wagged it before their startled faces. As she did, an unmistakable scent bloomed in the air.

With wonder, Jada neared. This wasn't a simple craft project. The wand was beautiful, with a round head covered in a rainbow of faux gems. A thick ribbon, the same rare blue as Fancy's eyes, wound up the stem.

Beneath the ribbon, sprigs of rosemary peeked out. Dark green and sharply scented, they were wound all the way up the wand's stem.

Determined to make her point, Fancy continued waving. A sprig came loose and fell to the floor.

Jada picked up the rosemary, held it to her nose. "Leave the basket, take the wand," she decided with a catch in her voice.

Philip chuckled. "Let's sneak the kid past the bride and groom." He brushed his nose across Jada's. "They may not like the last-minute change to their carefully orchestrated wedding."

Fancy patted his hip. "They won't mind, Daddy. Wishes *are* more important."

"They are," Jada agreed.

Taking Philip's arm, Jada tucked the rosemary in her hair.

Epilogue

Six months later

For emphasis, Linnie scooted her chair around the side of the desk. She swung her foot into Jada's unsuspecting lap.

"You see?" Linnie tugged off her sock and turned her ankle sideways for better viewing. "Huge. The other one is too. Like swelling balloons."

Jada knew where this was going. "Are you following the doctor's orders and walking at lunchtime? A quick jog around the inn, a brisk stroll on the beach? The third trimester will be easier if you get more exercise."

"I *am* getting enough exercise. Less than an hour ago, I chased Cat from my office. I nearly broke into a run. I was sweating and everything. Sometimes she drives me crazy with her complaints." Blind to her own litany of woe, Linnie wiggled her toes. She appeared uncertain if they still functioned. Then she pinched the puffy skin of her calf. "If this gets much worse, I'll have to resort to compression stockings."

"Not a biggie. I'll buy them for you."

"Oh, why don't the Sirens have an herbal cure for swollen ankles? I'm miserable."

Jada wiggled a chubby toe. "I don't know how to break this to you." She pointed at Linnie's navel. "Your ankles aren't the only thing that's swelling."

At the remark, Linnie reverently caressed the blossoming curve. She'd conceived during her honeymoon with Daniel in Aruba, and the expectant couple was over-the-moon happy. The baby was due in January.

"Yeah, but the baby isn't bothering me. Well, unless I have to pee. From the waist down, I'm beginning to look like Daniel's great-aunt Martha. I don't want my legs to resemble tree trunks."

With her free hand, Jada navigated the mouse to close down the file she'd been working on. It was nearing the end of October, and Linnie's pregnancy complaints were now part of the daily routine. It hadn't escaped Jada's notice how the complaints came with greater frequency as each weekend approached. On this particular Friday, she was *not* being sucked in.

Steering Linnie's foot gently to the floor, she said, "FYI, Millicent and Rosemary are in town. Spur-of-the-moment visit. They're unpacking in their suite."

"They're here?"

"And staying until next Tuesday."

"They came in at the end of September. Not even three weeks ago!"

"They're retired, Linnie. Spending time with Fancy is their favorite pastime. Actually, Philip is on his way over with the munchkin. They'll be here any minute." The flight from Chicago was never easy for Rosemary, and Jada had suggested they all meet for an early dinner in the Sunshine Room.

Since learning of Fancy's existence, Millicent and Rosemary flew in from Chicago regularly to visit their granddaughter. Millicent never arrived without an armful of books for the six-year-old she was determined to mold into a scholar. Rosemary, a talented artist, had filled Fancy's bedroom with all variety of art supplies—including a child-size easel she'd beautifully stenciled with a design of rosemary sprigs.

Philip often joked the doting grandmothers ought to surrender the long-distance commute and move to Sweet Lake. He made the comments in jest, but Jada suspected they were actually thinking about it.

Linnie's face fell. "Guess you have weekend plans, then."

"If Rosemary is up to it, we're driving to the Cincinnati Zoo tomorrow. Fancy has been begging to go."

"So . . . you can't bail me out and work my Saturday? Even though my ankles might explode? We're talking about swelling of epic proportions."

"No can do. I *will* drive to the drugstore if you'd like to give compression stockings a whirl."

"Thanks for nothing." Linnie gave her a glum look. "I can drive myself."

From the doorway, a low, gasping belch interrupted the conversation. Cat stood with her long brown hair tangled and her golden complexion unusually pale. "Not fair," she muttered. Pressing her hand to her waist, she glared at Linnie. "Did you talk her into working your Saturday?"

"It's your Saturday too," Jada reminded her. Now that she enjoyed a busy social life, Jada insisted on drawing up a monthly schedule to ensure they worked equal hours. As co-managers of the Wayfair Inn, it was only fair. "Check the schedule. You and Linnie are both on deck. This is my Saturday off."

"I was hoping you'd work my shift with Linnie."

Linnie grunted. "Get over it, Cat. She's bailing on us." Linnie shoved her foot back into her shoe. "She's going to the zoo."

Cat weaved her way toward Jada's desk. "Can't she reschedule? I'm at the point where I can't walk by the kitchen without feeling like I'll retch." She grabbed the wastebasket hugging the side of the desk and eased into a chair. "Is there something with cloves on the menu tonight? The smell is really getting to me."

She did look ill. Concerned, Jada asked, "Have you caught a bug?"

"Don't ask."

"What's the big deal? If you've caught an autumn bug, it's not the end of the world." She glanced out the window at the trees beautifully adorned in crimson and gold. Perfect weather for a trip to the zoo.

Cat slumped lower in her chair. "I can't talk about it, not while Mami's in Columbus."

Linnie settled her hands on her baby bump like a peevish Buddha. "What does your mother's shopping trip have to do with your dubious illness? I can't help but wonder if you're wiggling out of work to spend the weekend in bed with Ryan. Don't you two ever let up? If Ryan keeps giving you love bites, I'm buying you nothing but turtlenecks for Christmas."

"Oh, give it a rest."

Jada said, "I'm sorry, Cat. I can't work your shift. What about Mr. Uchida? He might pull a double. Would you like me to talk to him?"

"It's not like you to foist your responsibilities on Mr. Uchida." Cat hugged the waste can to her chest. "Where's your sense of honor? I'm your friend, Jada. You should help me out in a pinch."

"I'm no longer the black woman's version of Atlas."

"What's that supposed to mean?"

"I've stopped carrying the weight of the world," Jada explained with a warm rush of emotion. "I love you and Linnie, but Philip is right. I'm not responsible for every problem my friends encounter. I need to focus my energies on him, Fancy—and myself. Why should I always put myself last?"

Linnie regarded her with something akin to awe. "I guess you shouldn't," she agreed. "Jada, you've always been a great friend. The best. I love you for that."

Cat wiped the irritation from her face. "I love you too," she said. A burp popped from her mouth.

Then she vomited into the can.

Philip halted in the doorway, with Fancy a step behind. At the stench, Fancy smacked her palm over her nose. She bolted for the lobby.

Sauntering inside, Philip gave Cat the thumbs-up. "Ryan told me." He grimaced as she leaned back into the can. "Congratulations."

Jada was already out of her chair and hovering above her nauseous friend. "Wait. Are you saying she's . . . ?"

"In the throes of morning sickness? Why *do* they call it morning sickness when some women puke all day long? But, yeah, that'd be my guess." Philip brushed a kiss across Jada's lips. Drawing away, he added, "Daniel went over to Ryan's place. They're doing shots. They invited me to join them, but I said I have plans."

Cat moaned. "Why do men have all the fun?"

Linnie squealed. "You're pregnant? We're pregnant *together*? Oh, Cat—that's wonderful! Why didn't you want to tell us?" Considering, she puffed up her cheeks. "Oh. Right. You should let your mother in on the happy news before telling your besties. Silvia will pitch a fit when she hears we found out first."

Philip chuckled. "Silvia will get over it." He regarded Jada. "I spotted Frances and Penelope dining in the Sunshine Room. I'm sure they'll take Cat home."

"I'll take her," Linnie announced. Heaving Cat from the chair, she asked her, "Want to hang out at my house tonight? If the boys are getting toasted at your place, it'll be a whole lot quieter. Let's go online and check out baby names. I'm leaning toward Natalie for a girl and Tucker for a boy. I can't decide if I want to peek at the ultrasound or not."

Together, they shuffled from the room.

When they'd gone, Philip waved a hand through the foul air. "Call Housekeeping," he suggested. "Tell them to get in here with Lysol."

Jada sent the text. Grinning, she tried to wrap her brain around the new development. Cat and Linnie both pregnant. Both of her business partners bringing children into the world at the same time. The patter of little feet was sure to usher in a new era at the Wayfair.

Her spirits fell. Did she need to rethink her workweek, volunteer for more Saturdays?

Philip tipped up her chin. "Not your problem." The saying was his new mantra. "Their babies, their problem. You work enough hours at the inn."

She nodded. "Right."

"They'll find a solution. Just because they're both having babies doesn't mean you go back to carrying the world."

"I'm sick of carrying the world." Grateful for his protection, she landed a kiss on his cheek. "Thanks."

"You're welcome."

In the lobby, they found Millicent affectionately bent over Fancy. Leafing through the pages of a book, Fancy paused at a colorful illustration. She held up the book for Jada's inspection: *A Children's Guide to the American Revolution.*

Jada fingered the pages. "Another gift?" she asked. Dense type was interspersed with the illustrations. "Millicent, this might be a little beyond a six-year-old's comprehension."

"Nonsense. We'll tackle the book together. My granddaughter is precocious." She hugged Fancy. "Aren't you, sweetheart?"

With pride, Fancy straightened. "Sure am." Her brows puckered. "What's precocious?"

Philip patted her cheek. He asked Millicent, "Where's your better half?"

"Still fussing. She threw me out of the suite, informed me to take the stairs—not the elevator." Millicent patted her generous middle. "I don't know why Rosemary insists on unpacking every suitcase before dinner. It's not like we brought an abundance of clothing, and the gifts for you-know-who can wait until after we eat."

"Gifts?" Fancy rolled forward on the balls of her feet. "Are they for me, Grammy?"

"Who else?"

"Can I open them now? Maybe just one?"

Millicent glanced at the stairwell. "Why don't you surprise Grandma Rosemary and go on up? She can't wait to see you. Room 216."

Fancy patted Jada's hip. "May I?"

Surprise lifted Jada's head. Fancy never looked to her for guidance. She always asked Philip. With a questioning glance, she regarded him.

He winked.

Millicent nodded approvingly. "Once a child embroiders you onto her heart . . ."

The conversation from last spring wheeled through Jada. *She'll have expectations.*

Jada had a few of her own. Good health, happiness, family—she didn't mind working for what she wanted. She knew how to salt her expectations with determination and sweeten them with hope.

"Sure," she told Fancy. She turned her toward the stairwell to the right of the front desk. "Go upstairs and surprise your grandmother." Rosemary would be delighted.

Her hair flying in waves, Fancy scampered up the steps.

AUTHOR'S NOTE

Dear Reader: If you've enjoyed *The Season of Silver Linings*, I encourage you to post a review on Amazon or Goodreads. I'd love to hear from you as well at: Christine@christinenolfi.com.

ACKNOWLEDGMENTS

WITH HEARTFELT THANKS

To my wonderful editor, Christopher Werner, for his brilliant suggestions and enthusiasm for Jada's story, my developmental editor, Kelli Martin, for all her fabulous insights, and Lake Union's editorial director, Danielle Marshall, for making every phase of the publishing journey a joy and a delight.

To Rebecca Frank, for her enthusiastic comments during the plotting stage, and the advice on herbal remedies that inspired the development of the character Penelope Riddle, and Jan Crossen, for her patient read of the book's earliest drafts.

To my agent, Pamela Harty, for her generous advice, and Rachel Adam Rogers, for the beautiful cover art design.

To my copy editor, Stacee Lawrence; my production editors, Nicole Pomeroy and Elise Marton; and my proofreader, Sarah Engel—for both their patience and their careful edits. To Elizabeth Brown of Swift Edits for proofing the original version of the manuscript under tight deadline; to my author relations manager, Gabriella Dumpit, for guiding me through the publication process; to Devan Hanna and the marvelous team in Lake Union's marketing department.

To my amazing daughter, Marlie, for helping with Lucy, and for giving me reasons to smile on the longest writing days.

To Barry, for reading every review throughout the years and believing even when I entertained doubts. I love you, always.

THE SEASON OF SILVER LININGS BOOK CLUB QUESTIONS

1. At the beginning of the novel, Jada Brooks feels overburdened, especially with regard to her relationship with Linnie Wayfair. For a friendship to endure, must each person take turns carrying the heavier load? Do you have a friendship you cherish even though it seems you carry more of the weight? If so, why is the friendship worth keeping despite the obstacles?

2. The importance of family provides a strong theme in *The Season of Silver Linings*. Both Philip Kettering and Millicent Earhardt go to extreme lengths to protect the family members they hold dear. If you were a widower like Philip, would you refuse to allow your child to meet relatives from "the wrong side of the family"? Why, or why not? If you were Millicent, would you spend years searching for a missing loved one? In your own life, do you know of family, friends, or neighbors who have faced either Philip's or Millicent's dilemma? How did they handle the situation?

3.   Jada Brooks was not able to save Bodi's life on the fateful day of the snowstorm. Late in the novel, when Jada is wrapping bridal shower gifts at Frances's house, Frances urges her to share those final minutes on the frozen lake with the Sweet Lake Sirens. Why is it important to share the most traumatic moments of our lives? Why did Jada refuse to do so until her meeting with Rosemary and Millicent toward the end of the book?

4.   General discussion: If a friend or loved one has undergone a traumatic event, should you encourage them to talk about it? Should you encourage them to see a therapist if the trauma is too great? Why can group therapy sessions be successful in helping people deal with difficult events, such as the death of a child?

5.   Although Penelope Riddle quickly uncovers Millicent's true identity early in the novel, she keeps Jada in the dark. She believes Jada must discover the truth for herself. Did Penelope make a good choice?

6.   Group discussion: Children and young adults often learn through their mistakes rather than by heeding the warnings of older adults. How should parents provide loving guidance, without telling a child what to do? How do you respond to your own mistakes? Do you fall into self-chastisement, or view the mistake as a lesson from which you may learn?

7.   List three of the silver linings represented in the book. Is Rosemary's discovery of Fancy's existence the greatest silver lining? What would young Fancy view as the most important silver lining by novel's end?

ABOUT THE AUTHOR

Photo © 2016 Melissa Miley

Award-winning author Christine Nolfi writes heartwarming and inspiring fiction. She is the author of *Treasure Me*, a Next Generation Indie Awards finalist, and four other Liberty Series novels as well as the Sweet Lake series: *Sweet Lake*, *The Comfort of Secrets*, and *The Season of Silver Linings*. A native of Ohio, Christine currently resides in South Carolina with her husband and four adopted children. For the latest information about her releases and future books, visit www.christinenolfi.com. Chat with her on Twitter @christinenolfi.